Hidden

Mark Sekela

Hidden

ISBN: 978-0-9879059-0-1

First Edition 2012

Printed in the United States of America

Please visit www.MarkSekela.com for details about the other books in the Convergence Series.

For Luca and Matteo,

Find your *Hidden* talents.

ACKNOWLEDGMENTS

Thanks to Sigrid Macdonald and Dian Yu for their expert manuscript evaluation. I remain in awe of the incredible editing skills of Mark Hooper and the professionals at Angel Editing; they transformed *Hidden* from a manuscript into a novel. I received endless positive feedback from Dr. Chris Eckley, who kept my thoughts focused on the big picture. But it was the incredible patience and superhuman endurance of Melissa Gledhill, who had to suffer years of "talking book," that I owe my greatest gratitude; if it wasn't for her, *The Convergence Series* would not have been possible. Thank you, Melissa, for holding my reins as tight as you did and the certain embarrassment you saved me. Finally, I owe all of my inspiration to Luca and Matteo.

Hidden

By

Mark Sekela

CHAPTER 1

IT'S A MIRACLE

Hidden in the branches, the red-tailed hawk was unaware of the light penetrating its body. It waited with the devotion of a Swiss Guard for the resurrection of the late-afternoon thermals. The silver leaves of the cottonwood languished in the sunlight while heat waves danced over the ends of the asphalt driveways of the quiet rural street, blurring the distant hilltops of the Okanagan Valley.

Startled by the movement, the hawk tilted its head to observe a woman and child below. Elizabeth held her son's hand while escaping to the shade of the carport. Jasper shook off his mother's grip and darted to the small red tricycle parked in the corner. Elizabeth followed, helmet in hand.

"Jasper, if you don't wear your helmet, you can't ride your bike," she stated forcefully, struggling to put the helmet on his head.

Jasper slammed the lever on his tricycle bell in protest; the shrill pierced the afternoon heat, causing the hawk to take flight. Elizabeth, well seasoned by her son's antics, ignored his outburst and paused to watch the raptor soar.

"No, Mommy, no!" Jasper objected while shaking his head defiantly. He grabbed the bright red handlebars with both hands and peddled furiously to secure his escape. A squeal resembling a train braking emanated from the wheels with every rotation.

"Fine, don't wear it, but you can't leave the carport," snapped Elizabeth, wincing at the bike's noise.

She smirked and hung the helmet from a nail on the wall, delighted with the compromise. Elizabeth began her work in the garden now that Jasper was sentenced to the safety of the carport. She knelt before the ceramic statuette of the Virgin Mary gleaming in the afternoon sunlight. Elizabeth made the sign of the cross before yanking at the dandelions protruding from the base of the shrine. The smile lingered on her face, slow to disappear as she savored her small victory. Jasper's determination was formidable, even for a three-year-old.

Jasper perched his tricycle on the edge of the carport where the smooth flat concrete intersected the rough steep asphalt of the driveway. He brushed his hair out of his eyes and glanced to see if his mother was watching. His face full with defiance, he lifted his feet off the pedals and began to accelerate toward the road.

"Weee!" he squealed, his hands held high above his head.

The shrill of the wheels over the uneven surface of the driveway was unmistakable, and Elizabeth lifted her head from the garden. It wasn't humanly possible to get to Jasper before his bike reached the road, but like any mother would, Elizabeth desperately tried, bolting after her son with no hope of intercepting him.

"Jasper, stop!" she shouted, but her plea was muted by the screech of tires.

Without warning, the hawk descended from the sky like a missile, slamming its body into Jasper's. They disappeared into a translucent blue-grey haze just as the van and tricycle collided.

Horror crippled Elizabeth with the intensity of a bolt of lightning.

"Jasper!" Her scream shattered the stagnant summer air.

Elizabeth's hands shook uncontrollably, and she grabbed her head. The sound of the tricycle meeting the van had permeated every pore of her body, like the feedback from a loudspeaker. Weakness crippled her legs first and then consumed her completely. A curtain of smoke from the melted tire rubber hung in the air, obscuring the scene. The stench forced her to breathe through her mouth.

Elizabeth collapsed to her knees, her long charcoal-black hair masking her face. Death filled her mind, not the death of her son, but her own. The delivery van had taken the wrong life; surely it was hers God beckoned. She cleared the hair from her eyes and raised her head as the smoke slowly dissipated. Elizabeth then witnessed the unimaginable.

Jasper sat motionless on the road, holding his right knee in his hands. Blood dripped from the small crescent-shaped scratch on his forehead where the bird had collided with him. Glowing like sapphires in a crown, Jasper's crystal blue eyes remained dry as he lifted his hands to his mother. The only tears were hers.

"It's a miracle. Oh thank God, thank God!" she repeated as she ran to her son and lifted him from the road.

Elizabeth instinctively inspected Jasper's body to assess his injuries. A trickle of blood seeped from the two-inch cut above his knee, and a golf-ball-sized lump was emerging on the side of his head where it had hit the pavement.

"Wow, lady, is he okay? I don't know how, but he's one lucky kid," said the young delivery van driver as he stepped down from the vehicle, still shaking from the ordeal.

"Did you see it? It's a miracle. God sent an angel to save my boy," sobbed Elizabeth, unable to control the flood of emotions racing through her mind.

"All I saw was your kid in front of my van. He should... look like that," said the driver, pointing to the shiny red pieces of twisted metal under the front tire of the van.

"Lady, I've got a huge favor to ask. I really need this job and... well, if my boss finds out what happened... We don't need to involve the cops, do we?"

"No, no police. Let's keep this miracle our own little secret," said Elizabeth, looking into Jasper's eyes and deciding that she didn't want her husband to know of the incident. Professor Nikolas Stewart was extremely protective of his only son and would have left his research lab in an instant if he knew what had just taken place.

"Great, then I'll finish my deliveries before someone else calls them."

The driver backed his van off the flattened tricycle, and Elizabeth tossed it on the driveway as the vehicle drove away.

She kept her word and never mentioned the exact details of the incident to anyone—including her husband. Elizabeth's faith prevented her from lying, so she skillfully told Nikolas selective parts of what had happened that morning: how Jasper fell off his bike and cut his knee, and how the tricycle rolled onto the street to be crushed by a van. Her ability to form evasive answers and a vague description of the incident was a skill she passed on to Jasper.

Elizabeth's faith remained pivotal in every aspect of her life, and Jasper's miraculous survival simply intensified her dedication to God.

Nikolas had little use for religion but accepted his wife's cult-like faith. He knew exactly what had taken place that morning and how exceptional Jasper was. Nikolas also knew it wasn't God that had saved his son's life.

He had.

CHAPTER 2

ALTAR BOY

"Get up, Jasper! We're going to be late for Mass. If you make me even one second late this week, you'll have *my* hell to pay!" shouted Elizabeth from the bottom of the staircase. "Jesus, Mary and Joseph, you'd think I was dragging you to prison," she said more to herself than for Jasper to hear.

"Okay. Mom. Okay, I'm coming," Jasper shouted back. "I hate going to stupid church," he then whispered to himself.

Jasper leaped down the steps, ran out the back door and jumped into the car, which Elizabeth had already started.

"Mom, why do *I* have to go and Dad doesn't?"

"You just don't give up, do you? We've been over this a thousand times. Your father and I differ on this. You're going to church as long as you live in my house—that's final!"

"Fine! I don't want to live in your house," whispered Jasper just loud enough for Elizabeth to hear.

"That's okay with me. I'm sure the orphanage would love to have another nine-year-old to feed."

Jasper's rebuttal provided the final bit of convincing Elizabeth needed—it was time for him to start catechism.

***

In a loud and thundering voice intended to grab the attention of his students, Father Franklin opened his class as he had done for the past six weeks with his signature affirmation.

"Jesus died for us all!"

Father Franklin continued proclaiming the virtues of God, all the while staring directly into Jasper's eyes. He hoped to avoid another of Jasper's frequent outbursts intended to invoke dissent in the class.

Jasper, however, couldn't contain himself. He had endured weeks of this opening ritual, and the words flew from his mouth like a weapon.

"Prove it!" he shouted in a clear and cynical voice more like a nineteen-year-old than a nine-year-old.

Father Franklin's face collapsed with rage, and without a single second of hesitation, he commanded Jasper to leave the room and sit in the hallway. That one simple, two-word question ended his formal Catholic education.

That day Jasper's mother arrived late to pick him up. Father Franklin paced in the hall, avoiding Jasper while he waited for her arrival. Spotting her through the window as she walked up the steps, Father Franklin met her at the entrance. Without allowing Elizabeth to finish closing the door behind her, he pulled her aside.

"What's he done this time?" asked Elizabeth, turning her gaze toward her son.

"He questions everything the Sisters and I tell him— refusing to believe. I've read him countless passages from the Bible only to have him openly question them. I've never seen anyone so determined to refute the word of God—especially at his age."

"I'm sorry, Father. I'll speak to him at once."

"I don't want him back in our class, and I'll be discussing this matter with Father Malkin. I suggest you do the same."

Father Franklin cast one last glare at Jasper before marching down the hall, leaving Elizabeth open-mouthed.

***

Snow chased them into the church when Elizabeth pulled open the heavy wooden doors. The late November sunlight failed to fully illuminate the stained-glass windows crowning the ceiling. A candy-store smile appeared on Jasper's face when he inhaled the sweet aroma of vanilla from the scented candles burning next to the altar. This was quickly replaced by a scowl as they walked farther into the church.

"I'm not doing it!" protested Jasper.

"Enough!" snapped his mother.

The church pews resembled children's furniture next to the towering figure gliding down the center aisle towards them. The wind from the open door floated his purple robe from the floor as Father Malkin raised his hands to greet them. His childlike face hid the secret of his years, only to have his mousey grey hair reveal it.

"Ah, Mrs. Stewart, I'm so happy you came on such a miserable day. And you, Jasper, what a very special day for you," he said while bending down on one knee to tousle Jasper's hair. "Now, how old are you, ten?"

"I'm eleven," Jasper responded, brushing back his hair to make sure Father Malkin knew he was unhappy with the error.

"Eleven. Well then, you are a young man now, aren't you? Your mother tells me that you would like to help me with Mass. Would you like to be an altar boy?"

"Sure, I guess," said Jasper, struggling to sound sincere as he turned to face his mother. He knew this was her way of trying to further his Catholic education and strengthen his faith.

Father Malkin, described as 'gifted' by the parents in the congregation for his extraordinary way with children, instantly recognized the nuance of Jasper's retort and returned to his feet. Towering over Elizabeth with his six-foot-three stature, he bowed his head so his chestnut brown eyes delved deep within Elizabeth's, seeking confirmation.

"Are you sure? I have spoken with Father Franklin."

"Oh yes, Jasper is ready," Elizabeth insisted, quickly moving her eyes from his to Jasper's.

A smile filled Father Malkin's face. "Excellent, bring Jasper by on Saturday at one o'clock, and we'll get him a cassock and cotta and go over some of the procedures he'll have to learn."

"Thank you, Father. We'll see you on Saturday."

Father Malkin returned to his knee, deliberately aligning his eyes with Jasper's, and took the boy's hands in his. "I think we are really going to get along well."

Jasper glanced down at the robe spread over the marble floor like a purple carpet and, unlike most eleven-year-olds, cast his eyes directly into Father Malkin's.

"Great," said Jasper without expression.

Being fully aware that Jasper was lying didn't prevent the delight from flooding across Elizabeth's face. She was the lone fighter in a battle to ensure Jasper followed the ways of the Catholic Church. Her husband never prevented Jasper from participating in church functions, but he never recognized any part of the religion either.

***

Most Okanagan falls contrast with the warm summers, and the fall of Jasper's twelfth birthday was no exception. The clouds settled over the mountains, confining the late October rain to the valley for over a week. Jasper returned home from school to find his father's car parked in the carport. Dr. Stewart never arrived home from work early, and Jasper felt the rush of blood to his cheeks when he opened the front door.

"Dad?"

"In the living room."

Jasper rushed down the hallway, uneasy with his father's uncharacteristic early arrival. Dr. Stewart was speaking softly to Elizabeth as Jasper entered the room.

"Dad, what's going on? Mom, what's wrong?"

Elizabeth stood in her husband's arms, her face buried in his chest, sobbing uncontrollably. Dr. Stewart caressed her back as she turned to face Jasper, but before she could say anything, her husband spoke.

"Jasper, I want you to sit down; we need to talk."

"I don't want to sit. I want to know what's going on."

"Honey, please, sit down," said Elizabeth through sobs, pointing to the large leather couch.

Jasper sat at the end of the couch as his parents joined him. He wrapped his arm around his mother's shoulders.

"Mom, what's happening? Why are you crying?"

The sound of Jasper's concerned voice initiated another bout of uncontrollable tears.

"Your mother is very ill, she…"

"What do you mean?" Jasper demanded, leaping from his seat to stand directly in front of his mother.

"Please, Jasper, sit down."

"No! I don't want to sit!"

Dr. Stewart waited for his son to finish his outburst before continuing.

"You can't see it, Jasper, but your mom has cancer."

"Cancer? They can fix it though, right?"

"The doctors will try, but it doesn't look very promising."

The room began to disappear as Jasper processed what he was hearing. *This has to be a mistake; God couldn't do this, how could he? She prays every day and never misses a Sunday Mass.*

Upon hearing her husband's words, Elizabeth's breathing shortened and became irregular, complicated by the force of her sobbing and rendering her nearly incoherent.

"I'm… so… sorry… Jasper," she said between sobs.

"Stop it! Just stop it! You're going to be fine," he said and ran out of the room, heading up the stairs to his bedroom.

The sound of his mother's tears filled the house, giving Jasper no escape from the misery permeating his every thought. As he lay on his bed, staring at the poster of Albert Einstein his father had given him, his thoughts reassured him. *If God won't fix her, science will. The doctors will know what do—they must.* Jasper unconsciously rolled his fingers through his hair, lifting it from his head. No tears filled his eyes, only desperation.

***

A few remaining clouds gave way to a late spring sunrise. The aftermath of countless injections and drugs had taken their toll on Elizabeth. Her frail arms, no thicker than a broom handle, placed a brightly colored Sunday hat over the few remaining strands of hair on her head. The early May breeze carried the sweet smell of apple blossoms and lilacs through the air as Dr. Stewart held the car door open for her and helped her in.

"Let's go; you know how your mother hates to be late for Mass," he called to Jasper.

"I'm coming; I just needed to find my good shoes."

Jasper flew out the carport door and jumped in the back of the car carrying his shoes in his hands.

"Dad, you can leave right after Mass today. I'll walk home."

"Why?"

"Father Malkin asked me to stay again. He needs some extra help."

"Again? That's great, Jasper. He must really like you," Elizabeth put in.

"Yes," Jasper replied, hiding the fact that he only continued being and altar boy to please her.

Dr. Stewart joined the line of cars stopped at the curb directly in front of the church. Jasper got out and quickly opened the front passenger door to help his mother.

"I'll pick you up in an hour," said Dr. Stewart, leaning toward the passenger side so Elizabeth could hear him before Jasper closed the door.

Elizabeth waved at her husband through the window as he slowly drove away. Jasper held his mother's arm in his, like a father walking a daughter down the aisle, as they approached the church doors. He escorted his mother to the front of the church and helped her into the first pew before quickly making his way to the dressing room behind the altar to put on his vestments.

Jasper stood to the right of Father Malkin, holding the paten as he delivered Communion to the parishioners. A smile broke across Jasper's face when he saw the joy in his mother's eyes as she approached.

Father Malkin saw this show of affection from the boy. "The Body of Christ," he said, placing the Eucharist in Elizabeth's hands. His hypnotic eyes bore down on hers as he formed a near unperceivable smile—more sinister than affectionate.

"Amen," Elizabeth responded as she placed the Eucharist on her tongue and returned to her pew.

The final notes of the organ faded as the hymn ended, signaling the congregation to take their leave, and Jasper stood with Father Malkin on the front steps of the church to greet the parishioners as they left.

Elizabeth walked slowly toward them, her face hidden from the bright spring sunlight by the brim of her hat. She strained to raise her hand to Father Malkin.

"Wonderful sermon, Father."

"Thank you, Elizabeth, you're too kind."

"How's my son doing?" she asked as she lifted her hat to look into Jasper's eyes.

"You have a very special boy; you must be proud of him."

"There is nothing that makes this weary heart warmer than to see my Jasper on the altar next to you."

"Maybe a future in the church for him?" suggested Father Malkin, giving no indication of whether he meant the words or was simply paying a kindness to Elizabeth.

"I could only hope to live to see the day."

Dr. Stewart stopped the car at the front of the church to limit Elizabeth's walk and lowered the passenger widow.

"Jasper, help your mother into the car please."

Jasper rushed to the side of the car before Elizabeth, opened the door and helped his mother in.

"Thank you," Elizabeth said with a wan smile.

"Are you sure you don't want me to pick you up? You can call when you're ready," asked Dr. Stewart turning to his son.

"No, Dad. I won't be long, and it's a nice day."

Jasper closed his mother's door and waved good-bye before turning around to rejoin Father Malkin, who was waiting for him at the church door.

"Can you get the boxes out of my minivan and put them in the basement, and then join me in my office? It's the silver one out back."

"Sure, Father. What are we doing today?"

"Today your work will be religious."

An uneasiness accompanied Father Malkin's answer, and Jasper held his place momentarily, unaware of why he didn't move. Like walking on a frozen pond on a warm spring day, instinct urged Jasper to leave immediately, but his commitment to his mother overpowered it.

Jasper walked to the back parking lot and retrieved the boxes from the minivan. He carried them to the basement as requested and then went upstairs to change.

He left the change room and walked the short hallway to Father Malkin's office, where he knocked on the office door still feeling uneasy.

"Come in."

Jasper found Father Malkin sitting on a small tan loveseat. His long black robe was untied at the waist so the ends of the thick white rope hung close to the floor. The blinds were lowered so that only slivers of natural light entered the room. Jasper's throat closed as the repulsive smell of incense filtered through his nostrils.

"Come sit," said the priest, pointing to the barely visible

section of empty cushion next to him.

Jasper's feet wouldn't lift off the floor. Unfamiliar surroundings, unfamiliar thoughts and unfamiliar feelings crippled his movements—something wasn't right.

"We need to talk. Come."

Jasper reluctantly did as he was told.

"Is there a problem, Father Malkin? Have I done something wrong?"

"No. You haven't done anything wrong, Jasper. It's your mother."

"What's my mother done?"

"Nothing. She's an angel. There isn't another in this entire parish as dedicated as your mother. That's what I need to talk to you about. Your mother's very ill, and right now she needs all the help we can give her."

"How can I help?" asked Jasper, forgetting the apprehension which moments ago had overwhelmed him.

"You need to get closer to God—for He's the only one who can save your mother. You do want to save your mother, don't you?" asked Father Malkin as he cast his eyes directly into Jasper's and slid his body closer to the boy.

"Yes, more than anything in the whole world. How do I get closer to God?"

"First you must get closer to me, and by getting closer to me, you are closer to God. This is the only way we can truly save your mother."

Violation tore through Jasper like a wild fire, scorching his senses until he felt nothing at all. He would do anything to save his mother, and Father Malkin knew it. He slid his robe open, and Jasper disappeared into darkness.

CHAPTER 3

THE DEER

The pungent fumes of antiseptic filled the room as the rhythmic sounds of the monitors faded to silence. Jasper reached over the hospital bed and interlocked his mother's frigid fingers inside his. He couldn't look at her anymore; the last six months of pain had seared his heart until he felt nothing but anger. It was cruel for a child to witness his mother's insidious transformation. Her snow-white body, whittled away by the cancer, lay motionless except for the faint upward movement of her chest as she inhaled.

Two men towered over her bed and witnessed this, her last breath of existence. Father Malkin completed her last rights and blessed her departure with holy water while Dr. Stewart caressed her forehead.

Jasper knew the instant it happened. He didn't see it, but he felt it. The seed of anger inside him exploded, spreading to every cell of his body and leaving him saturated with hate. He was angry at everyone: at his mother for dying, at the doctors for not saving her, and most of all at Father Malkin. Jasper loathed his very existence.

Jasper's eyes reached across the room and grabbed Father Malkin's.

"There is no God—I wish it was you," he uttered with vulgarity then rose from his seat and bolted out the door, ignoring his father's plea to stop.

Jasper sprinted through the ward to the stairs at the end of the hallway. He skipped down two flights and kicked open the exit doors. The feeling began with a burning sensation followed by blurred vision, but he fought the urge to cry and ran faster. He darted between two ambulances parked in front of the entrance to the ER and sat on the curb. Tears had yet to form in his eyes, seeming to evaporate from the pain burning deep inside him. A moment later the large glass doors of the hospital slid open and his father walked out. Seconds passed before Dr. Stewart's crystal blue eyes adjusted to the bright summer sunlight and he was able to locate his son. Relieved Jasper hadn't gone far, Dr. Stewart returned into the hospital.

***

"Hi, Jasper," said Diana, a pleasant-looking fifteen-year-old as she walked up to his locker.

"Hey," was all he could manage.

Jasper flipped the hair out of his eyes with a quick snap of his neck and turned to face Diana. His skin tingled with fear. Girls scared Jasper, especially older ones like Diana.

When Jasper opened his locker, Diana's attention was immediately drawn to the small poster hanging on the inside of the door. It was a photo of the sun setting over Waikiki Beach as three surfers rode a turquoise blue wave.

"You surf?" she asked in a tone filled with surprise.

"Not yet, but I'm gonna one day," replied Jasper, slightly embarrassed.

Her eyes then turned toward the mountain of books piled on the shelf in front of them. She pulled one off the top and scanned the cover.

"No wonder you skipped grade ten. Is this what you read for fun?" she asked while lifting a three-inch-thick textbook on human genetics out of his locker.

"Not for fun," he said defensively. "I just think science is kinda cool, that's all. I want to be a geneticist when I go to..."

Jasper's sentence was cut short when his locker door slammed into the side of his head. The door pushed his head into his locker and nicked the skin near his temple. A droplet of blood oozed from the small cut. The blow left him disoriented for an instant and allowed Diana to catch a glimpse of the back of his neck.

"Hey, faggot, I didn't think homos talked to girls," said Kurtis Hodgeson while the small group of teenage boys next to him laughed.

Rage surged inside Jasper as he regained his composure and clenched his right fist. He turned to face Kurtis, but Diana stepped between them, blocking Jasper from taking a swing.

"You're such a Neanderthal, Kurt. Leave him alone," Diana snapped.

"Ohhh, look everyone, the faggot's got the girls protecting him now!" said Kurtis as he and the other boys walked off down the hall laughing.

"Just ignore those guys, they're idiots," Diana said, trying to console Jasper.

"Yeah. And I now know where they can find the Missing Link," he said, rubbing his head and unknowingly smearing the blood, which was covered by his hair.

Diana crumpled her forehead before casting a smile even though she didn't understand Jasper's attempt at humor.

"That's cool, you have a tattoo," she said, clearly not expecting to see one.

"What?" replied Jasper in a moment of confusion.

"On the back of your neck; it looks like a fish."

"Oh that, it's not a..." he started, but Diana cut him off with a gasp when she noticed the trickle of red snaking down his forehead.

"You're bleeding!" she exclaimed and pointed to his head.

Jasper touched his forehead where he felt the pain from the door and looked at his now red fingertip.

"It's okay, I'm fine," he said, not wanting any more

attention than he was already getting. He pulled a dirty gym shirt off the hook in his locker and wiped the blood off his head.

"You sure? We can go to the nurse."

"No, no, I'm fine, really," he assured her.

"Okay," she said, still a little skeptical. "What I wanted to ask you before that idiot came was, do you want to go to a movie sometime?"

"Sure, that sounds great," Jasper said, knowing it was a lie. Still, Diana's request left him stunned, and he stayed standing only with the support of his locker door. He felt more afraid of her than any bully he had encountered.

Jasper had never asked a girl out, but now, one had asked *him* on a date. Skilled at avoiding girls, he was a master at deflecting what few requests he got. His thoughts quickly turned to the reason for his abstinence and the problem haunting his fourteen-year-old life: after many attempts, he still hadn't even masturbated successfully. Deep down, Jasper was convinced this was a result of what happened when he was an altar boy.

The thought of not being able to bring himself to completion in the presence of a girl conjured such an intense fear inside him that it left him no choice but to avoid dating altogether. He was determined to suppress the sexual urges he had. Like most teenage boys, Jasper lied to his friends, including his best friend Greg, about his sex life, but it wasn't long before the cruelty of teenagers saw through his lies, and they labeled him gay.

***

"Jasper, can you come down here!" shouted Dr. Stewart as he entered the house.

Jasper was lying on his bed working on his laptop when he heard his father's request.

"Coming!" he called.

He placed the computer on the bed and leaped onto the floor, heading downstairs.

"What's up, Dad?" he asked, instinctively aware something was wrong the moment he saw his father's face.

"I got a call from the school today…"

"For what?" interrupted Jasper.

"Come sit down," said Dr. Stewart, and he led the way into the kitchen so they could sit at the table.

"What's wrong?" Jasper asked again, desperately trying to recall what he may have done to warrant a call from the school.

As they sat at the kitchen table, Jasper could see the concern covering his father's face.

"Dad, what is it?" he demanded.

"Counselor Pierson called me today."

"Great!" snapped Jasper, certain he knew the reason for the call and his father's troubled expression.

"How long has this been going on?"

"What?" responded Jasper, knowing full well his father knew about the bullying.

"The bullying."

"It's nothing; I can handle it."

"If it was nothing, would the school be calling me?"

"Dad, it's nothing, so just leave it alone."

"How long has this been going on?" he asked, unable to conceal the anger in his tone.

"I don't know,—since grade nine?" Jasper replied with no attempt to hide his sarcasm.

"What? Three years? Why didn't you say anything?"

"There's nothing to say, and don't go making a scene over this. I'll be graduating soon and never have to see those idiots again."

"Jasper, you listen to me. This is going to stop right now. I'm calling Pierson in the morning. If they don't do something about it, I will."

"Dad, please, don't. Grad is only two months from now,

and then it's over."

"Why are they doing this?" Dr. Stewart asked, even though Counselor Pierson had informed him of the homophobic nature of the harassment.

"What?"

"Picking on you?"

"I don't know," Jasper replied, letting his shoulder length hair fall over his face to partially obscure his eyes.

"Jasper?" demanded Dr. Stewart, well aware of his son's attempt to avoid eye contact.

"I told you, I don't know. Can you just leave it alone?"

"Fine, I'll set up a meeting with Counselor Pierson for tomorrow."

"Dad!" Jasper pleaded.

"I'm listening?"

Jasper remained silent as a battle raged inside his head. The urge to finally tell his father pulled at his thoughts, but the embarrassment was overwhelming, and he was determined to deal with it himself. *I've made it this far, I'm not about to cave now,* he thought and flipped the hair off his face.

"It's nothing, Dad. Really, I'm fine."

Dr. Stewart knew the power of Jasper's conviction and that once he had made his mind up, nothing or no one could change it. He left the table without making eye contact with his son.

***

The July sun, still high over the valley, painted the mountains in hues of silver and blue. Swallows darted over the meadows, gorging themselves on mosquitoes and black flies. The deep roar of a fully loaded logging truck echoed up the valley like approaching thunder, and the aromatic fragrance of the Ponderosa pines was replaced by the choking dust from the truck as it charged down the gravel road past the lake where the two boys had spent countless hours fishing.

"Aren't the mosquitoes driving you nuts? They're eating me alive," said Greg as he slapped his forearm for the tenth time.

"Nope, I don't think they like my blood," Jasper replied with an intended degree of smugness.

"Well, I'm getting out of here."

Greg zipped up his leather riding jacket, pulled his helmet over his head and slammed the kick-starter of his dirt bike. The resulting crack of the motorcycle sent a group of wood grouse flying from the top of a nearby spruce tree. Greg took off, and Jasper jumped on his bike, accelerating hard to catch up, a trail of dust bellowing up behind them.

The next lake was like glass when they pulled up and got off their bikes. Greg and Jasper spent most of their summer holidays exploring logging roads and fly-fishing the dozens of mountain lakes above Kelowna.

"Aren't you worried about drowning, Jasper?" asked Greg, watching Jasper skip between floating logs while holding his fly rod.

"Nope, haven't fallen in yet. Anyways, what's the worst that can happen? You get wet."

"I guess... I just don't like the thought of drowning; it freaks me out—that's all."

"Well, I don't like the thought of riding home wet."

"So, are you going to ask her to the movie?" Greg asked in a clear attempt to catch Jasper off guard.

"Who?" replied Jasper, knowing full well Greg was referring to Diana.

"Come on, Diana! You know she likes you, and man, she's hot!"

"Are you kidding? She doesn't even know I exist. What about you? Are you going to ask Linda?" Jasper asked in his own attempt to catch Greg off guard and to deflect the topic away from himself.

"Already did."

"You dog! What did she say?"

"Yes, of course," said Greg as smugly as possible. "That's why I wanted you to ask Diana, so we could go together."

"Hey, I got one!" Jasper shouted suddenly.

The water erupted with the thrashing of a rainbow trout trying to release itself from the hook. An overwhelming feeling of relief filled Jasper as the fish surfaced at the perfect moment to end the conversation. He intentionally played the fish longer than necessary to keep the topic of dating from re-emerging. After fighting hard for ten minutes, the fish took one last run for freedom and spit the hook as it leaped clear out of the lake.

"Shit," Jasper said in a feeble attempt to fake disappointment at the loss.

"Too bad, that was a nice one," Greg observed.

"I'll get another."

"Hey, have you decided where you're going to university yet? My parents keep bugging me to go to UBC, but I'm not sure."

Jasper was thrilled the fish had worked its magic and the subject of girls was finished. He was looking forward to going to university and talking about it made him even more excited.

"Yes, didn't I tell you? My dad got a position as the Dean of Sciences at the University of Windsor—that's where I'll be."

"Really, Ontario? Do they even have a law school?"

"I think so, but not a very big one. Is that what you're taking—law? You want to be a lawyer?"

"My parents said they'd pay for my school if I take medicine or law. I hate blood as much as I hate working, so law it is," Greg stated with a shrug.

"A lawyer, that's cool," replied Jasper, somewhat in disbelief.

"And if you're going to Windsor, so am I," Greg stated.

"I don't think I'll be able to help you with your homework—I know nothing about law," said Jasper with a grin, knowing he had done more than one of Greg's science essays for him.

"Tell me about it; that's the scariest part of going."

"And you'd better get your application in soon—the deadline's next week."

"Great," Greg replied, his laziness getting the better of him.

"We better get going—it's getting late," Jasper said, looking at his watch. "I'll race you to the top of Dead Man's Hill."

"You're on!"

They packed up their fishing gear and mounted their dirt bikes as the sun slipped below the mountaintop. The relief from the heat was instant. Greg and Jasper aligned their bikes in front of an imaginary starting line in the middle of the gravel road; the noise from the revving engines was painful even with their helmets on. The two turned to face each other, and the moment their eyes met, the race began.

Greg resembled an NFL linebacker; at least six inches taller and forty pounds heavier than Jasper. This additional mass combined with a much older dirt bike rendered the race over before it began. Jasper shot out to an immediate lead, leaving Greg in a cloud of dust so thick he was forced to pull off the road.

Completely unaware of his lack of competition, Jasper continued accelerating up the gravel road towards the blind hilltop. The remaining daylight filtered through the thick forest on either side of the narrow road, so Jasper felt like he was racing through a tunnel. The loose gravel on the top of the road caused the back of his bike to fishtail with each shift of the gears; but the poor conditions weren't enough to slow him down. After four years of riding, Jasper's skills were excellent.

Jasper could taste victory as he climbed the hill faster than he had ever done before. Adrenaline flooded his body, and the muscles in his legs began to tense in anticipation of the thirty feet of air he expected at the crest of the hill. With a final snap to his wrist, he opened the throttle to its fullest less than fifty feet from the top.

All of a sudden, instinct interrupted the high his mind was expecting. Without even thinking, Jasper wrenched the handlebars to the left as he slammed the back brake pedal with all his strength. The bike turned hard, sliding on the gravel and just missing the backside of a deer as it leaped past him. Jasper held the bike up, and it skidded to a halt in the ditch.

The huge animal disappeared in a cloud of khaki-colored dust just as a fully loaded logging truck barreled over the crest of the hill and ripped between them.

Jasper dropped his bike to the ground and fell to his knees, too shaken to support his own weight. Road dust filled his eyes, providing the perfect excuse for the appearance of large tears, which snaked down his cheeks leaving a worm trail in the dust on his face.

Jasper didn't thank God, but knew he owed his life to a deer.

CHAPTER 4

FINAL JUSTICE

The stone walls of the tiny cafeteria were painted bone white, making the room appear larger. A long wooden picnic-bench-style table extended the length of the room, leaving just enough space for a person to walk between it and the life-sized crucifix hanging from the wall. The traditional red and white checkered tablecloth was barely visible between the bowls of pasta and plates of cheese. Heated discussion filtered out the windows as the cream-colored Italian moon cast shadows on the walls.

The banter halted when a middle-aged man arrived. He had silver-grey hair and ink-black eyes, devoid of light, like a starless night sky. He commanded the room as he stood at the head of the table and addressed the now silent group of eight men with authority.

"There is no time to waste. You must begin at once. They have to be found." His English was perfect but burdened by a strong Italian accent.

"Why is it so urgent?" asked a much older man sitting halfway down the table. He wore a turban and was dressed in traditional Indian attire.

"Yes, what's going on? Why have you called us here on such short notice?" interrupted an Asian man sitting next to him.

"We are running out of time, and they must be stopped," said the grey-haired man, causing the room to erupt into discussion.

None of the men crowding the table heard the ring of his cell phone through the din. The grey-haired man reached deep into his breast pocket and retrieved his phone, looking at the caller ID while making his way outside.

"*Pronto*," he said as he placed the phone to his ear.

"We have another," answered the caller.

"How many this time?"

"Who knows? Ten for sure, maybe a dozen or more."

"Where?"

"Canada."

"I want it dealt with at once. You know what to do."

"Yes, sir."

"Make it immaculate, understand?" instructed the grey-haired man as he prepared to hang up the phone.

"Of course. I'll send the Australian."

"These abominations could jeopardize my plans. I want to know when it is done. Have him call me."

"Certainly."

"Wait, the name?" asked the grey-haired man.

"Malkin."

***

All of Kelowna was asleep at three in the morning except the few who worked the trade. Two teenage boys stood on the curbside wearing only cut-off jeans and tattoos. A silver minivan cruised slowly toward them, the driver was invisible in the shadow of the streetlights. The van stopped directly in front of the two boys and rolled down the passenger window.

"How much?" asked the driver in a thick Australian accent.

"That depends," said the taller of the two boys.

"What are you looking for?" asked the smaller boy.

"Fifty for an hour," said the driver.

The two boys laughed out loud.

"For both of us? You'll have to do better than that," said

the taller boy.

"No, just you," replied the driver, pointing to the smaller boy.

"Okay, but I charge more for anything weird—you know—kinky," the small boy said as he entered the self-opening side door of the van. The door slowly slid closed, and the van drove away into the darkness.

The driver and boy stood at the front door of the rectory, and the driver removed a pair of black leather gloves from his jacket, pulling them on before pressing the doorbell.

Father Malkin lay fast asleep in his bed when the chime woke him. The bell rang three more times as the priest made his way down the stairs. Still not fully awake, he opened the front door to find a man equal to his height standing with a teenage boy.

"What in heaven's name brings you two here at this hour?"

"Father, we have an emergency," said the driver.

"Are you hurt? What is it? Please come in." Father Malkin was now somewhat concerned.

"Nothing like that," replied the driver as he and the boy entered the rectory, shutting the door behind them.

"What is it then?" asked the priest, still clearly concerned that there was some sort of medical problem.

"You haven't been a very good servant of God, have you now, Father Malkin?"

"What do you mean?" replied the priest, his concern evaporating and replaced by apprehension.

"Do you like this boy? Does he turn you on, Father?" asked the driver, obviously enjoying the immediate reaction on Father Malkin's face.

"What the hell are you talking about...?"

"Now, Father, that's not language becoming of a holy man, is it? But you're not much of a holy man, are you?"

"Get out of here, I'm calling the police." The fear in the father's voice was evident.

"Look, buddy, I don't do priests," interrupted the boy.

"Shut up and get over there with him," said the driver as he pulled a revolver from under his jacket.

"What are you doing?" Father Malkin shouted.

"Shut up, the both of you—not another word. Move upstairs to the bedroom," demanded the driver as he pointed the gun at them.

They went upstairs, and the driver ordered Father Malkin to remove his nightclothes and lay naked, face down on the bed. "Hold that pillow over your head," he demanded.

"Please, I beg you…"

"Shut up and do it!"

Father Malkin began to pray to himself as he buried his face into the bed and slid a pillow over the back of his head.

The driver reached into his jacket and pulled a second gun from the inside pocket.

"If you want to live, you'll do exactly what I say. You won't get another chance," said the driver as he handed the second gun to the boy and held the muzzle of his own gun to the side of the boy's head.

"Move over there." He pointed to the side of the bed where Father Malkin lay.

Fear silenced the boy and tears fell from his face as he walked to the bed.

"Put the gun to his head—now!" shouted the driver.

With a trembling hand, the boy lifted the gun and placed it a few inches from the pillow over Father Malkin's head. His tears were replaced by open sobbing as he looked back at the driver.

"Pull the trigger."

"I can't!" he cried.

"Do it!"

The crack of the gun caused the boy to stumble backwards, and the salty smell of the gunpowder filled the room. The boy lowered the gun to his side as the driver approached, still pointing his own gun at the boy.

"Keep your hands down," commanded the driver.

The boy didn't respond. He just stared, catatonic, at the stream of crimson blood trickling from beneath the pillow and pooling on the pearl-white sheets.

The driver positioned himself to the right of the boy and grabbed his right hand, which still held the gun. He slowly and purposefully lifted it to the side of the boy's head and pulled the trigger.

***

Two days later, Jasper sat at the kitchen table eating dinner with his father and watching the evening news. The weather forecast was interrupted by the anchorwoman.

"We have breaking news—this just in: a murder-suicide has been discovered in Kelowna tonight. It appears to involve a well-known local priest."

Jasper's stomach formed an instant knot as he put down his fork. Goosebumps formed on his arms and legs in anticipation of the news report details. Dr. Stewart turned in his seat to get a better view of the TV.

"We're now going live to the apparent murder-suicide location, where our correspondent Brett Keta is on the scene. Brett, what can you tell us?"

"I'm here at St. Alphonsus Catholic Church, where police have just confirmed they have found two bodies in what appears to be a murder-suicide. Our sources have told us one of the dead is the head of this parish—a Father Allen Malkin. The other is an unidentified male believed to be in his teens."

The blood rushed to Jasper's face, singeing his cheeks auburn red. His heart pounded in his chest as the warm feeling that began in his face filled his body. Afraid to be discovered, Jasper didn't let his father see his growing smile, but he savored the sweet taste of vindication. This was final justice for Malkin, and ambrosia to Jasper's mind.

The euphoria was short lived as Jasper's thoughts moved

to the dead teenager. *That could have been me,* he thought as his mind filled with the darkness of Malkin's office.

"Dad, why would Father Malkin kill a boy?"

"Why would anyone want to kill anybody?"

The next day, the headlines on the morning paper read: 'Child Abuse at The Church—Teenager Kills Priest.'

Dr. Stewart read the first three columns of the story and stopped after the part where it said the police had found an eyewitness who identified Father Malkin's silver minivan as the one seen picking up the teenage boy prostitute. The article went on to explain how the boy had killed Father Malkin, and not the other way around.

Dr. Stewart boiled with anger as he waited for Jasper to arrive in the kitchen for breakfast. The paper remained open on the table next to his empty coffee mug. Fury painted his normally smiling face stoic. Jasper walked into the kitchen and immediately recognized the look on his father's face.

"I want you to sit down, we need to talk," Dr. Stewart said in an unusually calm voice.

The last time Jasper had heard these words from his father was the worst day of his life; he knew nothing good was about to follow.

"What's up, Dad?"

"I need you to be completely honest with me, Jasper. Can you do that?"

"Always, why?"

"What went on at the church when you were an altar boy and helping Father Malkin?"

A bitter coldness gripped Jasper's body, his flesh tightening as his eyes met his father's. Silence engulfed the room, leaving only the sound of their breathing. Dr. Stewart closed the paper so the headline could be read and tossed it across the table to Jasper. Jasper bowed his head to read the caption, allowing his hair to cover his face.

"It was nothing..." he replied, his face hidden behind a cloak of hair.

"What was nothing?" interrupted Dr. Stewart, leaping from his seat.

"Dad, relax, it was nothing," repeated Jasper as he flipped the hair out of his face.

"What did that fucking pervert do to you?" yelled Dr. Stewart nearly at the top of his voice.

This was the first time in Jasper's life he had heard his father curse.

Dr. Stewart leaned on the table, his face inches from Jasper's. "What did he do?" he repeated through clenched teeth.

"Dad, stop. I'm fine. Just leave it alone," Jasper begged.

"I'm not leaving it alone. You need to get help. I'm taking you to the doctor today."

"There's no way I'm going to some shrink if that's what you mean!"

"You need to get help! You've been abused, Jasper."

"Dad, listen to me. I'm not going, and if you drag me, it will be a total waste of time because I won't talk."

Dr. Stewart knew his son well; his stubbornness had become legendary by the time he was three. There was nothing he or any psychiatrist could do to make Jasper talk if he was determined not to; pushing the matter would only fuel his stubbornness.

***

The warm Italian sun was setting behind the Roman hillsides when the grey-haired man's cell phone rang.

"*Pronto*," he said.

"It's done," said the caller simply.

"I trust it went well?" asked the grey-haired man.

"Immaculate."

CHAPTER 5

ANGELA

The small dimly lit boardroom buzzed with the sound of the projector. Light reflected off the screen behind Jasper, barely illuminating the faces of the students crowded around the long oval table. Dr. Sierra Peterson and the other graduate students from the Advanced Developmental Biology class filled the boardroom.

Jasper looked at his captivated audience, and a smile erupted on his face. He paused for just the right amount of time before clicking the mouse to summon the final slide. Instantly the screen filled with Jasper's favorite quote from the Bible: 'God created man in his own image...'

The audience joined in his amusement as low whispers broke the silence. The words faded off the screen, replaced by a larger-than-life image of Adam and Eve standing naked in the Garden of Eden with an apelike Neanderthal hanging from a palm tree. The room filled with laughter.

"In conclusion, clearly the recent advancements in forensic DNA analysis will finally put to rest the theory of Creationism—the missing link was never missing! Thank you for your time."

The audience sat silent, stunned by the graphic on the screen and Jasper's provocative conclusion. Dr. Peterson initiated the clapping with a few loud cracks of her hands. This approval was the cue for the others to follow, and the group of students gave Jasper an extended round of applause.

"Well done, Mr. Stewart. Your presentation skills are excellent, and your opinion on the merits of evolution versus creationism is very thought provoking. I'm sure that many wouldn't agree with your findings, but we'll leave that for the theologists to debate," said Dr. Peterson.

"Thank you, Dr. Peterson."

Dr. Peterson's course, along with Biochemistry and Human Genetics, were the last three courses Jasper required for his doctorate. Like his father, Jasper excelled in genetics, although after becoming the Dean of the Faculty of Science, Dr. Stewart now spent most of his time in his office doing administrative work.

Jasper finished accepting congratulations from his classmates and left the Biology building on his way to the Chemistry building, where he crossed paths with Greg. Ten minutes into their conversation, Jasper glanced at his phone to get the time.

"Oh man. I'm late for the lab, and I'm going to end up sitting with some loser who just wants to copy everything I do," said Jasper. "Sorry, I've gotta go—if the weather holds, maybe this weekend we can head to the river? I'll call you."

Jasper raced up the front steps of the Chemistry building, taking them two at a time. When he reached the second floor, Jasper kicked the stairwell door open and flew down the hall to his lab door. It was closed, which meant the TA had already started the lesson.

Great, he thought as he slowly swung the door open, hoping no one would notice. Normally it was no big deal to arrive late for a class, but since this was the first class of the semester, that meant lab partners would be determined based on where people sat.

Unfortunately for Jasper, no one was at their seat. The fifteen students were all at the back of the lab getting glassware and other equipment for the day's experiment. Jasper searched around for a bench with no books or personal belongings on it. He finally found the one unclaimed seat left in the room. The last bench available was right at the front of the room, no more than three feet from the TA's desk.

Ah, crap, he thought as he walked to the seat. He threw his backpack on the bench and took out his biochemistry lab manual.

"Not the way I hoped to start the semester," he muttered to himself, but then things went from bad to worse. Jasper was casually flipping through the pages of the manual to find the day's lesson when the air filled with the exquisite scent of perfume.

"I'm Angela," said a soft voice. The words entered his ears as a female hand placed a large Erlenmeyer flask on the bench next to him.

"Jasper," he said without looking up and in a manner intended to be rude.

Still seated on his stool, Jasper turned his head to face the girl, accidentally placing his eyes directly onto her breasts. His burning crimson face provided a noticeable contrast to her loosely buttoned blue blouse. Thinking quickly, Jasper turned his eyes to the small gold cross nestled in Angela's cleavage.

"What a beautiful cross," he said, hoping both his eyeballs were still attached to his face.

"My grandmother got it for me in Italy for my sixteenth birthday," replied Angela.

Jasper unlocked his eyes from her chest and looked up to find the face from which the soft voice had originated.

A familiar sick feeling overcame Jasper without warning—the feeling of riding on a rollercoaster just as it approaches the highest peak, or when the flight you are on hits turbulence at 35,000 feet. Jasper remained glued to his stool for what felt like a lifetime. The manners his mother and father had worked so hard to instill in him evaporated. He completely ignored her reply and sat paralyzed with fear.

Angela was beautiful; there was no other way to describe her. She was of medium height with long dark brown hair which she wore in a ponytail held up with a blue scrunchy to match her blouse. Her eyes were as big as quarters and filled with the most beautiful dark-chocolate brown tint imaginable. Still sitting on his stool, Jasper continued to take in Angela's presence. The most noticeable part of her beauty was that all of this was accomplished without the use of any makeup. Angela had perfect genes; she was naturally gorgeous.

The time it took him to complete his visual assessment of her provided enough distraction for him to ignore his insides. His mind regained control of his body, and like accelerating down to the bottom of that rollercoaster ride, reality struck him hard. Jasper had just met the most beautiful girl in the world, and the only thing he consistently failed at was women.

"I'm so sorry," Jasper said as he finally emerged from his stupor and stood up to properly introduce himself. "I was late for class and didn't want to get stuck with..." Jasper caught himself before he said something he might regret. "I didn't intend to be rude and ignore you just then."

"It's okay," she said, followed by a little giggle that helped relieve some of Jasper's apprehension about his recent less than stellar behavior.

"I guess you're stuck with me then," he said in a higher, less masculine tone than his normal voice.

"No, I think it's the other way around—I'm not a great lab partner. I've broken more glassware than I can count," Angela said.

"Well, how about I handle the setup and you take care of the note taking?"

"Sounds like a deal to me," she replied, holding out her right hand for the two of them to shake on the deal.

Jasper took her hand in his, grasping it gently but firmly and shook it as he announced, "Deal."

It was another five minutes before Jasper took his eyes off of Angela long enough to notice that every other male in the room, including the TA, was looking at him with envy. This led Jasper to wonder, *How could this happen? There's no way my luck will hold—Angela won't want to stay my lab partner after today no matter what the rules are.* The vultures were already circling, and there was no doubt they would quickly move in if they had a chance. Jasper resolved to enjoy the rest of the two-hour class with his partner, knowing full well that next week's class would find Angela sitting with someone else.

The rest of the class flew by, with Jasper hardly taking his eyes off of the girl next to him. They kept to their deal, and Jasper finished the practical part of the assignment, producing the exact amount of caffeine expected: 1.6 grams from the 100 grams of tealeaves. Angela completed near-perfect, detailed notes on the procedure.

A few minutes before the class was to end, the TA made the announcement Jasper didn't want to hear.

"Time to clean up and place your used glassware in the wash-up area."

Jasper glanced over to Angela and was about to thank her for taking such great notes when she cut him off.

"Partners next week?"

Without hesitation and with a little too much enthusiasm, Jasper blurted out, "Sure, if you want to!"

"Yeah, I'd like that—and look, no broken glass," she said.

"Okay, I'll see you then." Jasper started to head for the door before she could change her mind. He was nearly out of the class when Angela's voice called out to him.

"Jasper, wait, the notes!"

He turned and happily headed back toward Angela.

"I have a Genetics class that starts in fifteen minutes on the other side of campus, can we link up later? Say at the library so I can photocopy them?"

Jasper quickly pulled a pen from his backpack and ripped a small piece of paper from his notebook. He wrote his email address on it and handed it over.

"Here, email me and we can set a time to meet," he told her.

Angela responded, "Great, but it might not be today—I have to take my grandmother shopping after class."

Jasper acknowledged her with an "okay" and they parted.

As he picked up his pace to make it on time to his Genetics class, a small part of him couldn't resist thinking, *Late for Biochemistry, met a beautiful girl. Late for Genetics, meet two Victoria Secret models? Get a grip—that was the best encounter you've had since sixth grade square dancing.*

Jasper was nearly jogging by time he got to his Genetics class; the exhilaration streaming through his veins was consuming his every thought. It had been so long since Jasper had let his guard down and allowed himself to fantasize about a woman, and the effects were intoxicating.

Maybe this is the one.

Mark Sekela

CHAPTER 6

GET LUCKY

Jasper had never felt a tingling this strong race through his body. And not since eating instant coffee to pull an all-nighter for undergraduate exams had he felt jitters like this. All his senses were acute in anticipation of Angela's email. The dozen false alarms that arrived as spam on his phone further tightened his stomach and shortened his patience. Jasper was a master at suppressing his sexual fantasies, but now he couldn't hold them back. Countless scenarios raced through his mind, each one more exciting than the previous.

Every time his phone signaled the arrival of an email, Jasper nearly ripped the zipper off the pouch of his backpack to get it. The first email that wasn't spam arrived the next day at noon.

"Please be her, please be her, please be her," he repeated as he slid the phone from his pack and touched the keys to reveal the contents of his inbox.

This time the new mail symbol on the screen was accompanied by the name 'ARossi' which caused Jasper to begin chanting, "Yes, yes, yes!" The subject line of the email displayed the words 'BioChem Lab Notes'. Jasper read the contents of the very short email:

Hi Jasper, I have made a copy of the notes I took in our last Biochem class and would like to give

> *them to you. Are you free this evening around*
> *seven o'clock? If so, we can meet at the Starbucks*
> *on University Ave. Let me know either way,*
> *Angela.*

Jasper felt like he had just won the lottery. He was unable to make his fingers work fast enough to type his reply:

> *Hi Angela, I can make it for seven, will see you*
> *there, Jasper.*

And he pressed the send key.

Jasper's thoughts immediately turned to the increasing butterflies in his stomach. In an effort to gain control, he tried to convince himself of how stupid he was thinking that this would lead anywhere. He tried to focus his thoughts on getting to his class, which started in ten minutes, but his mind raced even faster out of control. *What shall I wear? What cologne should I use? I better get home and shave. I hope my best jeans are clean…*

The rest of that day was a complete write-off as far as his classes were concerned. Normally Jasper would take at least five pages of notes in a lecture, but when he walked out of Developmental Biology he had barely written five lines in his notebook.

His last class of the day was Genetics, something he was more qualified to teach than take, but he needed the class to gain enough credits to graduate. Jasper had never skipped a class in his life, only missing a few school days due to illness. The thought of not going to class hit him like a hangover. *Just this once; this time it's going to be different*, he thought in an attempt to convince himself. Jasper looked at his phone for the time and realized he had no choice. *I have to leave soon or I won't make it back.*

It was nearly four o'clock, and he had a half-hour drive home. Jasper didn't have his own car and shared his commute to the university with his father, so he needed to ask if he could take the car home early.

Jasper hurried to the main Faculty of Science building located next to the campus library in hopes he would find his father in his office. The dean's office was located on the eighth floor, where his father despised working. Jasper could hear his father's voice in his head as he entered the elevator and pushed the number eight button, *'Remember Jasper, no meaningful work ever happens in an office building—the lab is where real research occurs.'*

With his mind tangled in thoughts of Angela and not expecting anyone to be waiting for the elevator, Jasper walked through the slow-moving doors with his eyes on the floor. An older couple waiting for the elevator was equally surprised by Jasper's appearance. The resulting collision sent the man's leather business case tumbling to the floor. Embarrassed by his absentmindedness, Jasper scrambled to pick up the case.

"I'm so sorry," he pleaded, handing the man his case, his eyes drawn to the large gold MBG letters embossed on the rich black leather.

"No, excuse my inattentiveness," replied the man, his foreign accent unmistakable.

"Are you okay?" asked the woman in a soft-spoken voice with an American accent.

"Really, I'm fine," replied Jasper his attention focused on the unusual kindness in the woman's voice.

When the man raised his arm to activate the elevator, the luster of the gems in his watch made Jasper stare like a crow mesmerized by a shiny object. The woman's faced filled with a smile before the couple disappeared behind the stainless steel elevator doors.

Jasper walked out to be greeted by the warm and welcoming voice of Ruth Davidson, the Faculty of Science administrative assistant. Ruth was a very large woman in her mid-fifties. She had long red hair she kept disheveled in what could only be described as a Klingon hairstyle.

When Ruth smiled, it always reminded Jasper of his

mother, even though they didn't look anything alike. Maybe it was that Ruth was always glad to see him. She never failed to offer him one of the plentiful candies stored on her desk.

"Hi, Jasper. I haven't seen you in ages. You're in luck, he's in and doesn't have anything left in his planner for the afternoon," said Ruth as if she were reading Jasper's mind.

"Great, so can I go on in?"

"Sure. Would you like an M&M—they're almond," Ruth said. Her smile stretched from ear to ear as if to say how much he would like them.

"No thanks, but maybe next time," Jasper replied as he made his way down the hall to the large corner office overlooking the Ambassador Bridge and the Detroit River.

"And when are you going to cut that hair?" shouted Ruth in a motherly fashion as Jasper disappeared into Dr. Stewart's office.

Dr. Stewart had his back to the door and was typing vigorously on his computer keyboard.

"Hey, Dad, how's it going?" Jasper said to get his father's attention, and at the sound of Jasper's voice, Dr. Stewart stopped his typing mid-word and stood up to greet his son.

"Hi, Jasper, what brings you here so soon—is everything all right?"

"Everything's fine, Dad, and why do you always jump to the conclusion that something's wrong when I show up in your office? You know, I'll be twenty-one this December. I think you can stop worrying about me," Jasper replied with a slightly acidic tone.

Dr. Stewart responded more with his facial expressions than his words and said, "I'm sorry, Jasper, but it's a father's job to make sure everything's okay when his son arrives unexpectedly at his office. Now what's the occasion?"

"I was hoping you might be able to catch a ride home with Professor Petra today. I'd like to head home now if that's okay with you."

Dr. Stewart immediately replied, "Are you sure you're

okay? Are you feeling ill or did some...?" Jasper cut his father off mid-sentence with his retort.

"Yes, Dad, I'm fine. Now stop!"

"Don't you have a class right now?"

Jasper responded in a much lower, more sheepish tone. "Yeah Genetics, but I've been acing that class and missing one lecture isn't going to kill me."

"This must be important for you to miss a class and make me wait for Professor Petra to finish her lecture. You know how long she goes on," said Dr. Stewart with a small smile on his face.

"I'm meeting a friend at Starbucks tonight to go over some of our Biochem lab notes," Jasper explained, hoping his father would drop the questioning at this point but knowing it was highly unlikely.

Sure enough, Dr. Stewart asked in a voice of astonishment, "Starbucks, do you mean you're going to drive all the way home so you can turn around and drive right back here to meet someone across the street?"

Just as the words left Dr. Stewart's lips, an unmistakable expression of understanding spread across his face.

"Oh," he said. He paused for a second then turned to his computer to see the screen saver bouncing around the darkened monitor before returning his eyes to Jasper.

"Tell you what, I'll pack up now and finish this email at home, that way we can both hit the road before rush hour."

"Thanks, Dad." Jasper wasn't sure if he was thanking him for the early departure or the fact that he had dropped the questioning about his early departure.

The ride home dragged on for what seemed like hours to Jasper even though his father was right and they missed the worst of the rush hour. Jasper was also thankful his father never asked once about who he was meeting. In order to prevent the subject from coming up, Jasper asked about the couple he had bumped into at the elevator.

"Dad, who was that couple that just left your office before

I arrived?"

"Oh, you met them."

"More like ran into them."

"What?"

"We collided in front of the elevator."

"I hope you were nice to them?"

"Of course, why?"

"You ran into the Mullers. They fund our genetic research."

"Really? That doesn't surprise me."

"Why?"

"They just looked very wealthy."

"They are. He's Derek Muller of MBG, the Muller Banking Group, and the woman is his wife Tanya."

"He sounded German, but she sounded American?"

"Close, he's Swiss, and his wife is from New York."

"What do they do?"

"Banking."

"Oh," said Jasper nodding his head with understanding but no better informed.

For the rest of the thirty-minute drive home their conversation was devoted totally to Dr. Stewart's research on human DNA from ancient artifacts.

Jasper had never showered, shaved and dressed as quickly as he did once they got home. The anxiety raced through his body like a drug, rendering him oblivious to his surroundings, including the time. Panic grabbed his mind when he glanced at the clock to find it was ten after six. He was cutting it close if he was going to drive back to the university by seven. One small fender-bender on the expressway would mean him arriving late for his meeting with Angela. Jasper wanted to make a great first impression and planned to arrive well before her so he could secure a table near the window; he would also have her coffee waiting on arrival.

So far everything was going as planned. Jasper had shaved

without hacking any part of his face—negating the need to stop the usual bleeding—found his favorite jeans clean enough to risk wearing and splashed on his best Hugo Boss cologne. With a quick shout, "Bye, Dad!" from the front entranceway of the house, Jasper opened the door and made his way to the car.

He had just opened the car door when Dr. Stewart let out a cautious, "Good luck," from the front door and waved good-bye. Jasper was well aware of the actual meaning of the two words his father had spoken. No one knew his record with women better than his father.

Luck, Jasper repeated the word in his head as he drove the car down the driveway and out towards the expressway. *Luck is what I want tonight, but what I really need is to get lucky.*

Jasper turned into the Starbucks parking lot fifteen minutes before seven o'clock. He slammed on the brakes while pulling into the vacant parking stall as a couple darted out from behind a large steel garbage bin to the left. Overcome with anticipation, Jasper smiled through the windshield out of courtesy but never made eye contact. The couple giggled like guilty school kids as they walked between the bin and the car. While waiting for them to pass, Jasper's eyes were drawn to the pallet of tattoos covering the man's left arm. Jasper left the car and repeated the words "Get lucky" out loud one more time as he walked through the parking lot towards the café entrance.

A middle-aged woman approached the entrance at the same time as Jasper. She was very distinctive and familiar looking; tall and slender with very long brown hair. Jasper grabbed the door handle just before the woman and held the door open. As the woman entered, her eyes met Jasper's, and for an instant, Jasper was certain he knew her.

"Thank you," she said and proceeded inside. Jasper quickly forgot the woman as a wave of fragrant air flooded out the doorway, and his nose filled with the aroma of roasting coffee beans. The loud sounds of coffee grinders and espresso machines steaming milk muffled the voices of the crowd waiting for their coffee.

Jasper scanned the tables one by one hoping not to see Angela's face. This was the first part of his plan—buying the coffees and getting a table by the window before she arrived. *So far so good*, he thought. Just as he was sure the coast was clear, on the far side of the coffee shop the long line of individuals waiting for their order moved to the left. Then Jasper spotted her; Angela was sitting by herself in one of the two booths by the window on the opposite side of the room.

Angela hadn't seen him yet; she was sitting in the booth with her view toward Jasper still partially blocked by the line of people at the counter. This also prevented Jasper from getting a clear look at Angela's face. When Jasper began walking closer, he noticed that there were two coffee cups already on the table in front of her.

Did she have the same plan as me? he thought. *Could it be I really am going to get lucky this time?*

When Jasper approached the booth, Angela noticed his arrival and looked at him with a heart-stopping smile. She lifted her hand and gave him a small wave, and Jasper slid into the booth opposite her.

"Hi, nice to see you again," he said, barely containing his enthusiasm. It took all of Jasper's strength to keep him from reaching across the table to hold her hand. Angela must have detected the awkwardness in Jasper's face, as she instinctively withdrew her hand and sat back in the booth to add some distance between them.

"Do you want a coffee?"

Jasper nodded his head and began reaching for the second cup of coffee on the table when Angela reached out to prevent him from picking it up.

"Not that one, that's Rob's. I'll get you another," she said.

The anticipation of the day blew out of him like air leaving a balloon. *Who's Rob? It's gotta be a boyfriend. What was I thinking?* Unconscious of his actions, Jasper's shoulders slumped and he released a sigh.

The noise of the espresso machines churning out steam for the lattes disappeared; the voices of the forty or so people laughing and talking vanished. Angela was speaking to him, but the words coming from her mouth were incoherent. At that instant, the only thing that existed in Jasper's mind was: boyfriend. *How could I be so stupid? Of course someone as beautiful as Angela would have a boyfriend*, he thought to himself.

"Are you all right? You don't look so well," asked Angela with a noticeable ring of concern in her voice.

Jasper scrambled to regain his composure and quickly thought of an excuse to cover his recent lapse. "Yes, I'm fine. I just felt a bit of a headache coming on; it's probably just low blood sugar. I didn't get a chance to eat before I left home," he explained.

"Are you sure?" Angela responded with considerable doubt in her voice. "Well then, let's get you something to eat right away. Do you want a scone or biscotti? You don't have to wait in that crazy line-up. My boyfriend works here, so he can get you something."

Like a bee sting, the word burned for an instant. Jasper was going to respond when a male figure standing at least four inches taller than him arrived at the side of their booth. His arms were the size of Jasper's legs and both of them were covered in tattoos. The artwork started at his wrists and covered his forearms right up to where the sleeves of his white T-shirt covered his shoulders. A crucifix overtop of the word "Faith" was inked onto his left forearm. Jasper had a sudden feeling of déjà vu but couldn't explain its origin. Rob's right arm had the words "Lancer Linebacker" scrolled up the inside of his forearm, leaving no doubt in Jasper's mind that he was a football player.

It was obvious he spent more time in the gym than he did making coffee based on his total lack of body fat and the unmistakable pecs stopping the front of his shirt actually touching the rest of his torso. His face wasn't 'model material' and appeared slightly hardened, but it wasn't unpleasant to look at and his hair was short, very blonde and quite curly. He was wearing a nametag with 'Rob' carved across the top along with the words 'Assistant Manager' on the bottom.

"Hun, can you do me a huge favor and get me a scone and a caramel macchiato right away?" asked Angela when Rob neared the booth.

"Sure, but I thought you weren't hungry," he replied.

He completed a full one-eighty and walked back behind the counter. He pulled a scone from the glass display case and asked one of the baristas to make the drink for him. A few minutes later he returned to the booth and placed the drink and scone in front of Angela. Without sitting down, Rob turned to Jasper and introduced himself.

"I'm Rob," he said while extending his right hand.

Jasper stepped out of the booth and clasped Rob's hand with his own. "Jasper. Pleased to meet you," he said, forcing the words from his mouth out of politeness. Saying them out loud made them even more difficult to believe. Jasper was not at all pleased to meet him.

"Thanks, hun, but these aren't for me. They're for Jasper. He's not feeling well and just needs something to eat," explained Angela. With that, she pushed the drink and the scone to where Jasper had been seated and demanded he sit and eat.

"Can you sit?" asked Angela while reaching for Rob's hand.

"No, I think I'll let you two do your homework—besides, the place has gotten really busy, and I better help Heather and Mary," he said, looking at the line of people waiting for their order. Rob leaned into the booth and gave Angela a quick peck on the forehead before returning behind the counter to help serve the growing line.

Jasper wasn't sure if it was the sight of Rob kissing Angela, the realization she had a boyfriend, or Rob's incredible physical shape, but nothing was more urgent to him right then than getting out of the coffee shop. Jasper's right leg bounced up and down wildly under the table as his mind searched for an exit strategy. He fought the urge to bolt, though desperation overwhelmed him.

Thoughts swirled in and out of his head as he began to search for excuses to facilitate his exit. He had to do it without causing the slightest suspicion of what his expectations had been for the evening—he had to be discrete.

The solution came to him instantly, like an email into his mind. Jasper's racing heart slowed as he took a deep breath. Jubilation provided relief from the darkness of his desperation, and he regained control of his emotions. *This is like high school all over again*, he thought and swallowed hard. The process of starting something he knew he was terrible at felt like swallowing cough syrup, but he began anyway and started his lie.

"Will you thank Rob for me please? For the coffee and the food, but I really can't stay long. I'm meeting a friend at the tunnel. We're going to Detroit tonight." Jasper paused long enough to inhale but didn't give Angela an opportunity to respond.

"Thanks again for the coffee and food," Jasper repeated, even though he hadn't even touched them.

In an effort to complete his quick escape, Jasper slid out from the booth, stood up and thanked Angela one more time before turning toward the door. He hadn't taken four steps when Angela called his name.

"Jasper, wait," she said.

Jasper felt like he had been struck by lightning, and he froze in place. He took two short breaths and turned around as Angela approached him.

"You forgot the notes," she said with a look of confusion painted over her face as she handed him a legal-sized brown envelope. "Are you sure everything's all right?" she asked one more time. It was obvious to her that he was uncomfortable.

Jasper again tried to avoid the embarrassment of Angela realizing his expectations for the evening by taking the envelope from her hand and repeating his thanks.

"Sorry I can't stay, but I'll be late if I don't leave now. Have a good night and thank Rob again."

Although in no actual danger, the adrenalin rush lingered long enough to cause his heart to pound so hard in his chest it made him short of breath. The pain of his teenage years returned with a vengeance, like he was asking a girl to dance for the first time or wondering when to lean in for the first kiss. Jasper hated the awkwardness of relationships and was certain he would never have to worry about seeing Angela again. He was positive she would find a new lab partner for their next Biochemistry class.

Without turning back, Jasper rushed to the door, trying not to run. When he reached the door, he found it held open for him. With a large grin shaping her face, the same woman he had opened the door for was returning the favor. She held a coffee in one hand while she pushed the door open with the other and allowed their eyes to meet.

"In a bit of a hurry?" she asked as he passed through the open doorway.

"You have no idea."

CHAPTER 7

THE MIRROR

J asper pulled into his driveway and turned off the car. The glow from the streetlight in front of the house entered the windshield and formed dancing shadows on the dashboard. He welcomed the silence and sweet solitude. A thousand images of the evening skipped through his mind, and for a moment, a single thought appealed to him: sleeping in the car and avoiding his father.

Time stood still as he stared at the mayflies circling the porch light. His indecision pressed hard against his body, forming its own gravity. The force of it was so great that it rendered his first attempt to open the door futile. The precious few moments he had with her played over and over in his head. The magnitude of his embarrassment grew like a summer wildfire, and his expectations remained just that, expectations—the ashes left behind. He sat in the car replaying everything he had said in his mind.

Jasper grabbed the steering wheel and put his head on the back of his hands while inhaling a long deep breath like he was about to dive into a swimming pool.

"I can do this," he said, but at that moment, attending a funeral seemed more appealing than going into the house. Dr. Stewart would be waiting, and he knew his father well—he would definitely ask. Hiding in the car just prolonged the suffering. His cheeks filled with fire as his pride rose from the ashes of his embarrassment. *I'm going in.*

He lifted his head from the steering wheel, grabbed the car door handle. The warm evening air was muggy and the leaves rustled on the large sugar maple in front of the house. He could smell the freshly cut lawn.

Jasper counted the steps as he climbed his way onto the porch. A small squeak occurred as he turned the handle and simultaneously peered through the three small windows in the front door. The light from the den reflected off the glass in the hallway pictures. The sweet smell of jasmine tea filled the air—his father's favorite nightcap. The only sound he heard was the dull clunk of his shoes hitting the hardwood floor as he kicked them off at the front entrance. Jasper walked down the hall to the den. His shoulders lowered in relief as the burden of meeting his father lifted from him, and Jasper felt victorious for the first time that night. The den was empty.

"Dad, I'm home!" he called out in the most cheerful voice he could muster. Jasper stood in the hallway for a moment waiting for a reply, but none came. Jasper made his way to the foot of the staircase and called out again.

"Dad, you there?" he yelled much louder than the first time, but there was still no reply.

Excellent, he must've gone out for a walk, he thought and made his way upstairs to his bedroom. Dr. Stewart often strolled through the neighborhood just before bed. It helped him unwind from a day at the office and cleared his head before trying to sleep. This was a lucky break for Jasper. The empty house allowed him to get to his bedroom without any interrogation. Dr. Stewart never bothered Jasper once he was in his bedroom, so Jasper could hide there pretending to study and avoid the inevitable questioning until the morning.

Jasper walked briskly up the stairs, worried his father would return at any moment. He entered his room without turning on the lights and closed the door. The light from the streetlamp was brighter on the second floor and filled the room with a dull yellow hue. He looked at the clock on the nightstand next to his bed and started talking to himself.

"Eight-seventeen. It's only Eight-seventeen on a Friday night, and I'm already home. Some night this turned out to be. Way to get lucky, Jasper."

Jasper turned towards his bed and began pulling his shirt over his head. *The best way to end this night is to get to sleep*, he thought as he made his way to the bed. He sat on the end of the bed and caught a glimpse of himself in the full-length mirror hung on his closet door. The fleeting image caused him to pause his undressing, and he focused his attention on the mirror. The poor lighting provided the perfect ambiance. Now shirtless, Jasper stood up, flipped his hair off his face and stared at his reflection.

Continuing to watch himself, he used his right hand to unbuckle his belt. The open belt allowed the top button of his Levi 501s to be freed. With his left hand he reached down and undid the rest of the buttons holding the fly of his jeans closed. His pants fell to the floor with a dull thud around his ankles. He stepped forward out of his jeans, leaving them piled where they fell, and then reached down to remove his socks. The bright white of his high-cut briefs glowed in the mirror as if he were standing under a black light. His breathing slowed and deepened as he assessed himself in the mirror.

Jasper's slight build made his average height appear taller. His boyish face and rounded cheeks made the dimple in the center of his chin more noticeable. Jasper's face was a younger, exact duplicate of his father's. Perfect strangers couldn't help but notice his eyes; they were a bright iridescent crystal blue like a malamute's. There was no doubt his eye color was a gift from his father.

His mother gave him a full head of shiny thick hair the color of black coffee. It was wavy in the back and naturally parted to the right. Jasper let his hair grow long enough to rest just above his shoulders, the perfect length to hide the birthmark on the back of his neck.

Jasper and his father shared more than their eyes; they

also shared the same birthmark. It was a peculiar-looking, incomplete figure of eight shape that they carried in exactly the same location. For as long as Jasper could remember, his father never liked the attention the birthmark brought when others noticed it. Jasper assumed this was a result of early childhood teasing, and like his father, Jasper preferred to keep his hair long enough to conceal it.

Jasper allowed his thoughts to wander while staring at himself in the mirror, and he drifted into a sort of hypnosis, focusing on the rhythmic sound of his breathing. The only thoughts he had were of Angela. His earlier expectations for the evening had been carnal in nature, and now his thoughts metamorphosed into fantasies when his right hand lay on his underwear. With his mind completely separated from his body, he made small circles with his hand over the top of his underwear. Jasper caressed himself until his arousal became uncomfortable. The restriction had to be released, and he used his left hand to pull down the waistband and slide his underwear off. His right hand instantly clenched his flesh.

The relief was short lived. The weakness building in his legs was matched by the willingness in his mind. Jasper allowed his body to fall backwards onto his bed in a single motion as if he was falling into a swimming pool. The sound of his body hitting the mattress was muffled by the duvet. The fall did nothing to interrupt the grip his right hand maintained. Jasper's eyes were glued shut, and he welcomed the events unfolding in his mind. The smell of her perfume, the warmth of her skin, and the sound of her voice whispering in his ear drew him deeper into his fantasy and further from reality, much further than he had gone before. Jasper was inching himself closer to the very pinnacle of climax when a familiar tension began to creep up inside him.

Jasper's entire body pulsed up and down in perfect harmony with his short, rapid breaths. A small droplet of sweat rolled off his forehead and into his right eye, slowly making its way through his tightly closed eyelid. The salty burn of his sweat wasn't enough to break his grip, however. Never before had he felt this close. His desire within reach, he continued for a second longer when the ecstasy suddenly disappeared into the darkness of a black robe.

"Stop it! I don't want to!" The words shouted inside his head.

Rage circulated through his veins, boiling anger through him until it replaced all sense of anticipation. Jasper knew the outcome of what he was trying to do—it was no use.

He opened his eyes and released his grip. His eyes glossed over as he stared out the window, comforted by the dim light. It wasn't going to happen now or ever. He had failed to bring himself to completion again, and the longer he attempted it, the more difficult his recovery would be. It was impossible to count the number of times he had tried over the years—never once with success.

CHAPTER 8

THE DOG

Songs of morning birds and filtered sunlight flooded the bedroom through the partially closed blinds. Its warmth caressed Jasper's face, coaxing his eyes to open. Blurry-eyed and still half-asleep, he peered at the clock to find it was just past seven. He closed his eyes again, looking for the solitude of sleep. No longer asleep but not completely awake, another three minutes passed before the memory of the previous night caught up with him. It wasn't the fantasy he recalled but the nightmare. He pulled the duvet over his head to shield his face from the rising sun and hoped for sleep to return. When that failed, he yanked the duvet off his head and inhaled a deep breath like a dog searching the wind for a scent. *No coffee. Maybe he's not up yet*, he thought.

He pulled himself out of bed and looked at the clothes lying on the floor. Wishing to remove any trace of the night before, he picked up his shirt and tossed it into the laundry. The smell of his cologne lingered on it. It was Saturday, so there was a good chance his father would go to work. It was the only time Dr. Stewart could work in his lab uninterrupted. Jasper really didn't want to speak to anyone today, so not wanting to take a chance, he decided he would leave.

What can I do to get me the hell out of the house today? The answer magically arrived—fishing. *It's Saturday, I told Greg I'd call if it was nice.* Jasper loved to go fishing, and there was no better way to pass a warm September day. He could spend the entire day away from the house down by the Detroit River. This would ensure he wouldn't be forced into a pleasant mood while at the same time allowing him to avoid talking to his father. Dr. Stewart hated going fishing, so Jasper knew he would be safe for the day at least.

Jasper pulled open his top left dresser drawer and started searching for one of his old shirts. He found the red one with a small tear in the armpit; it was still one of his favorites, so he pulled it over his head. He grabbed a new pair of briefs and stepped back into the jeans he had worn the day before. Sitting back onto his bed, he re-used the socks from yesterday, sliding them on his feet. Excitement gathered momentum in his outlook for the day. He stood back up and started walking out of his bedroom while buttoning his fly and securing his belt. He moved with haste since his father rarely slept in.

Jasper placed each foot down like a cat stalking a bird as he walked past his father's bedroom door. The house was quiet enough to hear the clock ticking downstairs on the kitchen wall. On his way towards the top of the stairs, his movement came to an abrupt halt when he heard a voice from behind the bedroom door. His heart instantly sped up to twice its normal rate.

"How'd it go last night? You were in bed before I got home," asked Dr. Stewart.

"I got all of the notes from my partner and then came home," responded Jasper, being vague but honest.

Dr. Stewart knew the answer was intentionally vague and sent out a softer and more subdued "Great."

"Will you need the car today?" asked Jasper in an effort to circumvent any further questioning.

His father paused for an instant and then replied, "No, I don't need it. Where you headed?"

"Fishing."

"Are you going with anyone?"

Jasper wanted to go fishing alone since his real intent was

to escape from reality for a day and not have to answer questions or fake some happiness. It seemed like the perfect solution, although he did remember that Greg had asked him to go this weekend. Greg was still in third-year law school and always went out for a few beers with the boys on Fridays, so he probably wasn't up yet.

Greg had gained twenty pounds after high school—likely a result of his fondness for beer. Since then, his voice had deepened and become raspy, commanding attention whenever he spoke, and it suited his current physique. He kept his hair brush-cut short, mostly because it was already receding, and his kind face slightly offset his large presence. If Jasper had to choose a profession for Greg, he would have made him a drill sergeant, although his voice would serve him well as a litigator.

"No, I'm heading out by myself. It was a last-second thing on my part, and I don't think Greg would be too happy about me calling him at this time on a Saturday morning. I'm just heading down to the old train wharf off Riverside Drive. I'll try Greg a little later; see if he wants to join me."

Jasper walked down the stairs toward the garage door to get his fishing gear when his father leaned over the staircase banister and asked, "Do you want some company? I could join you if you like."

Looking up the stairs so that his father could see his face Jasper said, "Dad," leaving no misunderstanding of what he meant, "I know how much you like to fish, but thanks anyway."

"Well, all right. Have fun and be careful. Will you be home for dinner?" asked Dr. Stewart.

"Dad," said Jasper in the identical tone to the one he had just used, indicating that he wasn't happy with the 'be careful' part. "I'll call and let you know later this afternoon if I'll make it home for dinner." He opened the garage door, yelled, "Have a great day!" and began gathering his fishing gear to load in the car.

It was just after seven thirty a.m. when he backed the car out of the driveway and headed toward Riverside Drive. The sun created a perfect dull orange sphere masked by the early morning haze as it rose above the horizon. Jasper could feel his armpits dripping from the humidity; it was going to be one of those 'dog days of summer.' In summer, southwestern Ontario could be the most humid place on the planet, with afternoon temperatures reaching nearly a hundred degrees and relative humidity in the high nineties. Spending a whole day baking in the sun on the end of an old wharf on the banks of the Detroit River wouldn't be easy without something to eat or drink. Jasper stopped by the Tim Horton's along the way and purchased a sandwich and a bottle of water.

It was another ten miles from the restaurant to the wharf where Jasper would fish for the day. The expressway was faster, but he drove the entire distance along Riverside Drive—the long route following the contours of the river. The scenery reminded him of a travel poster of some tropical destination.

The speed limit was thirty on 'The Drive,' as the locals referred to it, on account that every hundred yards or so there was an elegant cobblestone driveway winding its way to the road. The large estates finally gave way to Riverside Park, a long narrow strip of green along the banks of the river. The park had once been an industrial area and old rail yard but was now a public park gifted with spectacular views of the Detroit skyline. Riverside Park was considered the emerald of Windsor with its many miles of paved biking trails and walking paths, used by the locals to enjoy the splendor of the river while jogging, rollerblading or walking their dogs.

Jasper called Greg as he pulled into the parking lot. Still early on a Saturday morning for his friend, Jasper wasn't surprised to get his voicemail.

"Hey, Greg, I know you're still passed out, but if you can drag your hung-over ass out of bed, come join me at the wharf."

Jasper parked his car in the pay lot at the foot of Goyeau Street, only a few hundred yards from the wharf. The wharf had once been used to barge railcars across the river between Windsor and Detroit before the tunnel was completed. After the tunnel opened, the wharf was only used occasionally until it was finally decommissioned and the entire rail yard removed to create Riverside Park.

The warm morning breeze lifted the pungent odor of the river to the parking lot, and the early morning calmness was cracked open by the blast of a massive freighter signaling its presence in the shipping channel. Jasper left his lunch in the car for later and pulled his gear from the trunk. While holding his fishing rod in one hand and his tackle box in the other, he made his way toward the old wharf.

The sun had risen high enough to project a perfect reflection off of the silver-black windows of the Renaissance Center across the river. The reflected sunlight burned his eyes, blinding him as he stepped over the parking lot curb onto the paved path. Jasper turned his head quickly to stop the pain, causing him to stumble across the dividing line down the middle of the path. He ended up in the middle of the jogging track and directly in the path of a jogger.

"Watch it, buddy!" yelled the man as he jumped around Jasper to avoid a collision.

"Sorry!" yelled Jasper to no avail. The jogger's music screeched loud enough from his earphones for Jasper to recognize the song. He recovered from this near miss only to find it quickly followed by a second. Jasper stumbled to keep his balance and dropped his tackle box while trying to avoid another collision.

The metal lures and lead weights formed a high-pitched smashing sound identical to glass shattering as the tackle box bounced off the pavement. Jasper lifted his shoulders and winced from the noise. Out of the corner of his eye, he caught movement and, reacting solely by instinct, leaped off the path and onto the grass, but this time, it wasn't a jogger.

The brief glance coupled with fear induced by primordial instinct told him the grayish-white animal had to be a wolf. The rapid clicking sound of its claws scraping the pavement faded as it sprinted past him. Reason returned when Jasper got a clear view of the animal. Thick fur, bushy tail, pointed ears and the unmistakable crystal blue eyes meant it had to be a husky.

The summer heat and humidity were too much for the dog; its tongue hung inches from the ground. Jasper could hear the deep forceful sound of its panting, a sure sign it had been running for a while. No collar circled its neck, and the dog appeared to be following the jogger Jasper had nearly collided with.

What a cruel thing to do to a dog—making it jog on such a hot and humid day, thought Jasper as he collected himself from the near collision. He bent down, picked up his tackle box and continued his walk to the wharf, keeping his eyes open for oncoming traffic—in both directions!

A group of elm trees near the path housed a chorus of cicadas which filled the air with their vibrating buzz like a band of Mexican maracas. This had always been his favorite sound of summer because they only sang on the hottest days of the year. Jasper, still shaken from his close encounters, walked carefully down the hill to the old wharf.

'DANGER—Decommissioned Wharf—Use at Your Own Risk' was barely legible on the warning sign, spray-painted with graffiti, at the foot of the dock.

Approaching the wharf, Jasper could see that he would be sharing his favorite fishing spot with one other person: an older man apparently sleeping in a folding lawn chair. Jasper knew the man had to be a regular because he had wedged his fishing rod handle between two rotten wooden planks to keep it from being dragged over the side of the wharf when the big one struck.

The rotting planks emitted a dull creak as Jasper stepped on the deck. Fortunately, waves left by the passing freighter pounded on the rocks below, masking Jasper's movement. He walked within a couple of feet of the man's fishing rod before he noticed the small brass bell tied to its tip. Jasper didn't actually see the bell but heard it; his weight on the old wooden planks had caused the rod to shake slightly, setting off the bell.

With the reflexes of a rattlesnake lunging at its victim, the man sprang out from his slumber and snatched his fishing rod from the wharf. Surprise and embarrassment filled the man's face when he saw Jasper standing a few feet from him.

"I'm so sorry," said Jasper, trying to apologize for startling the man while suppressing the urge to laugh. "I didn't see the bell. This wharf is so old it feels like it's falling apart below my feet."

The man smiled at Jasper with his warm leathery face, lips parted just enough to show a few of his poorly kept yellow teeth. "No worry, this is the most excitement I see all morning," he said with a strong Italian accent.

An overpowering aroma of garlic accompanied the man's words, blended with the pungent smell of the Detroit River. Jasper strained to conceal his repulsion and began breathing through his mouth.

The distant wailing of a police siren soared across the river, causing both men to simultaneously look towards Detroit.

Jasper searched the area for the telltale sign of the day's catch, but the absence of a fish bucket on the wharf indicated slow fishing for the morning. He secretly grinned, knowing this meant that getting up at the usual five thirty a.m. to catch the 'early bite' would have been a complete waste of time.

"Any bites yet?" asked Jasper.

"Nothing. Just the one you give me. That was the first time I hear my bell since six o'clock this morning," said the old man. "I like to come early on hot days. I no like the heat so much and will go home soon."

Jasper knelt down and opened his tackle box. "I don't

think the fish really like the heat much either, but it's still a nice way to spend a Saturday." Continuing to rummage through his gear, he found the small package of fishing hooks he was looking for and removed one to tie on to the end of his line. Placing the rest of the hooks back into his box, he continued to hunt around for some artificial bait; it wasn't in its usual place on the top shelf of his tackle box.

It must've fallen to the bottom when I dropped the box, he thought.

Pushing the hordes of old lures and miscellaneous fishing gear to one corner of the box, he finally found the jar of fluorescent green bait. He baited his hook then shut his tackle box, moving closer to the edge of the wharf to make his first cast.

Fishermen loved this wharf because the missing railings made it simple to cast and easy to retrieve a fish. The swirling pools of turquoise water were mesmerizing. Jasper watched a small twig spin in circles, trapped by the water's grip, and vanish below the surface.

Using the same smooth motion he had performed a thousand times, Jasper flung the rod over his shoulder while releasing the reel trigger to launch his hook fifty feet from the wharf and into the swift-moving current below. He stripped out another twenty feet of line with his hand to allow the current to carry the bait downstream. Then he found a gap in the wooden planks and jammed the handle of his rod in between the planks to hold it in place. He picked up his tackle box and moved to a few feet from where the man was sitting and placed it back down on the wharf, using it as a seat.

"Hi, I'm Jasper," he said to the man.

"Alberto," said the man. "You can call me 'Albi.'"

"Do you fish here often?" Jasper asked.

"I come sometimes four or five times in a week if my wife lets me and the weather is nice. I no like to come on a weekend. Too many people on a weekend, but now school has started, it's not so bad, so I come today. You?"

"Not so much, I used to come more often, but now I'm too busy with university. What part of Italy are you from?"

"Roma. You go to Italy?"

"No, but I always wanted to; I love pizza and ice cream."

"*Buoni, si*, but everything here is better," said Albi, not attempting to hide his disdain for his homeland. "Here we have real freedom."

"What do you mean?" asked Jasper, unable to resist the desire to know what Albi was referring to.

"The Church. In Italy it controls everything—it's worse than the CIA. The Vatican control everything and everybody."

"Huh?"

"*Mio* son, Giorgino." Albi looked to the sky while raising both his hands as if speaking directly to God. "I work all my life in a factory, twenty years building cars, to make him some sort of computer expert, now he works for the Church. He never tells me what he does—everything secret. I tell you this, what my son does for the Church doesn't help people. There's something not right about what they do—it's not God's work, I tell you, this is for sure."

"What do you...?"

The small brass bell produced two sharp tinkles in the midst of Jasper's sentence. Their heads turned sideways in unison to witness the tip of Albi's rod bouncing frantically.

"Whoa, I think you got something big on, Albi."

With the speed of a teenager, Albi jumped up, clearing the few feet between his chair and his rod in the blink of an eye.

"*Mamma mia!*" Albi nearly shouted, his poorly kept teeth forming a grin you could drive a truck through. The ratchet screamed as the fish used the current to pull more line from the reel.

Jasper jumped off of his tackle box and followed Albi to the unprotected edge of the wharf. The excitement bloomed in Jasper even though it wasn't his fish. He stood beside Albi and looked over the edge, trying to glimpse the fish on the end of the line. Albi fought the fish with the enthusiasm of a marlin fisherman, lifting his rod tip high above his shoulders then rapidly reeling.

"*E grande, Molte grande!*"

It took a full ten minutes of reeling before Albi fought the fish to exhaustion. Keeping his line tight, the old Italian leaned over the edge of the wharf. Careful not to fall over the side, he lifted the fish from the water.

If I only had a camera, thought Jasper, unsure of who was more exhausted, the fish or Albi.

"*Bravo, bravo*," Albi said to himself. The enormous smile on his face refused to diminish. The walleye flopped on the wharf, still hooked in the mouth.

"That was the best fight I've seen all year—good one. It's got be at least five pounds."

"*Gracie, gracie*, I think I go now—I leave the rest for you," said Albi. He reached into the fabric shopping bag hanging off the side of his chair and pulled out a plastic garbage bag. He picked up his fish from the tail and slid it into the bag then turned the bag over three times to form a knot in the top. Still in a state of fish euphoria, Albi finished packing up the rest of his belongings and walked over to Jasper. Holding his lawn chair, fabric bag and the garbage bag containing his fish in his left hand, Albi reached out his right hand to shake Jasper's. "*Ciao*, Jasper," he said, and the bag containing the fish slipped from his hand, falling onto the wharf.

"*Catso!*"

Albi and Jasper bent over at the same time to retrieve the fallen bag and narrowly missed banging heads. Jasper was immediately captivated by the reflection of sunlight from Albi's chest, shinning like one of the lures from his own tackle box. His eyes were drawn to the light. The focus of Jasper's attention was a small gold cross dangling from a tricolor gold chain identical to Angela's.

An ache began in his forehead, ripping through his eyes like midday sunlight after leaving a dark theatre. The freedom his mind had enjoyed from last night's horror show evaporated. Jasper stood up and flipped the hair off of his face with his left hand as he handed Albi the bag with his right.

"You okay?" asked Albi as he accepted the bag.

"Yes, just a little lightheaded when I bent over."

"Okay, *buono*, nice talking to you," Albi said as he turned around and walked off the wharf.

Jasper watched him leave with his prized fish in hand. Just past the warning sign, Albi stopped and turned to face him.

"Oh yes, I forget to tell you *buon fortunato*."

Jasper was hopeless with foreign languages, nearly failing his high-school French, but even he understood the Italian words.

For the last three hours, his plan had been a success; he had escaped from the dread of the real world and hadn't let a single thought of last night cross his mind. That had all come crashing down with a tiny gold cross and two words—good luck.

Jasper stood frozen in place by the overwhelming flood of thoughts racing through his mind. The strike on his fishing rod caused it to lunge forward, but Jasper had slipped so deep into his memories that it didn't draw a reaction. The unnatural sound of his rod being dragged across the wooden deck broke his recollection. It took a second for the rod to slide to the edge of the wharf; the same amount of time it took Jasper to realize it was about to fall into the river.

***

Greg had parked his car in the same lot as Jasper and stood at the top of the hill in the exact spot where Jasper had nearly collided with the joggers. He had an unobstructed view of the park, the river and the events unfolding on the wharf. The hangover he had struggled to shake off suddenly evaporated.

"Jasper! Jasper!" he yelled, but the distance was too great.

***

Jasper lunged for the rod, grabbing it, but the power of his forward momentum was too great for the decaying railings. The cracking of old timbers sounded like distant fireworks as the sensation of weightlessness rushed through his body. He held on to his fishing rod as his feet entered the turquoise water.

A nervous laughter slipped from his lips while embarrassment rushed through his mind. Jasper's eyes remained sealed as water rushed up his nostrils. The low, eerie sound of submersion flooded his ears as the warm water engulfed him. Small convulsions in his stomach rolled quickly to his throat, and he gagged from the nasty taste of the river water in his mouth. The initial shock of submersion forced Jasper to swallow a mouthful.

After a few seconds, Jasper became slightly more aware of his situation, and he was surprised at how warm the water felt. *It's not that bad*, he thought, but the warm sensation of the water covering his body was suddenly replaced with a burning feeling in his right leg. Adrenaline sharpened his senses and filled him with a strong sense of urgency; things had taken a turn for the worse.

The burning feeling intensified to severe pain, and he reached for his leg. He tried to swim but remained submerged as if someone was standing on his back, the current relentlessly pushing his body forward, making it impossible to raise his head. In desperation, he opened his eyes in search of the surface, but no light could be seen. He was blinded by the constant stream of water mixed with bubbles moving past his eyes. Facing downward, bubbles rose and swirled from both sides of his face up past his cheeks and then his ears. The water in his ears amplified the sound of the rushing river. It was deafening, and the urge to scream for help welled up inside of him.

Panic overwhelmed him, filling him like a balloon about to burst. Jasper tried to reach back against the current to see what was causing the pain in his right leg but with no success. The river was alive, like a mythical creature determined to hold his body below the surface. The harder he struggled against it, the stronger its grip became. Jasper knew this could only mean one thing; he was weakening, succumbing to the relentless power of the monster—the water. At that moment, he realized he was still holding his fishing rod, and he used it to try and pry himself free. But his determination wasn't enough.

Jasper remained motionless with his eyes wide open. Darkness began to close in from all sides like the ending of an old movie. The river couldn't be heard anymore, and the monster pushing him from behind was gone. His arms and legs moved freely up and down, the pain in his leg vanished, and he was no longer holding his fishing rod. Panic didn't exist, he lost the incredible urge to breath, and calmness filled him. Only a pinhole of light remained as Jasper waited for the end.

CHAPTER 9

THE LIGHT

"Jasper!" Greg shouted at the top of his lungs as he sprinted down the hill to the wharf. His pace accelerated when he approached the wooden deck, having seen no sign of Jasper returning to the surface. Then, just yards before the wharf, Greg's stride suddenly faded. As surreal as a hallucination, a large dog flew by him as if he were standing still. The dog then leaped off the end of the wharf. The splash as the dog hit the water was so big it soaked Greg's face, and this wet slap brought him back to reality as he watched the dog disappear below the surface.

***

Light slowly began to fill Jasper's eyes. It grew from all directions, intensifying with every passing second. It was brighter and much whiter than the previous light, yet its edges were undefined. It had the warmth and comfort of an October campfire. Jasper was sure he had seen this light before on early fall days in the meadow near his childhood house. It continued to warm him; the light wrapped around his body like a blanket.

In the center of the light, from the brightest point, a figure appeared. It walked with intent directly toward him. It continued to approach Jasper, but in spite of its approach, Jasper still couldn't see the figure clearly. He sensed it was a woman—someone he knew. She reached out her arms to embrace him, and Jasper reached back. The moment their fingers touched, the figure disappeared, and Jasper began to float inside the light. Comforted by its warmth, he continued to rise higher and faster until the light disappeared. A searing pain spread through his entire body when the rush of air filled his lungs.

Intense pain radiated from his face like someone rubbing his cheek with sandpaper; and the smell and taste of the river tainted his mouth. A familiar stinging sensation returned—the burning pain in his leg. When his ears emptied of water, he could hear the low rumbling of a train engine in the distance. Jasper attempted to open both eyes but could only open his left. The rumbling sound was now clearer; it wasn't the sound of a train but the deep rhythmic panting of a large dog. Jasper turned his head toward the panting and saw the body of a dog at his feet. The dog was familiar; it was the same one Jasper had tripped over earlier. It was now apparent why the right side of his face and his leg were hurting; the massive dog was dragging him up the riverbank by the ankle, and his face was scrapping along the rocks on the shoreline. Jasper closed his eyes.

Greg shouted, "What the hell, you okay? Whose dog is that?"

Jasper's head began hurting at Greg's questioning. "Hold it, man," he snapped.

"You need to go to the hospital. Your leg's a mess, and so is your face. Man, you were under the water a long time. I can't believe you're not dead!"

Jasper replied immediately, "No hospital! My dad will kill me. I'm already going to get shit when he finds out I fell in."

Greg responded, "But, dude, your leg's a mess, and hell, I thought you'd drowned. If it wasn't for that dog..."

Jasper cut Greg's sentence short. "What about the dog?"

"He came out of nowhere, sprinting down the hill, onto the wharf and then dove into the river. He popped up seconds later with your leg in his mouth and swam you to shore. If I hadn't seen it, I'd never have believed it—no shit."

"You're joking, right? Don't mess with me."

With a small smirk on his face, Greg said, "I told you, no shit, that's exactly what happened. Wait until I tell my parents about this, they'll…"

"Don't you dare!" shouted Jasper. "You can't tell a soul what happened here today or I'll be in royal shit. Dad won't let me go fishing again unless he comes along, and he hates fishing."

"I don't know; this is too freaky to keep to myself. I don't think I can do it."

"Think of it as practice for your attorney-client privilege."

"Well, since you put it like that, I guess this'll be a great test for me, even though I won't be taking the Bar for another couple of years. What about your leg? Have you seen it? Looks bad to me. I think you need to get some stitches."

Jasper was sitting up by this point but still leaning against a large piece of discarded concrete on the riverbank. He twisted his leg to the side and peered down at the hole in his torn pant leg to see a two-inch cut in the side of his calf. It was still bleeding, and the blood mixed with the water draining off of his leg gave it the appearance of a much bigger wound.

"Oh yeah, I better get it looked at, but we can go to the walk-in clinic at the university. Not the hospital," Jasper said.

"If you say so, but I still think you're nuts and should go to the hospital. Maybe have your head examined too after all that just happened," Greg stated with a distinct tone of sarcasm.

"Help me up," Jasper demanded, not amused.

Greg bent down and grabbed hold of Jasper's right arm, pulling him to his feet while Jasper used his left arm to push off of the concrete block. He felt two things as soon as he got to his feet: the first and most noticeable was that his head began to spin with the same feeling you get when you go to bed after having a few too many drinks; the second was the feeling of warm mud squishing between his toes, like when he was a child playing in the mud puddles after a rainstorm.

"What happened to my shoe and sock?"

"I don't know. Maybe the dog took it," said Greg, half-joking.

This triggered a flashback for Jasper to the instant after his feet hit the water. When he fell below the surface and didn't pop back up, he remembered feeling as if someone was holding his leg. The right leg of his pants and right shoe must have caught on some old industrial debris hidden below the water, keeping him from getting back to the surface. Once the current got hold of him, he didn't have the strength to reach back and free himself. The more he had struggled, the weaker he had become until the foot entrapment had sucked the last bit strength from him.

Then he recalled the lights. *Was that brighter light God? Did God send the dog to free me*? This was too much for him to contemplate, and Greg's voice snapped him out of his flashback.

"You sure you're okay? You're starting to look a little pale. You're not going to puke, are you? Cause if you do, that's going to make me spill my guts too," confessed Greg. "If I see someone up-chuck, look out. I'll follow soon after."

"I'm fine. Let's get going; it can take forever at the clinic," said Jasper.

"Wait a second," Greg suggested. "I've got my workout clothes in the back of my car. Sit back down while I run and get my bag. Come to think of it, I have an old first-aid kit in the trunk too. That way I can at least clean up the cut and your face."

Jasper wasn't going to argue; the extra time to sit and regain his composure seemed like a great idea to him. He turned back toward the concrete rock and re-positioned himself back on it so he could sit without sliding off. While Greg ran back to his car, Jasper took the opportunity to search for the dog, but he could see no sign of the animal.

Why didn't I see a dog that big, especially if it swam right in front of me? Why did it save me?

Jasper's mind was racing faster than it ever had before, and a thousand more questions were coming when Greg returned to his side.

"Here, take these socks and put my shoes on but don't step in the mud with them. I use those in the university gym, and they won't let me in if they're dirty."

Jasper mustered a laugh and responded in a slightly sarcastic tone, "Oh, don't worry about me; I'll make sure your precious shoes don't get muddy—will it be okay if they have blood on them?"

"Yeah, that's okay, you know what they say in the gym— No Pain, No Gain. So blood's all right," Greg said and they both laughed.

Jasper removed the wet shoe and sock from his left foot and put on Greg's workout shoes and socks while Greg retrieved a large gauze bandage for Jasper's leg. He handed Jasper an old workout T-shirt from his bag so he could use it to clean the blood from his face and leg before putting the dressing over the wound.

"That's better," Greg said as he threw Jasper's shoes, socks and the bloody T-shirt into his gym bag. He helped Jasper on his feet again and they started heading up the hill to the parking lot.

"Are you all right to drive?" asked Greg.

"I'll be fine; it's just a flesh wound," Jasper assured him, and he continued to walk without aid from Greg but with a noticeable limp in his right leg.

Three hours and five stitches later, Jasper and Greg finally made it out of the clinic. Even though he was exhausted from his morning ordeal, the thought of going home and facing his father was unimaginable. *This is worse than last night,* he thought as they walked back through the parking lot. He knew his father wouldn't be happy with him.

"Let's go to the Pub, and I'll buy lunch. We can catch the Tigers' game on the big screen," said Jasper, knowing with any luck that the baseball game wouldn't end until after five and he could avoid going home until then.

"Free food, I'm in," Greg said, and they left for the University Pub.

***

Jasper arrived home just before dinner. His father had a plate waiting for him when he got there and was busy stirring some pasta sauce on the stove. Without turning to look at Jasper, he asked, "Thought you were going to call."

"Sorry, Dad. I had a bit of an incident on the wharf and forgot to let you know my ETA," Jasper explained.

Dr. Stewart stopped stirring the sauce and turned to face Jasper at once. His eyes locked on to Jasper's bloodied face. "What do you mean, an incident?" he asked in a surprisingly calm tone as if he already knew what had happened.

"Well, to make a very long story short, I fell off the dock and cut myself," said Jasper. Once again he wasn't giving the entire account of the events, but he also wasn't lying. Jasper had known since he was a very young child that his father had an uncanny ability to know when he was lying; it was like a sixth sense. There had been many times when Jasper thought there was no way anyone could find him out, yet his father somehow always knew. When he was younger, this ability had scared Jasper, and it finally got to the point that he wouldn't even attempt to lie to him, but it also developed Jaspers skills at being incredibly evasive in situations like this.

"Are you badly hurt?"

"No, just a flesh wound. I've had worse," Jasper said dismissively as he gently rubbed the back of his hand over the tender part of his face.

"Well then, I hope you're hungry. I've made a pot of

tomato sauce and there's lots of pasta."

"I'm starved," said Jasper, even though this wasn't exactly the truth either. He was more exhausted than anything else and really just wanted to go up to his room and lie down. "I'm going to go and change my clothes, and I'll be back in a minute to eat," Jasper added.

He went up to his room and put on a pair of old jogging sweats and a new T-shirt then headed back down to join his father for dinner.

***

Jasper finished his second bowl of pasta, surprising himself how hungry he actually was. He cleared the table of dishes and placed them in the dishwasher, then finished cleaning the rest of the kitchen and announced to his father he was heading to his room.

Jasper lay on his bed recalling the events of the day over and over in his mind, trying to make sense of it all. It was unbelievable that a dog had saved his life. And the most disturbing event of the day was the light that had engulfed him while he was under the water.

It wasn't only the light, but what it made him think that was disturbing. *God? Was it God I saw when I was about to die? Was it God who sent that dog into the water to save me?* He mulled these thoughts over while he lay on the bed. They shattered the very foundation of his beliefs.

"There is no God!" Jasper shook his head while repeating the words to himself.

He fell asleep not long after and didn't wake up until two thirty in the morning with a throbbing pain in his right leg and his bedroom lights still on. He made his way out of bed, still in his T-shirt and sweats, to find the bottle of painkillers the doctor had given him "just in case." He took two of them and walked across the hall to the bathroom for a glass of water to wash them down. After downing the pills, he went back to bed hoping they would soon take effect.

Other than a call from Greg to see how he was feeling, Jasper enjoyed a remarkably quiet Sunday. Dr. Stewart left early in the morning to do some work at his lab, and Jasper did some homework while watching baseball on the TV.

***

Tuesday's arrival brought a renewed sinking feeling in the pit of Jasper's stomach: that afternoon he would face Angela again in the Biochem lab. Not a hundred percent sure she had bought his excuse in the coffee shop, Jasper was on pins and needles the entire morning. When afternoon arrived, he made sure he got to the lab early so he could sit at the same bench he had the week before.

Angela arrived five minutes before the start of the lab and sat down next to him. She placed her notebook and pen on the bench and smiled at Jasper.

He was first to speak, offering a friendly, "Hi, how's it going?"

Angela responded in kind. "Great, how was your weekend?"

With a nervous laugh Jasper replied, "Fine, I did a little fishing."

"Catch anything?"

"No, but it was fun," replied Jasper, hoping to change the subject from his weekend to hers.

"What was your weekend like?"

"Nothing special. Rob and I went to Detroit to do some shopping on Saturday. On Sunday I took my grandmother to church as usual and then spent the rest of the day studying."

"You go often?" he asked.

"No, just when I need new clothes; they're way cheaper there."

"I meant to church."

"Oh?" she replied, and they both laughed. "Every Sunday

since I can remember. Why?"

"Just curious. Catholic?"

"Rossi?" she replied, lifting an eyebrow.

"Italian, of course," replied Jasper, feeling his cheeks light up.

"Oh yeah, my grandmother and I are very devout Catholics. We go every week. And every week she asks the same thing, 'Why don't you go to Italy, marry yourself a nice Italian boy, have children? Forget this university stuff.'"

"Rob's not Italian?"

"He's not even Catholic! He conveniently has to work every Sunday. My grandmother suspects but doesn't ask. He's promised to take the vows; he even got a tattoo of a crucifix."

"I remember it." The memory flashed in Jasper's mind like the spark from connecting two live wires. *The tattoo*, he thought, and Jasper remembered why Rob's tattoo of a crucifix seemed so familiar when Angela had introduced them. He had seen it before, only it was just moments before he actually met Rob.

What was Rob doing behind that bin? The thoughts raced through his mind, but Jasper kept his thoughts to himself, knowing there was no way Angela would believe him.

"What about you?" she asked with a smile. "You go to church?"

Jasper's face became stoic, and his muscles involuntarily contracted, causing him to recoil slightly. An instant of blindness filled his eyes when the flood of dark memories overcame his thoughts. He quickly flushed them from the front of his mind and forced a grin to his lips.

"Not anymore."

"That's too bad; you should come with me some time. I think you'd like it; the Church has changed so much. It can change your life in so many ways."

"It already has," replied Jasper.

CHAPTER 10

A DRY MOUTH

T he rest of the semester continued much the same for both Jasper and Angela. Each of them stuck to their original agreement: Jasper assembling the lab apparatus and Angela taking the notes. Over the three months, they shared many conversations and got to know each other quite well. Jasper remained thankful that Angela never asked about their first meeting, although he was certain she suspected something.

December arrived, bringing an end to Jasper's last semester of university and their final lab together. Sadness filled his thoughts knowing they would never see each other again. They had completed their final lab without incident and packed up their belongings to leave when Angela said, "See you at the finals."

"Yeah, I forgot about that," Jasper said. "So see you next week then." They left the lab and went their separate ways.

***

Dr. Stewart needed to be at work early the day of the Biochemistry final, so Jasper arrived at the student auditorium an hour before the three p.m. start. It was a cold and snowy December day with a bone-chilling wind blowing through the passageways between the campus buildings, so Jasper decided to go to the student cafeteria to wait. The bitter cold made him run all the way there.

The eating area was packed with students cramming for final exams, and it was impossible to find a seat. Jasper saw an open spot on the floor alongside a pole. He sat down and leaned his back against the pole. Pulling his notes from his pack, he began to read them over one last time before the exam. This extra bit of studying was a complete waste of time, as he had already reviewed the notes a dozen times. Reading them again did nothing but bore him.

Jasper shoved the notes back into his pack and decided people-watching was a better way to kill the forty-five minutes before his exam. Watching first-year students struggling to stay awake long enough to actually write the exam was great entertainment. Most had been up all night cramming. Small packs of first years chattered like monkeys, quizzing each other and hoping this last bit of effort would help.

The time flew by, and soon Jasper was making his way back to the auditorium. He raced to the front doors of the building only to arrive five minutes early. He waited outside with the growing group of students. No one was allowed in until the official start time of the exam. In an effort to locate Angela, Jasper rolled on to his toes to gain a better view of the crowd, but she was nowhere to be seen. He quickly pulled out his phone to send her an email before the start of the exam, as it was forbidden to use any electronic devices while in the auditorium. He scrolled through his address book to find her email address.

'Where are you? The exam is about to begin,' he typed.

The door swung open and the administrator commanded everyone to put any electronic devices away. Jasper pressed the 'Send' button and put the phone back into his pack, making sure the ringer was off.

Although Biochemistry was easy for Jasper, he was having a difficult time concentrating. They were thirty minutes into the three-hour exam, and Angela wasn't there. Just as he turned the page to begin answering the second question, he heard the auditorium doors open and watched Angela walk in, proceeding directly to the administrator at the front of the room. He handed her an exam, then looked down at his watch. Jasper assumed he was telling her she only had two and a half hours left to complete it.

It wasn't until Angela began walking toward the empty seat two desks in front of him that Jasper saw her face. She looked horrible, like she had obviously been up all night—not studying but crying. She looked like she had just attended the funeral of a loved one, with long drawn-out cheeks, bloodshot and puffy eyes, and completely disheveled hair.

I wonder what happened to her. Maybe her grandmother died, was the first thought Jasper had, although Angela had never mentioned her being ill.

Jasper finished his exam a half-hour before the allotted time, but he remained in his seat until the administrator instructed everyone to stop writing and leave their exams on their desks. Everyone put away their pens and started packing their belongings to leave, but Jasper walked straight over to Angela.

"What happened to you? You look terrible."

This was the worst thing he could have said. His words were like a spark igniting Angela's emotions into an explosion of tears.

"How stupid can I be?" he said out loud so she could hear him. He put an arm around her shoulders while picking up her coat and backpack with the other. Jasper began leading her toward the exit. They stopped in front of the doors and he swung her coat on for her. Angela didn't stop sobbing the entire time.

The wind outside cut through Jasper like a knife, but Angela didn't seem to notice the cold. The winter darkness had set in, and tiny snowflakes sparkled in the streetlights. Jasper suggested they walk to the student common room, hoping to avoid the crowd in the cafeteria. He didn't say a word as they walked, but his mind ran rampant with different scenarios of what could have caused her breakdown.

They were in luck; the common room was empty. Most students were unable to study in that room, distracted by the TV that was left on twenty-four hours a day. It also occurred to Jasper that since it was six p.m., most students would be getting dinner.

"It's okay," said Jasper, trying desperately to calm her crying, but it was no use. In fact, his words seemed to have the opposite effect, and her sobbing increased in volume and intensity.

Jasper removed Angela's coat and his and sat her down on the sixties era couch. He took a seat beside her, once again placing his arm around her shoulders. Angela buried her face into his chest and continued to cry so hard he could feel the dampness from her tears soaking through his shirt.

In an effort to be more sensitive, Jasper thought carefully about what words he would use next instead of blurting them out.

"What's wrong? Is your grandmother okay?" were the only things he could think of to say.

After a long pause, she lifted her head from out of his chest, revealing her once-beautiful chocolate brown eyes; now they were bloodshot red. Her face, distorted with sadness, resembled a dachshund's face, but her tears had subsided. Angela's first attempt to speak failed, and she returned to crying. Jasper continued to console her for another ten minutes before she tried to speak again.

"That asshole!" she said in an acidic tone. This caused Jasper to stiffen into a marble statue. He had never heard Angela swear, not even the time when she had knocked the flask off of the lab bench, causing it to shatter into a million tiny pieces.

Although he was pretty certain he knew who she was referring to, Jasper wasn't about to make the same mistake twice and assume anything when it came to Angela.

"Who's an asshole?" Jasper asked.

"He is," she snapped. Angela's eyes were beginning to well up with tears again, and Jasper knew another round of crying was about to begin. This time it only lasted a few minutes, and then she raised her head from his chest, revealing a look of anger instead of sadness.

"He's the biggest asshole I've ever known, and I hope he rots in hell—forever!" she said with disdain.

"Angela, who are you talking about? Did someone do something to you? You know...?" Jasper was scrambling for some way to finish this question without getting too personal. "You know, do we have to call the police?" he asked.

The thought of Angela being raped caused a feeling inside Jasper that he never imagined he would feel again. It wasn't a single emotion but multiple emotions swirling around in his head. His heart was pounding so hard in his chest he was sure she could hear it. He was fourteen again and wanting to hurt someone—wishing them dead. He felt an overwhelming urge to protect her and hunt down the person who had done this to her. Confusion ruled his mind; at the same time he wanted nothing more than to hold Angela as tightly as he could. The feelings crashed together in his mind, causing him to yell out.

"Who did this to you? What's his name?"

She responded with an equally loud, "Rob!"

Jasper froze again, waiting for his brain to catch up with her words.

"Rob raped you?" he asked.

"No, no, no," she responded, now starting to cry again. "He didn't rape me. He was fucking around on me. With not one, but with *two* of those sluts he works with."

The pounding in Jasper's chest began to subside as everything Angela was saying started to make sense. In a far more calming tone, Jasper asked, "What can I do for you?"

"Can you fix it so I pass Biochemistry? I'm sure I just failed that exam."

"I can't do that," replied Jasper. "But I can talk to the Dean of the Faculty of Science and see what can be done under these extenuating circumstances." Jasper had never asked his father to do anything like this before, and he wasn't sure if his father would be at all sympathetic.

"Are you kidding? I could never ask you to do that."

"I'll talk to my dad on the way home and explain everything. There might be some way we can get you a re-write. But please don't get your hopes up; I'm not sure if anything can be done."

"Thank you so much," she said, and then she leaned in and kissed Jasper on the cheek.

"My dad won't be heading home until eight or so. Do you want to go and get something to eat?" Jasper asked.

"I'm sorry; I don't really feel like eating anything right now."

"Oh yeah, I guess not after the day you've had. I wouldn't feel much like eating either," muttered Jasper in a consoling voice.

"Can I ask you a huge favor?"

"Sure, anything."

"I wouldn't normally ask this, but I'm not feeling up to driving right now, and the last thing I need is to crack up my car," Angela said. "Could you drive me home? It's not far, and I can come get my car in the morning."

"Not a problem," Jasper said with a shake of his head. "And I have an even better idea. I can drive you home in your car and take a taxi back here. That way you don't have to come back in the morning to get your car."

"That's a great idea, but only if you let me pay for the taxi," Angela demanded.

"How far is your place?"

"Just at the corner of Ouellette and University—the Royal Towers," Angela told him.

"Oh, that's not far at all. Let's get going."

They arrived at the Royal Towers, and Jasper parked

Angela's car in her underground parking stall. "I'll grab a taxi out front, there're lots of cabs running up and down University," Jasper said as he opened the car door.

"Why don't you come up for a bit, and I can make you a sandwich. You haven't had dinner and it's almost seven o'clock," Angela suggested.

Jasper's heart started pounding hard again, and his thoughts started racing back to when he had made that first critical mistake—assuming Angela was single. Once again, he didn't want to repeat his blunder and started searching for a reason why he couldn't go up to her apartment.

"I don't want to put you out. You've had a rough day."

"It's not a problem, and it's the least I can do for you after all of the support you've given me."

Thinking quickly and remembering she lived with her grandmother, Jasper countered with, "I don't want to disturb your grandmother by arriving unannounced."

"Again, not a problem. She's gone out of town on a church outing to London," replied Angela. "So it's settled, you're coming up and having something to eat."

When they entered the apartment, Jasper hung his coat on a hook on the back of the apartment door and removed his shoes, placing them on the rubber mat next to the hallway closet. Jasper walked the short distance down the entry hallway and found his eyes immediately captivated by the spectacular view of the Detroit City skyline filling the floor-to-ceiling windows in the living room.

"Wow, what a view! You've got a really nice place here."

"Thanks, but it's not mine. It's my grandmother's, and she's been here since my grandfather died twenty years ago. I'm just staying here while going to university. My grandmother doesn't charge rent, so it really helps me save money."

"I do the same thing. I live with my dad."

"Have a seat and turn the TV on. I'll make you that sandwich. Are the Wings playing tonight?" she asked, walking into the small kitchen.

"Don't know, but I'll take a look. Bet we can see Joe Louis Arena from here. I'll tell you in a second." Jasper stood looking through the sliding glass door leading to the large balcony. "It looks like there is a game tonight. Wonder who they're playing?"

Jasper sat down on the couch facing the TV and started looking for the remote. He found it sitting on a side table to his right. He picked it up and hit the power button. He started to flip through the channels to find the game but couldn't keep from watching Angela in the kitchen.

She noticed his preoccupation. "What?" she said, feeling self-conscious.

"What do you mean?" Jasper replied, feeling equally uncomfortable with being caught staring.

"Why do you keep staring at me?"

"I can't help it—you have perfect genes."

Angela immediately looked down at her pants.

"Really—thanks," she replied while her face contorted with confusion.

"Not those jeans, your other genes—you know, DNA."

They both burst out laughing.

"You're obsessed with DNA, aren't you?"

"I guess so. Other than space exploration, DNA is man's last unknown frontier. There's so much hidden inside DNA yet we know so little…"

"Okay, that's enough," she interrupted. "We're not talking any more school tonight."

"Sorry," he replied with a grin.

Angela walked out of the kitchen and placed a perfectly made ham and cheese sandwich, accompanied by a shiny red apple, on the side table where the remote had been. She then sat down on the couch uncomfortably close to Jasper and put her hand on his thigh. Like a well-trained dog given a command to sit, Jasper's body froze while his heart raced at a pace certain to cause him a heart attack.

Not at all sure of what was happening, Jasper turned and picked up the apple from the plate, taking a bite. The tension almost paralyzed him. He struggled not to look at his thigh to verify that her hand was really on it. Jasper's nerves cinched tightly into a knot. His mouth dried instantly, and he found it impossible to swallow. The bite of the apple was lodged in his throat. His eyes began to water, and he was using every muscle in his body to prevent himself from coughing and choking. He put the apple back on the plate and calmly tried to breath. Angela had no trouble detecting his struggle and turned her head from the TV towards him.

"Are you okay?" she asked with a discernable level of concern in her voice. "Is the sandwich all right? I didn't ask if you liked ham and cheese."

Jasper choked a little and said, "I'm fine; I'm just having a little trouble swallowing—my mouth is dry."

"Well I know what will fix a dry mouth." She immediately moved right into Jasper's lap and began kissing him firmly on the lips. She kissed him for what felt like hours to Jasper, but he enjoyed it so much he wished it would never end. When Angela finally relinquished her hold on his tongue and let their lips part, she asked, "Is that better?"

Jasper's eyes hadn't opened yet and with his tongue not completely recovered from the kiss, he was just able to murmur, "Yes."

CHAPTER 11

THE CLOSET

The moment was bittersweet for Jasper as he wrestled with his conscience. Three months ago, this had been his only wish—his fantasy come true—but now panic was stealing those precious feelings and leaving him unable to continue. Looking straight into his eyes was the most beautiful woman he had ever kissed, but something inside him was very unsure of what he was doing.

He started to question himself, and a flurry of thoughts ran through his head: *This isn't right. She just broke up with her boyfriend. You're taking advantage of her.* This last thought jolted Jasper into action.

Like a scene from one of the many bad movies he had seen over the years where this very situation happened, the words he was about to say seemed ridiculous.

"I can't do this. You just broke up with Rob, and you're not thinking straight."

Angela responded with a resounding, "Shut up. I know exactly what I'm doing."

She repositioned herself in Jasper's lap and gave him an even more passionate kiss, starting from the nape of his neck and slowly working her way up to his lips. There was nothing Jasper could do—or wanted to do—at this point, and he gave in to his want. Angela's hands moved all over his upper body, grabbing and clutching his arms, neck and chest. She ran her hand through his hair and kissed him behind the ear. Then they heard a phone ring.

Jasper halted his exploration of Angela's body and blurted out, "Shit, what time is it?"

Angela looked at the clock on the DVD player under the TV and said, "Twenty after eight. Why?"

"Oh crap!"

Jasper leaped off the couch and ran to his pack, hoping to get to his phone before the call went to voicemail.

"I forgot to call my dad."

Jasper pulled the phone from his pack and pushed the 'Receive' button, putting the device to his ear.

"Hey, Dad. I'm sorry for not calling you. I met a friend after my exam that needed some help, and I lost all track of time. Sorry about that... Yes, everything is fine... No, I don't need a ride. I'll make my own way home... Good night."

Jasper turned back to look at Angela, wondering if this was all a dream.

"Sorry about that. Can we pick up where we left off?"

"Not a chance," Angela replied with an incredibly mischievous look in her eye. "We're moving this to the bedroom."

Upon hearing this, Jasper's knees buckled, and he had to steady himself on the back of the couch. Angela walked over to him with an innocent smile on her face; it wasn't his legs he was worried about anymore. The roller coaster he had ridden nearly four months ago that had derailed in the coffee shop now appeared to be back on track and rushing to its highest peak. Jasper wasn't sure if he would survive the inevitable freefall that would follow.

Angela took his hand and towed him to her bedroom; his feet weren't moving fast enough. She stopped in front of her dresser and opened the top drawer to pull out a book of matches. She lit the three vanilla-scented candles on her night table and turned to look at Jasper. Neither spoke a word. She walked back to him and firmly grasped both his hands, freefalling directly backwards onto the bed, dragging

Jasper down in the process. Jasper braced his fall to keep his full weight from landing on Angela and began kissing her.

Her scent was intoxicating. Jasper slipped into an uncontrolled state, unable to stop kissing her body. He started on her neck and slowly made his way down toward her cleavage. When his lips finally reached the point where they were pressed lightly between her breasts, he felt the corner of her gold cross touch his cheek.

Instantly, shock ripped through his body, and his thoughts turned to his childhood. He fought back with a fury, using every ounce of his willpower. Nothing would stop him tonight, and with a light flicking motion, so as not to draw attention to his actions, he pushed the crucifix to the side with his nose. He then continued moving his lips down Angela's body without another thought of the past.

Moments later, they were only covered by each other, forming a single tight mass. Like musical instruments, each of his senses played its part, and when combined, their performance was an orchestra. The result was astonishing.

Jasper had dated only three other girls in his life, and none of them had come close to igniting such emotion in him. This hadn't been their fault; he still feared the humiliation that was sure to come. It had been more than a year since he had been with a girl, and as they continued to kiss, it became increasingly difficult for him to restrain the flood of primal urges he was experiencing. A war raged through every nerve in his body: on one side, the need to finally experience an orgasm; on the other, his desire to never let this feeling stop. Caught between these two forces, he found sanctuary.

Much to Jasper's dismay, Angela broke their embrace and rolled to the right. She reached into her nightstand and removed a condom from the top drawer. Angela ripped open the packet and handed it to Jasper.

The poor lighting and lack of experience, as well as his exhilaration, combined against Jasper and he fumbled with the condom. Angela took the condom back and came to his rescue.

Great, how embarrassing, he thought as he felt her unroll the condom.

Jasper began his thrusts in a slow and methodical manner, like the drumbeat in a military march. Angela responded back with her own thrusts, offsetting each of his while offering a gentle sigh of approval with each movement. Jasper was tormented; he hoped it would never end, but he begged for the climax he longed for.

Angela voiced her pleasure in a small cry-like whimper, and Jasper knew instinctively she had climaxed. Her climax subsided, and Jasper could feel her body moving to the more relaxed state of gratification. As her transformation occurred below him, Jasper's mind began to unravel. Visions of a darkened church office and Father Malkin invaded his ecstasy. He continued fruitlessly; his attempt to orgasm was growing futile. Each of his dying thrusts now only brought pain.

Jasper finished his last thrust when Angela raised her hand for him to stop. He rolled off of her and lay motionless. Angela laid next to him in perfect silence for a minute, and then turned her head so she could kiss him behind the ear.

"Thank you so much."

Jasper didn't say a word but found her hand in the bed next to his and gave it a tight squeeze.

Why is this happening? Something's wrong with me, he thought as anger and frustration mixed in his mind like vinegar and baking soda. Jasper let go of her and clenched his fists, fighting the urge to scream. He knew what was about to follow and loathed it. Angela lifted her head and placed it on Jasper's chest, facing towards his feet.

"God, Jasper!" Angela exclaimed. "I thought you'd finished?"

Jasper didn't know what to say. He knew this wasn't the time or the place to get into this conversation, but before he could even think of something to say, Angela had moved down to his waist. The pain was unbearable, but Jasper held silent, not wanting to embarrass her. His strength was no match for the pain, and he placed his hand on Angela's head, gently pushing her off.

"It's all right. I'm used to it."

Angela lifted her head and turned to look at Jasper in disbelief.

"What are you talking about?" she said as her face began to strain.

He didn't see any alternative but to say it out loud. "I can't cum," Jasper strained through tightly gritted teeth.

"What?" Angela was now even more noticeably confused. "Is it me?"

"No, you were great."

"You can't cum?" The words rolled off of her lips in unison with a nervous laugh. "You can't cum now? Or do you mean you can't cum at all?"

Jasper was about to begin with the sordid details of his inability when a loud and startling buzzing sound erupted from the entrance hall.

Angela immediately sprang to her feet, but not before the sound had bellowed three more times.

Jasper realized the sound was coming from the video-intercom system that let visitors into the building. Without covering herself, Angela left the bedroom muttering.

"It's one thirty in the morning, and those idiots next door are probably drunk again and pushing the wrong number..."

Still naked and now sitting half prone with his back against the headboard, Jasper heard two more buzzes before the sound of the headset being lifted from the wall. Then Angela's voice filled the entire apartment as she yelled. "What the hell are you doing here? No, you can't! Get out of here... Oh my God... Shit!"

Before Jasper could even speak a word, Angela screamed at him from the hallway.

"Get up! You have to get out of here!"

She ran into the bedroom holding his backpack and threw

it into the closet.

"There's no time. Get in here," she yelled, sliding the closet door open.

Jasper bent down and picked up his clothes from the floor. "What the hell is going on?" he asked in a slight panic.

"It's Rob," she blurted. "He's on his way up. I couldn't stop him. I could see him on the monitor, and I was telling him to leave when some guy leaving the building just let him in. If he finds you in here, he'll kill us both. There's no time; just get in the closet—now!"

Angela slid the mirrored closet door open a bit farther and took a terrycloth robe from inside, putting it on.

Jasper dove into the closet and slid the door completely shut behind him. He stood there in complete darkness, holding his clothes in his hands wondering what kind of mess he had just gotten himself into. A rapid pounding pressure erupted in his chest—his heart was begging to explode. He was trying to stand perfectly still so as not to make a sound, but pain emanated from his feet as he tried to stand on the shoes strewn across the closet floor. It occurred to him that the pain was due to being bare foot: his shoes and jacket were in the entrance hallway.

It was too late to warn Angela. He heard the front door open and Angela's angry voice ordering Rob to leave. Jasper thought, *Maybe she noticed them and put them into the front closet before opening the door...*

Their voices were so loud Jasper could hear everything.

"Please, you have to hear me out. It was all lies. Those two bitches," Rob pleaded for her to listen.

"I don't care, just leave!" Angela shouted, shutting down his argument.

They stood in silence—stalemate—until Angela finally gave in.

"Look, Rob. I wasted four years of my life on you, and I don't want to waste another second."

"I beg you, please—just two minutes to hear me out?"

"Fine, you've got two minutes. Then I want you out!"

Rob thanked her and began telling his side of the story.

"Heather lied to you about the whole thing. I've never touched either of those women, nor would I ever want to. Heather hates me because she wanted to switch to the day shift, and I told her no. She's been asking me for months, begging and pleading, but I told her she was hired for the nightshift, and if she didn't like it, she could leave."

Jasper closed his eyes and shook his head. He desperately wanted to stop the image of Angela's face forming in his mind, but it was impossible, and he could see it as clear as if she were right in front of him. Jasper's rage grew exponentially as he heard Rob's lies.

"The bitch changed her tactics last Thursday when she offered me sex anytime I wanted if I'd change her shift. I flat out refused and told her how in love I am with you. She stormed out of the back office and cooked up the story you heard. I'm not sleeping with either of them. She made sure Mary told you the same thing to get back at me. I fired them both today, and that's why I'm so late getting here—I had to work their shifts to cover until I get someone else. I've been calling you all night—why didn't you answer?"

Jasper placed his left fist into his mouth to keep from screaming. His heart told him to burst out of the closet and call the snake for the lies he was feeding her. But he couldn't; Jasper knew if they were discovered, nothing good would come of it. The sight of Angela's and his photos on the front page of the *Windsor Star* under a caption stating 'Two Dead in Lovers Triangle' might actually kill his father. His fist began to bleed as his front teeth penetrated the skin.

How can she believe this guy? This can't be happening, it just can't. It was clear from the dead silence in the apartment that only one thing could now be happening. *They're kissing*, he thought.

Jasper was devastated. He could feel the pressure welling up behind his eyes, but the final blow had yet to be delivered.

He was unprepared for what he heard next.

"What are you doing?" asked Angela in a surprised voice.

"Angela Rossi, will you marry me?" he asked in the most sincere voice he could muster.

Jasper exploded with hostility over what was happening. The darkness of the closet conjured the darkness of the robe and he slid the closet door open. He lifted his pants from the closet floor and yanked them on before pulling his shirt over his head. He burst out of the bedroom and stood in the living room. Rob was still holding Angela's hand when Jasper spotted the crucifixion tattooed on Rob's outstretched arm. But it was the word 'Faith' that ignited Jasper's temper.

"You liar!" shouted Jasper.

"What the hell?" uttered Rob in shock as he moved his eyes from Jasper back to Angela.

"Jasper—no!" cried Angela.

Jasper began walking to the center of the living room where Rob and Angela were standing.

"You fucking slut!" shouted Rob. "How long have you been cheating on me?"

Before Angela could speak, Jasper answered, "Not as long as you've been cheating on her."

"You son of a bitch, I'll kill you!" Rob shouted and he lunged toward Jasper, but Angela had not let go of his hand, trying to hold him back.

"He's cheating on you with one of those women—I saw the two of them that day we met in Starbucks; they were fooling around behind the dumpster."

Rob tossed Angela off his arm like a piece of clothing, sending her flying to the floor. He tackled Jasper as if he were in the finals of a football match. Jasper's back slammed into the hallway wall, and the two of them fell to the floor in a flurry of swinging arms. Jasper was no match for Rob and quickly found himself overpowered by the force of each blow.

Rob positioned his body on top of Jasper's, grabbed a handful of Jasper's hair and began slamming his face into the floor. Blood began streaming from Jasper's nose and mouth and splattered on the walls. Jasper struggled to fight back, but it was futile. The blood began to pour down the back of his throat after the third hit, making it more difficult to breathe with each inhalation.

The pounding continued for a few more seconds then suddenly stopped. Jasper was blinded by the blood and hair in his eyes and didn't see Angela throw herself onto Rob. She jumped between Rob and Jasper, breaking Rob's grip on Jasper's hair. The force of her body knocked Rob off.

"Leave him alone, you're killing him!" she shouted as Rob pushed her off of his body.

"Get away from me, you bitch!" Rob shouted as he jumped up and headed back toward Jasper.

Jasper had pulled himself up and was sitting on the floor leaning against the wall trying to wipe the blood from his face.

"Leave him or I'm calling the cops," she said, heading for the phone.

"Fuck you!" Rob said to Jasper before spitting on him.

Jasper tried to push himself up using the wall behind him, but the blood made the paint slippery and he fell back to the floor.

"Don't even bother," said Rob with a victorious laugh. He turned to face Angela and repeated himself, "Fuck you too," and left the apartment.

Angela retrieved a towel from the kitchen and knelt down in front of Jasper. He pushed her arm away as she attempted to clean his face and took the towel in his hand. Jasper wiped the blood from his eyes and saw the crimson fluid covering the front of her bathrobe like paint splatter. Jasper at last found the strength to stand and began searching for his shoes.

"Jasper, I'm so sorry," she kept repeating.

Jasper stopped his search and faced Angela, his eyes flooding with emotion. The rage then exploded inside him.

"Sorry!" shouted Jasper. "I'm the one who's sorry. I should have never let my guard down!" he yelled.

"What?" she cried, confused by his outburst.

"It was too good to be true. It's always too good to be true. It'll never happen, and I was stupid to think it could," he said with resentment. The anger with himself was painted in his words.

Jasper turned his back on Angela and resumed his search. He found his shoes behind the open front door and slowly bent down to pick them up. Placing them under his arm, he stepped out the front door and turned to face her.

Angela had followed him down the hall, trying to apologize while crying, but Jasper refused to acknowledge her. Suddenly, his eyes were captured by the sparkle of the hallway light off of the crucifix hanging between her partially exposed breasts. When he thought about how close Angela had brought him to climaxing, a grin formed on his lips, causing his cheeks to burn. A smile followed and sent a needle sharp pain through his face when he thought of her sanctimony.

"I'm so sorry, Jasper," she said, sobbing uncontrollably.

"Listen to your grandmother. Go to Italy and marry a nice Italian boy."

CHAPTER 12

CHRISTINE

The warm Hawaiian sun drifted across a smoky-grey sky to meet the Pacific Ocean. From the second floor lanai, Christine Anderson could see white wash soaring into the air from waves breaking on the black lava rock shore. To her these waves were a gift from God and not the distant storm swirling off shore. She also knew they wouldn't last long. Christine was staring into the distance dreaming about her next great ride when the chirp of her cell phone crashed the daydream. Recognizing the number at once, she flipped the phone open.

"Hey, Jess, you thinking what I am?" she asked.

"Of course," said Jesse Struger, his voice filled with excitement.

"Okay. I'll meet you there in fifteen minutes."

Christine rummaged through the pile of damp clothes hanging from the wooden railing of the lanai, looking for her favorite bathing suit. There were only a couple of hours left before sunset, and most of the good waves would soon be lost. Frantically flipping each piece of clothing off the railing, causing most to fall to the ground, she called down to her mother.

"Mom, have you seen my blue bathing suit? I left it to dry here last night."

"I put it where I always do," Sandra Anderson yelled back from the front yard of their small cottage.

"Thanks," Christine replied, feeling a little like a three-year-old; she really hadn't put much effort into finding what she was looking for.

Christine raced back into the house, grabbed her bathing suit off the fin of her surfboard and ran into her bedroom. She pulled her T-shirt and board shorts off and tossed them on the floor. She then closed her door to check herself in the mirror mounted on the back of her door. Her naked body was flawless, sculpted like a gymnast's from years of swimming in the surf. Christine bent her knees to see her face as the mirror had been positioned when she was in middle school.

She pulled her board shorts on over her swimsuit and rushed back to the lanai to find a beach towel. Sandra looked up and noticed her daughter's frenzied behavior.

"When I'm done with the garden, we're going to eat, so don't be taking off before dinner."

"I'm not hungry. Jess called and he said the waves are awesome."

"You're not leaving this house again without having something to eat. Besides, I made the sauce from scratch using these tomatoes." Sandra held up a pair of bright red Roma tomatoes in her left hand and waved her right index finger like a wand. "I mean it this time, get in the kitchen and eat, or I'm taking that board away from you."

"Ah, Sandy, you're so cute when you're angry," said Christine in a deliberate attempt to mock her mother. She hated being called 'Sandy.' "Mom, I'm twenty-five, and I'm pretty sure I'm old enough to decide if I need to eat or not."

"I could care less if you were fifty, if you live in my house you..."

"You live under my rules. Yeah, yeah, you've told me a thousand times."

Christine headed for the kitchen, grabbed a bowl from the cupboard and took a small serving of pasta from one of the two pots simmering on the stove. She covered it with a scoop of tomato sauce from the other pot and sat at the table. First making the sign of the cross, Christine recited her usual grace and completed the prayer with another sign of the cross.

"You're not even going to wait for me to sit down, are you?"

"Mom, I gotta go. There's only a little bit of daylight left, and you know how much you hate it when I ride in the dark." Christine tried to use her mother's own fears to her advantage. "I might get eaten by a shark or something."

"That's enough. I don't even like you joking about that kind of thing. You like the sauce?" she yelled after Christine, who was already halfway out the door—surfboard under her arm.

"Loved it—you too, Mom," she said as she leaped down the front steps.

Christine tossed her board in the back of her Jeep and jumped into the driver's seat. The Jeep raced down the crushed lava stone driveway, sliding to a stop where it met the pavement. Evening traffic on the Island Highway was worse than New York's; she waited ten minutes for a break. The short drive to the hidden beach she shared with Jesse felt like hours, especially when the surf was up.

The last mile was the worst; it was a narrow gravel track filled with potholes, coconuts and fallen palm trees. This penance was worth it though, as the road led to the finest few yards of powder white sand beach on the Big Island—completely untouched by tourists and natives alike. She parked her Jeep next to Jess's pick-up, not surprisingly the only other vehicle there.

Christine knew it was going to be a great couple of hours of surfing: the sea turtles were taking refuge on the beach, avoiding the pounding waves near the shore. She took her wetsuit and towel from the back seat, where she always left them, and pulled her board out. Christine ducked under the thick green brush in front of the Jeep and made her way down the path. The surf roared in the distance, and a white tern called overhead. Her bare feet were impervious to the still blistering hot sand of the beach. Having spent her entire life in Hawaii, she had gained some immunity to the hostile environment of the sun, sand and sea.

Jesse gave Christine a wave that she could barely see because he was so far out from the shore, avoiding the breaker line. She waved back and then stripped naked to put on her wet suit. Twenty-plus years surfing the endless waves of the Pacific had chiseled her to perfection, and the tropical sun left no portion of her body untouched, including her sun-bleached shoulder-length brown hair. Her honey-brown Hawaiian tan was flawless—uninterrupted except for the sandal lines on her feet. Her neck was laced with a snow-white shark's tooth necklace carved into a Virgin Mary. Its pure white was luminescent against her golden skin; a gift from her mother on her confirmation.

She paddled her way through the breaking waves and waited for Jesse to finish his ride; Christine wanted to catch the next set together. Jesse paddled his board over to hers and held it with his hand. They sat on their boards floating parallel to each other, facing directly into the setting sun.

"Hey, babe, you made it in record time."

"Couldn't stand to be away from you," she said with a smirk on her face.

"You mean the surf." He turned his head to the left and leaned over his board while she did the same until their lips met.

"Wow, never seen your eyes so blue. They're bluer than the water," Jesse said with sincerity.

"Stop it—I know what you really want. Now let's get going," Christine said.

"No, seriously, they're incredibly blue today."

"Bye, Jess." She paddled farther out to sea to wait for the next surge. Jesse quickly caught up to her and they paddled to where the waves started their rise. They sat upright, floating on their boards so they could watch the horizon for the next wave. A massive cruise ship drifted across the sunset on its way to one of the other islands.

"One of these days, I'm going to be on one of those," said Christine, staring longingly at the ship.

"Yeah, me too—but I never get sick of this, do you?"

"Never."

They both lay back down on their boards to paddle a little farther, but Christine sat back up when she heard a distinctive clicking sound.

"You hear that?"

"What?" asked Jesse.

"That clicking... Look at that." She pointed to the surface of the water fifty yards to their right. A pod of spinner dolphins erupted from the water, performing the aerial ballet that gave them their name.

"Awesome!" they said in unison.

They rode the surf until the last glimpse of sunlight had fallen below the horizon and then paddled back to the beach to sit on an old surfboard of Christine's that Jess had made into a makeshift bench.

"So?" asked Jess with a puppy-dog face she couldn't resist.

He reached behind her and began unzipping her wetsuit. Jesse carefully pulled it off—it was stuck to her skin from the seawater—and leaned in to kiss her. He lifted her from the bench so they stood pressed hard against each other without breaking his embrace. His skilled hands finished removing the suit from the rest of her body and continued to caress her as his breathing accelerated.

"Easy there, big guy," said Christine as she tried to slow his progress.

This momentary break in their embrace gave Jesse time to remove his wetsuit. He quickly re-engaged their embrace and grabbed Christine, pulling her tight against him, pressing his body against her skin. Jesse unlocked his lips from hers and started kissing his way down her neck, licking the sea salt from her skin.

Jesse's lips inched their way to the point where they

pressed lightly between her breasts. The crucifix etched into his cheek, and with a light flicking motion so as not to draw attention to his movement, he pushed the cross to the side with his nose. He continued his journey, moving his lips farther down Christine's body.

With her eyes closed and her head tilted backwards, Christine's heart began to pound louder than the surf with each delicate kiss, and pleasure surged through her skin. Captivated by her arousal, Jesse's movements became forceful, and he squeezed her body against his even more. Without warning, Christine's body tensed as if it had been doused with a bucket of ice water. She pushed hard against his body in an attempt to put some space between them.

"Jess no," whispered Christine, but he ignored her request and continued his pursuit.

"Really, Jess, no," she said more forcefully, but Jesse didn't want to relinquish his progress toward finally consummating their decade-long relationship.

"I mean it!" Christine nearly shouted as she pushed his body firmly away from hers, creating a safe distance between them. "You know my feelings about this; we've been over this a thousand times. Not until I'm married. It's my belief."

"Oh, screw your belief!" he shouted at her. "Screw your religion. I've had it. Ten years is long enough." Jesse's temper took hold of him, and he pulled their bodies back together.

"No, stop it, Jess! You're scaring me," Christine cried, pushing as hard as she could away from him.

"Fine, why don't you go back to your stupid church and pray a little more? Maybe God can fuck you. I sure as hell can't." Jesse shoved her away from him hard, put on his shorts and stormed away, leaving Christine crying on the beach.

She wondered how this monster could be the same sweet boy who had etched their initials into the lava rock at the top of the cliff.

Guilt filled Christine, knowing the torture she was putting

Jesse through. No matter how many times she and Jesse had tried to have sex, she was unable to—she felt her belief in God and her strong faith had always prevented it.

***

That night Christine's thoughts kept her awake. As long as she could remember, every Sunday, she and her mother had gone to Mass. They attended Saint Michael's, a small Catholic church on Alii Drive. Father Shannon was like a real father to her, always ready to listen to her no matter what the problem. He attended every one of her childhood birthdays and often showed up at school events. The Church and her mother were the two most important things in her life.

Bet I'm the only twenty-five-year-old virgin on the Island, she thought to herself as she lay in bed. She lingered in the state between consciousness and unconsciousness and wondered why she physically couldn't do it.

Her right hand slid below the sheets, and she began caressing herself. The evening's self-indulgence came quickly and easily without guilt, unlike every attempt with Jesse. They had started off great, but as they ventured deeper into the act, an overwhelming feeling of guilt always destroyed her arousal, leaving her repulsed. Christine still attributed it to her strong belief in God and the ways of the Church, although this gave her little comfort that the same wouldn't happen on their honeymoon.

Christine wasn't a stranger to Jesse's bad temper and knew he would be fine in the morning. She also knew a big part of his temper came from his sexual frustration, which she was responsible for. It had always concerned her that Jesse didn't feel the same way about God as she did.

***

The ring of Christine's cell phone woke her the next

morning. She glanced at her clock and knew why she couldn't lift her head—it was just after six. The morning light filtered through the half-closed curtains on her bedroom window, causing the dust to sparkle in the air. She wasn't surprised by the intrusion and saw Jess's name on the screen.

"Sorry, Chris, I just get so..." he started.

"Stop," she said, cutting his sentence off. "I'm sorry too. I just can't... I really want to, but I just can't."

"Meet me down at the beach; I've got a surprise for you," Jesse said, quickly changing the topic.

"Do I need my board?"

"Nothing."

"Okay, I'll be there in fifteen." Christine left a note on the kitchen table for her mother informing her she was going to the beach and would be back for nine o'clock Mass.

Christine arrived at the beach and parked next to Jesse's truck. She made her way through the thick bush and emerged on the other side to find Jesse standing in front of the old surfboard. A stack of two-by-fours and tools were sitting on the lava flow next to them.

"What's all this?"

"We're finally going to name our beach," Jesse said with a grin.

"Really, what are we going to call it?" Christine asked, excited by the prospect of giving their favorite place a name.

"That's entirely up to you—I'm only here to help."

They carried the old board up the lava flow, placing it high enough to keep it out of the surf. Christine hadn't used tools much, and the long spikes Jesse was using to nail the surfboard to the two-by-fours seemed impossible to hit straight.

"I can't do this," she protested after she pounded the third long steel spike on an angle into the wood.

"Just take your time and you'll get it," he said in an effort to encourage her to complete her side.

Christine put the sixth spike through the wood and

declared, "That's it—I'm done."

Jesse pounded the two wooden legs into cracks in the lava to secure them so the wind couldn't blow their makeshift sign over. He positioned the board so that the front could only been seen from the ocean.

"Well, have you decided?" he asked.

"Nope, not yet."

"Well, here's some paint. When you decide, you can use it to put the name on the board."

Jesse handed her a small can of bright red paint and a brush. "Make sure the board is dry before you paint it or it won't stick." Jesse picked up his tools and left the job of naming their private surfing beach to Christine. He kissed her on the cheek, still sensitive to the night before, and left.

Christine sat on the edge of the lava flow watching the sea turtles feed in the shallows for a while. Then her cell phone rang.

"Hello."

"Hey, Chris, it's Kerri. Do you and Jess want to join Ty and me for some awesome skim boarding this morning? The waves really suck for surfing."

"No, I can't. Mom and I are going to early Mass this morning. Oh crap, what time is it?" Christine asked in a panic.

"Almost nine," said Kerri.

"Sorry, Ker, I gotta go."

"Okay, I'll email you some of our best moves—show you what you missed," Kerri told her, trying to make her jealous, and they hung up.

It was twenty minutes to nine. She put the can of paint and brush in the back of her Jeep and raced home to pick up her mother.

"I didn't think you were coming," Sandra said as she climbed into the Jeep.

"Sorry, I got distracted at the beach and lost track of time."

"At least you weren't surfing. Why are you all dirty? Father Shannon should be really impressed by your appearance this morning," Sandra added with a high degree of sarcasm.

"He won't care—he's just happy to see me," replied Christine with a generous smirk.

"You're right about that," Sandra agreed.

Sandra and Christine took their regular pew near the front of the church and waited for Mass to begin. Christine stared blankly at the altar, unconscious of her surroundings. She missed the entire sermon, obsessed over finding a name for the secret beach.

Father Shannon started Communion, and Sandra had to poke Christine in the side to stand up and walk to the altar. Christine followed her mother to the front of the church to receive her Communion. She was walking back to their pew when she noticed the painting hanging on the back wall; it was her favorite painting in the church. As a child, she had daydreamed about being in the painting while Father Shannon was conducting the sermon.

It was a beautiful painting of Adam and Eve standing hand in hand on a rocky point, watching the sun disappear into the ocean. Walking back to her pew, she read the name engraved on the brass label affixed to the painting and decided it was the perfect name for the beach.

CHAPTER 13

DR. JEAN SABASTIEN

Jasper's voice gripped the room; captivating his audience with every word and building toward his conclusion.

"There is no missing link."

The crowded room erupted with applause. His fellow students and instructors rose to their feet to show their appreciation. The massive weight of four years of research lifted from his shoulders like a hot-air balloon taking flight. Unable to contain his exuberance Jasper exhaled a quiet "Yes," under his breath. He had just defended his doctoral thesis, and it was a home run. Two men stood near the back of the room and clapped in unison with the rest of the audience.

"Jean, you'll take good care of him?" asked Dr. Stewart.

"Of course, Nik. I'll treat him like my own son," replied Dr. Jean Sabastien.

"He's all I've got."

"Don't worry; he'll be working in the safest place I know. The security is tighter than Fort Knox!" Dr. Sabastien said through a smile in an effort to reassure his friend.

"I'll miss him."

They began walking toward the scrum of students gathered around Jasper at the bottom of the steps to the small stage.

***

The students were all trying to congratulate Jasper and shake his hand, but one hand stood out among the rest, moving over the top of the crowd towards him. It belonged to a very tall, slender, middle-aged man unknown to Jasper. He took the hand and shook it firmly. It was easy to see the owner of the hand, as he stood six inches above anyone else in the crowd. His sandy blonde hair extended to his shoulders and his smoky green eyes were welcoming in the light.

"Congratulations, that was a very impressive defense," beamed Dr. Sabastien over top of the crowd in a strong French accent.

"I'm Jean Sabastien. An old friend of your father's."

"Thanks," said Jasper, attempting to speak over nine or ten other voices all trying to congratulate him. "Wait a second. Are you *the* Dr. Jean Sabastien from the University of Paris? I've read all of your papers on genetics."

Dr. Sabastien nodded his head before he was swallowed by the mob of students. Jasper tried hopelessly to make his way toward the disappearing Dr. Sabastien to continue their conversation, but it was no use; he couldn't free himself from the mass of students.

"We'll meet again," said Dr. Sabastien as the crowd engulfed him.

Greg waited for the students to relinquish their hold on Jasper before pulling him aside. He pointed to the title on the one-page announcement of Jasper's doctoral thesis defense and read it out loud, "'Can Genome Identification Solve the Mystery of the Missing Link?' Using archeological artifacts for the acquisition of ancient human genetic material to validate ancestral heritage using gene mapping and identification.' What the hell does this mean?"

Jasper laughed, shook his friend's hand and said, "I wouldn't expect a lawyer to understand."

"I haven't passed the Bar yet, but soon. Really what will you be doing in Rome? And before you begin, dumb it down for us lawyers."

"I've been working with my dad, and we found a way to get the DNA left on old artifacts and match it with DNA stored in a database."

"Still not dumbed down enough," Greg stated with a blank stare.

"Okay, I'll give you an example. Say you have something from ancient Rome that you can prove belonged to Julius Caesar. It has to be something he's touched and left his DNA on. And someone else comes along and says they have his original battle shield. I can take remnants of DNA from those artifacts, compare them and tell you if they were handled by the same person—no matter how long ago."

"And this is important why?"

"How much would you be willing to pay to make certain the van Gogh you're about to buy wasn't made in China?"

Greg's face lit up with understanding, and he folded Jasper's defense announcement, putting it in his pocket.

"Have fun in Rome and get a big place for when I come and visit."

Jasper couldn't wait to start his new job at the Vatican. He knew there was no other place on earth that housed more ancient human artifacts, catalogued and documented. The Egyptians and Incas were a close second, but nothing compared to the Vatican. The Catholic Church had gone to great lengths to collect and guard tens of thousands of artifacts dating back thousands of years before Christ.

***

Four months later, Jasper couldn't believe his eyes; he stood under the hot Italian sun looking up at a gleaming white marble building in front of him. The intensity of the sun made him instinctively put his left hand to his face in a sailor salute so he could marvel at his surroundings.

I can't believe I'm here, he thought as he watched tourists march up the steps of St. Peter's Basilica. At that moment, he watched an enormous flock of pigeons burst from the ground in unison. Their upward flight darkened the sky for an instant, allowing Jasper to fully grasp the magnificence of the structure.

On both sides of the entrance two guards stood motionless like those seen in photos of Windsor Castle. For once, his high-school history proved useful: he knew they were the Swiss Guard, who for hundreds of years had sworn to protect the Vatican and the Pope. Jasper entered the Great Hall of the Basilica, the massive stone building providing an escape from the August sun.

Growing up in a house with a devout Roman Catholic mother hadn't been enough to prepare Jasper for Rome—the heart of her religion. Standing in the epicenter of Catholicism, in a building considered by a quarter of the planet to be the most sacred place on earth, Jasper still didn't waver from his own belief.

"There is no God." He had repeated these words to himself for more than twenty years. This mantra in his life, more than anything else, had directed his path forward and formed the basis of his scientific research. At his mother's funeral, Jasper had vowed never to step foot in a church again, but today he broke that vow.

She'd be so proud of me. Now in his twenty-fifth year, he wondered how his view of the Church and God would impact his work. After all, he had been hired by the Vatican to work in their state-of-the-art genetic research lab.

Jasper pulled the envelope from his backpack and held the Vatican documents he had received telling him where to go. It was no use; he couldn't understand any of the Italian printed on the map. He could hear a little sarcastic voice inside his head: *Seven years of university weren't wasted on you.* After a few more minutes of trying to figure how to get to his meeting with the Head of the Vatican Genome Project, Jasper began to look around the massive basilica for someone who could help.

As he wandered the corridors of the Great Hall, a small

crack began to appear in Jasper's lifelong distain for the Church. It was impossible not to be impressed by the historical significance of everything around him, from the polished marble floor with its intricate mosaic inlays to the painted ceiling showing passages from the Bible. Having spent his entire life in Canada, where nothing built by human hands was more than a couple of hundred years old, these ancient walls and stone pillars seemed to speak to him as he meandered past.

Completely lost in the ambiance of the paintings and stained-glass windows, Jasper forgot about his appointment and the reason he had entered the Basilica in the first place. Coming back to his senses just in time, he spotted a pair of men wearing black robes tied at the waist with what looked like a length of thick white rope. The men were walking briskly up the corridor toward him, and knowing they were definitely not tourists, Jasper waited for their approach.

When they were near enough for him to see their faces, Jasper noticed how young they looked—not much older than himself. One was clean-shaven while the other had a goatee. Both carried a small leather-bound black book with one half of a distinctive red ribbon hanging from the top.

"Excuse me, do you speak English?" Jasper asked.

Both men stopped immediately, looked at each other and began to laugh. After they finished, the man with the goatee responded in perfect English with a thick British accent.

"Course we do. We're from England, mate. That never gets old, does it, Father Scott?"

"Never, Father Brian," said the clean-shaven man with a similar British accent. "Now what can we do for you?"

Understanding the reason for the two priests' laughter, Jasper made a low groaning sound like most people do after a bad joke. He followed this with a small laugh of his own.

"That's funny. Is there any chance you can tell me where I can find this office?" he asked, at the same time pointing to the map and directions on the page.

The instant the two priests saw the writing on the page, their faces scowled, no longer beaming with the happy laughter of a second ago. As if they had been given some grave news, their faces quickly became expressionless, like the faces in the many paintings on the walls.

"You're in the wrong building," said Father Scott. "Go around the Basilica and look for the redbrick building with glass front doors. There'll be a sign out front with the letters 'VGP.'"

"Thanks," said Jasper, but his words fell on deaf ears. Both priests were already walking away. Their pace was now even more brisk than it had been before Jasper stopped them. Jasper noted their cold response to his paperwork but quickly let it slide; his jubilation in finally knowing where he was going was all that mattered.

He made his way back outside into St. Peter's Square. Without looking at anything that might distract him, he walked in the hot Italian sun to the back of the Basilica. Jasper spotted the brick building at once, not by its color but by the pair of Swiss Guards standing at attention on either side of the glass front doors. They never spoke a word, moved an inch or even blinked an eye when he walked up the three front steps to the doors.

Jasper pulled on each door in turn, but both were locked. His first reaction was to turn and speak to one of the Guards, but he quickly realized this would be useless and that neither would say a word. *It must be lunch,* he thought. He had heard that Italian office buildings and government facilities closed for lunch, which could last two or three hours. Trying to read the writing on the glass doors to no avail, Jasper was turning to walk away when he saw a video camera-intercom and electronic swipe pad mounted on the wall to the right of the doors.

He pushed the call button and waited a few seconds before a voice came on the speaker.

"*Pronto?*"

Jasper responded, "Hello, do you speak English?"

"Yes, your name please?" said the voice from the intercom.

"It's Jasper Stewart, and I have an appointment with the Head of the Vatican Genome Project," Jasper replied.

A few seconds passed and Jasper heard the click of the electronic door lock. He opened the door and began walking into the building when he was greeted by a young woman. Her hazelnut hair was pulled back into a ponytail, exposing her glacier-blue eyes.

"I'm Alica. Please follow me, Dr. Stewart," she said with an Italian accent.

"Thanks."

Jasper followed her down a long hallway toward the far end of the building. They passed office after office filled with people working on computers, talking on their cell phones and completing various other routine office tasks. This in itself wasn't noteworthy except that this was supposed to be a lab. Jasper's thoughts as they walked were not of his meeting but of his surroundings. *If this is a research lab, why are all these people dressed in business suits?* There were no lab benches, no DNA sequencers, no computers—or any of the other equipment he expected to see in a state-of-the-art research facility.

"Please have a seat, Dr. Stewart. It'll only be a moment," said Alica, pointing to a row of chairs. She knocked on the closed office door directly to the right of them and didn't wait for a response before turning the handle and entering.

"*Scusi, signore.* Dr. Stewart has arrived."

Jasper was wondering why she spoke in English. Then he heard the man's voice reply.

"Please bring him in." Upon hearing this, Jasper stood up from his seat and waited for Alica's return. She stopped in the open doorway and looked at Jasper.

"Please come in, Dr. Stewart."

A shock of excitement hit Jasper when he entered the office. Like he had jumped into an ice cold lake, Jasper's heart instantly began to pound inside his chest. He nearly tripped over his own feet rushing to the outstretched hand in front of him, one he had shaken before.

"Oh my God! Dr. Jean Sabastien!"

CHAPTER 14

PROOF OF A BELIEF

I t only took Jasper a few seconds to compose himself after the initial shock of finding out the head of the research facility he would be working at for the next few years was none other than Dr. Jean Sabastien. Jasper had spent most of his four years of graduate studies reading Dr. Sabastien's hundreds of publications. It was his work that had led Jasper to specialize in the field of artifact DNA. Now it was slowly sinking in: he, Jasper Stewart, would be working with Dr. Jean Sabastien. Jasper couldn't collect his thoughts.

"I'm sorry, Dr. Sabastien," Jasper said, looking up at the tall man's face and staring directly into his eyes.

"For what?"

"For my reaction, it just blurted out," Jasper replied.

"Let's get something straight right from the start. Not everyone who works for the Vatican is Catholic, or even religious. I myself don't believe in God," stated Dr. Sabastien. "Please have a seat."

It then occurred to Jasper that the only other person he knew who didn't believe in God was his father, who was also a geneticist. *An old friend of your father's.* Jasper remembered his brief introduction to Dr. Sabastien at his thesis defense.

"How are your accommodations? I trust you found everything to your satisfaction?" asked Dr. Sabastien.

"Excellent," Jasper answered. "I had no idea the Vatican had all these facilities; the place I'm staying in is like a hotel."

"The Vatican is a city unto itself. We have everything we need within a very short walk. I'm sure you have many questions about the research we do, and you would like to see the facilities, right?"

"Absolutely!"

"Good, but first, you must get signed in and get your security clearance and pass so you can move freely through our facility. I'll ask Alica to take you to security. When you're finished, I'll give you a tour and we can discuss our research," Dr. Sabastien explained.

Having only worked in a university research lab where there was limited security, if any, it was difficult for Jasper to comprehend the need for so many levels of clearance. Jasper had just finished filling out the ten pages of forms left for him by Alica when a short, fat and nearly bald man who didn't appear much older than him entered the room. He had a familiar, welcoming smile.

"Hi, I'm Gino Capozzi, Head of Security and IT. He spoke in perfect English without the slightest hint of an Italian accent.

"Hi," Jasper said.

"It won't be much longer now. Just a few more minutes and your electronic pass and computer access will be ready," Gino told him.

After having both his left and right hand fingerprints digitally recorded, the process finally ended with a retinal scan of both eyes. Jasper was growing more impatient by the second now and was surprised they hadn't taken a blood sample. He decided a little chitchat might help pass the time since Gino spoke English, but before Jasper could ask him where he was from, Gino's cell phone rang and he left the room speaking fluent Italian.

Jasper's eyes became heavy, and he struggled to stay focused. He couldn't believe how long the security process was taking; he had been at it for two hours, and the effect of the time difference between Canada and Italy was weighing heavy on him. He was starting to doze off and needed to get up and go for a walk before he fell asleep. Just then Alica arrived with his security pass and informed Jasper that he could leave.

Jasper returned to Dr. Sabastien's office on his own and knocked on the open door. Dr. Sabastien was working on his computer and motioned for Jasper to enter and take a seat.

"If you can excuse me for one minute, I'll just send this email off and we can get started."

Jasper could hear his fingers typing on the keyboard and sat quietly waiting for them to stop. Dr. Sabastien hit the keyboard with an extra bit of force, signaling that he had finished.

"Everything went okay at security?"

Jasper nodded.

"I thought we'd start with a little background of the Vatican Genome Project, what our research is and why we do it. Sound good to you?" Dr. Sabastien asked.

"Sounds great."

"Okay, let's get started. In essence, the VGP began thousands of years ago," Dr. Sabastien started.

"What?"

"Yes, you heard me correctly. In the early centuries A.D., Christians began searching for physical evidence of Christ's existence. They tracked down artifacts by word of mouth, gathered them together and kept them safe. Over time, these artifacts came into the possession of the Catholic Church. No one knows which of these artifacts are worthless and which have been touched by the hand of God," he said dramatically. "For thousands of years, Catholics relied solely on their faith as their proof but now they have science. Think of it: if someone finds an artifact two thousand years old and claims it was touched by Christ, we have the technology to analyze and confirm if the DNA matches the DNA in our database."

"So if a match is found, the Catholics could have scientific proof of Christ's existence," added Jasper.

"Exactly."

"How many artifacts could possibly exist that Christ is believed to have touched?"

"The Church has many thousands actually, and new ones arrive almost daily," replied Dr. Sabastien. "All those people you saw working in those offices out there—that's what they're doing; scouring the globe looking for anything that could be linked to Christ."

"I was wondering why there were no lab coats or research equipment to be seen," said Jasper.

"But what they're really looking for is evidence of his remains," Dr. Sabastien pointed out.

"Remains? How can there be remains if the Catholic Church believes He was resurrected?"

"Think," said Dr. Sabastien, waiting for the imaginary light bulb to illuminate over Jasper's head. "Remains don't have to be a body."

It then occurred to Jasper that 'remains' could exist, and astonishment erased the confusion from his face.

"The spear that stabbed Him, the nails which held Him to the cross, or the crown of thorns from his head—those would all have remnants on them!"

"Well done. We already have one such item," Dr. Sabastien explained.

"Which one?" asked Jasper in disbelief.

"The most famous one of all—the Holy Grail."

"No way!" fired out of Jasper's mouth as if he were back in his catechism class.

Jasper quickly apologized for his outburst but the smirk on Dr. Sabastien's face was a clear indication that no apology was necessary.

"Those were my exact words when I first saw the Grail," said Dr. Sabastien, then he chuckled out loud. "So to sum things up, you will be spending a lot of your time in the lab extracting artifact DNA as well as DNA from ancient human remains, sequencing that DNA and looking for matching codes. How does that sound?"

"Excellent! And I'm going to be actually handling these priceless artifacts—like the Grail?" Jasper asked.

"Yes, and they're certainly not 'priceless'—if you haven't gathered from the security process you just completed," replied Dr. Sabastien. "The Church has spent hundreds of millions of dollars on the VGP, and I assure you, they know the exact cost of everything inside this building."

"Now it's all starting to make more sense," said Jasper.

"Good, then let's go down and show you the lab—shall we?"

They left the office and made an immediate right turn down a second hallway until they got to a set of double steel doors.

"Scan your pass, then wait for the first light on the reader to turn green. Then grab the ocular scanner, place one eye in the receiver and wait for the beep. Once you've heard the beep, remove your eye and wait for the second light on the pass reader to turn green. When everything checks out, you'll hear a voice indicate you're cleared to enter, and the door will unlock.

"Everyone entering the lab has to do this, even if they have clearance to enter the lab. If you are escorting someone, like we are now, remember the same procedures are required to exit. If someone makes their way into the lab with someone else and the person with the security pass leaves, the other person will be stuck in the lab. No doors will open without a previous entry point registering your pass on the way in."

"So I guess you don't want to lose your pass while you're working alone," Jasper said.

"Not unless you like sleeping on lab benches," replied Dr. Sabastien.

They began walking down the long corridor to the elevator. "The lab is underground?" Jasper asked.

"Three stories underground. Positive pressure with nano-filtration to ensure the purity of the air and to prevent any foreign DNA from entering. Have you worked in a total isolation suit before?" asked Dr. Sabastien.

"I've seen them but never worked in one. Is that what we'll be doing?" asked Jasper.

"Yes, as soon as we exit the elevator we'll enter the suit-up area and put on the isolation suits. We can then enter the working area of the Extraction and Sequencing Labs," Dr. Sabastien explained.

The elevator doors opened and the brightness of the room caused Jasper to squint for a second. The entire room, which was about the size of a large bedroom, was filled with light, and everything from the ceiling to the floor was white. This included the large door on the opposite side of the room. On the right side of the room were two rows of hanging isolation suits that looked more like space suits than any isolation suit Jasper had seen before.

They were single-piece jumpsuits with a large helmet equipped with a clear face shield and a zipper that started from the crotch and ran the length of the front of the suit to the base of the helmet. Gloves were integrated seamlessly into the arms of the suit, and a light boot was attached to the bottom of each leg. Hanging from the back of each helmet was a long corrugated tube that reached just past the shoulder area.

"You look like a medium," said Dr. Sabastien. "Try it first, and if that doesn't work, we can change it. Put your shoes in the boxes over there and make certain the box is sealed." He pointed to a line of boxes stacked neatly behind the suits.

Jasper removed his shoes, placed them in the box and sealed it as instructed. He then walked back to the hanging suits to locate one with medium written on the inside label of the helmet. Dr. Sabastien demonstrated how to lift his suit from the inside so as not to contaminate the outside.

"Before you get too far, I need to explain a few other things to you regarding the suit," Dr. Sabastien started.

"First, safety protocols: once fully sealed, there is no way air can pass between the inside and the outside of the suit, and the average person will have about ten minutes before they black out and another five before they're dead. The tube hanging out the back is what we call a snorkel; it exchanges the air within your suit. Each lab will have a number of similar snorkels hanging from the ceiling. Take any one of them, connect it to the end of the one on your suit and just breathe normally.

"Second is the comm panel on the outside of the left sleeve." Dr. Sabastien pointed to sleeve of the suit. "See those five buttons numbered one to four and the red one with an exclamation mark? Each of these is a separate communication channel. By pressing a button once, you've activated that channel and you can communicate normally with everyone else who has activated the same channel. The channel stays open until you press it a second time. This is how we talk to each other while working in the lab.

"The red button is the panic button, and it is only used in the case of an emergency. It sends a signal to everyone wearing a suit as well as our main security computer. In order to activate it, you hold it down for a full three seconds. Once activated, it will flash on and off to indicate help is on the way.

"Finally, I should warn you: some people, when they first put the suit on, feel a little claustrophobic. Have you any tendencies to feel claustrophobic?" asked Dr. Sabastien.

"No," answered Jasper without hesitation, but knowing this wasn't quite true. He remembered the one time he had felt claustrophobic: hoping not to be discovered, his insides ripping apart as if they were going to explode when all he could think about was getting out of that closet.

"Okay then, let's seal the suits and enter the lab. Follow me once we exit this room," Dr. Sabastien told him.

Jasper nodded and stepped into the suit, pulling the legs on like the pair of fishing waders he had donned fly-fishing as a kid. Now standing in the suit legs, he pulled the rest of it over his torso by putting his arms in each of the suit arms while sliding his head into the helmet. The gloves felt a little strange, but he was surprised how easily he was able to grab the small end of the front zipper and pull it up.

Dr. Sabastien was completely suited and waiting for Jasper to finish even though he had started a minute or two after him. Making sure Jasper could see him, Dr. Sabastien lifted his right hand and showed Jasper a single index finger then pressed the number "1" on his left sleeve. Jasper did the same.

Instantly, Jasper could hear the muffled sound of Dr. Sabastien's breathing.

"We'd better get going," said a voice in the back of the helmet, which was clearly Dr. Sabastien's but with a very tinny ring to it as if he was speaking on a cell phone.

"I'll follow you," Jasper replied.

Dr. Sabastien opened the white door opposite the elevator and they entered a space no bigger than a powder room. Once inside, Jasper couldn't see any other door in the room, but this room was even brighter than the last one. The door they entered closed behind them.

"We need to wait here for thirty seconds. This is the holding area. The entire volume of air in this room will be removed and replaced with the filtered air of the labs. When the door opens, walk in and connect to one of the snorkels from the ceiling," Dr. Sabastien said.

"Okay," Jasper replied. Just as he began his next sentence, "What door..." the entire wall in front of them slid to the left and they were standing in a short hallway flanked by floor-to-ceiling glass walls. Looking through them, Jasper could see two labs, one on each side of the hall. They were huge compared to what he had been working in at the university, and his eyes couldn't take in all the equipment he was seeing. He was unable to stop his head from turning left and right, and he began subconsciously counting the pieces of equipment: three DNA sequencers, four ultra high-speed centrifuges, four digesters… the list went on.

"Jasper…, Jasper, connect your snorkel." Dr. Sabastien's voice knocked Jasper out of his daze. "You need to connect your snorkel before you hit the floor."

"Okay, right away," Jasper answered. He reached up and pulled one of the snorkels down from the ceiling, attaching it to the end of the snorkel on his suit. As soon as the two ends were connected, Jasper heard a click in his helmet, and seconds later fresh air entered his suit.

"I bet that's better," said Dr. Sabastien with a small laugh. This time the voice was sharp and not the least bit tinny like before.

"Wow, I hear you much clearer now."

"Once you connect the snorkel, you're hardwired to the comm center. When the snorkel isn't connected, we use cellular phone technology to communicate. It's for safety reasons; we don't want to be in the suits and not have communication."

"That makes sense."

"So, what do you think?"

"I'm speechless," Jasper responded. "It looks like you have two of everything here. This place must be worth millions!"

"Hundreds of millions as a matter of fact," said Dr. Sabastien. "The Vatican considers the VGP to be its top priority and will do whatever it takes to get the proof it seeks!"

Even though Jasper couldn't see his face, there was a distinct underlying tone of cynicism in the way Dr. Sabastien's voice spoke the words 'whatever it takes,' sparking a subtle uneasiness in Jasper.

After their tour of the lab, Jasper and Dr. Sabastien returned to the main floor and walked back to Dr. Sabastien's office.

"Have a seat," Dr. Sabastien said and pointed to one of the two chairs in front of his desk. "We just need to iron out the final few details for your work here, and then I'll let you go and take care of that jet lag."

Jasper's jet lag was subdued by excitement after seeing the state-of-the-art lab he would be working in. At that moment, he could run the Ironman; his body surged with more energy than he had felt in the last three days.

"What time do you want to start work in the morning?" asked Dr. Sabastien.

"Anytime works for me."

"You're not a student anymore, Jasper," said Dr. Sabastien with a small laugh. "If you haven't already noticed, things move a fair bit slower here than they do in North America. How do you feel about starting at nine o'clock?"

"Sounds great."

"Extended lunches are the norm here, and they seem to me more like siestas than lunches. Most here finish work around seven; will that work for you?"

"Not a problem."

"Good. Now take note of this, as it is important," stated Dr. Sabastien in a firm voice. "Under no circumstances are you to work on Sundays or religious holidays. The Vatican doesn't look kindly on that, as you can imagine."

That caused Jasper to think of a question he really didn't want an answer to, but felt obligated to ask.

"Do we need to attend Mass, you know, since we work for the Church?"

Dr. Sabastien erupted into a roaring laugh. Once he had calmed down a little, he responded, "Our employer looks very fondly on those who attend Mass on a regular basis, but it's not mandatory."

Jasper wasn't sure what that meant, but he let it slide and decided he would figure it out later. He was starting to feel tired again, and the thought of going back to his flat and sleeping began to override all other thoughts. It wasn't until they both stood up and were starting to say their good-byes when it occurred to Jasper, *Where's the other lab staff? A million-dollar-lab and no one's using it?*

"Sorry, Dr. Sabastien, but I have one more question."

"Yes?"

"Why were there no other people working in the lab today?"

"Yes, I forgot to mention that, didn't I?" replied Dr. Sabastien as he lightly tapped his head in a gesture of momentary lapse.

"You're the only scientist other than myself who'll be working in the lab. However, I don't get a lot of opportunity to do the hands-on work anymore, even though I do enjoy it. So the lab is really your lab to manage. You do have a technician to support you, but he won't be back until tomorrow. I'll introduce you to Tonino then."

Jasper didn't hear a single word past "your lab," so when Dr. Sabastien held out his hand to shake his, Jasper was caught off guard but instinctively reached out.

"Welcome aboard," said Dr. Sabastien with a large grin.

"Thanks," Jasper replied, and he walked out of the office with his head spinning from the remarkable day he had just had.

CHAPTER 15

FATHER CAVALLI

The next morning, Jasper arrived at the VGP building twenty minutes early, still suffering slightly from the effects of the time difference. He swiped his pass and entered the building. He hadn't discussed a meeting place with Dr. Sabastien, so Jasper wasn't sure whether he should go straight to the lab or wait in his office. He decided to head to Dr. Sabastien's office. It was the closest one, and he could send his dad an email while waiting. Jasper hadn't heard from his dad since he left Canada, even after sending a couple of emails to let him know he had arrived in Rome. This didn't concern Jasper; his father was notoriously bad at emailing.

Jasper sat down in one of the chairs outside of Dr. Sabastien's office and pulled out his phone. Just as he did so, the office door opened and Dr. Sabastien filled the doorway with a look of amusement on his face.

"You're here early. The jet lag still messing with your sleep?"

"Yeah, a bit."

"Well it won't be long and you'll be accustomed to it. Go on into the office, and I'll see if Tonino has arrived yet."

Jasper put his phone back into his pocket, entered the office and sat in one of the chairs facing the antique wooden desk. It was a large and open office; three expansive windows located on the opposite side of the desk provided a panoramic view of the back of the Basilica. Through the windows, Jasper watched massive flocks of pigeons make their way to St. Peter's Square as the summer sun began to light the many crosses atop the Basilica. The faint sound of hymns from the chapel drifted into the office as the nine o'clock Mass began.

Dr. Sabastien returned to his office accompanied by a man who appeared to be short, but only because Dr. Sabastien dwarfed most people who walked next to him. The man was about the same height and build as Jasper with black eyes. His short, grey hair was well kept and imparted a distinguished look to his weathered face. From the wrinkles lining the sides of his mouth and the corners of his charcoal black eyes, he appeared to be about fifty years old. It had never occurred to Jasper that a lab technician could be older than himself, as none of the university lab technicians he had worked with were much over twenty.

"Jasper Stewart, Tonino Fabro," Dr. Sabastien said.

"Nice to meet you, Tonino," replied Jasper and he stood from his seat, offering his hand.

"*Ciao, Professore* Stewart. *Per favore*, please, call me 'Toni,'" said Tonino with a very strong Italian accent.

"Only if you call me 'Jasper.'"

"Jasper, I'll have an office set up for you later today with a phone and a computer," said Dr. Sabastien. "It's right next to Tonino's. This will make it easier for you to check your emails rather than having to use the computer in the lab. In the meantime, maybe you two can get to know each other in your office, Tonino."

"Yes, of course, *Professore* Sabastien," replied Tonino.

"Please, *Professore* Stewart, Jasper, follow me," said Tonino as he led the way out of the office and down the hall. He opened the door to his office and escorted Jasper in, asking him to take a seat in front of the desk.

This office was much different from Dr. Sabastien's, both in size and brightness. It was a third the size and contained only one window to the right of the desk. The computer keyboard and monitor were positioned on the desk next to a telephone, and an assortment of files and papers as well as a ten-inch-high statue of the Crucifixion. Jasper's nose tingled from the distinctive musty smell in the air. It reminded him of the smell of an antique shop—although this was much more leathery than dusty.

The reason for the odor became apparent as soon as Jasper scanned his surroundings: the walls were covered from floor to ceiling in bookshelves, and each shelf was stuffed with books. Based on the condition of their spines, many of the books appeared to be ancient and most of them were leather bound, accounting for the musty smell. Tonino's office looked more like a small library than an office.

"Toni, you like to read?" asked Jasper, trying to be humorous.

Not getting the joke, Tonino replied, "These are not reading books but research books."

Embarrassed and not wanting Tonino to think he was making fun of him, Jasper removed the smile from his face.

"Of course… how long have you been working on the VGP?" asked Jasper, hoping to change the subject and rid himself of the awkwardness.

"Many, many years."

"Before Dr. Sabastien started working here?"

A smile broke through the rough edges of Tonino's mouth and his face brightened.

"Long before *Professore* Sabastien. I've worked here for over thirty years, before it was called the Vatican Genome Project. I worked for Father Cavalli. He was the Head of the Vatican Antiquities Department, which is what we were called then. The name was changed to VGP only this year when *Professore* Sabastien took over from Father Cavalli as head of the lab."

"Dr. Sabastien started this year?" Jasper asked with an audible tone of surprise.

"Yes, everything you see here is new. The lab downstairs

was completed three months ago, and *Professore* Sabastien and I started working together a few weeks ago, after the Vatican acquired the artifact."

"You mean the Grail?" asked Jasper.

"You know?" snapped Tonino, clearly not expecting Jasper to be aware of the Vatican's most recent prized possession.

"Yes, Dr. Sabastien told me yesterday."

"Did he also tell you we were successful in extracting a perfect DNA code from it?"

"No, we didn't discuss much work yesterday on account that I spent most of the day in security."

"Well, this is the reason you see so many people working around here; they're all looking for His remains," said Tonino in an acid tone.

"Christ's?" Jasper stumbled to say the word.

"Yes, the Son of God—Jesus Christ, our Savior. I think this is all a waste of the poor people's money. We give our money to the Church to spread the Word of God, not to prove He exists. What more proof do you need than to look around and see all the miracles He has given us: the air we breathe, the water, animals, plants and our children? What more do you need?"

Jasper struggled to contain himself. He clenched his teeth and swallowed his urge to refute Tonino's words. He didn't want to start off on a bad note with his new co-worker.

"There are many others here who think the same as I do, but they dare not voice their thoughts as..." Tonino stopped midsentence, his face compressing so that his grey eyebrows were almost touching. His eyes formed such narrow black slits that Jasper could barely see them. Anger was written all over his face as plainly as the titles on his books.

"I apologize, Jasper. This isn't how you should start your first day."

"No problem."

It occurred to Jasper that this could be the reason the two British priests, Father Scott and Father Brian, had become ice-cold after reading the information he handed them. *Like Toni, they must not agree with the Vatican spending so much money on the VGP.*

"Shall we go down to the lab and get started?" Tonino asked in a cheerful manner. His face returned to its more pleasant form.

"Yes, let's," Jasper responded.

They both stood at the same time and began walking toward the door. Jasper asked Tonino, "Where's Father Cavalli now? Did he retire?"

"He has many other responsibilities in the Vatican and still finds the time to hold Mass in the Basilica every Sunday," Tonino explained.

***

Tonino spent the rest of the week showing Jasper around the lab and helping him familiarize himself with the equipment. The first sample Jasper processed was his own—this was mandatory. Everyone who worked in the lab had their DNA profiled and stored in the database. This way they would know if one of the lab staff had contaminated a sample.

It didn't take Jasper long to get used to the instruments. They were brand new and practically ran themselves. The biggest difficulty he had in the lab was working in the isolation suits, especially when handling the glassware. No matter how hard he tried, he couldn't work his hands well inside the gloves, so Tonino spent a good amount of time sweeping up broken glass from the benches and floor.

The morning chat Jasper and Tonino had shared the first day became a ritual. The two of them would sit in either Tonino's office or Jasper's and talk about the old days of the VAD. It was evident from these morning conversations that Tonino, like most Italians, was deeply religious, and that his belief in God was fundamental to the core of his existence.

Jasper didn't dare mention his views on the matter.

Intrigued by Vatican politics, Jasper continued to absorb as much information from Tonino as he could. The internal workings of the Vatican fascinated Jasper; he had always seen it as just a bigger, more complicated parish and not the incredibly complex bureaucracy it actually was. He was astonished by the political nature of the city-state, and the enormous amount of secrecy and the infighting over the VGP among the cardinals.

The majority of the cardinals on the Vatican Council had voted in favor of funding the VGP, but the vote had been very close, and the funding could be terminated if just a few of the 'yes' voters were swayed to 'no'. Just as in any political arena, there was plenty of backroom lobbying at work, where deals were negotiated to gather support from both sides. As Jasper understood it, the VGP was safe for the next three years. So many resources had already been invested in the program that it would be foolish for the Council to pull the carpet out from under the project at such an early stage. After that, the project's future was uncertain.

***

It was Monday morning again. Jasper turned on the computer in his office and sat down, looking out at the morning sunrise. He entered his password and launched his email to find a message in his inbox from his father. This was the first correspondence from him since Jasper had arrived in Rome three weeks before. He had received emails from Greg and other friends from university but nothing from home until today.

It was a typical email from his father consisting of five lines: *'Hope you are well, Happy to hear things are going well, Nothing new here, Be careful and Good Luck.'* The email also had a P.S.—*'Say Hi to Jean for me.'* Jasper smiled.

There seemed to be no end to the backlog of samples

Jasper and Tonino had to analyze. They were all samples Dr. Sabastien and Tonino had prepared in the weeks prior to Jasper's arrival, and they were all DNA samples taken from artifacts, not human remains. Jasper was a little disappointed to learn that Dr. Sabastien had sequenced the DNA from the Holy Grail himself. This meant Jasper wouldn't actually get to see it. His disappointment was based purely on wanting to brag one day that he had held the Holy Grail—if in fact it was held by the hand of God.

Jasper was thinking about the Grail, the samples and the week ahead as he scanned through the rest of his emails. No sooner had he finished this than Tonino arrived in his office for one of their chat sessions. The two men caught up on weekend events and had just started to discuss the day's work when there was a knock and Dr. Sabastien appeared in the doorway.

Jasper hadn't seen much of Dr. Sabastien in the last week other than the occasional glimpse of him entering and leaving his office. He didn't give much thought to this since Jasper spent most of his time three stories below working in the lab. But it still surprised Jasper a bit to see him show up unannounced on a Monday morning, and he wasn't alone. Before Jasper could stand up and introduce himself to the guest, Tonino leaped out of his chair.

"*Buon giorno, Don Cavalli, avanti,*" Tonino said while enthusiastically kissing the man on both cheeks.

Not understanding a word of their conversation, Jasper didn't try to introduce himself but instead turned to look at Dr. Sabastien. Making a motion with his eyes, Dr. Sabastien communicated to Jasper to wait for the two men to finish their greeting.

Tonino finished his conversation and stepped to the side. While looking directly at Jasper, the man spoke with the same accented English as Tonino and introduced himself.

"I am Father Cavalli, you must be *Professore* Stewart?" asked Father Cavalli.

"Yes, it's a pleasure to meet you, Father Cavalli. Please call me 'Jasper.'"

"I have heard many great things about you, Jasper, from *Professore* Sabastien and *Signore* Fabro. You're the best in your field they say."

"I think it unwise of them to lie to a priest," responded Jasper, and the three other men laughed.

Father Cavalli was a very distinguished-looking older man. He was large in stature, both in height and girth. His snow-white hair was brush cut short and matched his eyebrows. His face was welcoming, but round and full and didn't have near the number of wrinkles as Tonino's on account of his extra weight. He wore glasses, which hung from the end of his nose to make him look like a well-dressed Santa Claus. It was difficult for Jasper to picture him as a priest, as he was wearing a suit and tie.

"Now, Jasper, do you have a few minutes so we can talk?" asked Father Cavalli.

"Absolutely."

"Would you like to use my office?" asked Dr. Sabastien.

"No, here will be fine, thank you," answered the priest.

"Okay then, we'll leave you two to chat," said Dr. Sabastien, and he and Tonino left Jasper's office.

"How are you liking Italy?" asked Father Cavalli in a clear attempt to break the ice.

"Very much. There are a lot of beautiful... uh... buildings here," said Jasper, catching his tongue before saying what he was actually thinking.

Father Cavalli laughed and said, "Jasper, I too was once your age and could appreciate the magnificence of a beautiful 'building' or two." He peered over his glasses directly into Jasper's eyes and gave him a wink.

With his office door still open, Jasper and Father Cavalli could hear Dr. Sabastien asking Alica to prepare some hot water for tea and coffee.

On hearing Dr. Sabastien, Father Cavalli's face went cold and his voice deepened. "But I chose another path, one that has allowed me to see beyond the beauty of one's exterior and to the true beauty that lies deep within. Listen to me carefully, Jasper, and remember this: what you see on the outside of a person is not always—"

"Can I get you some tea or coffee?" interrupted Dr. Sabastien through the doorway.

Father Cavalli turned his head to look back at Dr. Sabastien and replied in a noticeable tone of annoyance, "No thank you." It was clear that he wanted to be left alone.

Dr. Sabastien removed his head from the door and disappeared.

When Father Cavalli turned back to face Jasper, Jasper was taken aback by the unmistakable seriousness in his eyes. The pronounced smile of a few moments ago had been replaced with a face full of concern.

"Now, let's get down to business," he said in a firm voice. "I've not seen you at Sunday Mass yet. I hope you're not working on Sundays."

This wasn't what Jasper had been expecting to hear. What he really wanted to hear was the rest of the sentence that had been cut off when Dr. Sabastien had interrupted them. There had been an unmistakable 'word of warning' tone to it, and the manner of his speech had made Jasper certain that he was referring to Dr. Sabastien.

"No, I'm not working on Sundays," answered Jasper. He was now starting to feel very uncomfortable with where the conversation was heading.

"Good then, I hope to see you at Mass this Sunday." Father Cavalli knew the sensitivity around this statement; he couldn't officially ask Jasper to attend Mass. He quickly asked another question before Jasper could respond.

"I was hoping you would explain the details of the VGP research to me."

Jasper had the feeling Father Cavalli already knew the details of the research quite well, but he felt obligated to answer.

"The process we're using to identify the DNA recovered from artifacts is really quite simple. DNA is a chemical fingerprint left on an item by an individual who has handled that item. What we can do is meticulously remove the chemical fingerprint with no damage to the artifact. We can then put the fingerprint in a machine called a DNA sequencer. The results from the sequencer go into the computer, which allows us to compare them to many other results very quickly. Since no two people have the same DNA except identical twins, if we find a match, we know for certain the same person has touched both artifacts."

Jasper paused for a moment to give himself time to assess Father Cavalli's interest. The priest sat patiently waiting for Jasper to continue.

"This process confirms that DNA has come from the same person, but it tells us nothing about when the DNA was left on the artifact. There's no difference between one-hour-old DNA and one-thousand-year-old DNA—if it's a good sample.

"That's why we must know the history of the artifact; it'll give us the 'time of reference' for the DNA. Only when these two pieces of information come together can we potentially identify the DNA donor. If multiple artifacts date to the same time in history, and were handled by the same person, they would have matching DNA on them—this would provide substantial evidence to collaborate any verbal history associated with the artifact."

Father Cavalli held his attention on Jasper for the entire explanation and looked genuinely pleased.

"Jasper, that's the first time in two years someone has been able to explain to me what's going on in here and how important it is to the Church. God bless you, and keep up the good work. I have faith our proof will come soon," said Father Cavalli as he stood up from his seat.

"I will let you get back to your work."

Dr. Sabastien appeared in the doorway behind Father Cavalli as he walked out of Jasper's office.

The priest then turned to face Jasper and stopped. He pulled down his glasses so they rested on the tip of his nose and smirked. "*Arrivederci a domenica*," he said and walked away.

"What does that mean?" Jasper asked Dr. Sabastien.

"See you on Sunday," replied Dr. Sabastien as he began to laugh.

CHAPTER 16

THE HAIRCUT

After spending the rest of the week finishing up the last of the backlogged samples, Jasper was exhausted. Even though it was Thursday, he still thought about Father Cavalli and what he had said to him on Monday. Jasper couldn't focus on anything else.

That night Jasper prepared dinner in his flat and turned on the small TV for company. The only English-speaking channel was an all-news network. The story already in progress caught his attention instantly and made his stomach lurch. The frozen dinner he had been unwrapping fell from his hands and shattered on the floor, his attention focused solely on the TV.

"Interpol suspects a possible link between the deaths of more than thirty Catholic priests and their involvement in child abuse. Over the past three years, thirty-two Catholic priests have been found dead in countries from Brazil to Canada, as well as here on the European continent. Interpol investigators are now in Italy interviewing high-ranking officials within the Vatican to help in their investigation. We'll be following this story closely as more information becomes available," reported the news anchor.

A sense of smug satisfaction warmed Jasper's insides at the thought of a serial killer roaming the planet after pedophile priests. The warmth quickly subsided as the dark memories of Father Malkin began to emerge from deep inside his mind. Then, for the first time, the excitement of his new job took a back seat to another emotion—loneliness. Jasper was unsettled and isolated in Italy; he was surrounded by people all day, but he didn't have much interaction with anyone other than Dr. Sabastien and Tonino. The language was more than a barrier; it surrounded him like an isolation dome, allowing him to see and hear other people but not to communicate with them. Jasper was like a ghost walking among the living but never making contact.

With his dinner melting on the floor, Jasper decided he should go out and get a sandwich. He often left his flat in the evenings to pick up a Panini and some bottled water from a local bakery.

He got his food and then returned to his room to watch some Italian TV and study his 'Learn to Speak Italian' book. Watching Italian didn't seem to help his language skills much, but it did make him laugh; he found the commercials much funnier than those at home.

During his school years, Jasper had shown a natural gift for the sciences but this had never been the case for the arts—especially languages. His struggling started in grade-eight French and had continued to the end of high school. If not for weekly tutoring from a high-school friend, he never would have passed. What he really wanted now was an Italian tutor to help speed his progress. Jasper shut the TV off and tossed his book on the floor; he was going out to relieve his frustration.

***

Jasper arrived at work the next morning and devoted the entire chat session to learning the basic words needed to tell a barber how he wanted his hair cut. Tonino offered repeatedly to accompany him and to be his translator, but Jasper refused his offer, not wanting to feel like he was eight years old again. He was embarrassed enough about having to ask for Tonino's help for such a simple thing.

Jasper had been putting off the haircut for a while. Every time he put on an isolation suit, his hair would fall into his face, making it impossible to work. In the suit, his hands were unavailable to him, and Jasper couldn't brush the hair out of his eyes. He had resorted to using a rubber band to keep it tied back in a ponytail. The thought of trying to explain how he wanted his hair cut to an Italian barber was frightening; he hadn't even mastered some of the basic language skills yet—like please and thank you.

Jasper feared his haircut would be too short for two reasons: simple vanity and his birthmark. The only thing worse than people commenting on the strange mark on his neck would be people speaking in a language he couldn't understand. He practiced the Italian words Tonino had given him and even wrote them down to show the barber—just in case.

The rest of Friday, Jasper and Tonino worked in the lab finishing the last few analyses on the DNA sequencer and entering the results into the database. Tonino was cleaning up the lab bench for the day when Dr. Sabastien sent a communication to them through the internal security system. This still startled Jasper; hearing a voice other than Tonino's magically appear in his helmet was unsettling. On more than one occasion, it had caused him to literally drop what he was doing. Tonino laughed in a kind way, knowing that the unexpected voice bothered Jasper a little. It was funny to see the young doctor jump inside his suit as if he had been poked with a sharp needle.

"The Vatican Acquisition staff have secured a new find, and it will arrive Monday. This find displays excellent promise; the artifacts were completely undisturbed," Dr. Sabastien announced.

Jasper couldn't contain his excitement. An undisturbed acquisition was exceptionally rare because most gravesites had been looted or disturbed at some point in their history, making the integrity of the artifacts or remains questionable. In an artifact contaminated with multiple samples of human DNA, it was more difficult to separate and analyze the sequences.

"Did you hear that? Undisturbed!"

"Yes, Monday will be a big day for us," said Tonino, not exhibiting the least bit of excitement compared to Jasper.

"I can't wait. Let's finish up and get upstairs so we can talk to Dr. Sabastien and find out more about the remains," said Jasper, now over the top with enthusiasm.

"Don't pop out of your suit, Jasper. I don't fancy having to wipe down the entire lab because you've contaminated it," Tonino piped.

"Okay, but this will be our first new artifact, and it's promising," he stated in a voice two times higher than his normal tone.

Tonino was finishing the recalibration of the DNA sequencer, so Jasper took the opportunity to whip through the rest of his duties. He decided to get a head start on Monday by pulling out all of the glassware they would need for the extraction process. He placed it on the bench ready to go. When Tonino had finished, the two of them made their way back to the office level and waited for Dr. Sabastien to have a free moment to speak with them.

Dr. Sabastien called them into his office just after five to brief them on the acquisition.

"They found these artifacts two days ago."

"Where?" asked Jasper, noticing the look of slight annoyance on Dr. Sabastien's face at the interruption.

"At a road construction site in Jerusalem. The heavy machinery hit the top of a crypt in the middle of the night."

"Was it opened?" asked Tonino.

"No, fully intact. The company wasn't happy to have unearthed a burial site, knowing it would cause significant delays to their completion date. The company was already working twenty-four hours a day, and the delay in completion could result in huge losses in bonuses for them. The company wanted the entire discovery to disappear as quickly and as quietly as possible, so the Vatican was notified."

"How fortunate," Tonino pointed out with a raised eyebrow.

"Yes, isn't it? The construction company foreman ordered the heavy machinery stopped for an unscheduled maintenance inspection, and the site was vacated long enough for Vatican operatives to move in. In less than an hour, the artifacts had been acquired."

"Wait, is this how the Vatican acquires remains? Clandestinely in the middle of the night?" asked Jasper, unable to keep it from sounding like an accusation.

Jasper and Tonino were both sitting with their backs to the doorway, and to their surprise, a low, deep voice answered through the open door.

"This is one of the ways... but not the one we prefer," stated Father Cavalli.

Tonino leaped from his chair and approached the father, delivering the customary kisses to each cheek. At the same time, Dr. Sabastien and Jasper stood from their chairs to greet him.

"We do not like to acquire our artifacts in this manner, but unfortunately, sometimes it is necessary in order to preserve them for the good of all humanity. If we had not arrived in the nick of time, those priceless artifacts could have been buried forever below an overpass. Now we can catalogue and preserve them for all to enjoy," Father Cavalli said smugly.

It was clear to Jasper that this wasn't the whole truth. He hadn't seen a single newspaper story, YouTube or Twitter indicating the Holy Grail had been discovered. Something that significant 'preserved for all to enjoy' would never escape the mass media. Jasper began to wonder, *How many other lost artifacts aren't actually lost? Are they just stored safely in the ironclad safes of the Vatican? The Vatican's secrets*

are starting to make Area 51 look more and more plausible.
Maybe the US is storing Aliens in Nevada after all.

"I am certain Dr. Sabastien has informed you that this particular artifact shows some extreme promise. I am personally interested to see the results. Will you be conducting the analysis yourself, Dr. Sabastien?" asked Father Cavalli.

"No, Jasper is better qualified than I. After all, that's why we went to great lengths to bring him here," replied Dr. Sabastien.

This was a great relief to Jasper.

"Are you sure that is the correct decision?" Father Cavalli inquired, turning to look at Jasper's face.

"Absolutely. Jasper and Tonino will have no difficulties completing the work," Dr. Sabastien assured.

"Good then. When should I expect to see the results?"

"That depends on when we get the remains," interjected Jasper.

Father Cavalli turned to Jasper and snapped, "You will have them first thing Monday morning."

"Then you'll have your results on Tuesday," said Jasper with more confidence than he felt.

"Excellent," replied Father Cavalli, his face softening back to a mild sneer. "I will see you Sunday morning?" he said and left Dr. Sabastien's office without giving Jasper time to answer or Tonino and Dr. Sabastien time to say good-bye.

"Well, I think you two have your work cut out for you on Monday. Father Cavalli has never taken such a keen interest in any of the other artifacts we've analyzed, except the Holy Grail of course," commented Dr. Sabastien.

"Yes, I have never seen him display this much interest before," agreed Tonino.

They spent the next couple of hours discussing the details of the following Monday's work. A good portion of their conversation was spent speculating over the little details that Father Cavalli had given to Dr. Sabastien about the find. It was after eight o'clock when they ended their discussion and started to pack up.

"Do you want to practice one more time?" Tonino asked Jasper as they left Dr. Sabastien's office.

"Sure."

Jasper repeated the Italian phrases he had memorized, correctly for the most part, but he had to cheat and look at the notes scrawled on his sheet for the final few.

"*Bravo, e Buona fortuna*," said Tonino. He smiled, gave a little chuckle and left the building.

Jasper stood watching Tonino leave and feeling like he was once again looking for something he wasn't able to find. *Luck won't help me learn Italian. Why can't I do this?* Repeating the Italian words over in his mind didn't help him understand them. Burdened with regret, he wanted more than anything at that moment to call after Tonino and accept his offer to come with him to the barber's.

Jasper didn't sleep well that night. He was tormented by the last thing Father Cavalli had said before leaving: "See you Sunday morning." Jasper wanted to believe he had actually meant to say "See you Monday morning," but inside he knew Father Cavalli expected him to attend Mass, and worse, to take Communion. Jasper hadn't been to Sunday Mass or taken Communion in almost two decades.

The sun was shining when Jasper finally got up late Saturday morning. Early September was a beautiful time to be in Rome: most of the tourists had left, and the weather was still perfect. Jasper walked to St. Peter's Square, where the pigeons now outnumbered the tourists. The sound of church bells rang in the distance, and the smell of espresso greeted Jasper as he left the square and made his way to his usual morning coffee shop.

Determined to end the language barrier, Jasper forced himself to order his breakfast in Italian. After devouring a couple of pastries and finishing his latte, he couldn't procrastinate any longer. He started his walk to the barber's shop—the one Tonino had told him about a few days earlier.

Jasper found the area Tonino had described and spotted the shop across the street. All he had to do was to take his life in his hands and cross the street. Traffic in Rome could only be described as chaotic from a North American's point of view, and Jasper still wasn't used to it. The Italian citizens seem to accept it as normal to try to put their cars in a lane where no lane existed or to race as fast as possible between stoplights. But by far the worst thing was the scooters—they were everywhere. They would come out of nowhere going faster than most of the cars, endlessly honking their horns in hopes pedestrians would jump out of their way at the last second. These driving nightmares on two wheels even drove on the sidewalks; scooter drivers had no boundaries to where they believed they could drive.

Jasper took a deep breath and seized his opportunity when the traffic light up the street stopped most cars for a moment. He jumped off of the sidewalk and made a dash for the other side. He made it to the barbershop without incident, although he wasn't sure if the pounding in his chest was from the dash across the road or the anxiety of what was to come.

The barber's shop door was propped open, so Jasper walked straight in. The barber was an elderly man with very little hair himself. He was using electric shears to cut the hair of another elderly man sitting in the chair with a white apron draped around his body. The noise from the shears and the soccer game playing on the TV hanging in the corner of the shop made it impossible to talk, so Jasper nodded hello and took a seat in one of the three old vinyl chairs lined against the wall.

The small knot sitting in the pit of Jasper's stomach tightened when the barber looked towards him, indicating he was almost done. Jasper calmed himself by repeating the Italian words in his head over and over. This worked fine until the man in the chair rose, paid, and left.

Jasper's mind went blank.

The barber turned and said, "*Sedere, per favore.*"

Jasper assumed it meant "Take a seat" since the barber was pointing to the chair with his hand. Before Jasper sat down, he tried repeating the words Tonino had taught him. The barber tilted his head to the left and looked at Jasper through squinting eyes.

"*Scusi?*"

Jasper tried again to no avail. He then reached into his pants pocket to remove the paper on which Tonino had written the instructions. They weren't there. His heart raced as fast as his hands flashed between his pants pockets. He tried his left front pocket and then both his back pockets, but there was no paper in any of them.

The barber just looked on in confusion. Then Jasper remembered he had left the paper in his other jeans.

"Do you speak English?" Jasper knew it wasn't even worth asking, but he tried out of desperation.

"*Non*, no English. Pay later," he said, looking at Jasper's pants pockets hanging inside out.

Jasper felt doomed as he sat down in the seat and the barber began putting the apron around his body. He turned the chair so Jasper was looking directly into the mirror. In the reflection, Jasper could see the barber holding his fingers in the air indicating, "This much?" with the two first fingers of his right hand while making a scissor cutting motion with the two first fingers of his left hand. Jasper nodded and pulled his right arm out from under the apron to also indicate a length of about an inch.

The sound of the electric shaver gave Jasper goose bumps. The barber cleaned up the sides, back and top of his head using the shears and then finished off by cutting his bangs first then trimming the back of his neck. In order to make certain this area was cut evenly, the barber pushed Jasper's head downward so he was facing his lap. Halfway through the neck trim, Jasper instantly knew that the barber had discovered the birthmark hidden behind his hairline; the cutting came to an abrupt halt.

"*Mio Dio, segno del pesce,*" whispered the barber while looking directly into Jasper's eyes through his reflection in the mirror.

Jasper shrugged.

The barber smiled and also shrugged before returning to his cutting.

When the haircut was finished, the barber placed his scissors on the shelf in front of Jasper's chair. He then picked up a small round handheld mirror and held it facing the large wall-mounted mirror so Jasper could see the back of his head. Jasper forced a smile to his lips.

The haircut was fine except that the barber had cut his neckline about an inch too short. It was just long enough so the birthmark remained covered when his head was up and looking forward, but if he looked downward, it was clearly visible. Jasper struggled a bit with paying for the haircut and left the barber's shop thinking; *All in all, it could have been worse*.

Since it was a beautiful sunny day, Jasper decided to do some people watching. The best place to do this in Rome was the Spanish Steps. Even on a weekday when there were far less tour groups coming to the city, the Spanish Steps would be filled with locals and tourists alike—many of them around his age. On days like this, many of the best-looking young Italian girls would gather in small packs on the steps just to be noticed. They would remove a good portion of their clothing to better their tans and sit in packs receiving cat whistles and propositions. This made for great entertainment, and at the same time, it provided an escape from Jasper's isolation. No language barrier existed between twenty-year-old women and men, even for Jasper.

He headed directly to the Metro from the barber's even though it was lunch and he was starting to get hungry. Jasper had been to the Spanish Steps four or five times before, and he knew a good place to eat close by so he held off getting some food. The area was so filled with people it resembled St. Peter's Square during a Christmas Mass. He picked up pizza and a bottle of water, finishing the pizza while walking to the Steps. Once there, he wasn't disappointed: the steps were packed with young people.

Jasper's escapism was short lived, however. Just as he sat down, the distant sound of church bells sobered him like a glass of ice water in the face. Waves of anguish and uncertainty lingered in his thoughts.

How serious was Father Cavalli? I can't do it.

Jasper's mind conjured the darkest of images: his mother's funeral, Father Malkin. He stood up and began walking back to the Metro, resolving that nothing good could possibly come from breaking his childhood vow.

CHAPTER 17

LAST COMMUNION

Sunday morning arrived far sooner than Jasper wanted. He awoke early; before the sun had entered his room. The reprieve that sleep provided vanished the instant he opened his eyes. Across the far side of his bed, his alarm clock read 6:30. Jasper's stomach emitted a roar which he hoped was a hunger pang.

The good news was it was early enough to walk across the square and get a coffee and breakfast; the bad news was he would now have to suffer for two and half hours, fighting the anxious thoughts that exploded in his mind like fireworks.

Images of his childhood attending church with his mother returned. *How do they take Communion here?* Jasper began to hear the Mass in his head and wondered, *Will Mass be in Italian or Latin? Will Father Cavalli even be there?*

He decided to arrive early at St. Peter's Basilica so he could get a seat in the back of the small Chapel of the Blessed Sacrament. This would let him watch the parishioners ahead of him to see how they received Communion.

Jasper sauntered up the front steps of the Basilica just before eight thirty. When he reached the doors, he was amazed at how many people were already inside. His plan of getting a seat in the back had to be adjusted—it didn't look like he would find a seat at all. Making his way through the crowd into the nave, he remembered the side corridor he had stumbled into on his first day at the Vatican. He located the place where Fathers Scott and Brian had helped him and walked down the side corridor, glancing at the statues before stopping alongside one of the massive marble columns in front of the entrance to the chapel.

Jasper walked through the ornate metal-flanked entrance and gasped when he saw the sea of people preparing themselves for Mass. Many were already praying, using their rosaries or reading from the Bible. The weight of concern lifted from Jasper a bit when he spotted an arm waving above the crowd. A smile filled his face and a rush of relief filled his chest. Jasper couldn't believe his luck: there was Tonino, sitting at the end of the third pew from the front. Jasper made his way into the crowd and walked up to his lab assistant.

"Do you think there's room for one more?"

"Yes, sit here next to me," said Tonino with an enormous smile on his face. It was clear he wasn't expecting to see Jasper at the Mass.

Tonino spoke in Italian to a woman sitting next to him and she moved to her left. Tonino moved next to her, freeing the last seat for Jasper.

"Thanks," Jasper said.

"*Gabriella, questo è Jasper Stewart, il mio collega*," said Tonino to the woman sitting next to him.

"*Ciao, Signore Stewart*," she said in a whisper.

"*Ciao, Gabriella*," Jasper whispered back.

"I see I'm a good tutor. You are happy with your haircut?" asked Tonino while casting a glance at Jasper's hair.

"Not bad for my first time, but he cut it a bit too short in the back."

"It looks fine."

The conversation was cut short by the sound of the organ bellowing through the Basilica. Two altar boys carrying incense and candles walked on to the altar, which resembled a small theatrical stage. Flanking the altar, two gilded bronze angels knelt; but it was the massive painting of the Holy Trinity behind the altar that brought the chapel to life.

The crowd of parishioners stood up and silence fell. Two priests wearing red and white vestments filed behind the altar. They were followed by two more altar boys using a slow and methodical walk.

Jasper closed his eyes and tried to conjure happy visions: fishing in the Okanagan or eating watermelon in the summer heat. He tried to keep his mind from the dark and sinister memories the sight of the altar boys unleashed.

When he finally re-opened his eyes, Jasper saw that a third priest had walked behind the altar. Wearing pearl white vestments lined with intricate gold inlays, Jasper recognized the tall and overweight priest at once; making his way to the center of the altar was Father Cavalli. Once there, the priest conducted a blessing and then raised his arms toward the ceiling to begin the Mass in Italian.

Jasper listened to the prayers, amazed how similar they sounded to the English version; he could tell at once when Father Cavalli began conducting the sacraments. The vision of the large gold chalice raised high in the air over Father Cavalli's head sent Jasper back to Kelowna and his altar boy days. The flesh and blood symbolized by the breaking of the Eucharist and the drinking of wine had always disgusted him. Jasper felt that old feeling return when Father Cavalli drank from the chalice; he struggled to swallow at the thought of drinking blood.

Equally familiar to Jasper was the feeling that Mass dragged on, even when he didn't understand the language. His thoughts started to wander to other things, ignoring the Mass completely. Jasper thought about Monday morning and his first chance to work with the new artifact.

Will there even be remains left on the artifact? Will it be someone important or just a common person of the time? Will they be a man or woman's DNA? Could they even be the remains the Catholic Church so badly desires?

Jasper's daydreams rendered him oblivious to his surroundings, and before he realized what was happening, he was being ushered out of his row into a Communion line. In order to accommodate the parishioners in a reasonable time, all three of the priests offered the Eucharist—a priest on either side of the altar, and one, Father Cavalli, centered in the middle. Jasper followed Tonino down their pew toward the center aisle, even though it would have been much faster to take Communion from the priest directly to their right. Jasper saw that this was a deliberate move by Tonino so that Father Cavalli could present the Eucharist to them—and most importantly to Jasper.

Aversion gripped Jasper so tightly he had to use every bit of his willpower to keep from turning and leaving the Basilica. He felt sick from the pungent smell of incense and the broken vow to himself.

Jasper knew that while entering a church to attend Mass was difficult, taking Communion from a priest was completely hypocritical. Shame flooded his body as he approached the priest, leaving him disgusted with his own actions; he wanted to shower. The urge to leave grew stronger with each step he took. Father Cavalli was only feet away as the parishioners filed past one by one before him. He had only seconds to decide how to accept the Eucharist. The only way he could get through this was to watch Tonino and do exactly what he did. Jasper's mind slipped back to his childhood memories of attending Mass, and he followed Tonino as if on autopilot.

Gabriella took the Eucharist on her tongue, made the sign of the cross and knelt down on one knee while bowing her head. Father Cavalli held the large gold chalice filled with the Eucharist in his left hand and made the sign of the cross with his right. He finished delivering Communion with a short blessing. Jasper watched again as Tonino followed the same procedure as Gabriella before taking the Eucharist on his tongue. Jasper also knelt down on one knee while Father Cavalli looked down at him and gave a blessing. Tonino stood up and made the sign of the cross while walking away. Jasper was next, and he stepped in front of Father Cavalli.

Their eyes met, and Jasper saw an unmistakable look of conquest on Father Cavalli's face. The priest's glasses couldn't hide the sense of victory in his eyes, as if he had won a battle. This ignited a hot flash inside of Jasper so intense that it evaporated all other thoughts in his mind.

Jasper knew his presence at Mass was a small triumph for Father Cavalli, and he felt like a trophy—a feeling he despised, as it conjured dark memories of Father Malkin. This simply strengthened Jasper's hatred for the Church. He accepted the Eucharist on his tongue and forced himself to kneel down on his right knee. Not having to look at Father Cavalli was welcome when he bowed his head toward the floor. And as he did, he reminded himself: "*There is no God.*"

Father Cavalli held the chalice directly over Jasper's head and peered down at the young doctor to recite his blessing. From this vantage point, the birthmark on the back of Jasper's neck was suddenly clearly visible. Father Cavalli's fingers stiffened and his breathing stopped. The chalice then slipped from his hands and collided with Jasper's head.

The priest staggered back, gripped his chest and let out a blood-curdling scream. The noise filled the small chapel and echoed through the nave. The procession of parishioners lined up to receive Communion came to an immediate halt. The resulting silence allowed the priest's final words to resonate through the room, bouncing off the stone walls as if shouted through a loudspeaker.

"*La Convergenza! La Convergenza!*"

The chalice clipped Jasper on the left side of his forehead as he stood up to see what was happening. The weight of the metal cup combined with his upward movement was enough to cause him to lose his balance. The chapel began to spin, and his disorientation accelerated as something warm ran into his left eye.

Jasper heard many voices screaming and men shouting in Italian over the top of the sounds of women crying. Men in dark suits were arriving from all directions shouting at each other. His final vision was of three men ripping the robes off of Father Cavalli, who was lying in front of him, before Jasper sank into absolute silence and total darkness.

***

When Jasper regained consciousness, he was lying on his back in a dimly lit room. The distinct smell of rubbing alcohol filled his nostrils. He didn't know the time, but he knew it must be sometime in the late morning or early afternoon because the curtains were drawn to block out the bright sunlight forcing its way around the edges. He sat up, but the movement initiated a throbbing inside his head. He lifted his left hand to his forehead and felt something attached to it above his eye.

A nun dressed in traditional vestments walked into the room and began talking sternly to him in Italian while making a motion with her hands to lie back down. He froze in position. She had a warm face, although it wasn't smiling at the moment, and a few strands of light-brown hair dangled from the wimple partially obscuring her sapphire blue eyes. She tried again to make Jasper lie back down on the hospital cot.

"Where am I?" he said without thinking.

The nun looked at him for a second before turning to leave the room, talking to herself all the way out. A moment later an older man wearing a lab coat entered the room and introduced himself in English.

"Hello, Jasper. I'm Anthony Collins, the Vatican resident doctor," he said with an American accent.

"You're American?" Jasper asked.

"Yes, sir, born and raised in Michigan."

"I went to university in Windsor!"

"Well that makes us neighbors," Dr. Collins said. "You need to lie down for a bit; you took a nasty hit to the head.

Can you tell me what happened?"

"I don't... it's like a bad dream. I remember kneeling down after taking Communion and then hearing someone screaming in Italian. I think it was Father Cavalli; I saw him fall—is he okay?"

"I don't know, please continue," Dr. Collins requested.

"I saw Father Cavalli falling to the ground, and then I felt a pain in my head—like a bee sting. Men came running from all directions and they were ripping his robes off, then I could hear shouting and crying. After that I started to feel dizzy and everything went black."

"Good, it seems like you haven't had any memory loss. That's pretty much exactly what your friend said," Dr. Collins explained.

"Toni? Is he here?" asked Jasper in hopes of getting more information about what happened.

"No, I sent him home an hour ago. I told him you'd be fine."

"An hour ago. What time is it? Is this a hospital?" asked Jasper, progressing further out of his initial daze.

"You were out for a couple of hours. You banged your head pretty hard when you hit the marble floor. You're in the Vatican medical center; it's not a hospital per se, but it's just as well equipped, or maybe even better. And it's just past noon," Dr. Collins told him as he peered down at his watch.

"Hit the floor? Did I faint?"

"Not exactly. I think the chalice hit you hard enough for you to lose your balance, and when you fell, you knocked your head on the floor. That's when you lost consciousness," Dr. Collins explained.

"Oh—that's what made me think I was stung by a bee."

"Probably. Now I didn't stitch the wound in order to minimize the scarring, but you'll have to watch it. The skin is very thin on your forehead, and the butterfly tape holding the cut closed needs to be treated gently for a few days or the cut will open and start to bleed again. I want to watch you for another hour just to make sure you didn't get yourself a concussion, and then I'll let you go home to get some rest."

"Will I be able to go to work tomorrow?" asked Jasper, hoping for a positive answer.

"That depends. What do you do?" asked Dr. Collins.

"I'm a research scientist."

"Sounds interesting. Well, I'll leave it up to you and see how you feel in the morning. I'm sure you're going to have a nasty headache for the next day or two. I'll give you some pain medication just in case," Dr. Collins said. "I'll send the nurse back in when you can leave."

"Thanks, do you mean the nun?" asked Jasper.

Dr. Collins nodded his head and left the room. Jasper lay back down on the bed and tried to recall everything he could of the events of the morning. Father Cavalli yelling in Italian, and the men coming out of nowhere to his aid. Then he started to wonder again, *What happened to Father Cavalli?*

As he lay on the bed replaying the morning's events in his mind, Jasper didn't notice the young nun re-entering the room carrying a small plastic bag. She acknowledged her own presence in a soft voice.

"*Ciao, Signore,*" she said, looking right through Jasper with her gorgeous blue eyes. She placed the bag containing his shoes at the foot of his bed and presented him with a smile and a hand gesture indicating he was free to leave.

Jasper, startled for a moment, collected himself and then tried with all his might to pronounce "*Grazie.*" Pain tore across his forehead as he tried to sit up. He reached for the bag, and his head pounded like he was standing in the tail draft of a jet engine. He hid his discomfort from the nun for fear of giving her a reason to keep him in bed. Jasper put both his shoes on, though much slower than normal; the pressure from bending down to tie his laces caused the pounding in his head to intensify to the point that he couldn't hide the agony. He took one last look at the nun to reassure her that he was okay and left the clinic for home.

As Jasper walked to his flat, the late afternoon sun forced him to squint. This made the cut tingle and tighten, forcing a small droplet of blood from the wound. The pill bottle rattled in his pocket with each step up the stone steps of his building, but Jasper's thoughts centered on the fate of Father Cavalli. The image of him sprawled on the floor in front of the altar was etched in his mind like a stained-glass window in the Basilica.

Why was he yelling 'La Convergenza'? What did that mean? Jasper remembered the metal hitting his skull as he neared the top of the staircase and the throbbing intensified. Jasper finally recognized the rattling sound, and he pulled the small plastic bottle from his pocket. Standing on the topmost step of his floor, he flipped open the lid with his thumb and shook two capsules into his hand. The surging feeling of a needle piercing his head grew so great that he threw the pills into his mouth without water and swallowed as hard as he could to get them down.

Jasper entered his room with only one thought remaining in his mind—sleep. Without removing his shoes or getting under the sheets, he lay down on his bed and sighed deeply. This brought instant relief from the pounding in his head. While he lay there waiting for the drugs to take effect, the pain radiating through his head subsided enough to allow him one last thought: *Nothing good came from this day.*

CHAPTER 18

LONG SEQUENCE

The effect of the painkillers lingered as Jasper floated between realities. In one, he was attending Sunday Mass to receive Communion from Father Cavalli; in the other it was Monday morning and warm sunlight was filtering through his blinds to tap him awake.

The confusion slowly lifted as the throbbing in his head increased and solidified both realities. He had attended Sunday Mass, and now it was Monday morning—six thirty to be exact. Jasper lay in bed and stared at the ceiling until his thoughts and memories became clear again.

What happened to Father Cavalli?

The pain intensified; his cue to take more pills before the pounding became unbearable. Fully dressed from the day before, Jasper lifted himself from the bed and made his way to the bathroom for a glass of water to wash down the capsules. Dr. Collins had been right; he did have a hell of a headache. It wasn't coming from his forehead where the chalice had cut him but from the side of his head where he had hit the marble floor.

Jasper glanced at himself in the bathroom mirror and was horrified. He looked like he had just been run over by a train, so he decided to take a shower. Still looking in the mirror, he removed his clothes and noticed a lump the size of a chicken egg on the left side of his head above his ear. He gently touched it and winced.

Should be some fun getting into the isolation suit today, he mused.

This triggered his memory further.

"The isolation suit. Today we start on the new artifact!" he said to himself out loud.

In the turmoil of the past twenty-four hours, Jasper had forgotten how much he had been looking forward to analyzing the new and mysterious acquisition. It may have been this sudden recollection or the painkillers taking effect, but something helped alleviate the pain a little, and he hopped into the shower. The relief was only temporary though as the water splashing on his head caused the throbbing to return. It didn't take long for the dressing covering his cut to fall off, signaling the end of his shower. Jasper dried himself, carefully patting his forehead dry.

The cut, now completely visible in the mirror, was longer than he had imagined. A row of six evenly spaced butterfly strips held the thin crescent shaped cut together. The warm water of the shower had dissolved some of the dried blood, and a droplet of fresh blood oozed from the wound. Jasper grabbed a small piece of toilet paper and dabbed the blood from his forehead. He returned to his bedroom and slid open the drawer of the antique wardrobe where he kept his travel kit to retrieve a new dressing. Since the kit had a limited assortment of dressings, he was forced to use one barely long enough to cover the entire cut. He placed it over the wound, pulled a shirt on gently to avoid catching it, and finished getting dressed.

Jasper made his way to his favorite café and got his usual coffee and pastry before going to work. He was early and hoping to get a head start on preparing the instruments for the day's work. It was half past seven, so he had at least a half-hour before Tonino or Dr. Sabastien arrived.

He entered the VGP building and made his way down the hall toward his office to start his computer and check his email. Jasper had just walked into his office when a deep voice from behind startled him. He turned to see Dr. Sabastien leaning on the doorframe, arms folded.

"How are you feeling? You took quite a blow to your head."

"I'm fine. How did you know?" asked Jasper with a puzzled look on his face.

"Oh, Tonino called me. Are you sure you're all right? You know, it's okay if you take the day off after all that's happened."

"No, I'm fine. It's just a small cut—it's nothing," Jasper replied in a casual tone. "I wanted to get an early start on those 'promising remains' before Tonino comes in."

"Jasper, I don't think Tonino will be in today," said Dr. Sabastien, watching Jasper's face change from exuberant to disappointed.

"Why not, is he sick?" Jasper asked.

"Jasper, Tonino was a very good friend of Father Cavalli's. They worked together for almost twenty-five years!" stated Dr. Sabastien in a surprised tone.

Jasper blurted out, "Father Cavalli... was... Oh shit, you mean...?"

"I'm sorry, Jasper. I thought you knew. After Father Cavalli collapsed during Mass yesterday, he never regained consciousness. He died in hospital last night."

Jasper took a seat in his chair; he was starting to feel a little lightheaded. Even though he hadn't known Father Cavalli very well, it was still an incredible shock to realize the man had died right in front of him.

"Are you sure you don't want to go home and get some rest? This has been a big shock to us all."

Jasper considered Dr. Sabastien's suggestion.

"No, thanks anyway, but I think it best I keep myself occupied. I'll get started on the extraction of the new sample. Did the artifact arrive?" he asked.

"Yes, it came in early this morning. That's why I'm here so early. I put it in the lab an hour ago."

"Great. I'm going to go down and start the primary extraction. Do you think Toni would mind if I just got a little head start?" Jasper asked.

"No, he won't mind. He must have done fifty of those with me before you arrived, so I don't think he'll miss doing this one."

"Thanks," responded Jasper. He lifted himself from his chair and followed Dr. Sabastien out of the office to make his way down to the lab.

A fog of disbelief surrounded Jasper. The sadness associated with death was accompanied by astonishment. The swiftness with which a person could move from the living to the dead occupied his thoughts. The buzz from the elevator as it descended went unnoticed by Jasper as he recalled his last thoughts of Father Cavalli. He remembered the bitterness and hatred.

The elevator opened on the lab level. Jasper entered the isolation suit-up area and bent over to begin unlacing his shoes. The rapid movement caused a head rush that made him nauseous. He pulled off his first shoe and placed it in a container. A second head rush occurred when he bent over for the other shoe. This time, the surge of blood caused a butterfly tape to pull loose, releasing a tiny droplet of blood onto his forehead. Jasper unconsciously wiped his forehead with his left hand while placing the other shoe in the container.

He then walked over to the isolation suit rack to remove his suit from the hanger. Jasper lifted the helmet off the hanger with his right hand while at the same time grasping the suit with his left hand. He got into the suit using extra caution so as not to bang his head on the inside of the helmet.

Fully suited, Jasper entered the isolation room. Once the door to the lab opened, he connected his snorkel and entered the Extraction Lab to find the sealed cooler containing the newly discovered remains. He was surprised to see that the cooler was about the size of a large lunch box; he had been expecting to find the remains of an entire human.

Disappointment filled his thoughts. *This could only contain a hand or foot at most. Even a human skull couldn't possibly fit into such a small cooler.*

Jasper opened the cooler and removed a sealed bag containing a small woven wreath. It was perfectly round and completely desiccated. It appeared brittle but was remarkably intact for having spent thousands of years buried. The individual strands of the wreath were various shades of brown, ranging from beach sand to nearly black.

Jasper unzipped the plastic bag and carefully lifted the artifact out with his forceps, placing it in a glass Petri dish on the lab bench. Using a second pair of stainless steel tweezers, he positioned it in the dish so that he could take a photo. He did this to catalogue the sample prior to beginning the extraction process. He placed a second Petri dish on the bench next to the one containing the artifact and removed a scalpel from the drawer in the bench in front of him. Carefully holding the wreath in the air with the tweezers, he suspended it over the second glass dish. Jasper then used the scalpel to scrape small shavings from the surface of the artifact. He scraped until a fine dust covered the glass dish. Then he returned the artifact to the bag, resealing it.

Jasper opened the bench drawer and removed a small stainless steel spatula. Using his left hand, he reached for a clear plastic squeeze bottle located on the shelf directly in front of him. The squeeze bottle contained a dilute acid reagent used to begin the extraction process. Jasper grasped the spatula while squeezing the reagent into the Petri dish. He stirred with the spatula until the mixture of dust fragments and reagent made a thick brown slurry resembling cake batter.

He repeated this process of squeezing reagent into the dish and stirring a couple more times. On the third squeeze, he forced the reagent out of the bottle with slightly more effort than the last. The reagent splattered onto the spatula and his right glove.

Jasper spent the rest of the morning working up the sample in preparation for analysis in the DNA sequencer. By noon, he had reached the final step, digestion, which required a minimum of an hour to complete. Jasper decided to leave the lab and get some lunch while he waited.

He swung by Dr. Sabastien's office to see if he had heard any news from Tonino. It was clear to Jasper from the way Dr. Sabastien had spoken about Tonino and Father Cavalli's relationship that they had been very good friends.

As Jasper neared the office, he could hear the doctor's deep voice in conversation. The office door was partially ajar, so Jasper rapped quietly and pushed it open. Dr. Sabastien's eyes acknowledged him, and without interrupting his conversation, he pointed to one of the two chairs in front of his desk. Jasper was a little confused, thinking that Dr. Sabastien must be on speakerphone with someone. He continued toward the chair without speaking a word.

Just then, the midday sunlight that normally filled the office was obscured, replaced by a massive shadow. Someone else was in the room. Jasper turned to the right to see the figure of a very tall man standing in front of the large office window. The man stood with his back to them, looking directly out the window and leaving his shadow over half of the office.

The intensity of the sunlight flooding through the window made it impossible for Jasper to make out any more details of the silhouetted figure other than his height and his long black robe. Dr. Sabastien pushed himself back from his desk and stood up.

"Father Derksen," he said.

The figure didn't move and continued to face the window.

"Yes," Father Derksen answered in a crisp snap, allowing his voice to bounce off the glass.

"I'd like to introduce you to Dr. Jasper Stewart. He is our new research scientist conducting the genetic analyses on the artifacts."

The figure turned around, causing the lower half of his robe to swing outward in a way that made Jasper instantly think of Darth Vader. He walked toward Jasper with his right hand extended, and Jasper stood up.

"Father Helmut Derksen."

A shiver rippled through Jasper the instant their hands met. The priest's hand was as cold as ice and twice the size of Jasper's hand, which disappeared completely inside his when they shook. Emptiness filled the pit of Jasper's stomach, forcing him to withdraw his hand prematurely. Though the handshake had been unsettling, Jasper was compelled to absorb every detail of Father Derksen's face.

It was the granite face of a fifty-five-year-old man perfectly suited to a military uniform not a robe. Brush-cut steel grey hair stood straight up from his head, adding to his military presence. Deep lines crossed his forehead like battle wounds, and two perfectly straight eyebrows lay overtop a pair of coal-black eyes. His eyes seemed hollow, and yet they penetrated Jasper, looking directly through him as if he weren't even in the room.

"Nice to meet you, Father Derksen," Jasper said.

"The pleasure is mine, Dr. Stewart," responded the priest in an English accent.

"Please call me 'Jasper.' You're from England?" asked Jasper.

Father Derksen laughed for a brief moment. "No, I'm German born and raised. In Germany we learn English from the Brits, so we pick up their accent along the way. I've heard many great things about your work, Jasper."

"My predecessor, Father Cavalli," here Father Derksen paused to make the sign of the cross, "spoke very highly of you."

"I'm very sorry to hear of his death. I didn't get to know him very well," said Jasper.

"Yes, the Lord does take some of his flock far too soon in my opinion, although I'm sure He's happy to have one as dedicated as Father Cavalli. Now, I was just speaking to Dr. Sabastien about the most recent acquisition our good Father Cavalli obtained. Have you had a chance to look at the artifact?"

"As a matter of fact, I started it this morning, and it's almost ready to run through the DNA sequencer. That's why I came up here; the sample has to digest for a couple of hours now."

"Can you tell me how long it'll be before we have some results?"

"I'll finish the DNA sequencing today and will immediately run the results on the computer to check for a match in our database. This process can take a very long time—days or sometimes weeks—there are potentially billions of different combinations of DNA codes to be compared. However, based on the computer resources we have here, I'm optimistic it shouldn't take that long—hopefully a day or two at the most," Jasper explained.

"Wonderful," Father Derksen said before turning to face Dr. Sabastien.

"You'll let me know as soon as you have the results, won't you?" he said with no attempt to conceal the urgency in his tone.

"Yes, of course we will," Dr. Sabastien assured him. "Your team will be the first to know—after us, of course."

"Good then, I look forward to hearing from you. Now I need to get back to my office. Good-bye." Father Derksen nodded his head toward Dr. Sabastien, turned his head and did the same to Jasper. He spun himself around to leave the office, and his robe once again made the ominous sweeping motion. He left and walked down the hallway towards the front entrance.

"Wow, he doesn't really strike me as a priest," said Jasper.

"I wouldn't disagree with you there," Dr. Sabastien responded.

"The longer you're here, the more you'll find that many of

the Vatican priests have hidden talents not always becoming of the Church. But what were you coming to see me about?"

"Well, as you just heard, I've completed the extraction of the artifact, and it's digesting right now, so I thought I'd come up and see if you've heard from Toni. I won't start the sequencing until about two this afternoon, so I'm going to get some lunch now. Are you interested in coming along?"

"Tonino called this morning, and he'll be in on Wednesday. Father Cavalli's funeral is tomorrow. I'll pass on lunch today; Father Derksen's visit has put me behind in my work this morning, but thanks anyway. And, Jasper, you may need to check the dressing on your forehead."

"Okay, thanks. I'll take a look on my way to lunch. I'm going to get a Panini; do you want me to get you something?" asked Jasper as he raised his hand to his forehead in an effort to locate any blood running down his face.

"No thanks. I brought my lunch today. By the way, do let me know first if you find a match for the artifact," he said with a smirk on his face and a snicker in his voice.

"Sure."

Jasper left the office and headed for the washroom to check his forehead. He looked at his reflection in the mirror above the sink. He could see the remnants of the dried blood that had leaked from below the dressing while he was in the isolation suit-up room. Jasper wetted a paper towel and removed the blood from his skin but left the dressing intact. He washed his hands and headed out for lunch.

As Jasper walked across the crowded square, he couldn't stop thinking about what Dr. Sabastien had just said. It wasn't what he had said but how he said it that was troubling. It sounded to Jasper like Dr. Sabastien didn't really think they would find a match to the DNA on the artifact; it seemed like an inside joke to him. *Why would he take the position as the head of the program if he didn't think there was a reasonable chance of success? It can't be the money; he's the premiere geneticist in Europe and could've taken tenure at any university he wanted.* It then occurred to Jasper that Dr. Sabastien wasn't even really doing any research at the moment, only administrative work.

He put these thoughts aside for the moment as he turned toward *Café Piazza*; he had far more pressing issues to deal with now—having to speak Italian again to order his food weighed heavily on his mind.

The crowd of tourists in St. Peter's Square distracted him for a moment as he approached the street. The shriek of car horns replaced the bustling sounds of the square as the smell of diesel exhaust from a passing bus filled the air.

Jasper sprinted across the busy road to the narrow sidewalk on the other side. Just when he thought it was safe, a few feet from the café entrance, a scooter came screeching up and nearly ran him over, its horn blaring.

The driver, a kid no older than fifteen, jumped off the scooter and left it idling and propped up on its kickstand at the entrance. He glared at Jasper and spat out an Italian profanity as he adjusted his shoulder bag. Obviously in a hurry, he ran into the café ahead of Jasper, letting the door close in Jasper's face. He caught it just before it slammed shut.

Jasper followed him into the café, wishing he could at least fire back a retort, but he was still overcome with the fear at having to face the café owner to order his lunch.

"*Ciao, Zio*," said the kid.

"*Ciao, Bernardo*," replied the owner from behind the counter.

The owner tossed a Panini to Bernardo, who stuffed it in his bag and left.

Jasper reluctantly approached the counter. "*Uno Panini...*" he started, his attempt to speak Italian frozen in his mind while he pointed to a sandwich in the display case.

The owner understood Jasper's gesture and removed a Panini. Jasper took out enough Euros to more than cover the cost and slid them across the surface of the counter. "*Grazie*," he said.

"*Prego,*" said the café owner.

Jasper took his Panini and bottle of water and walked back to St. Peter's Square to watch the tourists and feed the pigeons his crumbs. He finished his food and walked back to the lab. As he walked, Jasper again started thinking about why Dr. Sabastien had taken the position at the VGP. *What's in it for him?*

The more he thought about it, the less it made any sense. To abandon his research to be an administrator at a private lab wasn't going to further Dr. Sabastien's research career at all. *Unless,* Jasper thought, *it's the artifacts. Maybe he knows the Vatican possesses artifacts unknown to the rest of the world. Maybe Dr. Sabastien is enticed to run the lab knowing this will give him exclusive access to these artifacts.* Jasper decided this must be the reason he had taken the position. It would explain why he could work for the VGP when he didn't seem to believe in its purpose.

Jasper returned just in time to take the sample out of the incubator and to start the final preparations for injecting it into the DNA sequencer. He took the small glass vile containing the final extract and walked across the hall into the DNA Sequencing Lab. He placed the vial into the stainless steel holder on the bench next to the machine and removed a small glass syringe and a needle from the bench drawer in front of him. Jasper struggled to place the needle on the tip of the syringe; it required fine motor skills and a delicate touch. He often had trouble completing tasks like this in the isolation suit; the suit gloves didn't offer the same amount of 'feel' as normal lab gloves. He finally got the injection needle on the syringe and withdrew a sample from the vial. Opening the injection port of the DNA sequencer, Jasper placed the tip of the needle through the membrane of the port and depressed the plunger slowly, injecting the sample into the sequencer.

Now all he had to do was wait. If he had completed the extraction process correctly, it would only take about an hour or so to complete the DNA sequencing. In an effort to make the time pass more quickly, Jasper returned to the Extraction Lab and began cleaning up his workstation. Tonino would normally do this, but under the circumstances, Jasper felt it best for him to leave the lab in the same shape Tonino usually left it. He thought it would be a nice surprise for Tonino to return and find the first extraction of the artifact already completed.

It was well after six p.m. when Jasper started worrying that something was wrong with the DNA sequencer. It hadn't completed the coding yet.

Jasper checked the DNA sequencer terminal screen, expecting to see an error message or some other indication that something had gone wrong, but nothing appeared out of the ordinary. The sequencer was working normally. Finally, just before seven, the DNA code was complete. Not wanting to waste any time, Jasper decided to start the computer analysis of the DNA code immediately. He wanted to search the database for a match using his office computer. When he was at university, the network computers had been notoriously slow, and Jasper assumed the lab computers connected to the Vatican network would be as well. The matching process required an enormous amount of computing resources. He expected the database search to take at least forty-eight hours to complete, even on his computer, so he saved the sequencer results to a flash drive and left the lab for his office. He booted up his office computer, copied the results to the hard drive and initiated the database search.

CHAPTER 19

LA CONVERGENZA

A low rumbling sound woke Jasper on Tuesday morning. As he opened his eyes, a brilliant flash of light flickered through the bedroom blinds. The distant sound of thunder accompanied the first real rainfall since his arrival in Rome.

Jasper lay in bed, anticipating the next clap of thunder and taking comfort in the sound of the approaching storm. The familiarity of it lulled him partially back to sleep as his thoughts drifted back to warm humid nights in Windsor.

Summer storms in the Windsor area were a natural phenomenon that often resembled a Fourth of July fireworks display, especially at night. Accompanied by fierce winds, hail and the occasional tornado, they almost always triggered power outages. At this thought, Jasper snapped out of his trance-like state and bounded from the bed. He suddenly realized that this thunderstorm could have the same effect.

Could the power be knocked out? They must have a back-up power system for the computers at least and a surge protector.

The thought of a computer system failure and losing the data on the DNA he had just sequenced was too much for Jasper to take. It was only seven thirty, but he dressed quickly, hoping to get to the office as soon as possible. He put his shoes on and pulled an old blue sweatshirt from his suitcase. This was the only piece of clothing he had that could keep some of the pounding rain off of him.

He didn't own an umbrella or even a raincoat, and Rome was in the middle of a downpour. The flash of lightning followed immediately by a crack of thunder as he left the apartment meant the storm was directly overhead, and there would be no break in the rain for a while.

Jasper prepared for the dash from his residence to the cover of the next closest building. The intensity of the rain hitting the ground made it sound like a drum roll. Jasper left the front of his building and raced across the lane to the cover of the building across from his. In the middle of the lane, another flash of lightning blinded him and caused the hair to stand up on his arms and neck. He jumped in reflex to the deafening thunder overhead. He tried to make his reaction appear intentional, as if he was just leaping over the raging river of water running down the middle of the road. He continued hopping from building to building until he finally arrived at the VGP building.

He entered the building soaking wet, but relief obscured the cold dampness covering his body. Everything appeared normal; the sound of the storm was inaudible inside the thick brick walls of the VGP building. Jasper tugged at his cotton sweatshirt, now heavy with water, trying to remove it from his torso as he made his way down the hall to his office, where he removed his soggy running shoes and placed them over the air vent to dry.

Alica hadn't arrived yet, and Jasper was uncomfortable asking anyone else about the building's back-up power protection. The more he thought about it, the more he felt incredibly ridiculous. *Of course, a hundred-million-dollar research lab would have everything to prevent damage from a simple thunderstorm.* Fortunately for him, no one had arrived yet, as he would have been more than a little embarrassed standing in the hallway, soaked from head to toe, asking if the building had an uninterrupted power-protection system. If anyone asked why he was in so early, he decided to tell them that it was because of the sample he was analyzing.

"*Buon giorno*," said Tonino.

Jasper was stunned and excited to hear Toni's voice and turned to see him entering the building. It was an unexpected surprise, as Father Cavalli's funeral was that afternoon. Jasper looked at Tonino's face and didn't see sadness flowing from his eyes, only an emptiness.

"Toni, I'm so sorry to hear about Father Cavalli. Why are you here today? You should be at home."

"I won't be long. I need to collect a few things from my office to give to his family," replied Tonino, his voice emotionless. "You need to get yourself an umbrella, Jasper—and a pair of sandals," he continued with a hint of a smile on his face as he looked at Jasper's dripping sweatshirt and shoes sitting on the air vent.

"Yes, I figured that much out this morning—a little too late." They both offered a small laugh and then there was a noticeable and uncomfortable pause in the conversation as both men looked at each other.

Tonino broke the silence. "How is your head? You took a very big fall in the Basilica. I was worried about you. I went to the Vatican clinic with you, but you did not wake up right away. Dr. Collin said you would be fine and I should go."

"He told me. Thanks, I'm fine," Jasper assured him.

"How many stitches did it take to close the cut on your forehead? It was bleeding quite badly in the Basilica." Tonino took a seat in the chair in front of Jasper's desk.

"None actually. The doctor said he wanted to limit the amount of scarring so he used butterfly tape. It's been okay, but I've had a little bit of bleeding every once in a while. Nothing too bad though."

"That's good. That was a very large chalice that hit you," replied Tonino in an effort to keep the conversation going.

But Jasper wasn't focused on their discussion. He was thinking more of the questions that remained about that day. *What really happened last Sunday morning? Father Cavalli yelling 'Convergenza', his collapsing to the altar, men in black suits arriving from every direction coming to his aid.* Jasper couldn't hold it inside any longer, and just as he had always done, he blurted out the question even though he knew it wasn't the polite thing to do.

"Toni, what happened on Sunday morning? Why was Father Cavalli yelling, and who were all those men?"

Tonino looked into Jasper's eyes and took a deep breath so that his chest and shoulders rose up and down in unison. He paused for a moment before standing up and walking across the office to close the door. He then turned and faced Jasper, who now had a look of intrigue on his face, knowing he was about to hear information for his ears only. Tonino returned to his seat and settled into a comfortable position.

"Jasper, there is much you don't know about the Vatican. What I tell you, I'm not proud of—in fact it pains me to speak of it."

Excitement rushed through Jasper, heightening his senses. Like a high-school student about to hear gossip, Jasper held his breath in anticipation of what might come next and let Tonino continue.

"The Church is only one small component of the Vatican. It is what most people who do not know, like you, believe is the reason the Vatican exists. This is far from the truth. The Church is the face of the Vatican; it is what those of us who work here want you—the people—to see. We want you to see the face of God, represented by all the good things the Church does. Things like providing support to families in need, offering a place to gather and pray, sending representatives on missions to spread the Word of God. These wonderful things, as well as many others, help spread love and friendship around the world.

"Sadly, not everything done in the Vatican is in the name of God. Many of the efforts put forth by the Vatican are focused on gathering more followers to increase the Vatican coffers. It is not just about money, but power. The more Catholics there are, the stronger the Vatican becomes, and the wider its network can extend."

"So this is what the Pope really does?" Jasper interrupted as a feeling of vindication filled his entire body.

"No, no, no," Tonino cut the question off and continued. "The Pope, like the Church, is only a figurehead. He knows nothing of what goes on in the Vatican. He signs papers, makes guest appearances and travels the world gathering more followers for the real rulers of the Vatican: the Vatican Council."

"What?" asked Jasper incredulously.

"The Vatican Council. The Council is made up of four Bishops or Cardinals, each responsible for a different department of the Vatican. You already know one of the departments: the Vatican Acquisitions Department, where we work. The second is the Department of Diocese, where the day-to-day Church operations are conducted. The third is the Department of Papal-Intergovernmental Relations, and the fourth and most powerful department is the Vatican Secret Service."

It took a few seconds for this information to sink into Jasper's mind. Tonino stared at him, knowing this last statement had caught Jasper off guard. But as hard as he tried to string the thoughts together, it just wasn't making any sense.

"What do you mean, Secret Service?"

"Father Cavalli was the Head of the VSS for the past twelve years. The primary function of the VSS is to protect the Vatican Council and the secret workings it conducts. Its mandate is to know everything that goes on within the Catholic Empire."

"The Catholic Empire?" Jasper repeated, his feeling of vindication returning.

"Yes, an empire, although few really know this. Like all empires, its ultimate goal is to expand, even at the expense of its citizens. In this case, the hard-working, devout Catholics all over the world. They think—no, they believe—they are working for the good of the Church and God, but the reality is they are working on expanding an empire controlled by the few in the Vatican Council."

"How long has it been going on?" Jasper had more questions, but this was the first to escape his lips.

"For as long as records have been kept, there has been a Vatican Council in existence. Few people know why the Council exists; its purpose is known only to its members. It remains one of the greatest mysteries of the Church itself. I can tell you it has power greater than any country, and its influence reaches to the very roots of humanity."

"So those men I saw rushing to Father Cavalli as he fell were part of the VSS?" Jasper was stunned as he began to finally understand the events of that day.

"Yes. They are everywhere. There is no way of knowing who they may be or where they may be working. The VSS take their orders directly from the Council, and their loyalty remains unwavering, even in the face of death."

"What about those words he was yelling as he fell to the ground? '*Convergenza*' or something like that. Do you know what that means?" Jasper asked.

"This troubles me," replied Tonino, his black eyes showing a measurable level of anguish. A perplexed expression crept across his face as he continued.

"Father Cavalli and I had not spoken about *la Convergenza* in years. When I heard him shout this, I was confused and quite astonished. Even when we did discuss *la Convergenza*, it was never in the company of others. Up until a few years ago, *la Convergenza* was the biggest concern of the Council. In fact, when I started working here, I was assigned to research *la Convergenza* as my first task. Now I would say most people, including here at the Vatican, have never even heard the word before. I think the best way for me to explain what *la Convergenza* is is to show you. I will get my old file. Give me a moment."

Tonino stood up from his seat and proceeded out of the

office. A few minutes later, he returned holding a briefcase. He unlocked the case and removed a large red file folder crammed so full of documents that it had to be bound shut with a large rubber band. Tonino put the folder down on the desk in front of Jasper.

Jasper could clearly read the large black letters on it spelling 'Convergenza 97/07.' Tonino grabbed the back of the chair he had been seated in and dragged it to the other side of Jasper's desk so they could sit side by side. Tonino removed the rubber band and opened the file to reveal the first document.

Jasper was surprised to see a photo of an ancient stone tablet covered in small and barely discernable scratches.

"This is the first evidence we have of *la Convergenza,* although we are quite certain its existence predates even these 4000-year-old stone tablets. They were found encased in a tomb near Luxor, Egypt. The Vatican acquired the tablets more than two centuries ago, but it was not until I began working on the file that their significance became known. The writing is called 'Cuneiform' and was used in ancient Mesopotamia."

Jasper continued to scan the photo, focusing on the small pictures carved into the stone.

"I'm sorry, Toni, but I still don't see anything. What am I supposed to see? What is *la Convergenza?*" he asked.

"Here, let me show you," Tonino pointed to a symbol on the stone tablet that resembled a figure eight with the very top portion missing.

"I still don't get it. Is that *la Convergenza?*" asked Jasper.

"This symbol has been found at every single ancient site discovered on the planet, from the jungles of Peru to Easter Island. The Egyptians displayed it on the walls of their tombs, and the creators of Stonehenge scratched it into their stone blocks. The Aboriginal Australians painted it on the sides of rocky outcrops, while the ancient Africans drew it on the walls of their caves.

"This one symbol unites all of mankind, transcending race, culture and—most importantly—religion. It has been found in the ancient scrolls and writings of all of our present-day religions, including the ancient pottery writings of the Hebrews, the first written scriptures of the Koran, the Bible and Chinese Daoism. Even the walls of the Mayan pyramids and jewelry of the Inca contain this symbol."

"But, Toni, this doesn't tell me a thing," Jasper interjected, beginning to lose his patience with Tonino's ramblings about ancient ruins and religion.

"It was not until scholars were able to complete the translation of ancient Greek, Arabic and Hebrew writings into Latin that the first modern reference to the word *la Convergenza* occurred. All of these ancient languages used the incomplete figure eight symbol when they referred to *la Convergenza*. *La Convergenza* is not a person but an event. It is described in all of the ancient literatures as an event of Biblical proportions, greater even than the Great Flood. In English I think you call it the Apocalypse."

Jasper's face froze in disbelief, and he looked at Tonino. For an instant he was seven again, listening to the priest in church wanting to scream "Liar!" He was stunned at what he had just heard. He refused to believe it possible that anyone could consider *la Convergenza* fact. It would be like believing in Adam and Eve or the parting of the Red Sea or any of the other stories in the Bible. This was clearly just another fable, contrived to convince people to behave in a certain way or to follow a leader blindly and without question.

Then realization flooded Jasper's thoughts as if he had just solved a difficult mathematical problem. Remembering his childhood, he saw that it was possible for others to believe in *la Convergenza*. Like the parishioners in his mother's church; they had faith.

Jasper's mind raced with questions: *Why has the Vatican Council invested so much of its resources in la Convergenza? Surely they aren't governed by the stories of their own faith.*

What would make them spend so much time and money chasing down a fable?

Tonino continued to flip through pages and pages of documents while pointing out the symbol to Jasper and explaining to him when and where the information had been collected. Jasper lost his focus; much of what Tonino was saying sounded the same.

Suddenly, like a distant flash of lightning, he saw it; but so much doubt clouded his mind that he wasn't certain he had actually seen it. It was the incomplete figure of eight symbol that he had just seen a hundred times, but it was different. This time the symbol was on its side, which made it look like a fish. More importantly, it made it look exactly like the one on the back of his neck.

Jasper's body filled with panic, starting from his head and rushing through every pore. He froze with fear as if a bear had appeared from nowhere on a hike—yet there was nothing to fear. The panic raced through his mind, compelling him to flee, to leave the office. He felt that he was in danger, that he had to escape.

Jasper slapped his hand onto the page to prevent Tonino from turning it, unaware that he had used far more force than necessary and caused a loud slapping sound. His eyes were transfixed on the symbol while his heart raced and a horrible feeling of anxiety filled his veins. Tonino raised his head from the folder, obviously startled, and looked at Jasper. But before Tonino had a chance to ask Jasper what he was doing, Jasper picked up the photo and examined it closely, his hands shaking.

"Is this the same symbol as all the others?"

"Yes, it can be drawn in any direction. Why? Is something the matter?" Tonino was now aware of Jasper's out of character reaction and had stopped turning pages.

Jasper slammed the photo face down on the desk without realizing it and quickly tried to regain his composure. He tried unsuccessfully to hide the emotion from his face.

"No, I realized I've seen the symbol before. I've seen it on the back of a lot of cars at home."

"Yes, it is very common here in Italy; you can see it on many necklaces and earrings. This is a symbol that many Christians use to identify themselves to others; it also symbolizes the miracle of the loaves and the fishes."

"Toni, does the Council believe in *la Convergenza*?" asked Jasper out of the blue, even though he felt he already knew the answer.

"That is a silly question," responded Tonino with a chuckle. He lifted his arms and pointed to the walls. "Do you think they would have spent all these years and all of this money if they didn't believe?"

"Do you?" asked Jasper.

Tonino's face instantly shifted from the sarcastic one he had used to answer Jasper's last question to one of contemplation. He took a long time to answer, and Jasper guessed that the answer wasn't a simple one.

"I spent many years of my life tracking down leads, translating ancient artifacts and investigating new discoveries to find proof of my belief, but I have yet to identify anything that can prove to me or the Council that one day there will arrive *la Convergenza*—it remains a matter of faith."

"Why do you think Father Cavalli was yelling *la Convergenza* before he collapsed?" Jasper asked.

"I can only guess he was experiencing some type of seizure at the time which caused him to hallucinate. After all, he must have known much more about it than I," Tonino replied with a shrug.

Jasper nodded and stared at the desk. He knew perfectly well the real reason Father Cavalli had yelled it. He had witnessed the mark on the back of Jasper's neck; it would have been easily visible to Father Cavalli when Jasper knelt down. The shock of seeing the birthmark had caused the priest to collapse. This meant one thing to Jasper: there were some members of the Council who truly did believe in *la Convergenza*.

CHAPTER 20

MORTO DERKSEN

"Toni, look what time it is. Don't you need to get going?" Jasper asked.

Tonino looked at his watch. "It's eleven thirty; the service will start in half an hour. You are right. I have to leave soon. Luckily, it is just around the corner from here in the Vatican Chapel."

Jasper was still thinking about Father Cavalli as the realization of what had caused his death sank in. *How could my birthmark, which by mere coincidence resembles an ancient religious symbol, have caused his death? Of the billions of people on the planet, odds are there must be hundreds or thousands of people with a mark like mine.* The idea a man could drop dead on seeing it was insane to Jasper. A smile filled his face, and he laughed nervously to himself just thinking about it.

The series of events unraveled in his mind like a black comedy: a change of pants, poor linguistic skills and a slightly too-short haircut had started it all. Then he had gone to church for the first time since he was eleven and had to receive Communion. Finally, the exposure of a small birthmark on the back of his neck had caused a heart attack. But this comedy ended badly: there was no humor in Father Cavalli's death. It reminded Jasper of the many years his father had spent concealing his birthmark. *Does he know?*

Tonino had been busy closing up the file folder, getting all of the papers back into it and securing the large rubber band around it. With the task complete, he looked up at Jasper to find him lost in thought. Jasper realized Tonino was still next to him, watching him, and pulled himself back to the present. As he did, he remembered that he had completed the extraction of the new remains.

"Toni, I forgot to tell you. I extracted and sequenced the new sample Father Cavalli acquired. It's running through the database as we speak," said Jasper, happy to provide Tonino with some good news and change the subject.

"Excellent, any problems?" asked Tonino.

"No, none. Everything went really well. The only odd thing was it took nearly four hours for the sequencer to complete the analysis."

"Four hours!" exclaimed Tonino. "Are you sure the instrument was working properly? That's an exceptionally long time for an artifact."

"Yeah, I double-checked everything. I think it was just a very large sample. It worked out in the end."

"Well anyway, don't get your hopes up. The odds of finding a match in the database are almost zero," Tonino pointed out.

"I'm not, but this is still my first one and, well, I like to dream. Besides, this artifact must be a little bit special. Father Cavalli said it showed promise, and so did Father Derksen."

"What?" asked Tonino. "Did you say 'Derksen?'"

"Yes, I met him yesterday in Dr. Sabastien's office when I went up to ask if he had heard from you. Why?" asked Jasper.

Tonino didn't answer immediately but began walking toward the small window in Jasper's office as if he wanted to know the weather. He paused in front of the window and then turned to face Jasper. Clearly hesitant to speak, his face indicated that he was searching for the right words.

"This can only mean one thing: Father Derksen has replaced Father Cavalli on the Vatican Council. He must be the new Head of the VSS."

"So?"

"Father Derksen conducts his business very differently than Father Cavalli did. This change is not good, not for the Vatican or the Church," said Tonino, shaking his head. "What exactly did he say?"

Jasper hesitated, his heart racing with anxiety precipitated by the tone of Tonino's questioning.

"What did he say?" asked Tonino again, this time in a demanding tone.

"Nothing really, he asked if I had any results for the new sample yet. I said no, I had just started analyzing them. He indicated it showed great promise, exactly the same way Father Cavalli did. That's it. Why?"

"Did you hear him say anything to *Professore* Sabastien?" commanded Tonino.

"No, nothing. Why?" asked Jasper. Impatience was replacing his anxiety. Tonino was asking all the questions and was not offering any meaningful answers to his.

"As I said, Father Derksen conducts his business much differently to Father Cavalli. He's referred to by some in the Vatican as 'Morto Derksen' or in English: 'Deadly Derksen.' He is far too comfortable using the full complement of powers at his disposal, with no regard to the outcome.

"The VSS have powers beyond those of any country, and now those powers are in the hands of Father Derksen. I'm afraid we are headed for very dark times. I must warn you, Jasper, please be careful. If you have anything to do with this man, I am absolutely sure no good can come of it. I must be going now, or I will be late for the funeral."

Tonino quickly picked up his file folder and left the office without turning to say good-bye.

Jasper looked at his watch and realized his hunger pains were justified. It was nearly noon, and he hadn't eaten a thing. Sitting with only his socks on his feet, he swiveled his chair so that he could remove his shoes from the air duct. He stuck his hands inside of them to feel if they had dried and was surprised to feel no dampness. He slipped them on and stood up from his chair to take a look out the window. The storm had finally passed.

Jasper made his way across the square to *Café Piazza* to buy his usual Panini and water. He was now comfortable going to this café: the owner was accustomed to his lack of Italian and always showed patience when Jasper picked his food by pointing through the glass case. The café owner placed his food in a bag and handed it to Jasper just as Bernardo walked through the door. The owner greeted him with a vibrant. "*Ciao, Bernardo,*" picked up the Panini he had pre-wrapped and tossed it across the café into Bernardo's hands.

"*Ciao, Zio, e grazie,*" replied Bernardo. He stuffed the Panini into his shoulder bag and turned to follow Jasper out of the café. Bernardo got back onto his still idling scooter and blew away at full speed, riding down the middle of the sidewalk as a couple of elderly women cursed him with hand gestures.

Jasper was so hungry that he started eating while he walked through the square. He glanced around and noticed how few tourists there were. For the first time, Jasper could sit on one of the benches in the square by himself. He took the opportunity and continued to eat his lunch. As he sat, Jasper recalled the conversation of that morning.

He continued having difficulty believing everything Tonino had told him regarding *la Convergenza*, but one thing troubled him more than the rest. It was not something he had seen in the file or anything Tonino had said; it was something Jasper had not done. Or rather something he *could not* do: show Tonino his birthmark. At the moment he had realized the symbol and his birthmark were the same, a hot flash had surged through his body. It had been more intense than anything he had ever felt before. He had felt like he was putting himself in grave danger, like at any moment something horrible was going to happen. Jasper's mind had tried to tell him there was no danger, but his body had refused to let the surge dissipate. Jasper finished his food and resolved that the hot flash had been a combination of the early morning rush to the office and his hunger and brushed it off as best he could.

The sound of church bells rang from behind the Basilica, sending the flock of pigeons that had been finishing his breadcrumbs into flight. Jasper hadn't heard these bells before, and they were ringing far more rapidly than the usual bells that came from the Basilica. He glanced at his watch and noticed the time: it was noon. Father Cavalli's Mass.

So much had happened in the last few hours that Jasper had completely forgotten about the sample again. He picked up his pace as he made his way back to the VGP building. Before heading back to his own office, he decided to see if Dr. Sabastien was in his office. Jasper started down the hall but Alica stopped him halfway.

"Sorry, Jasper. He's gone to the funeral and won't be back this afternoon," she said.

"Thanks, Alica," he said with a little relief.

Jasper was delighted that he didn't have to waste more time talking to Dr. Sabastien. All that he really wanted to do was go straight to his office and check his computer. Jasper made his way to his office and walked directly to his desk, grasping the mouse and shaking it to awaken the screen.

A mixture of relief and disappointment greeted him when he saw the screen. He was happy that everything was running properly but disappointed that the search was still processing. Jasper had been hoping to see a barcode and corresponding number on the screen. This would have indicated that the DNA from the remains matched a DNA sample from an artifact catalogued in the Vatican database.

Better no result than a negative result, he thought to himself.

Jasper let go of the mouse and noticed the photo left behind by Tonino. He picked it up and walked out of his office to Alica.

"Alica, can you give this to Tonino? He left it in my office and his is locked. I'll never remember to give it to him."

Jasper handed the photo to her, and her face grew pale the instant she glanced at it. She raised her head and sat motionless, her eyes glowing and remaining fixed in space.

"Alica, are you okay?" Jasper asked.

She snapped out of her stare and ignored his question.

"Tonino gave you this?" she questioned.

"He left it in my office by accident. Why?"

"Did he tell you what it is?"

"Yes. Why? What's the matter?" Jasper asked, surprised by the line of questioning.

"What did he tell you?"

"It's an ancient symbol and the Vatican has been looking for it for years. What's wrong, Alica?" Jasper quickly grew frustrated at her blank stares and lack of response and turned to leave.

"Where are you going?"

"I have work to do, is that okay?" Jasper responded, confused by the woman's tone.

"Dr. Sabastien will want to see you as soon as he returns."

"Since he's not coming back this afternoon, I guess I'll see him first thing tomorrow then," Jasper said, donning a smirk.

"Yes, straight away," she said with an unusual intensity.

It may have been Alica's strange behavior, the disappointment of having no results, or his early arrival at the office, but Jasper didn't feel like working that afternoon. He didn't want to risk slowing his computer's search by logging on to the Vatican network just to check his email, so he left work early to do some shopping.

His flat had a tiny cooking area equipped with an equally small stove and fridge. The only part of the kitchen that he actually used was the microwave, and his supply of frozen foods was diminishing. Shopping wasn't normally a bother to Jasper, but since his arrival in Italy, he had avoided it as much as possible: going to the store meant talking to a cashier—in Italian.

Jasper left the VGP building and started walking up the lane toward the narrow staircase between the chapel and administration building. This was a shortcut out of the Vatican and onto the main road that circled the Vatican wall. The staircase was covered by the low-lying branches of an enormous chestnut tree. Halfway down the stairs, Jasper heard two men arguing. Out of curiosity, he stopped to listen.

Disappointed that they weren't speaking in English, he resumed his walk. However, after two more steps, it occurred to him that one of the voices sounded surprisingly familiar. It was difficult to be certain because they weren't speaking Italian or English, but German. Jasper backed up a couple of steps and carefully pulled some of the leaves aside on one of the large branches so he could see the men below.

The two men were standing thirty feet from Jasper in a small stone courtyard. A fountain with a figure of an angel pouring water from a vase ran in the middle of the courtyard, making it even more difficult to hear. One man was facing directly toward Jasper while the other had his back to him. He knew the man facing him; he was unmistakable.

Jasper could clearly see the black eyes of Father Derksen as he stood in his long black robe tied at the waist with a bright red rope. His hand was raised as he yelled in German at the other man. It only took a second for Jasper to recognize the second man as well: it was Dr. Sabastien. He now understood why the voice had sounded familiar. It had only confused him at first because he had never heard Dr. Sabastien speak in any language except Italian or English. Jasper wasn't sure what surprised him most: the fact that Dr. Sabastien spoke four languages fluently or that he was in a heated argument with Father Derksen.

A sudden fear rolled over Jasper. He remembered the warning Tonino had given him that morning. *"Deadly Derksen, don't have anything to do with him."* The thought circled through his head.

Down in the courtyard, Dr. Sabastien obviously didn't like

where the argument was going.

***

"I'm in charge of the lab, and I think it best," Dr. Sabastien said, his voice beginning to strain. He was tired of yelling in German, but it was a matter of privacy.

"Don't forget who you report to. The artifact is our priority, not some archeological dig in the Middle East. He's to stay and finish, that's final!" commanded Father Derksen.

"I'll let him decide," Dr. Sabastien said in an elevated voice.

"It's not up to Dr. Stewart!" shouted Father Derksen, pointing his finger directly at Dr. Sabastien.

***

Jasper watched intently from his hiding place. *Why can't everyone just speak one language in this country*? he thought out of frustration. He wanted to know so badly what the two men were arguing about. It was clear the argument was coming to a head; both men's voices were escalating, and both were using wild hand gestures while speaking. The final words spoken in the argument came from Father Derksen, and Jasper was stunned when he heard them. They were "Dr. Stewart."

Once again, Father Derksen completed a dramatic turn so that his robe followed in a swirling motion and he marched out of the courtyard with his back to Dr. Sabastien.

With Father Derksen gone from the courtyard, Dr. Sabastien left as well. Jasper dared not move until the coast was clear, and he stood like a statue, watching Dr. Sabastien walk away. At the edge of the courtyard, Dr. Sabastien stopped and turned, casting his ice-blue eyes directly up into the chestnut tree where Jasper stood.

CHAPTER 21

THE MATCH

J asper finished his shopping without embarrassing himself and returned to his flat to make dinner. He tossed a frozen package of pasta into the microwave and turned on the TV to watch the news. He was fixated on the argument he had overheard, and his thoughts ran ramp. *Why were they having such a heated debate? What did I have to do with it?* And the part that annoyed Jasper the most: *Why did it have to be in German?* Not talking to Dr. Sabastien about it would be impossible for Jasper. It was only a matter of time before his inability to contain his questions would win over his willpower.

His thoughts dissolved, interrupted by the beeping of the microwave. He removed the steaming plastic dish with his fingertips to avoid burning himself and quickly placed it on the counter.

Jasper stood in the kitchen eating his food and watching the news. He hadn't kept track of the time and just realized the news was ending and it was already eight o'clock. He tossed the finished package of pasta into the garbage and went into his bedroom to retrieve his laptop; he was going to start searching the Web for information on 'the Convergence.'

Jasper sat on the chair in front of the TV and waited for his laptop to boot. He connected to one of the many unsecured wireless networks and Googled 'Convergence'. Not surprised, Jasper found over twenty-five million hits; he had to refine his search, as none of them referred to Tonino's explanation of the Convergence. When he entered 'Convergence Religion Symbol,' it reduced the hits to a few hundred thousand. Jasper began adding additional modifiers including 'Italy,' 'ancient' and 'Vatican,' yet nothing came close to what he was hoping to find. Finally, he typed '*Convergenza*' in Italian and the returns reduced to five.

The first two websites he opened were in Italian, and from what he could surmise, completely unrelated. When he opened the third website, butterflies filled his stomach; a photo of St. Peter's Square filled the screen except for a short paragraph of writing. This too was only written in Italian, so Jasper copied the entire paragraph and pasted it into an online translator. Even though the translation was poor, it was evident to Jasper that it was also unrelated. His eyes were burning with a grinding sand feeling with every blink as he grew further annoyed with his lack of progress. Frustrated and tired, he shutdown his laptop and headed off to bed.

***

Bright sunlight warmed Jasper's face from his bedroom window. Once again he had forgotten to close the blinds before going to bed. The six a.m. sunlight offered no forgiveness, waking him as easily as his alarm clock. Unable to return to sleep, he decided to make the best of the morning and get showered for work, offsetting his early departure yesterday. Jasper finished his shower and started shaving in front of the bathroom mirror when he noticed all but one of the pieces of butterfly tape holding the cut on his forehead closed had fallen off. He pulled the last one off with one quick yank and tossed it in the garbage.

He wiped the fog from the mirror to get a better look at his cut; it had scabbed over well. The wound was sealed everywhere except a very small corner where the cut intersected a wrinkle in his skin. The warm water of the shower had dissolved the scab there, allowing a tiny dot of fresh red blood to form. The amount was half that coming from the hacks he was putting in his face with the dull disposable razor he was using. Jasper pulled two squares of toilet paper from the roll and dabbed the blood off of his chin and forehead.

He then made his way to the office, arriving before seven o'clock.

Overflowing with the excitement of a five-year-old on Christmas morning, Jasper quickly scanned his ID and entered the building. The urge to sprint to his office was quelled by the sound of a voice. Not expecting anyone else to be there, Jasper's curiosity triumphed over his anticipation, forcing him to skip his office and walk toward the sound of the voice.

Jasper peered through the open door of Dr. Sabastien's office and astonishment froze his movements. Dr. Sabastien was already at his desk talking on the telephone.

The urgency in Dr. Sabastien's tone was evident to Jasper, even though he was speaking in Italian. Jasper knew better than to disturb him, so he walked back to his office, regaining his excitement to look at his computer.

Not waiting to sit down, Jasper stood behind his chair and shook the mouse to wake his screen. The three seconds for the screen to come to life lingered until Jasper released a yelp followed by, "Holy shit! Holy shit! Holy shit!" which he repeated faster and louder each time. He couldn't believe his eyes. The screen displayed only a barcode and a catalogue number.

He burst out of his office, sprinting down the hall to Dr. Sabastien's. Having forgotten he was on the phone, Jasper started to ramble incoherently.

"We got one, we got one!" Jasper yelled.

Dr. Sabastien held the phone to his ear, showing complete confusion.

"Got what?" he asked, moving his hand over the phone to

prevent the person on the other end from hearing the conversation.

"A match! A match! We got a match in the database," Jasper nearly shouted.

Dr. Sabastien's face turned to stone, and his blue eyes pierced Jasper's, unleashing a shockwave of confusion inside the young doctor.

Dr. Sabastien put the phone back to his ear and said something that Jasper presumed was a parting comment, as he immediately hung up. He then stood up and closed the door.

Jasper's incredible high began a collision course with the ground, and he was completely stunned as to why.

"What's wrong?" Jasper asked.

Dr. Sabastien didn't answer but asked his own question.

"What matched?" he demanded.

"I didn't look. I was so excited I just ran straight here."

Dr. Sabastien opened the door and walked briskly to Jasper's office. Jasper followed, unable to keep up.

"What's going on?" Jasper asked again.

Still no answer came from Dr. Sabastien, but now they were in Jasper's office, and Dr. Sabastien stood in front of the computer screen working the mouse.

"I don't believe it. It's not possible," he said in a low and concerned manner. "This can't be right." He clicked the mouse and instantaneously a photo of an old chalice appeared on the screen with the words 'Grail' below it.

"No way!" erupted Jasper.

Dr. Sabastien turned around and looked at Jasper for a moment before starting to type on the keyboard.

Jasper watched the screen in horror, unable to speak for an instant, disabled by the words on the screen— 'Reformatting in Progress.'

"What are you doing?" Jasper protested.

Dr. Sabastien began a complete hard disk reformat while Jasper protested over his shoulder.

"Are you insane?" Jasper shouted, now angry and forceful in his tone.

"Did you run this search on any other computer?" demanded Dr. Sabastien.

"No, just here. Why?" Jasper asked, still waiting for answers to his questions.

"Did you run this on the network?"

"What did you do to your eyes?" asked Jasper, caught completely off guard by the radiant blue of Dr. Sabastien's eyes.

"Just answer me!" Dr. Sabastien demanded.

"No, I figured the network would be slower. Will you tell me what's going on?" begged Jasper.

"I haven't the time now. Say nothing about this to anyone. Understand?" he said in the same tone Jasper had first heard the day before when he was arguing with Father Derksen.

"Okay," Jasper agreed, uncertain why.

"We've got to hurry, follow me," Dr. Sabastien commanded next.

Jasper and Dr. Sabastien made their way to the lab. While getting into the isolation suit, Dr. Sabastien started asking him question after question.

"Was this the cooler? Where are the original samples? Do you still have the extract you injected into the sequencer?"

Jasper answered all of these questions but was still unable to get a single answer to any of his own. Now angrier than ever, and out of patience, Jasper asked one more time before pulling the helmet on.

"Are you going to tell me what's going on?"

"Just get suited up and get into the transition room," snapped Dr. Sabastien.

Jasper yanked the helmet over his head in anger, hitting himself directly on the cut in the process. The intense pain felt like a bee sting but disappeared in a flash. He zipped the front of his suit and entered the transition room alongside Dr. Sabastien.

"It's critical I dispose of the entire contaminated sample before he arrives," came a tinny sounding version of Dr. Sabastien's voice through the wireless communication system in the helmet.

"Toni? Why?" protested Jasper.

"I haven't the time to explain, just don't speak of what we are doing. Understand?" Dr. Sabastien stated before he and Jasper connected their suits to the ceiling snorkel ends.

"Yes," responded Jasper, now knowing better than to even try and ask anything else, as it was clear he wasn't going to get an answer.

They went directly to the Extraction Lab, where Jasper showed Dr. Sabastien the cooler with the artifact still in it and the tiny bit he used to take his sample. Dr. Sabastien removed a new sample from the cooler and began the same process Jasper had followed, making certain that he used completely new equipment.

"You're not to help in any way unless I ask you to, understood?" said Dr. Sabastien, looking at Jasper.

Jasper nodded his head inside the helmet.

Jasper was impressed by Dr. Sabastien's lab skills, as most senior research scientists spend very little time actually conducting the day-to-day analyses so their techniques deteriorate over time. Dr. Sabastien was extremely efficient and completed the extraction procedures in half the time it took Jasper. Dr. Sabastien set the timer for one half-hour on the incubator and placed the sample inside. They then moved to the DNA Sequencing Lab.

"Turn on the sequencer and retrieve your file."

Jasper did as he was told without conversation.

"Click on the 'Check Sequence' icon," was Dr. Sabastien's next command.

Jasper had only used this function once before as part of a training exercise when he was learning to use the equipment. It was a built-in function of the DNA sequencer that could automatically conduct a scan of the DNA data to check for errors. It only indicated if the machine was operating correctly and if nothing failed in the analysis. It couldn't identify errors in the digestion or extraction procedures.

"Will this take long because the original sequence of the sample took nearly six hours to complete?" asked Jasper.

"Six hours? It shouldn't have taken more than an hour," said Dr. Sabastien loud enough that Jasper heard him without the communication system. "Why didn't you tell me this?"

"I was going to, but when it finally finished, it was late and you'd left early," Jasper replied sheepishly.

"The check should take less than an hour," Dr. Sabastien stated again.

Jasper glanced at the clock on the wall, which indicated it was just after eight a.m.—Toni would arrive soon.

"Dr. Sabastien," Jasper interrupted him from the sequencer screen, where he was watching the program results. "Is Toni coming to work today?"

"When he does, I'll speak to him," was all Dr. Sabastien said when they both noticed the light on the incubator timer flashing in the Extraction Lab. Dr. Sabastien stood up from the sequencer terminal and retrieved the digested sample. Jasper was unsure if he should prepare an injection syringe for injecting the sample into the sequencer, so he remained near the instrument, waiting for Dr. Sabastien's return.

The transition room door slid open as soon as Dr. Sabastien walked back into the DNA Sequencing Lab, and Tonino started making his way in. He connected his snorkel together and greeted them.

"*Buon giorno*. What brings you to the lab so early this morning, *Professore* Sabastien?"

"Jasper told me about the trouble he had sequencing the new artifact. He said it took six hours to run, so I offered to lend him a hand, seeing how promising this artifact is," he said with an air of sarcasm that was even detectable over the communication system.

"How can I help?" asked Tonino.

"We're about to inject a new sample, can you start cleaning the Extraction Lab?" replied Dr. Sabastien, obviously trying to keep Tonino out of the Sequencing Lab.

"Sure," Tonino said and he left for the Extraction Lab.

Dr. Sabastien prepared a syringe for injecting the sample without any of the trouble Jasper had. He drew up the new sample and injected it into the second sequencer sitting on the bench across from the one Jasper had used. He entered 'New analysis' on the command terminal and proceeded back to the lab bench. He retrieved a second syringe and needle and repeated the same procedure with the sample Jasper had prepared on Monday.

Dr. Sabastien injected this sample into the same sequencer Jasper had used and entered 'Re-analysis' on the command terminal. This was the only means to be certain Jasper hadn't contaminated the artifact itself, for if he had, there was no way for Dr. Sabastien to dispose of it without attracting attention from the VSS.

"Won't it take six hours?" asked Jasper, concerned over how long they may be waiting.

"It's a re-analysis, should certainly be less than an hour," responded Dr. Sabastien.

They waited in silence for the sequencers to complete the analyses as Tonino finished cleaning the other lab. Never before had Jasper felt awkward around Dr. Sabastien, but this silence wasn't normal—for either of them. The silence was short lived, much to Jasper's delight, when Tonino's voice beamed into their helmets.

"Have the analyses finished yet?" he asked as he entered the Sequencing Lab.

"Nothing yet, and we were just about to start cleaning this lab ourselves," Dr. Sabastien replied.

Dr. Sabastien stood from his seat just as the other sequencer, the one analyzing the new sample, flashed 'Analysis Complete.' The three of them moved directly in view of the screen and watched as Dr. Sabastien saved the file to a flash drive. Once the file finished saving, he removed the flash drive from the sequencer and walked back to the other machine to monitor its progress. The screen still showed the 'Analysis In Progress,' so they collected the dirty equipment for cleaning. Tonino returned to his chores, cleaning the equipment and allowing Dr. Sabastien to delete the file on the sequencer unnoticed.

"Dr. Sabastien, are you going to begin the database search?" asked Tonino while Jasper remained silent.

"I'll wait for the second sample to finish so we can run them at the same time," responded Dr. Sabastien, trying to buy some additional time.

Jasper speculated that Dr. Sabastien hoped they would finish cleaning the lab before the analyses were complete. This would allow them to return to their offices, keeping Tonino clear of what he was doing. This wasn't the case, as a moment later, the second sequencer screen flashed 'Analysis complete.' The three of them walked over to the second terminal and watched as Dr. Sabastien repeated the file saving procedure.

Jasper was impressed at how well Dr. Sabastien knew the sequencing process, as he was exactly right in his estimate on how long a 're-analysis' would take. Unable to see his face inside the isolation suit, Jasper could only guess that Dr. Sabastien was disappointed they didn't get the work completed before Tonino arrived. It was no secret to Jasper; Dr. Sabastien tried his best not to run the database with Tonino present. Jasper thought, *How is he going to explain to him why we aren't running the database without raising suspicion?*

Dr. Sabastien didn't move his head from the screen while he saved the file. The isolation suit constricted his peripheral vision so he was unaware that Tonino had walked over to the computer and signed in.

Tonino worked on the computer for only a few seconds more before he spoke over the communication system. "I have begun the database search."

"What?" shouted Dr. Sabastien, unmistakably angered. He turned in his seat to see Tonino still working on the computer with his back to him.

"Why did you do that?" he shouted while walking to the computer with Jasper following him.

"I thought that's what you said a moment ago. You wanted to wait until we had both samples analyzed. When I saw the second sample finish, I started the database search while you were backing the file onto a flash drive. Is this a problem, *Professore* Sabastien?" asked Tonino, not understanding the reason for his out-of-character reaction.

Silence filled their helmets, broken only by the sound of their own breathing.

Dr. Sabastien responded in a much more subdued tone. "No, but I was going to run these on my PC in my office since Jasper found this to be much faster than using the Vatican network system."

Jasper could only imagine what Dr. Sabastien's face looked like after he had gone through all the effort to make sure there was no trace of the results on Jasper's PC. Jasper couldn't see his face, as Dr. Sabastien was leaning over Tonino's shoulders while he worked on the computer.

"That's not the case at all, but the opposite," Tonino replied.

"The Vatican network should be hundreds of times faster than running it offline. The network system in this facility is part of the Vatican Secret Service, which uses the most powerful supercomputers available. We should see the results at any moment."

No sooner had Tonino spoken the words than the computer screen displayed 'No match found' for sample 'A.'

"Which was sample 'A'?" asked Jasper, unable to contain himself.

"The one from the second sequencer," said Tonino as he turned in his seat and pointed to the machine Dr. Sabastien had used to analyze the new sample he had prepared.

Moments later, the screen displayed a second message 'Error in processing sample B.' In a bid to derail any further attempts by Tonino to 'help' him with the database search, Dr. Sabastien tried to take control of the computer terminal from him.

"Let me take a look."

Tonino didn't move from the seat, as he was still unaware of Dr. Sabastien's attempts to remove him from further involvement.

"I have seen this before; I can fix it," he said and didn't move from the computer.

Dr. Sabastien was forced to allow him to continue or raise too much suspicion. Tonino clicked the mouse a few times, and the program began processing again, but this time it only lasted a few seconds when 'Sample contaminated' appeared on the screen.

"What's this? I have never seen this before," said Tonino as he made a few more clicks with the mouse so the screen produced a three-dimensional model of a DNA molecule.

To the untrained eye, it looked like two sets of railroad tracks, one in red and the other in green, destroyed by a very intense explosion, causing the red and green tracks to crisscross randomly. In contrast, a normal DNA molecule would look like a perfectly formed railroad track gently spiraling in three dimensions down the screen.

"Tonino, something must have gone wrong in the extraction step when Jasper prepared this sample. It is obviously no good, and we can delete this one and dispose of the sample. After all, it was his first time using the lab, so it is understandable."

A boiling feeling rose inside Jasper, bubbling up to the very edge of his tolerance. He knew he had completed the extraction process a thousand times before, and it had nothing to do with this. *Why blame me?* he thought angrily.

Jasper was no longer able to stand there in complete

silence and began to erupt, especially since Dr. Sabastien had refused to tell him what was going on. He clenched his teeth so hard his jaw muscles ached under the tension, but he stayed silent.

"Wait, *Professore* Sabastien, I think I see something," Tonino exclaimed.

He clicked the mouse frantically, and within a few seconds the screen split down the middle, displaying two perfectly normal but different DNA molecules, one in red on the right and one in green on the left.

"There, the sample was contaminated," Tonino pointed to the screen with his gloved finger. "These are two completely different DNA molecules; this is why we got the error."

He clicked the mouse a couple more times and the screen split in three. A third blue-colored DNA molecule appeared. All three were normal-looking DNA molecules.

"*Mio Dio*! This is astonishing. They're identical!"

The blue DNA molecule from the sample prepared by Dr. Sabastien was identical to the green one prepared by Jasper.

"You're right, *Professore*, Jasper's sample was contaminated. Likely thousands of years ago, and it was just bad luck he scraped the wrong part of the artifact."

Relief lifted Jasper's spirits like he hadn't felt since finishing exams, as this explained everything; it was all just a mistake. He waited with anticipation to hear Dr. Sabastien's voice confirm this to be the case, but there was nothing but silence. Jasper turned to face the doctor when he spoke.

"Excellent, we can wrap this up and start fresh," Dr. Sabastien said simply.

"We can re-start the search now the samples have been separated," said Tonino, still working at the computer.

Before Dr. Sabastien could say anything, Tonino clicked the mouse and the database search began. Instantly the words 'No match found' appeared on the screen next to the two identical DNA samples. The third sample was processing when Dr. Sabastien, still standing directly behind Tonino, tapped Jasper on the left arm. Jasper looked at him and watched as his right hand pressed the number two button on his suit. He nodded to tell Jasper to do the same. Jasper did and instantly heard Dr. Sabastien barking commands at him.

"Jasper, don't speak, just listen to me carefully. We only have a few seconds. You need to leave at once. Leave the Vatican, leave Rome as fast as you can, don't stop or speak to anyone until you get to Rocca Sinibalda. Trust no one, do you understand?"

"Why... what are you talking about?"

"Shut up and listen to me!" Dr. Sabastien continued. "Your life is in grave danger. If you want to live, you must do as I tell you. Go to Castello di Rocca Sinibalda and find the man with eyes just like yours; he's one of us. Understand? Don't speak to anyone else."

"Where, Rocca... what? My eyes? One of who? What are you talking about?"

"Jasper, it's imperative. Listen to me—everything depends on this! Castello di Rocca Sinibalda! Go!" he said forcefully.

"This is fucking nuts! I want to know what's going on!"

"Just get going! There isn't any more time," pleaded Dr. Sabastien.

Jasper could see Tonino had stood up and was trying to talk to them but hadn't realized they had changed communication channels. His face was filled with confusion, and it looked as though he was talking, but the isolation suit muffled his voice.

Jasper frantically unzipped his suit. In his haste, he forgot to disconnect the snorkel, so it remained hanging from the ceiling as though someone was still in it.

In his rush to get out of the suit, Jasper didn't open the front wide enough, and the hair on the back of his head became entangled in the zipper, instantly exposing his birthmark.

The instant Tonino saw the mark, shock filled his face. Tonino's voice rang clear, yelling from inside his isolation suit. "*La Convergenza*—It is you!"

Dr. Sabastien had removed the top portion of his suit to free his hands and untangle Jasper's hair. As soon as Jasper was free, he stood face to face with Tonino, who was still in his suit. Astonishment glazed Tonino's face, and he was momentarily frozen in place. Jasper turned his eyes for a second from Tonino to peer down at the computer screen; he whispered the words aloud as he read them.

"Sample match."

The moment his eyes focused on the bottom of the screen, his body began to shake uncontrollably and his stomach convulsed. The words read in large bold text: "Artifact #132 (Grail) + Reference DNA Sample #47 (Dr. Jasper Stewart)—positive match."

"I've never touched the Grail. It's a mistake," protested Jasper.

"Run, Jasper!" shouted Dr. Sabastien while removing the rest of his suit.

Tonino's face rapidly changed to a pasty shade of white, and he reached for the communication panel on his suit.

Jasper's face also changed instantaneously from the flush red brought on by the stress of Dr. Sabastien's request to chalk white. His legs felt like jelly, and his stomach curled into a knot as they both realized his DNA was an identical match to DNA found on the Holy Grail.

CHAPTER 22

BERNARDO'S SCOOTER

D r. Sabastien disappeared, Tonino disappeared, the entire lab faded away, leaving just the words on the computer screen etched in Jasper's mind.

Frozen in time, Jasper tried to move, but his mind wouldn't allow it. His body continued to ignore his every command. It may have been seconds or hours that passed before Jasper realized he wasn't moving. Dr. Sabastien opened his suit and was yelling a few inches from Jasper's face.

"Jasper, Jasper! Go! Get out of here right now! They'll be here any second. You're not safe!"

"Okay," Jasper responded, barely able to form the words as he continued to stare at the screen.

Dr. Sabastien gave Jasper a stern shake to pull his attention back to reality and the urgency of the moment.

"I'm going!" Jasper turned and ran for the lab door.

"Wait, Jasper, this is paramount; don't speak to anyone—I mean anyone—unless you see them with your own eyes," Dr. Sabastien reiterated as Jasper fled from the lab.

Jasper ran to the suit-up area and put his shoes on. The wait for the elevator invited further anxiety as well as the opportunity to speculate about what was happening in the lab. *Is Toni part of this, and who am I running from? Are they arguing or even fighting right now?* He hated not knowing anything; where he was going, how he was to get there or who he could speak to. "*Don't speak to anyone unless you see them with your own eyes?*" *What the hell does that mean?* Jasper thought when the elevator door opened.

He made his way to the office level and darted down the hall. He headed towards the front doors, but instinct pulled him to a halt; through the glass doors, the unmistakable black shape of Father Derksen appeared, approaching the front of the building. He was running up the steps flanked by two other men in suits. Dr. Sabastien was right; somebody already knew—the VSS.

Certain this wasn't someone he wanted to see, Jasper ducked into the first empty office he could find directly across from the reception area.

Alica was at her desk and noticed his uncharacteristic behavior. She looked directly at him first, then at the three men entering the building. Jasper put his finger to his lips, making the gesture for her not to give his location away, and he hid behind the open door of the office, listening as Father Derksen spoke to Alica. His tone was aggressive, and Jasper only understood two words of their very short conversation: 'Sabastien' and 'Stewart.'

The fading sound of their shoes clicking on the marble floor indicated that the men were walking down the hall toward the elevator. Jasper peered from behind the door to find Alica visibly shook up. Her blank expression told Jasper that his instinct was correct and he had made the correct decision to avoid the priest. Jasper nodded his head to the right in a wordless effort to ask Alica if the coast was clear. She nodded back and Jasper resumed his escape from the building.

Jasper had just pulled the front door open when he saw two more men approach the entrance. These men were clearly part of the VSS, but Jasper had no choice but to continue his exit from the building as a sudden course change would be a dead giveaway. He took the chance that these two men were uninformed of who they were looking for. He held his breath and opened the door for them as they walked into the building, the skin-tone earpieces clearly visible in their ears.

"*Prego*," said the larger of the two men as they passed through the door.

Jasper offered them a polite gesture and began walking as fast as he could into the square.

A typical lunchtime crowd filled the St. Peter's Square as swarms of tourists took photos, read their guidebooks and ate their lunches. Jasper had no idea where he was going or how to get there. The only thing he was sure of was that he had to get out of Rome. Out of habit, he found himself walking across the square to *Café Piazza*, although today he was nearly running.

Dodging in and out of the tightly formed packs of Japanese tourists following their guide, Jasper caught sight of an opening. The shouts of the tour guides and voices of the tourists didn't keep Jasper from hearing his name.

"*Professore* Stewart!" shouted the voice.

The voice continued to get louder above the crowd.

"*Signore, aspetta! Signore, aspetta!*" the voice shouted.

Jasper was afraid to turn and look, knowing this would only slow him down so he continued walking, just shy of a run. He heard the same voice shouting again, but this time it was much closer.

"*Signore Stewart! Aspeta per favore*—Stop, *Professore* Stewart!"

Jasper couldn't resist. He turned his head to find the two men he opened the door for at the VGP building running toward him only a hundred feet back. Jasper immediately broke into a sprint.

He scanned the square for a place to lose the men, but there was nowhere to hide. He weaved in and out of the tourists trying desperately to lose them, but it was futile; Jasper could feel them gaining on him.

Faces in the crowd locked on Jasper, watching the spectacle unfold as if it were a movie set. Looking to his right,

Jasper spotted a large flock of pigeons shuffling across the pavement following two small boys who were feeding them. He turned to the right, running straight through the middle of the flock. The mass of birds scattered at his feet before taking flight, flying directly into the faces of the men, slowing their progress for a few crucial seconds. It was enough time for Jasper to get out of the square.

Not knowing anywhere else to run, Jasper darted across the street to *Café Piazza*. Standing in front of the café, Jasper found Bernardo's scooter, still idling. With only a split second to decide, he jumped on the scooter and tore off down the sidewalk. Jasper had driven only a few yards when he heard a voice yelling at him and three or four loud popping sounds.

"*Aspeta, aspeta—Ladro*!" Bernardo yelled.

People on the sidewalk and walking in the street jumped into open storefronts and behind parked cars. The popping sound wasn't the scooter backfiring; it was gunfire.

"Holy shit! These guys are trying to kill me. Dr. Sabastien was right!" Jasper said aloud.

Jasper opened the throttle on the scooter and made his way off the sidewalk onto the road. The wind rushed through his hair as his eyes began to water. He hadn't been on a motorcycle since he was a teenager. He focused his attention on the chaotic traffic Rome was so famous for.

Jasper kept driving, getting as far from the Vatican as he possibly could. Still, he had no idea where he was going; he had to find a map. He remembered the map in his flat when it occurred to him where he got it: the train station tourist information booth.

Jasper searched in vain for a train station, narrowly missing cars and pedestrians as he weaved through the traffic. The exhaust combined with the midday heat began to take its toll, and a lightheaded, dizzy sensation floated through his head. Unable to focus as the scooter handlebars loosened in his grip, Jasper knew he had to stop as the muscles in his gut rolled and tightened. His stomach felt like he had been drinking all night. The stress of being chased and shot at was too much of a shock, and he had to stop.

Jasper found the first place he could park the scooter and jumped off. Not able to hold it down any longer, the acid started burning his throat on the way to the back of his mouth. He bent down behind the scooter and threw up. The cascade of events resulted in total exhaustion; his legs no longer had the strength to hold his weight, and he fell to his knees. Jasper continued to heave for another minute until there was nothing left but dry heaves.

Panting like a dog from the pain in his stomach, he had trouble catching his breath. He sat on the ground behind the scooter, unsure if anyone had seen the condition he was in, and remained there until the lightheadedness cleared a little.

He lifted his body to his feet, leaning against the scooter for support. Finding a map was no longer his priority, what he needed was a glass of water and a toothbrush.

Just down the block from where he stopped, he could see a pair of elderly men sitting on two old wooden chairs around a small oval table. Jasper walked toward them, and as he approached, he could see they were sipping espresso, the aroma of roasting coffee beans filling the air from a café behind them. Jasper walked into the café displaying none of his normal hesitation, marched directly to the counter and ordered.

"San Pellegrino," he said.

The young Italian woman behind the counter handed him a bottle of water.

"*Due Euro, per favore*," said the woman.

Jasper paid her and started to walk back to the door when he spotted three computers in the back of the room—it was an Internet café. He walked back to the counter and began gesturing as if he was typing.

"Computer," he said.

"*Si, due Euro per dieci minuti*," the woman responded.

"*Grazie*," said Jasper, and he walked to the back of the café, sitting in front of a computer to begin searching the web.

He started typing the letters of the Italian words Dr. Sabastien had told him. He made his best attempt to spell them phonetically in hopes Google's search field would find what he was looking for. In his first attempt he tried 'Rockabaldo' and versions of this spelling, but this got him nothing even close. He continued to type as many versions as he could. His frustration mounted when he remembered there is no letter 'K' in the Italian alphabet.

Jasper retyped 'Rocabalda' and this time the screen filled with hits. It was the last hit on the page which caught his attention—'Rocca Sinibalda'. *That's it*; he thought but had no way of knowing for sure. Jasper clicked on the webpage and up popped a photo of a beautiful sand-colored castle with an Italian caption reading *'Castello di Rocca Sinibalda, Rieti, Lazio.'*

Jasper selected the entire article and copied it for translation. The translation was slow, and it took a few minutes before Jasper could read it. Scanning the poorly translated English, Jasper found exactly what he was looking for—a map. The article described the location of the castle: 50 kilometers northeast of Rome near the city of Rieti in the Region of Lazio. This had no meaning to him; Jasper wasn't even sure which way was north. Using MapQuest, he found driving directions from the Vatican to Castello di Rocca Sinibalda. The Vatican was the only starting point he could think of since he knew he wasn't far from there. He printed out the directions.

Jasper stayed at the computer trying to remember everything Dr. Sabastien said to him. *Why me?* Was all Jasper could think of. Nothing made any sense to him, but the danger was real, more real than anything he could have imagined.

Great, I've the location but no idea which way to go, he thought as he began to leave the café. *Screw this! I'm asking for help.*

He stopped just before the door, turned and started to walk back to the counter to ask the woman for directions. Knowing he didn't stand a chance of getting the Italian right, he took the map out. He folded it in such a way as to hide his final destination but still showed enough of the roads that he could point to where he was heading.

"Excuse me," he said as he approached the counter and placed the map on top of it.

The woman responded with a polite "Si," and smiled.

She noticed the map Jasper was pointing at and came to see if she could help. After three attempts to give him directions, she took a pen from below the counter and drew them with arrows on the map.

"*Gracie*," said Jasper and left the café without getting anything to eat; his stomach was still too unstable for food. He got back on the scooter and took one last look at the directions. He committed Rieti to memory so when he saw it on a road sign he would know he was driving in the right direction.

The traffic in Rome was like nothing he had seen before. The closest he had come to traffic like this at home was trying to exit the Joe Louis Arena parking lot after a Red Wings game. Cars were everywhere, and it seemed like none of them were moving. The only traffic getting through were other people riding scooters. They dodged in and out of the traffic at unbelievable speeds with no notice by the cars. Only after the twentieth scooter passed him did he decide to drive like the rest of the Italians. He snaked through the parking lot of cars on the road like moving through the trees of an Okanagan orchard. Each traffic light he came to reminded him of a starting line at a Formula One race. The cars and scooters jockeyed for position only to race to the next traffic light and start the race again.

After an hour's driving through the worst of what Rome had to offer, Jasper finally escaped the craziness and got out of the city. Both green and brown hillsides appeared in front of him like a massive tapestry contrasting the stone walls of the Vatican.

The countryside was filled with farms, vineyards and olive groves. Perched atop every hill was a village, connected by a winding road that sliced through the vineyards. The air was filled with the scent of citrus blossoms. The peacefulness of the countryside was only briefly interrupted by the many small villages along the way. Here the sounds and smells were similar to Rome with one exception, the smell of coffee from roadside cafés provided relief from the car exhausts so dominant in Rome.

Jasper followed the map, sticking to Via Salaria, labeled as SS-4 on the occasional road sign. He was driving into the town of Poggio San Lorenzo when the fuel light came on. The calmness of the country drive evaporated, leaving a more familiar feeling of panic. Not knowing how long he had, Jasper began frantically looking for a gas station. He rode all the way through the small village in an effort to find one. He couldn't risk going any further, so he returned to the center of the village. He cruised slowly up and down the narrow cobblestone lanes, knowing it would be unlikely a gas station would be located in such a lightly traveled area. Finally, Jasper was left with no choice but to ask someone. He drove back to the main street and pulled up to the front of a small café to ask for help.

Sitting at a table on the sidewalk were four men drinking coffee and watching a soccer game on an old TV inside the café. The volume on the TV was turned so high that Jasper had to shout.

"Excuse me," he said while still seated on the scooter a few meters from the men.

None of the men looked as they carried on watching the game. Jasper repeated himself but this time louder.

"Excuse me, *signore!*"

Two of the men turned their heads to look at Jasper and then returned to watching the game. Jasper had no choice but to get off his scooter and walk over to the men. He placed the scooter on its kickstand and walked up to the table.

"Excuse me, *signore*. Gas Station... Petrol?" The man closest to Jasper turned his head and looked at him.

"American?" he asked through a thick Italian accent.

"No, Canadian. You speak English?"

"Yes, not so well," he replied.

"Is there a gas station in town?"

"Yes, but it is not open right now," replied the man, who followed his answer with a small laugh.

"When will it open?" asked Jasper, not understanding the humor in his question.

Jasper watched as the man nudged another man to his right and spoke in Italian to him.

"Flavio will open at half time," he replied with another laugh.

Jasper looked at the TV to see how much time was left in the soccer game—1:35. A few minutes later, the whistle blew and the first half of the game ended. The English-speaking man pointed to another man, who finished his coffee and stood up. Then he pointed to a small car parked on the opposite side of the street..

"Follow him."

Jasper jumped back on his scooter and drove it to the other side of the street directly behind the car.

The man, who was presumably Flavio, got in his car and drove up the road a short distance. He then made a right off the main street and drove another short distance before making a second right turn. Flavio pulled into a small gas station that only had a single gas pump and stopped his car a few meters from the pump, leaving it running. Jasper pulled next to the pump and shut the scooter off. Flavio held the gas pump in his hand and waited for Jasper to open the gas tank, but Jasper had no idea where it was.

"*Su su, andiamo,*" said Flavio in an obvious rush to return to the soccer game.

Jasper couldn't see anywhere to put the gas. He was beginning to feel quite embarrassed, knowing Flavio was in a hurry to get back to his game. After a few more seconds of waiting, Flavio turned the ignition key of the scooter to the left, causing a popping sound from the seat, and using his free hand, he lifted the seat up and pointed to the gas tank.

Jasper's face flushed as he filled it with a stupid smile, indicating his lapse of memory as to where the gas tank was.

Just as Flavio turned the pump on, the sound of church bells shattered the air of the tiny village. It wasn't until he heard the bells that Jasper noticed the old stone church across the street. The three-story bell tower was so close its shadows covered them. The bells continued to sound as Flavio filled the scooter with gas; it was so loud nothing else could be heard. Jasper watched the old wooden church doors open, and a few elderly Italian women walked out followed closely by a priest.

The priest, only a few meters from Jasper, caused the hair on his arms to stand up. The man was wearing the same sort of robes the Vatican priests wore—a long black robe tied at the waist with a bright red rope. This image snapped Jasper back to reality—Father Derksen and the trouble he was in.

Dr. Sabastien's words ran through his mind, particularly the part about not talking to anyone.

The priest finished saying good-bye to the afternoon parishioners, kissing them on each cheek while shaking their hands. The priest followed the last of the parishioners down the front steps as he gave his parting words and stopped. He didn't return to the church but stood for a moment staring directly at Jasper.

Silence suddenly returned to the village as the bells stopped ringing. From the gas station, Jasper could see the priest's face, wrinkled and weathered, like an old car seat, and he had dark black eyes. The priest continued to stare for a second longer until Flavio tossed him a wave as he removed the gas pump from the scooter. The priest waved back and then turned swiftly, causing his robe to swirl in the air in exactly the same manner as Father Derksen's.

It might have been the swirling robe or the eyes, but the little voice inside Jasper's head screamed at him to get going. Flavio held up seven fingers.

"Thanks, I mean *grazie*," Jasper said as he handed Flavio a ten-Euro note, not waiting for his change.

He got back on the main road, traveling toward the city of Rieti. His eyes strained with every road sign in an effort to find Via Salaria Vecchia or the village of Ornaro Basso. The signage on the secondary roads was nearly nonexistent. Even when he did find one, it was so old and weather-faded Jasper had to stop to read it. He finally spotted a sign indicating two kilometers to Ornaro Basso, so he pulled off the road to check his map.

Jasper found his way onto Via Salaria Vecchia and headed for Capannaccia. The road narrowed and gained elevation as it twisted and turned through the vineyard-covered hillside. The scene reminded him of the many car commercials he saw of a flashy convertible sports car racing around the blind hairpin turns. There was very little traffic on the road, and when Jasper met oncoming vehicles, there was barely enough room for the scooter to pass. *No cheating the corners here*, he thought, as the curves were so tight a head-on collision was a sure thing.

Things were going well when he left the tiny village of Capannaccia and headed for Convento, the last spot marked on the map before Rocca Sinibalda. His best guess had him no more than five kilometers from there when he spotted a car in his handlebar mirror. It was an average-looking small red car with dark tinted windows. Jasper wouldn't have even noticed it except it was the only car on the road. It was also coming up behind him quickly. Normally this was no reason to be concerned based on his first day driving in Italy, but this was no ordinary day, and the pit in his stomach told Jasper things were about to take a turn for the worse.

He rode as fast as he could. His experience on dirt bikes gave him a great advantage in navigating the hairpins and steep roads, but the scooter was no match for a car. His best estimate gave him thirty seconds before the car would catch up.

Jasper looked desperately for an escape route. He assessed every driveway, side road and path he passed, but none of them offered an escape.

The tension grew as he clenched his teeth, his hands welded to the handlebars. A quick glance in the mirror brought him back to the steep gravel roads of the Okanagan with Greg hard on his tail. The race to the finish line just around the corner meant he could leave nothing in the tank.

His next look in his mirror brought Jasper back to his immediate peril. The brief glimpse gave him a view of the two men in the car, leaving no doubt in his mind of their intent. They could have been clones of the guys who chased him in St. Peter's Square, and now they were three yards behind him. The roar of the car engine filled his ears as the squeal of rubber grew closer. Jasper braced himself for the impact.

The car accelerated to a few inches from the back of the scooter when Jasper leaned hard to the right, causing the scooter to move onto the gravel shoulder. The scooter fishtailed violently in the soft gravel, leaving a cloud of rocks and dust to shower down on the windshield the car. The driver momentarily lost sight of Jasper, allowing him to regain a small lead.

The car quickly regained its position behind Jasper and once again increased its speed to ram the back of the scooter. Jasper saw no other option than to leave the road. He repeated another hard right turn, but this time he launched the scooter off of the road. Jasper and the scooter took air for about ten feet before landing hard. The impact travelled through Jasper, leaving him with the feeling his kidneys had burst. He had landed in the first row of a large olive grove, and to his own astonishment, he hadn't crashed the scooter.

His amazement was short lived, as the car followed him off the road. Jasper was able to maneuver the scooter through the trees so he was no longer racing down the first row but the next row over. The spacing between the trees was too small for the car to fit, so this kept the driver from further attempts at running Jasper over.

They kept pace with Jasper as they raced parallel with the road. The passenger window lowered and Jasper saw a gun. The passenger leveled it and fired at Jasper. In an instinctive move, one he had completed a thousand times, Jasper slammed on the back brake of the scooter, causing it to instantly slide sideways and come to a stop. The driver followed suit and slammed on his brakes. The weight of the car was no match for the scooter, and the car continued to slide for another fifty feet; the grass they were driving on gave them no traction. Jasper snapped the throttle of the scooter and made his way back onto the paved road, having no other alternative.

It only took about five seconds for the car to follow. Having run out of options, Jasper knew in the next few seconds the scooter would launch itself from below him and the impact of the car would kill him. With the car less than three feet away, Jasper leaned hard to the left and took a chance to 'cheat' the corner. The scooter crossed the pavement and switched to the opposite side of the road.

A blaze of bright yellow suddenly filled his vision. He turned the scooter as hard as he could to avoid the oncoming vehicle. In the instant the yellow car passed, Jasper peered through the windshield and saw the face of the driver. The face stayed etched in his mind, and he recognized the driver. It was the nun who had nursed him in the Vatican clinic. Her eyes were unmistakable; they connected with his as they passed. Her car accelerated as it passed, barely avoiding him on the right.

Jasper heard no screeching tires, only a thunderous crash. The sound of breaking glass and buckling metal was deafening even over the noise of the scooter. Jasper didn't stop; he couldn't, not even slow down. Disbelief overwhelmed him, like watching a tornado approach, leaving Jasper feeling nothing—he was numb.

He continued down the winding road, peering into his mirror for a second to witness a cloud of deep black smoke billowing up into the cloudless blue sky.

CHAPTER 23

TEMPLUM

Jasper couldn't drive any farther and pulled off the road, parking the scooter in a vineyard. He lay down in the freshly mowed grass carpeting the ground between the rows of grapes. The smell reminded him of his childhood days playing in the orchards. The silence Jasper enjoyed was punctuated by the buzz of insects and the distant call of a crow.

Adrenalin rushed through his veins, making his senses more acute than they had ever been in his life. Everything moved in slow motion—the clouds drifted magically across the sky while the wind rustled the grape vines. The pounding in his chest subsided and he began to shake. The tremors began in his hands, spreading slowly up his arms until they flooded his entire body. It was a warm summer day but the shaking was uncontrollable, as if he had hypothermia. Emotions surged inside him like a tide, welling up to the point where he couldn't keep them from the surface. Water pooled in his eyes, filling them to the brink of overflowing. The warm liquid rolled from the corners and made a trail along the side of his face. He fought the inevitable, but he was no longer able to hold back his tears. Jasper couldn't remember the last time he had cried, but there was no strength left inside of him to prevent it.

The tears continued to roll down his face as he lay with his eyes closed, feeling the late afternoon sun warm him. It wasn't until he heard the distant sound of sirens that he regained some composure. It was at that point he realized what had caused his emotional breakdown—a combination of fear and frustration.

He had never known fear like this before. This was no ordinary fear but the kind of fear a twenty-five-year-old never thinks about—the fear of death. Like most males his age, he always considered himself invincible, like when jumping off the cliffs into Okanagan Lake or taking an extra-long leap off a snow cornice on Whistler Mountain while snowboarding—dying never entered his mind. Jasper's fear was aggravated by the frustration of knowing someone was trying to kill him—the VSS wanted him dead, and he didn't know why. More than anything, the not knowing infuriated him.

Jasper had never wavered in his belief; he alone was in control of his life. He had never questioned this and took responsibility for his life—there was no such thing as Divine Intervention.

Nothing could explain what was happening to him. His scientific background could not come close to explaining it. *How did the VSS find me so quickly?* It was humanly impossible to explain how the same nun who nursed him in Rome happened to be driving down the same road as him in the middle of Italy at the very moment he was about to be killed. Jasper's analytical mind struggled to make sense of what was unfolding around him. *I don't know what's happening to me.*

The late afternoon sun slipped behind the mountaintops before Jasper regained enough composure to drive. He mounted the scooter and read the map again. He was just outside of the village of Convento, placing him five kilometers from Rocca Sinibalda. Jasper took a closer look at the photo of the castle and started the scooter to make his way back to the pavement. Although anxious to get to his destination, the scooter's handlebars still shook in his hands, forcing him to keep his speed down.

He spotted a road sign indicating one kilometer to Rocca Sinibalda. There was no sign of a castle or even a village from the road, which crisscrossed through steep forest-covered slopes. Knowing he was almost there caused his chest to tighten; his heart wanted to burst with anxiety. The trembling in his hands had stopped, and he was suddenly filled with desire; the desire to get there was greater now than it had been all day, the desire to know why all this was happening. He wanted answers. Jasper was no longer prepared to continue blind to what was happening around him.

When he rounded the final turn in the road, his heart exploded with every beat when he saw the castle perched atop the hill. It was magnificent and surrounded by a village like jewels in a crown. He instantly recognized it from the photo and knew he had made it. Feelings of relief and anticipation swirled inside him, making the drive down the narrow main street of the village seem endless. He passed a church on his left followed by rows of stone and brick houses on both sides. The main street was very short, no longer than three hundred yards, and ended at the foot of the castle.

Jasper drove to the castle entrance and parked his scooter to the right of the massive dark brown wooden doors. The doors were ancient, at least fifteen feet high and flanked with black iron along the edges. He pushed on the door handle, but it didn't budge. Jasper took two steps back and stood looking at the massive doors.

"Now what?" he said aloud.

Knocking on the doors was futile; they were at least a foot thick. *There's got to be a way into this place*, he thought.

He walked around the perimeter of the castle walls, filled with frustration. *Why here? What makes this place so special? There must be a thousand castles like this in Italy*, he thought while continuing to look for a way in.

He walked up a long set of stairs which hung from the mountainside between the castle wall and a row of houses.

He didn't see anyone; the village and castle were deserted, which Jasper knew was a good thing since he couldn't speak to anyone. He continued as far as he could up the steps, hoping they would end at a back entrance, but they led to a dead end.

Anger rose inside him, fueled by his lack of progress. He jumped down the steps two at a time, making his way to the bottom in half the time it took him to climb to the top. Jasper stood in front of the massive doors and looked up the main street. An elderly couple left a building four doors down from him. Backed by his anger, the decision was easy—he was going to ask for help. Jasper walked to the building they had just left.

The windows of the stone building were completely covered with posters of local community events. The door was held open by an old wine press. Jasper coughed as his lungs filled with cigarette smoke, the stench indicating that he had entered some kind of bar. This was confirmed by a long counter lined with stools and a wall filled with liquor bottles.

The only people in the bar were the bartender talking to two old men smoking at the bar across from him. Jasper jumped as the men erupted in cheers. The TV hanging in the corner displayed a soccer game playing without the sound. To the right of him the bar opened into a slightly larger room which had half a dozen tables and chairs. Four teenage boys were playing an old pinball machine against the middle of the far wall.

Jasper's need to get answers prepared him for the inevitable difficulty he was about to encounter. He walked to the bar and addressed the men.

"Excuse me," he said, looking at the bartender.

"No English," the man replied.

Jasper continued.

"*Castello*," Jasper said, knowing this meant castle but not knowing how to say open.

The bartender responded, "*Castello e chiuso*," but Jasper had no idea what this meant. The bartender recognized Jasper's frown and desperate eyes as an indication that he had no idea of what he just said.

"*Steffano, vieni qua, subito*," yelled the bartender to the boys playing the pinball game. The smallest of the boys came running over to the bar.

"*Si, Papa*?" he replied in a high-pitched voice.

"*Inglese*," said the bartender and pointed to Jasper.

The boy walked over to Jasper.

"Can I help you, sir?" he asked.

"Yes, you speak English?"

"I study in school."

"You're doing very well. I'd like to visit the castle. Can you tell me when it opens?"

"The castle no open, sir. No visitors for many year." Jasper couldn't hide the disappointment from his face.

"Is there any way I can go inside? I've come a very long way to see this castle."

"*Mi dispiace, sir, no possible*. Castle closed for many years—no tourists."

"*Gracie*," said Jasper, and he walked out of the bar in complete frustration.

Jasper questioned himself, *Is this the place?* He walked back to the castle entrance, where he had left the scooter. He glanced across the street and saw the word '*Polizia*' written across the top of the last building on the street.

Indecision was new to Jasper, and he loathed it. His life was on the line, and he didn't know what to do. He had to get inside the castle. He wanted answers. Asking the police seemed like the right thing to do, but it could also be the worst thing to do. The VSS had no trouble finding him this afternoon, and now knowing their power was even greater than he imagined, going to the police could be sending a message directly to them.

Jasper walked up the sidewalk until he was directly across

the street from the police station. He paced back and forth, trying to decide what to do. Finally, after ten minutes, he decided to take the risk and ask for help. He crossed the street and began walking to the station when he passed a small bakery.

The smell of the fresh baked goods filled his nose, intoxicating him. He responded without reservation when an audible hunger pang erupted from his stomach. Jasper hadn't eaten all day, and it finally caught up with him. He peered through the window at the front of the bakery and eyed a piece of focaccia. Jasper opened the door, ducking his head as the bells hanging over the door rang, announcing his entrance to the shop.

"*Aspetta, uno momento,*" a man's voice shouted from the back.

Jasper waited without answering for the man to arrive. A few seconds later, a short man walked from the back of the shop with his arms filled with small square pastry boxes stacked so high Jasper couldn't see his face. He placed the boxes on the counter. The man appeared to be forty years old with a well-trimmed beard peppered with flour, which matched his full head of brown hair.

Jasper's eyes met the shopkeeper's and instantly a tingling sensation ran through his body.

"Do you speak..." but before Jasper could finish his sentence, the shopkeeper cut him off.

"We've been expecting you, Jasper."

"How do you know my name?" he asked as his hunger quickly vanished and turned to fear. *I should run*, was all Jasper could think of at the moment, but then he noticed the shopkeeper's eyes. The possibility of finally getting some answers all of a sudden seemed closer.

"Animus told us you were coming."

"Who?" asked Jasper.

"You know him as Dr. Jean Sabastien."

This is starting to sound like some kind of cult, Jasper

thought as he scanned the bakery for other signs of weirdness.

"Don't be concerned. Right now we must get to the castle before you're seen."

"What do you mean 'seen?' I've already been seen in the bar asking for help to get into the castle."

"Who did you speak to?"

"I don't know... some locals," he replied in frustration.

"You must get inside the castle."

"How do you expect us to get in that place when it looks like it was built to withstand a medieval rebellion?"

"Did you speak to anyone else?

"No, that's it."

"Good, follow me."

"Where are we going?

The man looked at him as if Jasper didn't understand his English. "We are going..."

"I know, to the castle," Jasper snapped.

"Good, you understand."

"What's your name?"

"Matteo."

"Before I take one step farther, I want some answers."

"Dr. Sabastien will tell you everything. Right now, it's most important we get to the castle before anyone sees you."

"The castle," repeated Jasper as his patience grew thin and he thought, *I was nearly killed getting to the fucking castle. What's so important about the castle?*

Matteo locked the front door to his shop and flipped the sign hanging in the window. Jasper followed him through the back of the shop filled with the prospect of finally getting some answers. The back of the shop had two rows of counters filled with Italian pastries and breads, reigniting Jasper's hunger.

"Matteo, can I have one?" asked Jasper as he pointed to a tray of chocolate-covered pastries sprinkled with powdered sugar.

"Yes, take what you like but don't stop. There'll be plenty to eat at the castle."

They stepped out the back door of the bakery into a small, cobblestoned lane. Matteo locked the bakery door, and they began walking up the steep slope. The sun had left the sky, and the bluish grey hue of twilight lit their way. The sound of their footsteps bounced off the backs of the buildings lining the winding alleyway. The steepness of the route combined with the two chocolate pastries in his mouth forced Jasper to breathe as if he was in the last seconds of a marathon. Lucky for him the castle was close.

They followed the perimeter of the same immense stone wall Jasper tried earlier, but this time from the opposite side. The walkway curved around the back of the castle and terminated at another ancient wooden door about half the size of the one at the main entrance. Matteo pulled a key from his pocket and pushed it into the lock, opening the door. He signaled Jasper to go in.

When Jasper entered the door, he found himself in complete darkness. A vision formed in his mind of the halls of Hogwarts lit by torchlight and covered in spider webs. This quickly evaporated when Matteo clicked the light switch. The dull yellow light cast by the single bulb illuminated a large staircase winding upward out of sight. The walls were made of hand-cut stone blocks resulting in a rough texture. The ceiling looked to be twenty feet high, giving Jasper the impression he was in Joe Louis Arena making his way to a balcony seat.

Matteo led the way up the spiral stone steps to the top where they entered a large open chamber about the size of a school gym. The lighting resembled a darkened movie theatre as the dozen or so wall sconces barely cast enough illumination to see the ceiling. Jasper could see the first of the evening stars through the large open windows surrounding the far side of the ballroom.

"This way," Matteo said, and they began to cross the floor.

They walked towards a set of French doors directly across from them. Their footsteps echoed like the sound of horse hooves over cobblestone.

Jasper's eyes finally adjusted to the low lighting, and he got a better view of his surroundings. The walls were covered in huge tapestries, each depicting a different Biblical scene. When they reached the halfway point of the hall, Jasper peered toward the ceiling.

Awe brimmed out of him as he took a deep breath and gazed in astonishment. The ceiling was covered in a massive fresco. The most spectacular depiction of the Garden of Eden spanned the entire length of the ceiling. The word 'Templum' was written in large ancient lettering across the bottom. The point of view was from behind a young man and woman holding hands. They stood in the middle of the image facing a setting sun while gazing over a turquoise ocean. It was clear to Jasper they were Adam and Eve.

Suddenly, Jasper froze in his footsteps, his head locked upward. He stepped backwards to position himself directly under the two naked figures above him. Matteo continued to walk a few more steps, unaware he was alone.

"Jasper, what is it? Is there a problem?"

Jasper didn't answer but continued his upward stare. He was straining so hard to see the ceiling that his eyes began to water. He blinked and looked away as everything began to blur. His focus returned, and Jasper resumed his fixation on the ceiling; he had to be absolutely certain of what he saw.

After another moment of fixation, Jasper removed all his doubt. Depicted on the back of Adam's neck, exactly the same as his own, was a birthmark. Jasper moved his eyes to the painting of Eve. There, painted as clear as the one on the back of his own neck, was a birthmark—a mirror image of Adam's.

"Jasper, what's wrong?" Matteo insisted.

Jasper was oblivious to Matteo's question, his mind imprisoned by the image. He had seen this scene countless times, Adam and Eve in the Garden of Eden, but never like this. Jasper stumbled as his legs weakened from looking upwards for too long. He couldn't take his eyes off the ceiling. Matteo's voice echoed through the empty room and unlocked Jasper's stare.

"Are you all right?"

"What... no, I'm fine," he said, although he was anything but fine. "I just had to stop for a moment to admire the painting. Let's go."

"Yes, magnificent, isn't it! Hundreds of years old and one of the first we had painted," Matteo explained as they continued their walk toward the doors.

Jasper squinted after they left the massive hall, his eyes adjusting to the well-lit corridor. Matteo opened a door to their left, and they entered a much smaller room. Immediately Jasper felt it out of place; it was furnished like a modern office boardroom except for the long, thin ancient wooden table in the center. The surface was rough and grey, and it had a two-inch split in the top running down the edge of the left side.

Three large paintings hung on the left wall, but it was the right wall that caught Jasper's attention. The entire thirty feet was covered by a life-sized mural of the Last Supper. *It must be by the same artist*, he thought. The wall directly opposite Jasper was split into four large windows, each arched and glassless with fully opened solid wooden shutters. The evening breeze rushed through the room from the open door.

A thin, dark-haired man sat at the far end of the table staring blankly into the air. Jasper's entrance failed to interrupt his stare. A tall, blonde-haired man stood with his back to the doorway and continued to gaze out one of the windows. He too ignored their presence.

"Animus," Matteo said.

The tall man turned his body from the window, and Jasper recognized him at once. Dr. Sabastien's face filled with a large smile and obvious relief.

"Jasper, we're so happy you're safe," said Dr. Sabastien as

he began to walk toward Jasper.

"Safe?" repeated Jasper in anger. "I was nearly killed twice! Why are people trying to kill me?" He fought back tears when he repeated his last request, the pent-up emotions from the day's events flowed out from his body like a tide.

Dr. Sabastien pulled a chair from the table and put his hand to Jasper's shoulder in an attempt to guide him to a seat.

"Jasper, please sit…"

"I don't need to sit!" he shouted and brushed Dr. Sabastien's hand from his shoulder. "I need to know what's going on!"

"Please, Jasper. Sit down. I'll tell you, but you must remain calm."

"How can you expect me to be calm when people are trying to kill me?"

"I understand, but it's difficult to explain, and unless you're able to think clearly, you won't have a chance of understanding."

"Fine, I want to know everything," he said like a three-year-old being scolded.

"You will."

Jasper sat in the chair in front of the doctor at the end of the table. He grabbed the edge of the table and pulled himself closer so he could lean on his arm. Dr. Sabastien remained standing while Matteo took a seat at the far end of the table next to the other man.

"First, it is rude of me not to introduce you. You've met Matteo. This is Luca."

Luca nodded his head and smiled.

The two men were looking directly at Jasper, and it was impossible to ignore their eyes. Four identical crystal blue eyes stared back at Jasper—the same eyes as the nun's, Dr. Sabastien's, and his own.

CHAPTER 24

PRIMORIS AND VACARE

D r. Sabastien returned to the window and resumed his gaze into the evening light. It was obvious to Jasper he was looking for someone. Matteo and Luca sat at the table in silence while Dr. Sabastien spoke.

"Jasper, do you remember what happened before you left this morning?"

"How could I forget? Tonino finished the database scan of the sample I prepared and an error occurred. It matched the Holy Grail."

Dr. Sabastien turned from the window and faced Jasper.

"Exactly, but it wasn't an error," he said, looking straight at Jasper in expectation of a reaction. "They're a match and I knew it. I was desperately trying to delete the files and dispose of the sample."

"What are you talking about? How can they match? That artifact is more than two thousand years old."

"Your DNA and the DNA on the Grail are a match," he said while making sure he maintained eye contact with Jasper.

"That's impossible. I've never even seen the Grail, let alone touched it."

"You haven't, but your DNA has."

"What?"

"Come and look at this painting. Tell me what you see?" requested Dr. Sabastien as he moved toward the fresco.

Jasper got up from his seat and walked along the narrow

table toward the painting. While he stared at the image he thought, *I've got to be hallucinating.* The subtle differences in the artwork were like nothing he had ever seen before. At first glance, the image was like every other scene of the Last Supper, but as he analyzed the details more closely, he could see the image was filled with peculiarities.

All twelve disciples were portrayed with brilliant blue eyes, including the image of Christ. There was a woman standing behind Christ at the center of the table. Her eyes were blue, and she was holding the hand of Christ as it rested on his right shoulder. And if this wasn't strange enough, the most startling part of the image was that the woman was clearly pregnant.

"Obviously someone had a sense of humor when they painted this," Jasper stated.

"It is painted as it was," said Luca.

Jasper turned and looked at Luca and Matteo in disbelief but decided not to ask further questions and asked instead, "What does this have to do with me?"

"They are your ancestors," replied Dr. Sabastien, pointing to the image of Christ and the pregnant woman.

Jasper smiled with amusement, thinking it was some form of a joke as he made his way back to his chair. Looking at the others, he quickly realized no one else saw the humor in it.

"I know what you're suggesting, and it's not funny."

"Jasper, it wasn't meant to be funny. Can you explain how your DNA matched that found on the Grail?"

"Yeah, a computer error or a stupid prank, but it's not because I share the same DNA with..." Jasper cut his own sentence off, unable to say the words.

"Then why do you think these people are trying to kill you?"

"I don't know. You're supposed to tell me that. I think they suspect I tried to steal their priceless artifact," he replied, unable to hide his frustration.

"Jasper, I think you know that's not why. You know it. You

said it yourself—you've never even touched the Grail."

"Then why the hell are people trying to kill me?" he lashed out, unable to contain the anger rising within him.

"You have something far more valuable than an old cup—your DNA."

"What are you talking about? What about my DNA?"

Jasper leaned back in his chair and ran his hands through his hair in frustration. He paused for a moment then spoke. "Look, I don't understand anything you're talking about, but what I do get is that there are some people out there trying to kill me. And I don't have a fucking clue why! That's what you need to tell me!" he shouted.

"I am trying to," said Dr. Sabastien in a calm and fatherly manner. He paused for an instant as he took a seat next to Jasper, during which time Matteo got up and stood near the window and Luca went to the door. Jasper watched the men's movements but didn't want to delay getting the answers he desperately needed so he didn't ask why they were obviously guarding the room.

"I am an Animus," said Dr. Sabastien. He paused for a reaction but none came so he continued. "We are Primoris. The collective that created humans on earth in order to further expand existence throughout the universe."

"What the hell are you talking about?" snapped Jasper, taken completely off guard by what he just heard.

"It's impossible for anyone to truly describe what Primoris is—it can only be experienced. I think the simplest way to explain what Primoris is, is to think of it as consciousness; the purest form of energy in existence."

"Okay, this is getting too strange for me, and I'm starting to get a little freaked out," Jasper said, looking at Luca and Matteo as if they would back up his concerns.

"I appreciate it's confusing," said Dr. Sabastien as he folded his hands together and placed them on the table.

"The person you see and the voice you hear right at this moment is that of the human known as Jean Sabastien, but it is not his consciousness communicating with you."

Jasper's flight response was begging him to run from the insane people in front of him, but he resisted the feeling, knowing he had nowhere to go. The logical response that erupted from deep inside his mind was proof. He needed facts not words, and the ten-year-old child inside him exploded the question from his mouth, "Prove it!"

No sooner had he said it than a large brown bird flew in through the open window. It raised its massive wings in front of Matteo as it settled itself on the stone sill. Matteo showed no sign of surprise upon its arrival even though it landed just a few inches from him. The raptor stood motionless with its back to Jasper. When it turned its head, its brilliant blue eyes exploded with light. As the light floated closer to Jasper, the intensity grew so great he was forced to shut his eyes. It was then that Jasper heard a new voice.

"Has he been followed? Good."

Jasper couldn't tell whether he heard the voice through his ears or in his head. It didn't matter because at that moment what he saw with his eyes transfixed him. The bright bluish-white light had filled his eyes, making it impossible to see anything else.

Absolute comfort and warmth settled over his body as the fear and anxiety of the day vanished. He was drawn to the center of the light, wanting to touch it as it drifted a few feet in front of him. Unable to contain the urge, Jasper reach out and put his hand inside it. The instant his hand disappeared, he became the light. Total understanding and contentment enveloped him.

The sensation of weightlessness complemented his contentment. Jasper saw people and places he had been. They were all familiar and happy, releasing a sensation of euphoria throughout his body. He knew he never wanted to leave. Jasper could hear the sounds of laughter and children playing; the children's voices called out to him.

"Jasper, come and play."

"Jasper, let's go on the teeter-totter."

Jasper couldn't see where the voices were coming from, but somehow he knew them all. He looked deeper into the light for the source of the voices when he saw the silhouette of a person. The voices were children's, but the silhouette was an adult's. The person walked towards him, both arms outstretched, as if reaching for him.

Jasper just knew they were the arms of a woman. When the arms drew nearer, the shape became more familiar. The children's voices had disappeared and Jasper heard only one voice. This voice he knew. It was unmistakable; it was the voice of his mother.

Jasper lifted his arms to reach for hers. The moment his fingers touched hers, Jasper's eyes snapped open. He was back in the room holding Dr. Sabastien's hand. The bird was gone.

Jasper's emotions spun out of control, and his vision blurred from the upwelling of tears in his eyes. The feeling of utter contentment vanished, replaced by the fear and anxiety of moments earlier.

"Jasper, how are you feeling?" Dr. Sabastien asked in a subdued voice.

Jasper didn't answer and continued to stare at the table as he attempted to regain control of his emotions.

"He's having difficulty processing the information. I'm afraid he may run."

"You bet I am, and if I had somewhere to go, I'd leave," said Jasper, not realizing he heard Dr. Sabastien's side of the discussions with Luca and Matteo inside his mind.

"Excellent, Jasper. Can you understand the others or just me?"

"What do you mean?"

"You heard me in your consciousness not with your ears."

"I only heard one voice in my head, if that's what you mean," Jasper replied, unsure of his new talent and whether this was something he should say aloud.

"You'll understand the others in time. The return of Simone must have provided focus for your own consciousness. Already understanding me is an excellent sign."

"Simone?" asked Jasper, searching the room for a woman.

"Simone arrived with the owl."

"She was that light?"

"Yes. That is how we appear when not sharing consciousness."

"I felt her before; I had that feeling in the river."

"Yes, we have been protecting you from the moment of creation."

"Protecting me—from what?" he asked, hoping to get some more meaningful answers.

"The Vacare."

"What?"

"That which is searching for you. It's the opposite of the Primoris. It moves throughout the universe focused on spreading its darkness."

"The Vacare is trying to kill me?" Jasper said as if he knew exactly what the Vacare was.

"Not exactly. The people chasing you are the VSS."

"Oh that's better," he said, sounding even more sarcastic.

Dr. Sabastien ignored the sarcasm and continued. "The VSS are controlled by the Vacare. I made a terrible mistake bringing you to the Vatican. If you hadn't given Alica that photo from Tonino, I would have never known."

"Known what?"

"The total resources of the Vatican are now in the hands of the Vacare. I'm afraid nowhere will be safe."

Jasper found his thoughts wandering in multiple directions, and he began to realize his lack of sleep was taking its toll on his ability to focus, and the sheer amount of information he was trying to absorb was overwhelming. Questions raced through his mind at light speed, making it impossible to decide which was the most important to know first.

"Are the VSS all Vacare?"

"No, most of the people working within the VSS believe they are working for the good of the Church."

"What does it look like, the Vacare?"

"Like I said, it's the opposite of Primoris. The brilliant blue you see when you look into our eyes, your own eyes, is the essence of the Primoris. You can't see Vacare; it has no light—only the darkest black imaginable."

Jasper moved the hair off his face and paused for an instant to gain the courage to ask, "What if they get me?" and he cast his eyes directly into Dr. Sabastien's.

"The Vacare will have succeeded. All consciousness, existence itself, will be rendered to the darkness, the absolute nothingness which can only be found in a vacuum."

"And if they don't?"

"Your DNA carries a genetic code. When the time is right, your DNA will combine with another's and plant the seed of existence—and the Convergence will have begun."

CHAPTER 25

CONVERGENCE

"Convergence!" shouted Jasper. The word started a cascade of thoughts rippling through his head.

"You mean *La Convergenza*?" The sound of Father Cavalli's voice yelling it, and his image lying on the altar whisked through Jasper's mind. Clarity of understanding flushed through his thoughts for the first time since the discussion began; he finally understood.

"I understand Tonino provided you information on the Convergence. What did he tell you?" asked Dr. Sabastien.

"Not much other than the *La Convergenza* has existed in the artifacts from the beginning of written communication and it transcends nearly all ancient religious beliefs. The symbol for it looks something like a broken figure eight or fish."

"Did you recognize it?"

"Yes, it's the same shape as my birthmark and..." started Jasper, but he was interrupted by Dr. Sabastien.

"But do you understand what it means?"

"Not really," replied Jasper, not fully grasping what he was expected to know.

"Where else have you seen this shape? Think of your genetics class."

Before he could give Jasper any further clues to the true meaning of the symbol, a look of total embarrassment filled Jasper's face. Dr. Sabastien smiled and waited.

"Of course, why didn't I see it? It's part of a helix—like in a DNA molecule."

After a moment the reality of the true meaning began to surface. The elaborate fresco on the ceiling formed vividly in his mind. Jasper hesitated. Anxiety raced through his thoughts as the image materialized in his mind. Unable to contain his need to know, the words rushed from his lips.

"Why do I have the symbol?"

"I think you already know."

"It's something to do with Convergence, but I don't know what?"

"It has everything to do with Convergence. The mark has been passed to you over millennia. Jasper, you are one of two Vectors, each carrying half of the primary DNA. Only after your DNA combines with the other's can Convergence begin."

Jasper didn't know where to start; his mind was working faster than he could speak. *What do you mean 'primary DNA?' What other half?* This frightened Jasper, but the most unsettling thought to enter his mind remained the Convergence. He blocked these thoughts for the moment and started looking for answers.

"What exactly is primary DNA?"

"Your DNA is the male half of the original DNA used to create humans on earth. The other half of course is female DNA. When these two…"

Jasper interrupted his sentence with another question even more difficult to comprehend.

"What do you mean the 'first?'" asked Jasper, grabbing a handful of his hair in his hands with his elbows planted on the table. He knew what the answer would be but had to hear before he could believe it.

"Over time, human religious beliefs gave the male name 'Adam' and the female 'Eve,' but we call them primary DNA. Not nearly as human as Adam and Eve."

"If I have Adam's DNA, then there is an Eve, right?" asked Jasper with some apprehension.

"Yes. We have also protected her. The Convergence can only occur if the two of you combine your DNA."

"Combine? Do you mean have a kid?"

"Yes. We call it a Terminal Vector."

"That's never going to happen," said Jasper, grunting a laugh from deep inside his throat.

"I'm certain it will. When the time comes, even I can't prevent the union of the Vectors. When you approach the female Vector, a force stronger than anything you could imagine will overcome you. This is why we've kept you apart."

"We're talking about a human woman, right?" blurted out Jasper, feeling embarrassed to ask.

"Yes, what where you expecting?" replied Dr. Sabastien with a smile.

"And she exists somewhere, right now?

"Yes, of course."

"What's her name?" asked Jasper, intrigued at the thought. "Christine."

"Well, I have news for you. We may be unable to resist each other, but there won't be any transfer of my DNA," Jasper scoffed.

"Jasper, I've been with you from the instant you were created. I know everything about you."

Jasper struggled to understand exactly what that meant.

"Your sexual frustration was programmed into your DNA—it's a safety measure to ensure you don't pass your DNA to anyone other than Christine. You were designed that way."

Jasper's face began to crumple with realization. Anger boiled his blood as the resentment for his years of sexual frustrations emerged. Only his eyes spoke the anger in his mind.

Dr. Sabastien turned and faced Luca when Jasper heard the voice in his mind again. "I think he needs to rest; I can see he's unhappy. It's too much for anyone to handle at one time."

"I'm not leaving!" barked Jasper, his determination to know everything remained unwavering.

"You must," pleaded Dr. Sabastien.

"Get him some food and water," demanded a voice inside Jasper's mind.

Luca left the room.

"Forget the food; just tell me more about the Convergence. Tonino said it was catastrophic, of Biblical proportions. Why would anyone be a part of that?"

"He's wrong. Others think this because of the past."

"This has happened before?" asked Jasper, unable to contain the surprise in his tone.

"Yes, there have been other attempts at Convergence. When it failed, the result was devastating. Humans of that time could not understand what was happening and saw them as religious events."

"When?" demanded Jasper.

"The first attempt you know as the Great Flood. Your history records the male primary DNA as Noah and the female his wife, Naamah. There was a flood, as the Bible states, but that's not what caused the devastating genocide."

"The Bible was right?" he said in astonishment.

"Yes, nearly the entire human population was lost at that time, thus destroying critical mass. It took us another five thousand years before we could rebuild critical mass and attempt a second Convergence."

Jasper's face filled with a stunned look, *Noah?* he thought in disbelief as Luca returned with a plate of food and a bottle of water, which he placed on the table in front of Jasper.

"The second attempt of Convergence was nearly successful; we combined the primary DNA and created the Terminal Vector. But once again, genocide occurred."

"Who was it?" asked Jasper, realizing the Vectors where his direct ancestors.

"Human history records the male primary DNA as Joseph and the female Mary."

Of course, thought Jasper. The names rang in his head. *Joseph and Mary, Mary and Joseph.* The place his mind led him was incomprehensible. He was saying it before he finished his thoughts.

"That would make me a direct descendant of Jesus Christ. It wasn't an error," he said out loud as if that would make it more believable.

The full magnitude of what Dr. Sabastien had said didn't faze Jasper. A minute passed before he could think straight; his mind was re-booting like the hard drive in a computer. The explosions in his chest from each heartbeat gave him the first indication of the full implications of his own words.

His fingertips felt like icicles and his breaths became shorter. Everything in the room became fuzzy as the early onset of shock flooded through his body. Jasper suffered little impact when Dr. Sabastien first told him he was the living descendant of Christ. But his own realization made it truly inconceivable.

His lips became dry, and he reached for the bottle of water but knocked it over. Dr. Sabastien grabbed it before the entire contents spilled onto the table and placed a napkin from the food tray over the mess.

"Does this mean you're…" he couldn't finish. The word wouldn't leave his lips. Jasper could not find a way to speak it.

"God?" whispered Dr. Sabastien, fearing what reaction the word may have on Jasper.

Jasper nodded as he pulled his hair into a ponytail in an attempt to keep it behind his ears then released it. The lack of sleep and food had whittled away the last of his determination. Hearing the word was the final blow that sucked the remaining strength from him. Jasper remained at the table, motionless and broken.

"If that's what you believe," said Dr. Sabastien as he reached over to place his hand on Jasper's.

Jasper looked down at the hand and could only conjure a nervous smile.

"What's amusing?" asked Dr. Sabastien.

"The Hand of God," said Jasper and he lifted his head to once again lock eyes with Dr. Sabastien. "I'm smiling because I don't know what to call you—Dr. Sabastien, Animus, Father or just God?"

"Call me what you wish, Dr. Sabastien or if you like, Animus, it's up to you. Please, Jasper, let me explain further before your thoughts spin out of control."

"It's far too late for that," Jasper said with a small laugh.

Jasper wanted to escape the room more than anything else at that moment. Like a prisoner under interrogation, he felt as though he were being forced to continue, but it was his own mind tying him to the seat. He needed to know.

"What do you expect me to say? I spent my whole life refusing to believe."

"I'm concerned for you. It's very late; I can see you're exhausted."

"I'm not going to bed. Do you really think I could sleep after everything I've heard?"

"Very well, at least eat something," demanded Dr. Sabastien.

Jasper picked a piece of cheese from the plate and placed it in his mouth. Dr. Sabastien spoke to Luca and Matteo, "Go and do the rounds."

They left the room at once.

"Jasper, I meant what I said; it's what you believe…"

"That means nothing," protested Jasper, interrupting.

Dr. Sabastien continued, "Listen, all humans have their own idea of what or who God is. Humans have religions to try and make sense of the concept of God. What unites a vast majority of these religions is one single belief—their God created them."

"I thought you created us?" asked Jasper.

"I created the humans on earth. Human creation is the reason an Animus forms and is fundamental to the expansion of Primoris."

"You keep saying humans, but you mean everything, right? Plants, animals, insects..."

"No, these creatures have a beginning and an end. They're not part of the Primoris. They evolved on earth. Evolution of living entities is common throughout the expansion."

"Other planets have life, and it's human?"

"Infinitely many."

"But there's only one God?"

"Think of it like this: for those who believe, there is only one 'God' for this planet, this galaxy, this universe, it's Primoris. Primoris isn't bound by time or space."

"What's so special about humans? Why us?" he asked with the initial shock dissipating, the scientist in Jasper returning.

"It's in your DNA. Humans are born with a tiny bit of energy. Think of it as a little piece of God within you, waiting to join the Primoris. It's the only place where new consciousness can be created."

"You're reproducing!" exclaimed Jasper.

"Yes, you can think of it that way. The earth is our egg, which I fertilized with humans more than ten thousand years ago."

"That makes us the cells," added Jasper, rapidly comprehending the concept.

"Exactly," replied Dr. Sabastien, delighted with Jasper's progress. "Humans continue to multiply, creating more and more DNA, until finally a critical mass of new DNA is formed—the consciousness we are made of."

"Critical mass?" interrupted Jasper.

"Our expansion of existence can only be successful if there is sufficient human DNA for Convergence to occur."

"And if it there's not?"

"It is imperative that we wait until there is. The timing is essential for the creation of a Terminal Vector. If we are wrong, I'm afraid Tonino was correct, the results would be catastrophic."

"But Convergence has failed before?"

"Critical mass has failed, not Convergence," he said with a tone of authority. "The only way for the Vacare to succeed is for the Primoris to fail."

"This doesn't sound too good to me."

"The Vacare will destroy humanity in order to prevent Convergence, leaving the earth no better than Mars, a barren rock floating in space."

"Great, any more good news?" Jasper asked sarcastically as the late hour took its toll on him.

"I'm afraid it's far worse than that: if humans continue to multiply on the earth without Convergence, the Vacare will have succeeded. The unabated accumulation of new consciousness will result in an implosion, causing the complete annihilation of existence. The Primoris, humanity... everything will cease to exist, leaving only the Vacare.

Chapter 26

Narrow Escape

"Luca, prepare a bedroom for Jasper. The Da Vinci room," Dr. Sabastien said without speaking.

"Thanks, I'm exhausted," Jasper admitted.

Dr. Sabastien smiled with pleasure. Jasper heard his thoughts although he was so exhausted he didn't realize the words occurred inside his head.

"Your room is ready, follow me," said Luca.

Jasper couldn't move fast enough; the thought of sleep consumed him. They left the room and walked a short distance to a stairwell filled with wide stone steps. Luca began climbing the steps with Jasper close on his heels. The stairway was spiral and poorly lit, making it impossible to know how many floors were above or below. They only climbed one flight before entering a massive corridor. Jasper found it difficult to see the opposite end, the lighting was so poor.

Large wooden doors, spaced evenly apart lined both sides of the corridor, giving the impression they were in a hotel. Their footsteps reverberated off of the marble floor as they walked down the empty hallway. Between each set of doors hung large paintings, each distinct from the next. Jasper recognized some of them as Biblical figures while others were just landscapes. They had walked past ten or eleven doors when Luca stopped. Directly to the left of the door was a life-sized painting of Leonardo Da Vinci's *The Vitruvian Man.*

"This will be your room," said Luca as he lifted the ancient iron latch and opened the old wooden door for Jasper.

Jasper entered a room that resembled a ballroom rather than a bedroom. It was immense. The left wall held an antique iron headboard which crowned the four-poster bed. The right wall was furnished with a white marble fireplace flanked by three-foot-wide marble pillars. Jasper walked across the room to open one of the two wooden shutters on the windows when Luca stopped him.

"Please leave those closed," he said.

Jasper didn't argue and began to remove his shoes when he noticed his backpack placed on the table next to the bed.

"How'd that get here?" asked Jasper, surprised to see it as he had completely forgotten about it until that moment.

"Animus got it. He filled it with as many of your personal belongings as he could—including your passport."

Jasper was excited to see it; his few remaining personal items reconnected him with reality. His MP3 player and headphones hung from the side pouch, and his phone was in its mesh holder on top.

"The bathroom is farther down the hall on the right next to the painting of the Coliseum."

"Did he get my toothbrush?"

"I don't know. *Buona notte*," said Luca and he left the room.

Jasper decided he was too tired to brush his teeth so he pulled his MP3 player out of his pack and threw himself on the bed without undressing. He placed the ear buds in his ears and scrolled to his favorite song—*She Sells Sanctuary*. The electric guitar introduction was still resonating in his ears when he passed out.

***

A troop of eight men dressed in military fatigues and wearing night-vision-equipped helmets emerged from the black panel truck. They moved like ghosts in the darkness as they approached the massive front door. Their formation was perfect; with guns drawn, six men supported the other two, who pressed the clay-like explosives into the iron hinges. With the wires inserted, the troop split into two groups on both sides of the entrance, positioning themselves flat against the stone wall for protection.

The commander broadcast the count down over their radio headsets. The explosives worked precisely, cutting the iron hinges and sending the door flying through the air into the castle. The power of the explosion shook the old building, and before the dust had settled, the commander waved his men through the entrance.

Jasper was still lying on the bed in exactly the same position he had fallen asleep in three hours earlier. His MP3 player muffled the full intensity of the explosion, but it was still loud enough to wake him.

Confused and disoriented from the abrupt arousal, Jasper thought he heard fireworks. He yanked the ear buds from his head and listened. The first thing he heard was Animus shouting inside his head.

"Get him out of here!" followed by a few seconds pause. "Now!" said the voice before it was replaced by a string of rapid bangs.

Jasper recognized them as the sound of gunfire. He launched himself from the bed and was putting his shoes on when the door slammed open. Matteo remained in the doorway while Luca entered the room and shouted at him.

"Come on, we must go at once!"

"What's happening?" protested Jasper.

"We don't have time. Just grab your stuff and come," commanded Luca.

Jasper grabbed his pack and slung it over his shoulder when he heard Animus yelling from out in the hall.

"You're wrong; he's not here..."

"Stop your lying! We've got the scooter!" shouted the

other voice.

"I don't know what scooter you're talking about. It could be anyone's."

Jasper's heart sank when he heard the word 'scooter,' remembering he had left it parked at the front of the castle. They knew he was in the castle, and it was only a matter of time before they found him. Jasper heard shouting in Italian and the sound of footsteps in the hallway. A flash of light resembling lightning filled the hallway, and Matteo shut the door just as a small explosion occurred. Thick white smoke began to billow from under the door.

"We have to leave, get him!" shouted Matteo.

Matteo remained right in front of the door waving his arm to come. Jasper ran over to him, followed by Luca.

"Once I open the door, we only have a second. Go out the door to the left and stay down. Continue up the hall and into the last door on the right. Got it?"

Matteo looked directly at Jasper. "Go, as fast as you can!"

Water poured from Jasper's eyes the moment the door opened. The hallway was black and filled with smoke, making it impossible to see the other side.

Luca pushed Jasper out the door so both he and Matteo were directly behind him, and they began running blindly down the hall. The more Jasper searched for the door, the sharper the sting became in his eyes; he struggled to keep them open.

It became harder to breath as the thick fumes filled deeper into his lungs with each breath. With his eyes barely open, Jasper saw a thin beam of red light flash over his head. He ran a few more yards and four more thin beams of red light reflected off the smoke ahead of him.

The crack of gunfire rang in his ears; the sound was so close it caused him to duck instinctively. A sharp pain erupted in his shoulder when a force from behind sent Jasper lunging to the ground. He landed in an open doorway, out of the hall. The door slammed behind him, and Matteo stood next to him, locking the door.

"Where's Luca?" he demanded.

"Don't worry about him. Get up," said Matteo.

"I can't."

"Get up! We've got to go!" Matteo commanded.

"Why don't you guys have guns? Why aren't you shooting back? They're trying to kill us!"

"We don't have time for this—just follow me," said Matteo.

"Where?"

"Out of here."

"Where can we go they can't follow?" Jasper snapped.

Matteo led the way as they ran to the far side of the room. He opened a pair of large French doors that led to a balcony. Jasper started to move through the doors.

"No, not that way, over here," Matteo said.

The VSS SWAT team had reached their room and was yelling in Italian as they pounded on the door. Using what little light that entered the room from the open doors, Jasper followed Matteo a few yards to the front of a small door in the wall. Based on its size, Jasper guessed it to be a broom closet; it was just wide enough for a man to enter sideways. Matteo opened the door and entered first. Lifting his leg, he kicked the back wall of the tiny space, causing a small door to open in the back.

Matteo pushed Jasper through the small opening at the rear and followed, closing the both doors behind him.

Standing in complete darkness, Matteo and Jasper could hear the SWAT team entering the room. The sound of their leather boot heels scrambling across the floor, resembled hundreds of hammers.

Instinct told Jasper not to speak while they stood in the pitch blackness. Jasper felt a tug on his right arm as Matteo pulled him. Jasper knew they were walking in a narrow tunnel; his pack was banging both sides as they inched their way through the darkness. He stumbled on the back of

Matteo's feet, forcing his pack hard into the wall. The collision activated a key on his phone, waking the screen. The light filtered through the mesh pouch, dissolving the darkness of the tunnel. Jasper pulled it from his pack and handed it to Matteo. Using it as a flashlight, they moved swiftly through the tunnel.

"Keep close, we are almost there!" whispered Matteo.

A faint glow of light appeared ahead of them. As they approached it, Jasper could see a large steel grate at the end of the tunnel. The light was coming from the early morning sunrise; the sky glowed behind the steep hillsides to the east. Matteo returned the phone to Jasper and unlatched the gate. They exited into the same lane they had used to enter the castle.

"We need to get back to the bakery," said Matteo.

They began running down the lane, the sound of their footsteps bouncing off the sides of the stone buildings. Adrenalin heightened Jasper's senses, and his eyes scanned the surroundings for any hint of a red beam of light. He expected to hear the crack of gunfire at any moment. They arrived at the back door of the bakery after a few minutes of sprinting and entered.

"We'll stay here. All the roads will be monitored," said Matteo.

"How long?"

"I'll wait to hear from the others. Until then, we need to hide you. They'll be coming soon."

Matteo opened the door of the large storeroom in the back of the bakery. It was filled to the ceiling with sacks of flour.

"Let's move these to get you behind them," Matteo said. Jasper tossed his pack in the corner of the room and began helping Matteo rearrange the sacks to make a hiding place just large enough for him to fit in.

"I'll open the bakery; it's almost seven o'clock. If I don't, it will draw their attention sooner. This is a very small village, and everyone knows when I open. Remember, you can't be seen."

Matteo left the back of the bakery and turned the lights on in the front of the shop, unlocking the front door as he did so. Jasper stayed in the back, listening for the bell on the front door to chime. This was his cue to move into the storeroom hiding place. Standing behind the flour sacks, Jasper could hear the faint sound of Matteo's voice as he chatted in Italian with the local villagers.

A little later, the door chime sounded again, sending Jasper into the storeroom. As he stood in the darkness behind the sacks, he knew something was different this time. Matteo's voice became clearer. He had entered the back of the bakery and was speaking to another man. Jasper strained to listen to their conversation and put his ear against a thin gap in the sacks.

Why me? How can this be happening to me? he asked himself as the endless parade of near-death experiences began to erode his will. *It can't be me, it's gotta be a mistake. They'll realize that soon, and this'll all go away*, Jasper thought as he tried in vain to convince himself. His moment of insecurity ended as the conversation outside the storeroom grew louder.

Jasper strained to listen. His effort was not to understand the conversation but to recognize a voice. Something seemed familiar about it even though he spoke in Italian; the second man's voice was one he had heard before.

Jasper froze in place when the conversation continued directly in front of the storeroom door. The door opened, the light was turned on, and Matteo continued to talk. Light penetrated the cracks between the poorly layered sacks. Jasper took a chance and pressed his eye to one in an effort to see the source of the voice, but the small crack only permitted him a very narrow field of vision. Jasper could see only the backs of three men speaking to Matteo. Matteo continued to speak to one of them, and the other two left. The man spoke for another five minutes and then turned around to shut the storeroom door.

The moment he saw the man's face, Jasper bit his lower lip so hard it began to bleed inside his mouth. *How could it be?* he thought to himself.

Tonino switched the light off and began closing the door when the unthinkable happened. A faint beep-beep sounded from the corner of the room. Tonino instantly stopped and drew his gun.

Jasper knew exactly what the sound was and thought, *I'm so stupid.* The low battery indicator on his phone was sounding. Tonino stood in the doorway like a hunting dog waiting for a pheasant. Matteo attempted to distract him, but Tonino was not fooled by his attempt and waved him silent. Just then, a second beep-beep sounded.

The backpack was still sitting in the corner of the room where Jasper had tossed it that morning, his phone hanging out of the thin mesh pouch. It sounded a third beep-beep and Tonino moved to the corner, picking up the pack. Tonino pulled it out and looked at the screen. Jasper's name was displayed across the front.

"Jasper, come out!" ordered Tonino.

Jasper hesitated until he saw Matteo nod his head. He walked out from his hiding place and looked directly at the gun in Tonino's hands.

CHAPTER 27

BURIED ALIVE

Tonino's face filled with anguish; he seemed to have become quite fond of Jasper. Still no words left his mouth. Jasper could see the struggle gripping Tonino as his arm wavered from the weight of the gun.

"Why, Toni?" Jasper asked, remaining motionless in front of the sacks of flour.

Tonino glanced away from Jasper as Matteo took a few steps closer.

"*Aspetta!*" barked Tonino, and Matteo halted his advance. "Isn't it obvious? I work for the VSS, and I follow orders."

"Orders? You're talking about killing—killing me!" yelled Jasper with indignation.

"It doesn't matter. I have my orders…"

"Listen to me, listen to yourself. This isn't right. How could killing be what God wants? Is this the will of God?"

Jasper tried to keep the dialogue going, looking for some way of convincing him not to follow his orders.

"Quiet!" he shouted.

Jasper continued despite the order, sensing the internal struggle Tonino was experiencing.

"You don't want to kill me. You don't want to kill anyone. This isn't what Father Cavalli wanted. This isn't what God wants."

Tonino's eyes seemed to grow darker at the mention of Father Cavalli. Jasper knew they were close, and he knew that

Tonino disliked Father Derksen. Jasper realized Cavalli must not have been a part of the Vacare, but Derksen surely was, demonstrated by his command of the VSS. He now ruled the VSS with the fist of a general. Tonino started to lower his gun as he responded to a voice in his earpiece.

"*Si, uno momento*," he said as he activated the microphone inside his suit pocket with his free hand. His partners seemed to be growing impatient with him, so Tonino ordered them to wait in the car.

He raised the gun back to its original position, pointed directly at Jasper.

"I'm sorry, Jasper, I have to…"

Jasper saw Tonino's finger move and heard the click of the safety release. He prepared himself for the pain.

"*Aspetta!*" shouted Matteo. "Show him, Jasper, show him the mark."

Jasper appeared confused and didn't understand.

"Show him the mark!" Matteo demanded.

Still pointing the gun at Jasper, Tonino looked back at Matteo.

"What mark?"

Jasper didn't speak but began turning his body so the back of his head faced Tonino. He grasped the hair on the back of his head, forming a small ponytail, and lifted it, exposing the birthmark.

There was no reaction from Tonino.

"Toni, listen to me. It's true, it's all true. The DNA you found on the Grail was a match. It was no error," said Jasper, now crouching down next to Tonino. "The ancient symbol, the mark on my neck, they're the same."

As Jasper spoke these words, he couldn't believe what he was saying. Until this moment, he really hadn't believed it himself. He had listened to Animus, seen the evidence, but it wasn't until he spoke the words that it became real.

"Toni, do you understand?" Jasper asked. "Matteo and I have to go."

Tonino paused for a moment to collect his thoughts and returned the gun to its holster.

"No, you can't leave. They'll find you. We have every road to this village blocked. I've got to get back or the others will suspect something is wrong." Tonino was leaving the storeroom when he turned around. "Tonight, I'll be at the checkpoint on the old highway. Hide yourself well, and I'll get you through at eight o'clock. Be on time." Tonino left the room and the chime of the front doorbell indicated that he was gone from the bakery.

Matteo and Jasper began planning how to hide Jasper and escape from the village. They had less then twelve hours to come up with a plan and make the preparations. It didn't take them long to agree: the bakery delivery truck was their only chance. Matteo normally drove his truck to the city to drop off baked goods and purchase supplies. The difficulty was finding a way to conceal Jasper inside the truck.

Jasper decided it best to use the flour sacks, to create a false wall just as they had done in the storeroom. But this time, instead of standing, he would lay flat on the bed of the truck, giving the illusion of a solid stack. Matteo would interlock the sacks around and overtop of him, making it appear a solid mass of flour. Once stacked correctly, it would be impossible to tell he was there.

Jasper helped Matteo load as many of the sacks as he could into the back of the truck. They stacked a three-foot-high solid wall of sacks along the back of the truck to act as support for the top of the hollow pile.

At seven thirty p.m., Jasper took his position, lying on the bed of the truck in front of this sack wall. Ensuring his phone was turned off, he placed it inside his backpack, which he used as a pillow.

Matteo continued the stacking process with the precision of a mason. Starting from Jasper's feet, he worked toward his head, alternating the orientation of each sack while slightly offsetting subsequent layers. This created a three-foot-high pyramid leaving a cavity large enough for Jasper to slightly raise his head and feet off the bed of the truck.

The box of the truck filled with a fog of flour dust. Jasper took a final breath, inhaling deeply in anticipation of his live burial. The smell of the dust produced a happy image from his childhood—watching his mother making pie dough on the kitchen table. This comforting image was replaced by the intense stare of Matteo's crystal blue eyes.

"*Buon fortuna*."

"Thanks," responded Jasper and blackness filled his eyes.

Matteo placed the final sack over his face, eclipsing the light provided by the tiny fixture on the ceiling of the truck. Instantly, the darkness combined with the confinement and resurrected the worst of Jasper's memories. Panic escalated inside him as he pushed against the sacks like they were the heavy black robe that smothered his innocence. He counted to ten over and over in his mind, like he always did, knowing if he did everything right, it would be over soon.

He struggled to clear his mind of the past but found himself thinking of his mother. Jasper hated her endless devotion to God and how her belief gave her the strength to continue even in the face of death. Tears welled up and combined with the flour dust to burn his eyes. With no way of touching his face, Jasper blinked rapidly to relieve the pain. The mixture rolled down the sides of his face.

If she only knew, he thought. *Her son is a direct descendant of Jesus Christ*. The image of his mother filled his mind. *Maybe she does know*, entered his thoughts as the memory of going into the light filled his thoughts and he smiled.

The muffled sounds of Matteo stacking the remaining sacks over top of him snapped Jasper back to the present. The bitter taste of the flour dust stung the tip of his tongue. .

Matteo worked swiftly, stacking the remaining sacks over Jasper. Neither of them knew how many minutes Jasper had before the air inside the hiding place would be exhausted. Matteo knew it was best not to fill the entire back of the truck with sacks, adding flats of bread and pastries with his routine delivery addresses fixed to the packaging to make sure the disguise was convincing. In a final attempt to gain any advantage, Matteo removed the bulb from the ceiling light before closing the back doors.

The vibration of the engine starting tingled through the base of Jasper's spine; the hard wooden deck of the truck offered no padding. Matteo slowly moved the truck down the cobblestone lane. The steep hill caused the heavily weighted truck to pick up speed. Jasper felt the acceleration and began to feel he was the recipient of voodoo doll torture, the uneven surface causing needle sharp pains to rip through his back. They only drove a few minutes before Jasper sensed the truck slowing, providing welcomed relief from the pain.

***

The headlights reflected the bright yellow police tape strewn across the road, and Matteo slowed the vehicle to a crawl.

He glanced at the dashboard radio to get the time: it was three minutes before eight. He slowed the truck further as he approached the roadblock. Through the darkness, Matteo could see the yellow tape was tied to cars parked on the side of the road. There were three cars, two on the left side and one on the right, making it impossible for a vehicle to pass on either side.

Two men stepped on to the road in front of the truck waving flashlights and gesturing Matteo to stop. Through the headlights, Matteo could see the taller and much older of the two men giving the younger man instructions. He stopped the truck and rolled his window down, greeting the older man as he approached while the other walked to the back. The older man at his window spoke politely in Italian and flashed a *Carabinieri* identification badge.

"We are looking for an escaped prisoner. Have you seen

anyone who looks like this?"

He produced the photo from Jasper's Vatican Security ID and directed the light from his flashlight onto it so Matteo could see.

"*Non*," Matteo said with a shrug.

"Please exit the truck," the policeman requested while pointing the flashlight into the cab. "And open the back," he asked, and they both walked to the back of the truck, joining the younger man waiting by the doors.

"*Si*," said Matteo, fumbling in the darkness for the right key to unlock the door. He opened the door and stepped back from the truck as the two men directed their flashlights into the truck. While the men searched, Matteo scanned the area for Tonino. The night was pitch black, making it impossible for him to see more than a few yards past the light coming from the back of the truck.

"How do you turn this on?" asked the older man, pointing to the ceiling light.

"It doesn't work. I haven't had time to replace it," Matteo replied.

"Where are you going with all this?" asked the older man, pointing to the sacks of flour.

"I'm a baker. I'm making my last delivery for the night."

"You deliver flour?" he asked with skepticism.

"My help didn't show-up today, so it didn't get unloaded."

"Do you mind if we take a better look around?" asked the older man.

"Feel free, but I'm not moving another sack today," Matteo said as he rubbed his back, indicating the soreness from lifting the flour sacks. The older man pointed his light at the stack of flour sacks and instructed the younger man to search the truck while he and Matteo stepped away from the doors.

The younger man placed his flashlight on the pile of flour sacks covering Jasper's head so the light pointed toward where he began to remove the sacks. He threw each sack onto the bed of the truck with enough force to shake the entire vehicle. Matteo continued to look around for Tonino, realizing it had to be eight o'clock and not long before Jasper was discovered or suffocated.

***

Jasper noticed his breathing becoming rapid and shallow, unsure if it was the adrenaline rushing through his body or the lack of oxygen. The force of his heart pounding inside his chest made his entire body shake, and he could feel it throb inside his head. A moment later, he realized it wasn't his heart he could feel but the bed of the truck pounding. The truck hadn't moved, so he knew someone must be removing the sacks and dropping them on the box.

Jasper was overcome by the urge to topple the sacks off his body and leap into the air, knowing any second one of the sacks would be lifted and his location discovered. Part of him welcomed the thought of having fresh air again as his willpower weakened from being buried alive.

The pounding of the sacks grew stronger and louder; it was only a matter of seconds before he saw light again and felt fresh air filling his lungs. The anticipation grew more intense; he could sense the release that was coming. He began to fidget, shifting left and right, turning his feet in small circles trying to free them from their bindings. Release arrived, and fresh air filled his tomb.

A few faint flashes of light met his eyes, and Jasper instinctively tried to pull his knees to his chest, the reaction triggered by the glimmer of light coming from his feet.

A familiar voice resonated in Jasper's head, but before he could identify the source, it was interrupted by the slap of a flour sack hitting the bed of the truck. The same sack that covered his feet.

***

Tonino left one of the parked cars on the side of the road and began yelling as he marched toward the older man. Without acknowledging Matteo, he shouted at both men.

"What are you doing? Do you want to be here all night?" Tonino yelled.

"We're searching the truck, sir," said the older man while the younger walked to the door of the vehicle.

"Do you think you could survive under a ton of flour? *Idiosi*! Let's get going, I'm needed at the Vatican at once," barked Tonino.

The younger man walked back to the flour sacks and retrieved his flashlight. He jumped out of the back of the truck and joined the other men. Matteo closed the back door of the truck and returned to the cab, watching the three cars race away.

Matteo navigated the dark lane like he was driving a Maserati, following every twist and turn with perfection, something he did every night. This night he was extra cautious when rolling through the hairpin turns, hoping not to cause his cargo to shift.

***

The five-minute drive to Pontoria, where Matteo kept a traditional Italian villa felt like a lifetime to Jasper. Every turn Matteo executed shifted the flour sacks from side to side, bringing them ever closer to collapsing on Jasper.

Darkness wasn't the only thing that returned when Matteo closed the truck doors, the feeling of claustrophobia welled up inside of Jasper, but a hundred times stronger than before. It didn't matter anymore where he was going or what was happening outside the truck—every ounce of his being begged him to get out of his tomb. He kicked the sacks in vain with the little legroom he had. It was hopeless; there was no leverage to move any of the heavy sacks. His arms lay pinned along his sides. The space around his torso afforded him only a few inches of movement, making his arms more useless then his legs. Jasper's frustration climaxed into panic when he felt the vibrations of the truck stopping and the engine turning off. He was getting out whether it was Matteo or the VSS.

Through the opening at his feet, Jasper heard the truck box door open.

"Jasper, you okay?" asked Matteo, not hiding his concern as he jumped into the back of the truck.

"No, I need out of here—right now!" he said with panic in his voice.

"Yes, yes," responded Matteo, frantically pulling the sacks off the pile.

Jasper sprang out of his tomb the instant Matteo freed his body. A faint ray of light emanating from the villa penetrated the darkness in the box. It was enough to illuminate an escape route for Jasper from his grave. He leaped over the sacks and pastry boxes strewn over the bed of the truck and bounded out the back doors. He stood motionless in the porch light, his chest heaving from the deep gasps of fresh air entering his lungs.

Matteo exited the truck and walked over to Jasper. Laughter rolled out off of his lips when he looked at him.

"What's so funny?" demanded Jasper, who wasn't the least bit amused.

"You look like a ghost," Matteo chuckled.

"You would too if you were buried alive," Jasper said, still not the least bit amused.

"No, it's not that," said Matteo, trying unsuccessfully to lose the laughter. "You are literally as white as a ghost."

Jasper had emerged from the flour-sack tomb completely covered in flour dust. This combined with the sweat pouring from him during his burial created a perfectly smooth white coating over his entire body. Jasper looked at his arms in the dim light and could see the fine white powder covering his skin. He began to laugh, but Jasper's laugh was different than

Matteo's; his laugh was that of relief, it was his body releasing the adrenaline that flooded through his veins.

His laughter served as the perfect antidote to the frayed nerves ripping his insides apart. Jasper knew he had come within inches of death. More importantly, for the second time he owed his life to Tonino.

CHAPTER 28

THE AMERICAN

Matteo parked the bakery truck in the shop out back of the villa, making sure it couldn't be seen from the road. Jasper entered the villa and was taken aback by its magnificence. The near complete darkness couldn't hide its splendor. Jasper's senses seemed to fire in unison with the flicking-on of the light. His nostrils were the first to react, tingling with the aroma of fresh basil and garlic, a glorious contrast to the hour-long torture they endured inhaling flour dust.

His eyes slowly adjusted to the brightness of the lights and were dazzled by the magnificence of the room. He was standing in a large room with a spiral staircase leading to the second floor and a large brick oven completely filling the opposite wall. Before Jasper moved from his position, Matteo entered the room from the back carrying his backpack.

"*Avanti*, come in, make yourself at home," he said.

"Thanks," Jasper responded, still standing on the spot.

Matteo walked up to him and handed him the backpack. "I think you may want to take a shower," he said with a very large grin. "There are towels in the vanity under the sink. The washroom is upstairs—the second door on the left. I'll get your bed ready; we'll be leaving early tomorrow to meet Animus."

Jasper had completely forgotten about the others. The last twenty-four hours hadn't come close to settling in his mind.

His only concern was for himself; not for a single second had he thought about the others.

"Animus... is he all right? I know he was talking to Father Derksen. I recognized his voice at the castle."

"He's fine. Now don't worry about him and get yourself cleaned up. I'll get you some clothes. We have a long journey."

"What journey?" he demanded.

"I will explain later. Now take a shower."

Jasper took his pack and walked up the staircase to the second-floor washroom. He found the towels and got in the shower. The warm water cascading down his back removed more than just the dust from his skin. It washed away the tension woven through every fiber of his body, enabling Jasper to relax. He directed the showerhead toward his face and leaned his body against the opposite wall, wincing when the cold marble pressed against his warm skin.

The washroom filled with so much steam it transformed into a sauna. This further calmed him as if injected with a tranquilizer. Jasper entered a state between conscious and unconscious normally experienced before sleep. Images flipped through his mind like a deck of cards, each time increasing in their realism—his escape from the castle, hiding in the bakery, being buried alive... all rolling faster in his thoughts. The images moved deeper and deeper through his mind, blurring his sense of reality. Jasper could hear the VSS hammering on the door.

***

His closed fist banged the wood with enough force to lift the coffee cups from their plates, but his actions rattled more than the Vatican dishes. The two men sitting across from him cowered backwards in their seats, focusing their undivided attention on the hollow black eyes before them.

The cathedral bells resonated through the tiny room, rendering even his loud voice mute. The grey-haired man paused for the interruption.

"What's the problem? If you can't get it done, you'll be replaced," he demanded.

"There's no problem, sir," replied the younger of the two men sitting across from him. "I'll get it done, it's just that the Chinese are being difficult because, after all, it was we who implemented the 'single-child policy' in the first place."

"I know what we did!" he snapped. "But things have changed in our favor. Don't you realize how fast a billion Chinese will add to our effort?" said the grey-haired man, slamming the table a second time.

"Yes, sir," replied the younger man.

He turned to face the older man. "And you, Father, what about India?"

"They're on board but request the food be delivered soon or our efforts will be..."

The grey-haired man interrupted, "I had the same request from our Africans."

"South America has already begun," said the priest.

"Good. I've taken care of the European and the North American Catholics. The pontiff will be sending a clear directive in his next public address bestowing the virtues of large families," said the grey-haired man and his smile evaporated. "What about the technology, you have acquired it?"

The younger man placed a laptop on the table and folded open the screen before typing a few short commands. When the screen displayed a map, he swung the laptop to face the other way. The bottom of the laptop stuck to the tablecloth, causing a coffee cup to spill on the younger man's suit, but he continued unabated. The grey-haired man ignored the fumbling and looked at the screen with little interest.

"Did American Intelligence give you any problems?"

"No, sir," replied the younger man.

The grey-haired man cast his cold dark eyes on the two men. "I want continuous updates from both of you."

"Yes," both men replied.

"Sir, I must warn you, even this technology only works when the device is turned on…" the younger man was silenced by the grey-haired man's raised hand.

"No excuses! Everything is contingent on us finding both of them. Prevention isn't good enough—I want elimination!" he shouted as he pounded the table for a third and final time.

***

The third knock on the door snapped Jasper back to reality.

"Yes," Jasper replied as he reached up and redirected the water out of his face.

"You all right? I was getting worried, it's been almost a half-hour. I've been banging on the door with no answer," Matteo asked.

"I'm fine, just tired," Jasper responded.

"I've got you some clothes."

"Come in."

Matteo opened the door, peering up at the wave of steam flooding out the door, and placed the clothes next to the towel on the sink.

"Get some rest. I have prepared the bed in the room next to this one. Tomorrow will be a long day." Matteo left the room without giving Jasper any opportunity to continue the conversation.

Jasper left the shower and got dressed as fast as he could. He wanted to continue questioning Matteo. He pulled the T-shirt over his head, soaking the front with water from his partially dried hair. He picked up the pants and held them up for a moment. *This must be a mistake?* He was holding a pair of dark blue Bermuda shorts. Jasper put them on and took a glance at himself in the mirror on the back of the door. *I look like a tourist on a cruise,* he decided and left the washroom to find Matteo.

Rejuvenated from the shower and hoping for some answers, Jasper put his pack on his bed and flew down the stairs.

"Matteo?"

"Yes?"

The voice came from upstairs, so Jasper turned on the spot and climbed back up the stairs to find him. Matteo was sitting in a small den at the end of the hallway gazing out a large window as the enormous yellow harvest moon rose above the distant hillside.

"Animus has made arrangements to fly from Switzerland tomorrow evening. We will drive there tomorrow. Be prepared for roadblocks and the police along the way. The VSS have every police force in Italy looking for you."

"Why Switzerland?"

"Because every airport in Italy has a photo of you posted in their security office. It is impossible for you to board a plane anywhere in Italy. Even Switzerland could be risky."

"Where are we going?"

Matteo didn't answer but just stared out the window as if Jasper had said nothing. It was then he realized that Matteo was communicating with Animus.

"Why can't I hear him?" asked Jasper with some annoyance in his tone.

"You haven't progressed enough to communicate over great distances."

"Where are we going?" Jasper asked again.

"I don't know," Matteo said, still transfixed on the rising moon.

"Ask him."

"He'll tell you on the flight."

"He is coming with us?"

"Not us."

"What do you mean? You're not coming?"

"No, you need to get some sleep; we will be leaving in a few more hours."

Unhappy with the information he had gotten from Matteo, Jasper said goodnight and headed for bed. He knew it was useless to further question Matteo. Jasper removed the phone and charger from his pack and plugged it in. He then pulled off his shirt and climbed into the bed, leaving his shorts on. Reaching down to get his MP3 player, the memory of gunfire erupted in his mind. He left the player in his bag and picked up his shirt. He put it back on and then wondered where he had left his shoes.

It wasn't hard for Jasper to find sleep that night. Even though not knowing where and why he was going kept his mind occupied, his body quickly released him from exhaustion and he fell into a dreamless sleep.

***

Matteo knocked on the door just after six o'clock and woke Jasper from the first real sleep he had had in days.

"I'll be right there," Jasper shouted, completely disoriented. He spoke instinctively, thinking he was at home and his father was trying to wake him for school.

"I have some breakfast ready for you. Don't delay—we need to leave," Matteo called back.

Jasper sat up in bed returning to the present as the sound of Matteo's footsteps faded down the stairs. The early morning sunlight cast a halo over the dark green hillsides when Jasper peered out the window. He unplugged his phone and checked the time. He replaced the phone in his backpack and made his way downstairs.

The fragrance of fresh-brewed coffee filled the air.

"Matteo?" Jasper called. There was no answer, so he made his way to the kitchen, where he found a plate of fruit and pastries next to a cup of coffee on the table. Not realizing how long it had been since he had last eaten, Jasper inhaled the pastries before trying the coffee. The door of the kitchen opened and Matteo entered.

"*Buon giorno*, Jasper. Sleep well?"

"Good morning. Yes, thanks."

"Good. Today we drive to Switzerland."

"Where, Zurich?"

"No, Animus will meet us in Lugano."

"Where?"

"It's a small city more than six hundred kilometers from here. It's located just over the Swiss-Italian border. Lugano has a regional airport where we will meet Animus before seven tonight."

"Why Lugano?"

"We'll talk in the car. Finish your food so we can go."

"Okay," said Jasper, feeling like he had just been scolded. He finished the rest of the food and stood up from the table to finish his coffee. Matteo stood in the doorway holding the door open while looking directly at Jasper, implying the need to leave at once. Jasper picked up his pack and headed out the door.

The small silver car was parked a few feet from the back door with the passenger door already open. Jasper took this as the final signal of the urgency to leave and immediately got in. Matteo locked the villa door and made his way to the driver's seat.

Jasper had been in Italy long enough to witness the driving habits of the Italians, but only from the window of a bus or taxi or the seat of a scooter. Matteo had the car nearing a hundred and fifty kilometers per hour in the slow lane when a BMW followed closely by a Mercedes passed them.

"Is this normal?"

"What?"

"Driving like we're in a Formula One race."

A large smile filled Matteo's face and he laughed. "Yes, it's the Italian way."

"Well, Italians are nuts. What happens if they have a blow-out or someone cuts them off?"

Matteo pointed to a white cross embedded in the hard shoulder of the road with the photo of a person mounted in the center of it and '2009' scrolled along the top. They were travelling so fast Jasper couldn't read anything.

"That's what happens."

After an hour of driving, Jasper counted over twenty crosses and then gave up.

Jasper struggled to keep his eyes open. The night's sleep wasn't enough to restore the countless hours lost over the previous week. He convinced himself he would only close his eyes for a moment to remove the gritty feeling every time he blinked. The sound of the engine combined with the rhythmic clicking of the wheels skipping over the cracks in the highway ended Jasper's self-imposed torture. He closed his eyes one last time and didn't open them until Matteo woke him.

"Wake up. We're at the border," Matteo said while he gently shook Jasper.

"How long have I been out?" he asked, feeling embarrassed.

"A couple of hours…"

"Hours?" interrupted Jasper, the flushness rushed through his face, and he wondered if he had been snoring.

"The border is a few miles north of here. I am concerned there may be a checkpoint at the crossing. I am going to leave you at the next stop."

Matteo pulled into the rest stop and parked the car on the far side of the building.

"It's an Auto Grille, just stay out of sight," Matteo told him.

"Okay," Jasper agreed and walked toward the side of the restaurant.

Matteo returned in less than ten minutes. Jasper got back in the car, and they continued their drive.

"Did anyone see you?"

"How could they? You were only gone a couple of minutes. Well? How does it look?" Jasper asked.

"Nothing at the border."

It may have been the subtle inflection in Matteo's voice or just intuition, but Jasper felt that Matteo was holding something back.

"That's great, right?" asked Jasper, searching for reassurance.

Matteo paused before answering. "Yes…"

"Yes, but?" Jasper insisted.

"Animus expected some attempt at the borders to locate you. It seems extremely unusual that the VSS have not tried to intercept you."

"Maybe they think I've already left the country."

"That's what Animus suspects."

"Matteo, why are we going to Lugano?"

"Animus arranged a flight from Lugano because the airport is not in Italy and is much smaller than Zurich's. You'll connect flights in Zurich without having to go through security again. Animus thinks it is safer to go through security in the Lugano airport."

"I'd offer to drive, but I'm not so comfortable driving like an Italian," Jasper said, watching a small red sports car streak by looking like a small fighter jet.

"Thanks, but it's not far."

Matteo had just finished his sentence when Jasper heard another voice; the words were in his head but the voice wasn't Matteo's.

"I'm pleased you made it without incident," said Animus.

Jasper sat frozen in his seat, his heart racing faster than the car engine.

"Thanks," was the only thought Jasper could materialize in his mind. He had forgotten the feeling of having someone else's thoughts enter his mind. It was like standing naked in front of a crowd; he wondered if Animus could read all his thoughts.

"Excellent, Jasper," Animus responded. "You've already grown stronger. You're now able to communicate with me without the need of your voice."

This hadn't occurred to Jasper until Animus mentioned it, but it did feel more natural to Jasper.

Matteo and Jasper entered Lugano Airport and made their way towards the Swiss Air sales counter, where they were to meet Animus. They arrived to find a single attendant speaking to a short, dark-haired man. Matteo stopped at the entrance to the roped switchback aisle leading to the counter.

"Good-bye, Jasper."

"What?"

"We will meet again," said Matteo and left without any further discussion.

"Where's Animus?" shouted Jasper, competing with the announcements over the public address system.

Matteo didn't answer and walked out of sight. No sooner had the words left his lips than Animus answered him.

"Jasper, I'm at the Swiss Air counter."

Jasper turned around to face the counter. The short, dark-haired man stood looking at Jasper with brilliant blue eyes. Jasper's stomach instantly tightened like he had been kicked below the ribs. The words entered Jasper's mind as if they had been spoken in his ear.

"Yes, it's me," said Animus as he walked toward Jasper. "Don't be alarmed," he added in an effort to calm the young man.

Jasper couldn't think. The flight announcements filled his head, and the words Animus placed in his mind became lost with each new announcement. The man walked a few feet from the counter to meet Jasper in the aisle.

"Jasper, it's me," Animus said, using his voice this time and offering his hand in an attempt to snap Jasper out of his shock.

The sound of the man's voice worked even though it had a strong American accent.

Jasper responded by accepting his handshake and answering back with a nervous, "Hi."

"I'm Bill Eckart, from Seattle," whispered Animus in Jasper's right ear, continuing to hold Jasper's hand with a firm grip. "We need to hurry if we are going to make our flight."

"Where's Dr. Sabastien?" asked Jasper, trying to make sense of what was going on.

"We'll have plenty of time to talk later. We need to get going. You got your passport?"

"Yes," Jasper confirmed.

"Good. I've purchased the tickets, but they need to see your passport before they can issue yours."

Jasper removed it from his pack and placed it on the counter for the attendant.

"Thank you, Mr. Stewart. Do you have any baggage to check?" asked the attendant.

"No, just my pack, which I'll carry on," replied Jasper.

"Very well. You must hurry to Gate 2. The flight departs in twenty minutes. The gate will close ten minutes before the flight departs, so you have no time to waste. I will call ahead to let them know you are coming. When you get to security screening, show your boarding card to the guard; you won't have to wait in line. Have a good flight."

Jasper and Animus made it to the gate to find two attendants awaiting their arrival. One walked them down the ramp to the aircraft while the other closed the gate door behind them. When they entered the aircraft, all eyes were fixed on them. The attendant that escorted them onto the flight closed and latched the door behind them.

Animus sat next to the window, leaving the second of the two leather seats for Jasper. He gestured with his hand for Jasper to sit next to him.

Jasper assessed Bill, the man Animus was sharing consciousness with, while he took his seat. He was in his late thirties with short, well-kept black hair. His clothing was impeccable, from the sparkling Oxford shoes to the three-piece designer suit. His left wrist was covered by a diamond-studded gold watch, exemplifying his wealth. They were sitting in the front row of the aircraft but not as a result of their late arrival, which Jasper initially thought, but because of the first-class tickets Animus had purchased. One thing was for sure, Bill Eckart was wealthy. Jasper looked at Animus, and without the need to speak or even think the words, Animus knew his thoughts.

"A surgeon," Animus stated, looking at Jasper seated next to him. "Bill Eckart was on vacation hiking in the Swiss Alps."

"Oh," said Jasper, not comfortable speaking to the complete stranger sitting next to him. The sound of his voice, with the strong American accent, unsettled Jasper and made it difficult for him to concentrate.

"I'd rather communicate without speaking if you don't mind," Jasper said in his head.

"Excellent. I'm pleased you're adjusting so quickly," Animus replied.

"Where are we going?"

"I can't tell you yet. You'll have to wait a bit longer…"

"Why not?" snapped Jasper before Animus could complete his thought. The verbal outburst was fueled by the frustration boiling inside him.

"I must be absolutely sure it's safe to tell you. That won't be until we board our last flight. I can't risk anything at this point."

"What do you mean?" Jasper responded.

The roar of the aircraft engines filled the cabin when the aircraft accelerated down the runway. "We're only a few hours away; there's too much to risk."

"How do you know I'll even go through with this? What if I don't?"

"Don't worry; it's what you were created to do. There's nothing you can do to stop it now. The closer we get, the more you'll understand."

Jasper didn't like that answer. The idea of having to do something he had no control over was unsettling. Not knowing exactly what he was going to do made it worse.

He pulled the magazine from the pouch in front of him and began mindlessly flipping through the pages as they started their approach into Zurich. Jasper remained silent while they de-planed, and he followed Animus through the airport to the international departures gates. They stopped at Gate 33, where Jasper read the monitor 'Swiss Air 736 to Amsterdam departing 20:36.'

"Why Amsterdam?" asked Jasper as they looked for a seat in the waiting area.

"We'll be spending a couple nights there. I need to make some arrangements, and you need to rest. We'll leave Friday."

"What, then where?" whined Jasper, growing tired of the travel.

"We have another connection in Seattle," Animus explained.

"Seattle!" he replied and perked up momentarily at the sound of a familiar place.

For the first time in weeks, he felt a little home sick.

Seattle was only hours from Kelowna. A fleeting thought whipped through his mind. *I could leave Animus and run to Kelowna.* Reality quickly settled in when he remembered he hadn't lived there in years and there was nowhere to run to.

"Will you tell me where when we get to Seattle?"

"When we're safely on board our final flight. I must prepare you for what will happen."

Jasper had become used to not getting answers from Animus, and with no attempt to hide the displeasure in his voice, he replied, "I can hardly wait."

CHAPTER 29

REALIZATION

T he layover in Amsterdam provided Jasper with little sleep. He spent the two nights awake listening to jets coming and going and staring at the ceiling while he relived the last forty-eight hours over in his mind.

Friday can't come fast enough, he thought and began to realize rushing through airports was better than being a prisoner in a hotel room.

When Friday afternoon arrived and they finally got on their flight to Seattle, Jasper immediately went to sleep. He thought he was dreaming when he heard a soft voice ask him to raise his seat. But reality arrived when the loud voice of the pilot announced they were on final approach to Seattle-Tacoma International Airport.

"How long have I been asleep?"

"About eight hours," Animus said through a small grin. "I'm happy you slept; it'll help ready you for the changes."

"Changes? What if I don't want to change?" Jasper said with apprehension in his voice. But before Animus could respond, Jasper answered himself. "I know, wait, wait, wait..."

They left the aircraft and cleared US Customs before proceeding to the street to flag a taxi. Jasper felt the cool, damp, northwest air flow over his bare arms and legs, causing goose bumps to appear on his arms. The evening sun was low in the sky, hidden by silver-grey clouds. The sound of jets taking off and landing flooded their ears before he and

Animus entered the taxi.

"I thought we were catching another flight—are we overnighting?" Jasper asked.

No sooner had the words left his lips than Animus said, "Boeing Field" to the taxi driver.

Jasper knew this small airport located in the heart of Seattle; it was the testing center for Boeing's new aircrafts.

Jasper continued to mull over the thought of him 'changing' while the taxi navigated heavy traffic on I-5. The faintest feeling of excitement, like butterflies before a first kiss, swirled inside his stomach when they approached Boeing Field. Jasper brushed it off as nerves of not knowing where they were going. Animus instructed the driver to take them to the far end of the airfield, where they stopped in front of a manned gate.

The guard left his seat inside the small booth and approached them. The driver and Animus rolled down their windows simultaneously.

"Good evening. What can I do for you fellows this evening?" said the guard.

Animus reached into the breast pocket of his suit and handed the guard some papers. The guard returned to his booth and made a telephone call. After speaking for a moment on the phone, he returned to the taxi and handed the papers back to Animus through the back window.

"Second hangar on the right," said the guard to the driver while peering in through the driver's window. "Have a good flight, Dr. Eckart," he said as he tapped the top of the taxi before walking back to his booth to open the gate.

With the sun well below the horizon, darkness settled-in much quicker than it had in Rome. The taxi followed the winding road until a large number '2' was visible on the side of the enormous grey building.

"Take us to the other side," Animus instructed. The driver acknowledged and drove the taxi to the front of the hangar, where two perfectly straight ribbons of blue lights mixed with an occasional red and yellow light stretched for more than a mile on either side of the runway. The vivid colors reminded Jasper of Christmas lights. The taxi stopped in front of the hangar doors. Jasper grabbed his pack and left the taxi while Animus paid the fare.

When Jasper entered the hangar, the enormity of the building became apparent. The lights hanging from the ceiling were so high they looked like stars. Their footsteps dissipated into the void as they walked deeper into the building. Along the back wall of the hangar were three small jets stationed in a row.

The size of the hangar made them look more like model aircrafts then actual jets. All three were identical in size and color when viewed through the limited lighting.

Animus led the way toward the jet furthest to the right, which had a set of stairs leading up to an open door. Upon their arrival at the foot of the steps, they were greeted from inside the aircraft by the pilot.

"Welcome aboard, Dr. Eckart. I'm Brad and this is John," said the pilot, pointing to the co-pilot, who was popping his head out the cockpit door.

Animus nodded his head toward John. "Hi, call me 'Bill.' This is Jasper." Jasper extended his hand to meet Brad's and after a brief shake, he gave John a small wave.

"Do you have any other bags?" Brad asked.

"No, these are it," said Animus.

"Good. Then we can go whenever you're ready. The flight plan puts us on the ground in Kona about five and a half hours from now."

"Kona! We're going to Hawaii?" said Jasper like his dad had just broken the news of a surprise vacation. It was the first truly good thing Jasper had heard in the past few days. His jubilation raised his spirits and released the first instance of positive anticipation he had felt in days.

"Oh, did I just spoil a secret?" asked Brad, looking concerned.

"No, don't worry about it. I was going to tell him as soon as we left."

"Okay, guys, take a seat, strap in, and we'll get under way."

Jasper, still jubilant from the news they were going to Hawaii, ignored the fact they were in a private jet. He was consumed with his childhood dream of learning to surf in Waikiki. His dream was interrupted by the sound of the jet engines starting and Brad folding the staircase in as he closed the door.

John had already started moving the jet toward the large hangar door, which was slowly sliding open, when Brad joined him in the cockpit, closing the door behind them. Unlike a commercial flight, the jet was on the runway and airborne within minutes of leaving the hangar.

Without wasting any time, even before the wheels had left the ground, Jasper began questioning Animus.

"Why Hawaii? What happened to Dr. Sabastien, Matteo, and Luca?" asked Jasper without taking a breath.

"Slow down. I'll get to your questions. We have much to cover."

"I've waited long enough," Jasper demanded.

"You needn't worry about anyone—they're Primoris now."

"My mother?"

"Yes," Animus said.

Jasper's body warmed instantly as he fought the tears of joy from breaking free. He felt as though he had just won a prize in a lottery he hadn't entered. Jasper filled with comfort knowing his mother still existed. Animus, aware of the fragile emotional state Jasper was in, paused before continuing.

"Do you remember what I told you about the Primoris?"

Jasper, still overcome by the memory of his mother, managed to formulate an answer.

"Yes."

"Good."

"But..." Jasper started.

"This is our third attempt on earth for Convergence. This is unique. Convergence has always occurred before human self-awareness."

Animus looked at Jasper for any sign of comprehension, but Jasper acknowledged nothing, so he continued.

"Humans can comprehend their own reality but haven't evolved enough to fully realize the concept of their own existence. In the beginning, to fill this gap mankind created a multitude of Gods. Over the last millennia, the concept of a single God has brought mankind to the cusp of discovering their existence—the Primoris."

Jasper thought about this. The words were simple, but the concept was complex. Animus waited patiently.

"Now I'm confused," Jasper admitted.

"Humans perceive the concept of a single God, but they haven't grown to realize where it exists," Animus explained.

'We're all born with this tiny bit of energy, a little piece of God within us, waiting to join the Primoris,' thought Jasper, as he remembered Dr. Sabastien's words, and the understanding rose from inside him, a tidal wave of unstoppable realization.

"Not every human has Primoris inside them. There are those, for reasons unknown, that are born without it, and with others, it just disappears like the light from a blown-out candle."

"But they're still alive?" asked Jasper, unable to visualize what he was being told.

"They live but are lifeless. You can recognize them by the vacuum in their eyes—all light disappears within their eyes, leaving them hollow. These are the humans that will hunt you and stop at nothing to find you."

"Why can't you stop them?"

"Do you mean kill them?"

"Yes. They won't hesitate to put a bullet through my head, why don't you fight back?"

"It's not possible for the Primoris to unwillingly take

another's consciousness."

"You mean kill them?"

"If that's how you see it, yes."

"What are you talking about? The nun, the VSS chasing me, Luca, Dr. Sabastien; they're all dead because of the Primoris."

"Their life is gone, but their consciousness exists."

"What?"

"It's part of the Primoris now."

Jasper mulled over the meaning of the words, not fully convinced.

"Why don't you just share consciousness with me and Christine? Wouldn't that be way easier?"

"The Primoris cannot share consciousness with a human until they've fully developed their own consciousness. The immature mind of a child is incapable of sharing consciousness until they reach the age of twenty."

"Why?"

"They are unable to separate their own consciousness from that of the Primoris. If the Primoris were to share consciousness with a child, the result would be devastating for the human."

"What about an adult?"

"When we share ourselves with a human, we become part of their consciousness. Their own consciousness remains, but it's locked away in their mind's subconscious. Our thoughts and theirs become one. When we leave, all the actions and thoughts we shared become part of their unconscious, buried deep within their mind, and their own consciousness returns, unaware of our presence.

"It's no different than the thousands of unconscious actions your mind performs on a daily basis: breathing, heart beats, standing upright. You do these things completely unaware you are doing them unless they are specifically brought to your consciousness."

"Should I be concerned when we get to Hawaii?" asked

Jasper with some apprehension.

"No, it's the safest place on earth. That's why we hid Christine there."

"Christine?" said Jasper. The mention of her name sparked a quiver to spread through his body with the force of an electric shock. He quickly moved his body in the seat so he could face out the window. Jasper pretended to gaze at the sunset in an effort to conceal his reaction from Animus. The maneuver worked, and Animus made no mention of his sudden movement.

"Yes, Christine," said Animus. "Hawaii is one of the most isolated places on earth. This allowed us to protect her while we waited for critical mass."

Jasper began to fidget like a child; his legs were bouncing up and down, and he continually adjusted his position in the seat.

"It's beginning, isn't it? You can feel the change?"

"What do you mean?" Jasper replied in an attempt to play dumb.

"You feel different—inside? The agitation you just experienced is only the beginning."

"What else is going to happen?" asked Jasper.

"The physical changes will be few: a tingling feeling passing through your body, difficulty sleeping and the constant sexual arousal."

"What? You're joking!"

"The closer you get to Christine, the more difficult it will become for you to control your need to unite—it will consume you."

"You mean sex."

The thought of having sex with a woman he didn't know was unnerving, but finally experiencing an orgasm was unimaginable. It might have been his train of thought or the fact that they were two hours from Hawaii, but Jasper found himself aroused. Just as Animus said, he couldn't get comfortable in his seat and tried to occupy his mind.

"Not just sex. You are going to feel something you've never felt before."

"I hope so," Jasper replied with a grin.

"I'm not talking about an orgasm," Animus said, the seriousness in his tone catching Jasper off guard.

"What are you taking about then?" he asked as his cheeks filled with color.

"I'm speaking about your feelings and emotions. The reason you've never been able to maintain a relationship with a woman is the same reason you've never had an orgasm—we made you that way."

Jasper sat up in his seat and made eye contact with Animus. "What are you talking about?"

"Your ability to experience feeling and emotions is controlled by your genes. We had to be certain."

"About what?" Jasper snapped.

"Certain you could only love one."

"Christine," he stated.

"Yes," said Animus, knowing this would be difficult for Jasper to accept.

Jasper's thoughts turned to the few relationships he had had, and he realized Animus was right. He had desired those women, even experienced lust for some, but he had never loved any of them. He inhaled a deep breath and held it a little longer than normal before letting it slowly escape between his pursed lips. He turned away from Animus and clenched his teeth to ward off the flood of sadness drifting through his mind. *Diana, Angela... all of them, that's why it never worked out for me.* He felt cheated.

"I'm sorry, Jasper. It was the only way."

"How's it going to happen... you know... us getting together?"

"That's up to you and Christine. But it'll take all of your effort to resist initiating the union the moment you see each other. Physical contact will help lessen the immediate urge; however, this won't last long. I've decided you will meet at

Christine's house. It's safe there, and her mother's expecting us."

"Her mother?" Jasper asked, not realizing Christine lived at home. "That makes things a little awkward, doesn't it?"

"Sandy Anderson is part of the Primoris and has been protecting Christine from the moment she was born."

"What's she like?"

"You mean, what does she look like?" said Animus laughing loudly. "It doesn't matter; you'll be unable to resist her. Christine is experiencing exactly the same feelings as you. But if you must know, she is a beautiful young woman."

Jasper stared out the window at the black water below. With each passing mile, his discomfort increased. Jasper's stomach churned inside him, but the rising anticipation of his future was not enough to bury the anguish of his past.

CHAPTER 30

HAWAII

T he moment the jet door opened, warm humid air flooded the aircraft. Jasper's lungs filled with the sweet aroma of tropical flowers.

Jasper and Animus thanked the pilots and left the aircraft.

A steady wind rustled the palms outside the terminal, causing Jasper to glance skyward. The cloudless night sky was glistening with more stars than he had seen in his life. A feeling of anxiety coursed through his body, calling every one of his senses to attention. The outdoor arrival area of Kona Airport was small and deserted; most of the Friday night flights from the mainland had already arrived. Animus led Jasper out of the airport to the street, where they stopped on the edge of the curb.

"There's a taxi. Do you want me to call it?" asked Jasper.

"No, she'll be here in a moment."

"She? I thought..." Jasper didn't finish his statement as a dark blue car stopped at the curb. Animus opened the front door and entered the front passenger side as Jasper reached for the back door handle. He opened the door and tossed his backpack on to the far side of the seat. Although not fully in the car, Jasper heard Animus talk without speaking.

"Let's get him there as quickly as possible—the changes have begun."

"Yes, it won't take long," replied an unfamiliar woman's voice inside Jasper's mind. The voice was much softer than any of the other voices, and this voice had no trace of an accent. The presence of a woman's voice inside his mind startled Jasper, causing him to not close the door properly.

"Jasper, your door isn't shut," said the woman's voice from the driver's seat.

Ignoring the door, Jasper whipped his head around to find the source of the female voice. With the door ajar, the overhead light remained on, allowing Jasper a clear view of the driver. Two familiar blue eyes surrounded by golden-brown skin glowed in the dim car light. Jasper continued to stare in disbelief at the beautiful middle-aged woman with sun-bleached blonde hair sitting in the driver's seat.

"Jasper, please shut your door," she repeated.

Without speaking, Jasper said, "Animus—I heard a woman's voice in my mind. I thought it was…"

"Christine's," said the same soft voice inside Jasper's mind, and the women he was staring at smiled at him.

Animus replied, "Jasper, you can communicate with others—this is excellent." Without speaking, Animus introduced Jasper. "This is Sandra Anderson, but you're speaking with Simone."

Sandra reached her arm over the front seat to shake Jasper's hand. Still stunned with confusion, Jasper shook her hand briefly and closed the door properly before they drove off.

"I'm Christine's mother," said Simone.

"What? Is that why I can barely focus my thoughts—because you share the same genes?"

"No, if that was the case, you would be feeling far worse. Sandra Anderson and Nikolas Stewart were the two Vectors preceding you and Christine," Animus explained.

"My father?"

"Yes. If we had approached critical mass sooner, your father and Sandra would've begun the process, and you and Christine wouldn't have been necessary."

"But Sandra and Christine have the same DNA, so what's

the difference?"

"Your background in genetics is showing through," Animus pointed out with a laugh. "The two Vectors who carry the genetic code are linked temporally."

"What?"

"Time imprinted. It's a safeguard to ensure only one attempt is possible."

"What do you mean?" asked Jasper, displaying confusion in his tone.

"You and Christine were conceived and born at exactly the same instant in time, so your genetic codes are precisely the same age..."

"As if they were a single genetic code," Jasper said, finishing the sentence before Animus could. "That's incredible! We literally are two halves of a single DNA molecule. That's why I'm so compelled to jump out of the car and start running in the opposite direction. She—Christine—must be in the other direction, right?"

"Yes. We're going to spend tonight in town. Tomorrow we'll begin."

"What do you mean? You're not going to stand there and watch us, are you? This sounds a little bit freaky to me."

"Of course not. Our function is to protect you and ensure you and Christine meet in an appropriate location. If we weren't here, what would you be doing?"

"I'd be driving in the other direction as fast as humanly possible. I have no idea where, but I know it's the other way."

"Exactly. And the closer you get to Christine, the stronger the attraction. This attraction would guide you directly to her. Can you imagine what would happen if the two of you met in the middle of a shopping mall? This is why we're here."

"Who's watching her if her mother's here?"

"Her boyfriend."

"What? She has a boyfriend—you didn't tell me that. What does he think of all this?"

"Don't worry. Neither of them knows anything. I wouldn't have told you either, but the VSS left me no choice. Luca's with her."

"You mean 'is'—her boyfriend, right?"

The car pulled into the parking lot of the Royal Kona Resort, and Jasper and Animus left to check in. Sandra didn't get out but waited for the doors to shut. She pulled away after they walked into the hotel lobby. Jasper then heard Simone's soft voice inside his mind.

"I'll pick you up Sunday night at five."

This was followed by the more familiar voice of Animus answering, "Yes," even though the car Sandra was driving was more than a mile from the hotel.

Jasper was glad he was wearing shorts and a T-shirt, even though he hadn't changed in days. The warmth of the tropical night clashed with the frigid air-conditioned lobby, which aggravated the adrenaline rush his body was experiencing. Although he was sweating like a marathon runner, his arms and legs felt the chill. Jasper obsessed about taking a shower, and this single thought overran everything else in his mind, temporarily masking the immediate urge to run towards the magnetic pull he was fighting. They left the elevator on the eighth floor and made their way down the hall to their room.

"Do you mind if I take a shower first?" asked Jasper.

"No, go right ahead. You have your own bathroom," Animus told him.

Jasper tossed his backpack on the bed and stripped his clothes off. He glanced at his completely naked body in the mirror, surprised that he was still aroused. Jasper brushed this off as a result of his overwhelming need to take a shower.

After standing for twenty minutes in the pulsating water, Jasper had found no relief from the compelling urge to leave or the intensity of his arousal. He stepped out of the shower and wrapped a towel around his waist in an effort to hide the state he was in. He looked at the dirty clothes on the bed. *There's no way I'm putting these back on.*

"Animus, do you have any other clothes I can borrow? I've been in these for days, and I can't put them on again," Jasper asked from his bedroom.

"No, but go ahead and use the laundry in the hallway closet if you want." The words entered Jasper's mind the instant he finished his question.

Jasper lay on his bed still draped with the towel listening to music on his MP3 player while waiting for his clothes to dry. The warning Animus gave him about not being able to sleep was true. The uncontrollable urge to leave surged in his body like the roar of the surf outside his window. The music did nothing to quell the rampant thoughts of what was expected of him.

When the laundry had finished, he put his shorts back on and returned to the bed. He directed his thoughts to Christine. *What does she look like? Will she like me? What should I say first?* Jasper continued to use thoughts of Christine to pass the time, but he didn't sleep.

***

Bright morning light entered the room through the open window, painting the ceiling orange. It was a beautiful Sunday morning just before six a.m. Jasper lay on the bed staring at the ceiling, watching the edge of the sunlight slowly move from one side to the other.

His second night in Kona was much better than his first, and he woke up remembering a childhood ambition. Jasper could hear the waves crashing on the rocks. *I wonder if I'll ever learn to surf*, he thought. This moment of mental freedom from the last week quickly vanished as the need to leave surged inside him again.

Not able to stay in bed another minute, he put his shirt on and walked out the sliding glass door to sit on the lanai. The ocean was as smooth as glass. A pod of spinner dolphins broke the surface on their way past the hotel. Jasper peered over the side of the lanai, transfixed on the water below. *I'll survive; it's only the eighth floor.*

The need to find Christine was like a seed growing inside him, slowly transforming every fiber of his being, leaving no part of him unaffected. Jasper unconsciously stepped closer to the railing. He grabbed it with both hands and gazed over the side. Staring blindly at the water below, he was oblivious to the height of the lanai or the perilous black lava below. The rhythmic action of the waves called to him, convincing him that finding Christine was all that mattered. He prepared himself to leap. Gripping the railing with both hands, he lifted his right leg to the top of the railing.

Animus slid the glass door open. Using his voice, Animus belted out a military command.

"Jasper, stop!"

The sound of his voice broke Jasper free from the rhythmic spell of the ocean and the relentless urge to find Christine.

"You must stay inside; as the time grows nearer, the forces acting inside you will consume your thoughts. Here, I ordered breakfast." Animus placed a tray of food on the table in the center of the living room. "Come in and eat."

"I'm not hungry. How can I just stay here and wait? It's tearing me up inside. Is she going through the same thing as me?" asked Jasper in frustration.

"Eat," ordered Animus. "You have to wait, but it won't be long now. And yes, Christine is experiencing the same discomfort as you, but she doesn't have the advantage you have—she doesn't know why she is feeling so compelled to come to town."

"Why isn't she looking for me?"

"She is, but she doesn't know it. As a matter of fact, Christine is in much worse condition than you. The same uncontrollable urges you feel are also racing through her. These feelings alone are overpowering her every thought. What makes it so difficult for her is her boyfriend. The strong sexual feelings she is experiencing are not for him—it's causing her tremendous confusion. Luca is doing everything he can to comfort her and keep her at home."

The morning felt like an eternity to Jasper. He just lay on his bed, staring at the ceiling and listening to music. Endless thoughts flashed through his mind, forming fragmented and fleeting images. His mind was a rapidly spinning merry-go-round, but instead of the usual horses, it was filled with images. They turned faster and faster, so quickly he couldn't make sense of any of them. He tried to concentrate, to see a single image, but it was too difficult. Jasper couldn't focus for more than an instant before a new image arrived in place of the old. There appeared no end to this mental torture until all at once the images vanished. They were replaced by the sound of Matteo's voice. It was clear and resonated in his head. It commanded his attention like a slap in the face.

"Animus, they're here," he said as he watched the aircraft land. Matteo was stationed at the airport as an immigration officer.

The familiar calm voice of Animus answered.

"When did they arrive?"

"The aircraft just touched down," Matteo replied as the concern in his voice escalated.

"Do you know who it is?"

"It's a Vatican jet. How did they find us, Animus?" he asked.

"Don't worry about that now—just let me know as soon as they exit the aircraft. I want to know who we're dealing with."

Animus walked into the bedroom, where he found Jasper sitting up on the bed in anticipation of his arrival.

"Things have changed," Animus said. "The VSS have found us, and we have no time to waste."

"How? I thought they had no idea where we are?"

"It doesn't matter now. What really matters is that they don't find you or learn about Christine."

"They don't know about Christine?"

"No, I'm certain of it, but it won't take them long to figure it out. Once they realize what we're doing, they'll use the full power of the VSS to stop us."

"You mean kill me."

"Yes. Every second counts. Jasper, you must do what I tell you—everything we've worked for depends on this. You can't leave; do you understand?"

"Yes, but..."

"There's no but," Animus said with a tone of urgency that Jasper had never heard before. "No matter how difficult it becomes, you must resist the urge to leave—you must not leave! Stay in the hotel until I send someone. Is that clear?" commanded Animus with even more urgency in his tone.

"What are you going to do? How will you stop them?" asked Jasper, attempting to restrain the concern in his voice.

"We have the advantage; we know they're here. But once the VSS have been given orders, nothing can prevent them from fulfilling them."

"What does that mean?" asked Jasper, quite sure he already knew.

Animus left the room without answering.

CHAPTER 31

GIVE ME YOUR HAND

The late afternoon sun filled the small living room of the Anderson home. The ceiling fan's attempt to cool the room was negligible; the temperature and humidity transformed the room to a sauna. The uncontrollable anxiety Christine felt was exasperated by the heat. She had grown tired of Luca, appearing to her as Jesse, and his efforts, unknowingly to her, to keep her prisoner in her own home. Her agitation was aggravated by the sexual urges, something she had never felt this strong before, racing through her veins. This emotional turmoil was confounded by her lack of interest in Jesse. With each passing moment, she felt more distant from him, and she began to resent his presence.

Luca's ability to keep Christine occupied until Jasper's arrival was failing; he knew it wouldn't be long before Christine left.

"Animus, I won't be able to keep her here much longer—send Simone. I'm sure she'll listen to her mother more than Jesse," requested Luca.

"I'm on my way," replied Simone. .

She left the shopping center where Sandra worked as a cashier and began the drive back to her home.

"While you're on your way, I'll make one last attempt to keep her here," Luca interjected.

"Chris, you have to relax," he begged, but it was no use.

"Shut up, Jess!" she barked. "I've had it! I need to get out of here."

"Where are you going?" asked Luca, knowing full well where she would be headed.

"Just out—I don't know where. I need to get away, away from here, away from you!"

"Why, what have I done?"

"I don't know why. I just need to go. I'm sorry, Jess, it's not you."

Christine stood up from the living room couch and began looking for the keys to her jeep when Luca asked one more time in an effort to try and determine her exact destination.

"Where are you..."

But before he could finish Christine yelled at him.

"I told you I don't know!"

She walked over to Luca, took his hand and looked directly in to his eyes. "I'm sorry, Jess—really I am."

This brought her within inches of his face, allowing her to notice the discoloration in his eyes. Jesse's deep chocolate brown eyes had been replaced by Luca's brilliant blue eyes. Luca had covered them with colored contact lenses to prevent anyone from noticing. He spent the entire day wearing sunglasses where he could and avoiding direct eye contact with Christine.

"What's up with your eyes?" she asked, now close enough to see the effect.

"Nothing," Luca replied, turning his head quickly to the side as if he was trying to hold back tears.

"Is there someone else?" Luca asked, pretending to be jealous.

Christine didn't answer. She couldn't endure another second with him and stormed out of the house.

"Animus, she's left," came a new voice in Jasper's head, which he identified as Luca.

"Did she say where she was going?" Animus asked.

"No," replied Luca. "But we know she'll be heading to town. She's very agitated and confused."

"It's expected," said Animus.

"Jasper, now more than ever, you must not leave the hotel." These words resonated in Jasper's mind, as Animus was no longer around to prevent him from leaving. "The closer she comes to you, the stronger your urge to leave will become—you must not leave!" commanded Animus.

"Okay, okay, I get it. I won't leave," replied Jasper, angered by the orders and frustrated by the prison cell he was confined to.

"Luca, make your way to the airport and assist Matteo," ordered Animus.

"What about Jesse? He's overwrought with anguish. I'm afraid he'll—"

"We have no choice. Leave him and get to the airport," demanded Animus without letting Luca finish.

Luca left Jesse at Christine's house and instantly arrived at the airport, joining Matteo as a second immigration officer. They waited for the unmarked private jet to stop on the terminal.

"Is it wise to let her go without accompaniment?" asked Luca.

"We have no choice. As long as they are unaware of Christine, she's safe. The VSS are only focused on finding Jasper. We can't let it happen. If it's necessary, I'll use everyone again.

"We were twelve last time and failed," Matteo pointed out.

"That was more than two thousand years ago—things have changed since then. We will not fail. I'll be at the airport in a moment," Animus responded.

When Jasper heard Matteo mention they were 'twelve last time,' his mind catapulted him back to the castle boardroom. It all made sense now. The additional voices entering his mind were confusing. He remained silent, listening to the instructions given by Animus without interrupting. His desire to know more was dwarfed by the rapid changes engulfing his body. The changes resonated from his heart, which pounded harder and harder deep in his chest. Each rhythmic beat fired another shot of adrenalin through his veins, leaving no part of his body immune from the torture. Jasper knew this could only mean one thing—Christine was close.

***

Christine drove down the road toward town without knowing why. Her body pulled to town like a riptide dragging her out to sea. Her repulsion of Jesse was complete; he never entered her thoughts. The minute she turned the corner onto Alii Drive, it became clear where she was going. The upwelling of emotions from a moment ago subsided when the old stone Catholic church came into view.

This is it, she thought. *This is the answer.* Her faith in God would halt the uncontrollable urges rushing through her body. Like it had a thousand times before, her faith would erase the urges and sexual desires. *If I pray, God will put an end to these feelings.* Christine glanced at the clock in the dashboard and knew she could make the five o'clock Mass.

She parked the jeep and entered the church. She went to the first open pew and pulled the kneeling board from the back, getting to her knees to pray.

Father Shannon and the altar boys were already in position behind the small wooden altar when Christine begged God for relief.

***

The stone church was only a few hundred yards down the road from the Royal Kona Resort. Christine's proximity to Jasper instantly began to take its toll on him. The strain was about to erupt inside him. It came in waves, like the winds of a severe thunderstorm pushing against the branches of a tree; twisting and bending them farther with each moment of its approach. Jasper paced from room to room in the small condo repeating over in his head, *I must not leave!* It was hopeless. Like the power of an approaching storm, the impact of Christine's arrival at the church was definitive. No thunder or violent cracking sound preceded the event, but it was just as decisive—Jasper snapped. He grabbed his backpack and left the resort. Holding back the urge to sprint, he began walking up the side of the road, unknowingly toward the old stone church.

***

Animus arrived at the airport and met the others. The jet rolled up to a position in front of the terminal and shut down its engines. Animus sent three more Primoris as ground crew to assist the others while he waited in the terminal. This was the first step in his plan to delay the VSS. Animus knew he would only be able to hold them for a short period.

The sudden appearance of additional Primoris voices in his mind at the same time made it impossible for Jasper to understand what was going on. The only voice he could comprehend belonged to Animus. When Animus gave an order, it silenced all the other voices. They would keep the jet on the tarmac for as long as possible. If it became necessary, he would send others to watch over Jasper and Christine. Animus knew Jasper was safe as long as they could keep him hidden.

Luca and Matteo entered the aircraft. "Animus, there are three aboard, and it's him," Matteo said.

"Just as I expected," replied Animus. "It's worse than I thought. They know how close we are."

Jasper couldn't hold his silence and he stopped walking.

"Who?" he demanded.

"Don't concern yourself, Jasper. There's still time. They won't find you, just stay where you are," he said.

Animus could hear the desperation in Jasper's voice and knew he had to act quickly. He sent another Primoris to watch over Jasper.

The Primoris arrived instantly in the lobby and found the hotel female concierge asleep behind her desk. She raced up to the unit and found it empty.

"We're too late, he's gone, Animus," said the Primoris after searching the empty hotel room.

"Jasper, where are you?" Animus demanded. "Come back. The danger is far too great, and we can't help you unless we know where you are."

Jasper didn't respond.

"Jasper, where are you?" demanded Animus in a desperate attempt to find him.

Jasper ignored him and approached the church. He stopped and stood motionless, looking at the front of the building. The sight of the cross on the building paralyzed him. Jasper took no notice of the small pick-up truck turning into the church parking lot.

***

After ten years of dating, Jesse knew Christine better than anyone else. He knew the one place she would go on a Sunday evening—to the church. Christine relied on her faith to guide her when troubled, as she had done this many times in the past. Jesse pulled his truck into the church parking lot and smiled when he saw her Jeep. He decided to stay in his truck until Mass ended; it was no use trying to speak to her in the church.

***

Jasper moved slowly up the lava-stone path to the front doors. He was no longer in control of his body. His every movement felt like it was being controlled by the pull of a string. Jasper couldn't stop his hand from reaching for the door handle. The steel handle was warm in his hand as he wrapped his fingers around it; he began slowly pulling the large wooden door open.

***

A single small tear slid from the corner of Christine's eye, and she left her pew to walk out of the church. Her faith in God had never failed her before. She asked herself why as she walked to the church entrance. God had always provided the relief she so desperately prayed for. She placed her trembling hand on the entrance door and began to push it open.

***

Twenty-five years and thousands of miles had kept them separated; nothing had divided them more than the church. But now, unknowingly working together, they removed the final barrier. Brilliant orange sunlight from the setting sun skipped over the Pacific Ocean, setting Christine's eyes aglow.

With the church door open, Jasper stood directly in front of Christine, overwhelmed by her presence. The urge to wrap himself around her was interrupted by the uncontrollable shaking of his body. He could see that Christine was experiencing the same reaction.

"Christine?" Jasper asked without using his voice.

"Yes... do I know you?"

Their bodies continued to shake. It was taking every ounce of Jasper's strength to keep from embracing her at that moment.

"What's going on? What's happening to me?" Christine asked, showing signs of distress.

"Give me your hand," demanded Jasper without speaking.

"Why?" she responded.

"Now!" Jasper shouted inside her mind.

Christine reached out to his extended hand and grabbed it.

As their hands touched, relief flashed up their arms, flooding their bodies with a sense of calmness.

"Who are you? How do you..." she was afraid to say the words; it was too incredible to believe.

"My name is Jasper. How do I... what?" Jasper didn't realize he was speaking to Christine without using his voice.

"I hear you talk, but your lips don't move—it's like I can hear you in my head."

Before Jasper could do anything, he had to be sure he and Christine would be able to function together.

"I'm going to try something, okay?"

"What are you talking about?" Christine asked.

"I want you to let go of my hand on the count of three and tell me what you feel. Ready?"

"What?"

"Just do it—1, 2, 3."

The moment she let go of Jasper's hand, they both began to shake, and their bodies filled with an uncontrollable lust. They both didn't care who was watching or if they would be arrested, fulfilling their need was all that mattered.

"Jasper!" shouted Animus, but only Jasper could hear him. "Where are you? Are you with Christine?"

The words entered Jasper's mind as if Animus was standing in front of him shouting in his ear. Jasper put his hand up in the air to silence Christine's attempt to speak.

"Yes, we're together."

"Have you...?"

"Not yet," Jasper interrupted, knowing exactly what Animus wanted to know.

"Where are you?" Animus demanded.

"In town," replied Jasper.

"Hide—immediately! Go! Now!" Animus shouted.

Jasper quickly grabbed Christine's hand, sending the flood of relief back through their bodies. Not only did it reduce the urges when they held hands, but Jasper also realized he couldn't hear anyone in his mind, not even Animus, but

Christine could still hear him.

"We need to get out of here—right away," Jasper said urgently.

"Why? What's going on? I'm not going anywhere until I know what's happening to me. Why do I feel like this?" protested Christine.

"Do you have a car?" Jasper asked.

"Yes," replied Christine as she pointed to her Jeep with her free arm.

Jasper pulled her toward the parking lot, but she protested, stopping abruptly to rip her hand free from his. "I'm not going anywhere until you tell me what's going on." Christine barely had enough time to get the words out of her mouth when the urges erupted inside her.

Christine jumped onto Jasper and wrapped her body around his, causing his pack to fall to the ground.

"What's happening to me?"

As Christine madly attempted to pull his shirt off, Jasper found her right hand with his. He grasped it as tightly as he could without hurting her and told her without using words, "I'll explain later, I promise. Trust me—right now we've got to get out of here."

Jasper picked up his pack with his free hand and slung it over his shoulder again.

"Do you know where we can hide?"

The shock of hearing Jasper's words inside her mind and the surge of relief from the handholding calmed Christine to the point where she let go of Jasper's body.

"Yes, I know a place we can go," Christine said, taken aback by the voice in her mind.

"Does anyone else know about it?"

"No, it's a great place."

***

Jesse had sat in his truck watching Christine and a guy

approach the parking lot holding hands. The initial jealousy boiling inside him was quickly replaced with a furious anger. Out of instinct, he ducked down in his truck as they ran to the Jeep.

Christine got in from the passenger side so she didn't have to let go of the man's hand. Jesse saw the man toss his pack in the back of the Jeep and follow Christine into the seat. The action of the two of them entering the Jeep without even letting go of their hands deepened Jesse's anger. He had little doubt that their secret love affair had been going on for some time. Jesse started his truck and followed them from a distance.

***

"Christine, I need to let go of your hand for a few seconds. I know it's uncomfortable, but I'll explain later."

The second Jasper released his grip, words came flooding into his mind.

"Jasper, where are you?" pleaded Animus. "We couldn't stop them. Have you found a place to hide?"

Jasper could see the stress not holding her hand was having on Christine and grasped it again to give them both relief. Christine appreciated the instant calming effect, and she smiled briefly.

"Sorry, I have to let go again, but only for another second," Jasper explained.

"Don't!" she begged.

Jasper quickly released his grip. "We're on our way," said Jasper.

"Where?" asked Animus.

"I don't know. Christine is taking us. I'll ask."

"Where we going?"

"A beach no one knows about," Christine said, straining to keep her composure while driving.

"We're headed to a beach," Jasper relayed to Animus.

"What beach? Where?" Animus demanded, clearly in distress.

Jasper took her hand and asked, "What's the name of the beach?"

"It doesn't have one. It's a tiny little beach away from tourists where I go surfing—north of the airport. You'll never find it unless you know where it is."

The words had just left her mouth when Christine pulled the Jeep off the highway and started driving over the black lava rock toward the ocean. The Jeep bounced up and down over rocks and ruts in the lava, making it impossible for Jasper to keep a firm grip on Christine's hand. Every time their hands separated, a shockwave of desire rushed through their veins, forcing Christine to drive faster. Jasper couldn't see the ocean through the windshield, as the crimson sunset was shining directly into his eyes.

"This is the last time," and Jasper let go of her hand to inform Animus.

"A small beach just north of the airport."

"Where, Jasper? I need to know exactly where you are so we can help you."

Jasper didn't hear this request, as he had rejoined the link between himself and Christine.

***

The VSS left the airport and headed south on the Island Highway towards town. High above the highway, a white tern followed their car—Animus wouldn't leave them unattended. After driving a little over a mile towards town, the VSS abruptly pulled off the road and made a U-turn. Animus tried in vain to contact Jasper to let him know they had changed direction and were headed north.

***

Linked like a pair of Siamese twins, Jasper and Christine left the Jeep. She had parked in front of the long strip of thick brush which concealed the beach like a stage curtain. She grabbed her beach towel from the back of the Jeep as Jasper took his pack.

"You can leave it; I'm sure it'll be safe," said Christine through a smile.

"Yeah, I guess you're right," and he tossed his pack back into the Jeep.

Jasper began walking toward the water when Christine pulled him in the opposite direction. They walked a few steps in front of the Jeep when Christine lifted a giant fan palm leaf to reveal a well-hidden path. They walked for a few hundred yards before exiting on the other side of the bush.

Jasper froze in place at the scene in front of his eyes. Christine tried to pull him farther down the beach, but his feet were cast in concrete while he absorbed the scene. Astonishment momentarily subdued his desire for Christine, and he stood motionless in disbelief. The sun was setting directly across the water, perfectly aligned with the front of the narrow white sand beach. Palm trees grew out of the cracks in the rocks and lined both sides of the beach, providing a near-perfect arch over the narrow patch of sand. They stood motionless on a strip of sand bordered on both sides by glistening black lava flows. The lava flows reaching into the ocean like the fingers of a giant's hand, each separated by the glistening white sand.

"Jasper, what's wrong?"

He didn't answer Christine but continued his silence.

"Isn't this the most beautiful place you've ever seen?" asked Christine in hopes of breaking Jasper's silence. She tossed the beach towel on the sand and completely forgot all the questions she had for him.

"I've seen it before," was all he could say.

"What?" said Christine in disbelief.

It wasn't the beauty before his eyes that had caused

Jasper's paralysis but the scene itself. This wasn't the first time Jasper had gazed upon it. He had seen it before on the fresco on the ceiling of the castle where he had first learned of the Primoris and first met Animus. The painting was of Adam and Eve, or so he thought. The image was etched into his mind—the palm trees lining the beach, the rocky shoreline, the perfect setting sun and the two naked figures walking into the sunset.

Jasper turned to look at Christine, who was removing the last of her clothing. Standing completely naked except for her necklace she quickly began removing Jasper's shirt. Nothing felt more right to Jasper. The very last rays of the setting sun gilded their bodies in a warm glow.

They began walking toward the ocean, their rapid breathing hidden by the sound of the waves crashing on the shore. The ocean breeze lifted Christine's hair from her shoulders, suddenly revealing her birthmark. Jasper smiled, knowing what was to come, knowing this was exactly how it was meant to be.

Their feet entered the water as the sun completed its final act, disappearing below the horizon to bring an end to the day.

CHAPTER 32

FIRST KISS

T he pick-up truck came to a stop on the solidified lava next to the Jeep as it had done a hundred times before. Jesse sat in his truck playing the image of Jasper and Christine holding hands over in his mind. The anger inside him grew with each passing moment, exploding into rage. The energy inside Jesse vanished like the final sliver of sunlight over the horizon. His eyes were now the color of the lava. Jesse was venomous.

Christine was his only love—his childhood friend and girlfriend. But now he wanted her to suffer, hurt the way he was hurting. Nothing else mattered, and he wouldn't stop until he confronted her. Jesse entered the bush to make his way to the beach.

***

A large car parked next to the truck. Three men remained in the vehicle with the engine off, scanning the surroundings. A grey-haired man was first to exit, straightening his suit as he stood on the warm lava rock. A second man stepped out of the back of the car and placed an open laptop on the roof so he could remove his jacket. The driver followed, removing his dark black robe and tossing it in the back of the car. The three men walked toward the water while Animus circled overhead.

"Where is he, Gino?" asked Tonino.

Gino clicked the laptop screen frantically. "He should be right here—I don't understand?" Gino replied. "It has to be right here."

"See if it's in there," said Tonino, pointing to the Jeep.

"Yes, sir, at once," responded Father Derksen. He grabbed Jasper's pack from the back of the Jeep and pulled the phone from the top pouch.

"It's here."

"Make certain it's his."

Father Derksen touched the key pad, which activated the phone's display; *'6:22pm Sunday September 26, 2010—Jasper Stewart'* appeared on the small screen.

"It's his."

Animus was now certain of what he had always suspected; Tonino was commanding the VSS, not Father Derksen. It was also clear how they had found Jasper so easily. The US Intelligence software on the laptop performed flawlessly. It had tracked Jasper's phone to within a few feet.

Tonino knew the moment he had found Jasper's phone in the bakery that it was a gift. The solution to his problem had been handed to him—how to find both Vectors at the same time. It was so simple; follow one and it would lead him to the other. The key was finding them before it was too late.

Looking at the two parked vehicles, Tonino's face broke into a smile.

"Excellent! They're both here. They can't be far—let's get this over with," he said.

The three men walked slowly toward the ocean, stumbling over the uneven lava flow. The twilight combined with their leather shoes made it difficult to walk. Standing at the water's edge, Tonino could see only the outline of two figures in the distance. They drew their handguns and approached the figures with the stealth of a SWAT team.

***

Jesse stood empty, as hollow as the darkness within him. He stood there, a shell of a human, void of all feeling. The evening light was enough to recognize the woman he loved standing naked with another man.

The crashing waves provided the perfect cover for Jesse as he pulled the wood from the back of the surfboard sign. Jesse wrenched the two-by-four Christine had nailed the sign to from the ground. The oversized spikes remained protruding from the end of the sign like the claws of a bear. He carried it with both hands as he walked through the sand to the bodies completely embraced by each other.

***

Jasper stood behind Christine and wrapped his arms around her body. He pressed his skin tighter against hers with every passing second, never wanting to separate. Waves crashed on the shore, surging the turquoise water between their legs. The inside of his chest tingled. Jasper felt as though he had just been born and every cell in his body came alive at once. He had never felt more alive than at this moment. He felt something he had never felt before—love.

Christine closed her eyes as Jasper slowly began to turn the front of her body towards his. The sheer power of their connection rendered them oblivious to their surroundings. Every nerve inside them seemed to fire at once.

Their other senses couldn't warn them of the approaching danger. They explored each other's bodies, their hands racing over each other's skin, releasing them from their prison of desire. Neither could wait any longer. Their uncontrollable urges would finally come to an end.

Christine slowly forced her hand between their tightly pressed bodies and gently held him in her hand. As she slowly guided him closer, Jasper felt the warmth of the penetration—it made his back burn, the pain was like nothing he had experienced before. It started in the center and radiated to his limbs. His arms and legs were no longer attached to his body. Like cutting the strings of a puppet, Jasper's body fell backwards into the water, Christine falling into the water with him.

Jesse had slammed the wood into Jasper's back with sufficient force to drive one of the steel spikes through his spine, severing his spinal cord. The other spikes completed the lethal damage, puncturing his lungs and rupturing his aorta.

Jesse stood for a moment, silently overlooking the two naked bodies lying in the water at his feet. Holding the bloody board in his hand, Jesse leaned backwards, bracing his body against the lava flow.

"No, Jasper, no!" screamed Christine as he collapsed in her arms.

Heads turned to search for the source of the scream, but the three men couldn't see Christine. The large black lava flow hid her and Jasper from view. The sound of gunfire shattered the air. Jesse slid downward against the lava onto his knees, clutching his chest. Blood poured through his fingers from the bullet holes in his chest, draining the life from his body. Hidden below the lava, Christine hadn't heard the gunfire over the crashing surf. She didn't notice Jesse's death; her only concern was Jasper.

Christine cradled Jasper's head out of the water in her arms. She rocked him slowly while tears filled her eyes. Waves swirled around their bodies, turning the water crimson red. Christine took no notice of the small white tern that landed a few feet from her.

The flash of the white wings caught Jasper's eye, but he was unable to communicate with Animus, as Christine held him tightly in her arms. He looked at Animus and struggled to speak.

"I'm so sorry. There can be no Convergence..."

"What?" asked Christine, confused by his words.

Animus looked back at Jasper and took flight. Now that Animus was gone, Jasper could see the writing on the surfboard with the last remnants of twilight. A weak grin formed on his lips when he read the hand-painted lettering and he spoke his final word, —"Templum."

Jasper coughed, sending blood into his mouth. He could taste it, and a small trickle seeped from the corner of his lips.

"Shhh," cooed Christine. "Don't talk," she whispered through a cry and squeezed Jasper's head tightly into her chest. Christine's necklace pressed into Jasper's cheek, and the image of the Virgin Mary formed in his mind.

"Kiss me," he demanded.

She heard his last request in her mind as clearly as if he had shouted it. Christine moved Jasper's head from her chest and pressed her lips tightly against his, kissing him for the first time on the lips. She kissed him with the passion of a newlywed saying good-bye to her husband. The metallic taste of his blood burned her tongue like a bee sting. Jasper couldn't feel her passion or the tender motion of her soft lips pressing his—Jasper didn't kiss back. Their first kiss was also their last.

Christine released her lips from his, and her breathing became rapid and difficult. The stinging progressed from her tongue to her lips and raced down her throat when she swallowed.

Animus flew back to the beach landing on a rock a foot from Christine. The appearance of the bird didn't register with her.

"Christine, you must leave," a new voice in her mind demanded.

"What?" she said out loud. She knew the voice wasn't Jasper's.

"You have to leave at once—your life depends on it," said Animus.

Christine's faith guided her; she was sure this was the voice of God.

"What do you want me to do?" asked Christine as she gazed skyward with tear-filled eyes.

"Swim," Animus said simply.

Christine's faith was strong, but it wasn't enough to let her enter the water without hesitation. The pounding surf and darkness frightened her.

"Swim now!" commanded Animus.

The three men approached with guns drawn. Christine crawled on her hands and knees into the pounding surf until she found herself floating in the water. She swam directly into the rushing waves, not nearly as comfortable as when on her surfboard.

"Dive below the surface," Animus ordered.

Christine did as she was told even though the rush of the surf was overpowering her. She took a deep breath, forcing her body below the surface. Waves rolled overhead, releasing the roar of a jet engine.

Christine panicked from the disorientation of the deep black water surrounding her. Doubt cast a shadow over her faith as she scrambled to find the surface, her mother's words racing through her mind, *"I don't want you in that water after dark."* Panic turned to horror as her lungs began to burn from the salt water. She was out of air when a familiar sound lifted her spirits. It was a rattle, like a baby's toy, clicking rapidly right next to her. She stopped struggling, stopped swimming and stopped breathing. Her body relaxed and floated in calmness. The water tickled her skin and her weightlessness caused euphoria within her.

Without warning, the clicking sound blasted inside her ears, faster and louder. Her body was thrust forward, destroying her euphoria and replacing it with the sensation of rushing water. She screamed in silence from the retching pain in her arms, which rose above her body. Someone was pulling her through the water by her arms, nearly tearing them out of her shoulders.

Star light peppered her eyes the instant the warm night

air filled her lungs. Christine surfaced a hundred yards past the surf line, unable to swim and unable to cry. Floating on her back, she began to pray.

"Our Father who art in heaven…"

Her prayer was cut short when the two spinner dolphins returned. Matteo and Luca positioned their bodies back under her arms.

***

Tonino gazed down at Jasper's partially floating body, the surge of the waves lifting it up and down like a piece of driftwood.

"This isn't what I expected," he said to Father Derksen and Gino.

"Someone has done our work for us. But who was this servant of God?" Tonino kicked Jesse's lifeless body so he could shine his flashlight onto Jesse's face. "Could it be they created such an abomination?" A sinister laugh escaped between his emotionless words. Tonino smiled while watching Jasper's naked body float in a mixture of blood and water.

"It appears the Vector preferred the company of men? A lovers' quarrel and something went terribly wrong," said Tonino, the smugness of victory clear in his voice.

"Throw him with his lover," Tonino commanded.

After tossing Jesse's body into the ocean, the three men walked back to their car.

"I'm surprised and disappointed," said Tonino, gazing into the blackness of the Hawaiian night.

"Shall I inform the others?" asked Father Derksen.

"Yes, tell them of our success and let them know things have changed," Tonino ordered.

CHAPTER 33

A MATTER OF BELIEF

Tonino decided to conduct some business before leaving Hawaii since they had come such a long way. The steeple atop the small stone church was glowing from the early morning sun when the three men entered St. Michael's Church. Father Andrew Shannon and his deacon, Richard Whyte, were repairing a pew and didn't take notice when the church door opened.

Father Shannon was a tall, thin priest with salt-and-pepper hair and a pleasant smile which accented his middle-aged face and warm and welcoming grey-green eyes. Richard was the opposite, his face cold and lifeless, rarely cracking a smile in his sixty-plus years.

Father Shannon ran swiftly down the steps of the altar to greet the men as they proceeded up the aisle. He recognized the traditional robes from his early work at the Vatican. He met Tonino first, as he was slightly ahead of the other two men and made the sign of the cross before offering his hand to introduce himself.

"Welcome to our parish. What a nice surprise to have your Holiness in our humble church," said Father Shannon with his slight foreign accent.

Richard caught up to the men and stood to the right of Father Shannon.

"I'm Andrew Shannon and this is Richard Whyte, a deacon with our parish."

Richard didn't offer his hand but instead nodded to the men.

"I apologize for our unplanned arrival, Father," said Father Derksen. "We were on the Island dealing with another matter and thought it impolite not to visit." Forcing a fake smile to his lips, Father Derksen handed both men his business card.

"No apology necessary. How wonderful! Can I offer you some coffee?" asked Father Shannon.

"No, thank you," said Tonino. "We only have a few minutes. However, we would like to ask you a few questions, if you don't mind." Tonino turned and gestured to Gino, who was already removing his laptop from its case.

"Yes, of course, anything," Father Shannon assured them.

"How long have you been at this parish?" asked Tonino.

"More than twenty-five years—it was my first and only assignment after the Vatican. I do love it here and have a very strong congregation," said Father Shannon, concerned the visitors were there to move him from his parish.

"Don't worry, Father, we're not here to relocate you," responded Tonino with a laugh.

Father Shannon's face glowed with relief.

"During your time here, have you come across any parishioners with a mark like this?" Tonino pointed to the screen on the laptop, which Gino held so that both Father Shannon and Richard could see the image. The screen displayed a symbol of the Convergence.

"No. Is it a tattoo?" asked Father Shannon, clearly confused by the oddity of their request.

"No need to worry—it's only of interest to us. Thank you for your time. Now, we really must be going," said Tonino.

Father Derksen made the sign of the cross, quickly followed by the other four men. The five of them bowed before the altar and left the church.

Father Shannon and Richard stood in the entranceway when Father Shannon offered a final wave as the men drove off. He knew there was more to their visit; an appearance from the Vatican was unprecedented in his twenty-five years on the Island. It left him confused and anxious, as something in the photo did seem familiar.

***

The sun continued its rise above the massive volcano, turning the sky a powder blue. Christine floated in the water, half dazed, supported by Matteo and Luca. Animus circled overhead and waited for Simone to make her way to Kua Bay beach. She waded into the water to help Christine to shore.

"Mom, I'm so happy to see you," Christine cried. "How'd you know?"

"It's okay," Simone said.

Shivering uncontrollably, Christine was frozen and exhausted from her night in the water. Unable to stand on her own, Sandra placed her on the beach.

"Sit while I get you a towel."

Sandra returned from her car and wrapped a towel around Christine's naked body.

"It was God. It was a miracle, wasn't it?" proclaimed Christine.

"Save your energy, Chris."

Christine couldn't hold back as emotions welled to the surface. The events of the past night entered her mind at random.

"I'm telling you, it's a miracle. I spoke to Him you know— God. He told me to swim. Dolphins came. He saved me from Jesse, God saved me. Oh, Mom, Jesse killed Jasper."

The events of the previous night began to fly through Christine's mind in small pieces.

"Come on, Chris. Let me help you to the car. You're exhausted."

Sandra lifted her from the beach and acted as a human crutch to get Christine over the lava flows separating the beach from the parking lot.

"I'm not crazy, Mom," said Christine while they drove down the Island highway.

"I know you're not. Just relax, we're almost home."

Christine's eyes drooped closed and she faded in and out of consciousness. When they entered the house, Sandra ordered her to bed, but as always, Christine ignored her mother and sat on the side of the bed shaking. Sandra entered her room and took a seat next to her.

"Mom, I met this guy—Jasper. I was out of control, and I couldn't stop wanting him—but I didn't know why. And then Jesse appeared out of nowhere... it was horrible!"

"Chris, listen to me. You need to get some sleep. We can talk about this later," said Sandra.

"I can't. I can't get him out of my mind. I never felt that way before. We were about to... and yet I didn't even know him. I couldn't help myself—it was like I was under some kind of spell."

Sandra gave her a glass of juice and a cookie then put her to bed. Sandra refused to talk to Christine about her ordeal until the morning, but she had one last question.

"Mom, how did you know where to find me?" asked Christine, now nearly asleep.

Sandra didn't answer as she pulled a blanket over her and left the room. Christine lay on her bed. Curled into the fetal position, she held her stomach from the tingling sensation inside.

***

Jasper found himself walking down a corridor towards a familiar bluish-white light. His steps were absolutely silent so he looked down to see the ground. He saw only light. He looked up and saw only light—everywhere only light. The light was soothing and warm, like the first sunlight of a spring day.

Absent was sound, gone was the rhythmic crashing of the waves, no more sand pressing between his toes, and lost was the smell of salt air. Gone too was Christine and the uncontrollable urges. There was only light and unexplainable peacefulness. Jasper continued his walk until a new feeling emerged, one he had never experienced before—it was time, or more precisely the lack of it. Jasper didn't know if he had been walking for minutes, hours, days or even years—time had vanished.

He walked a little farther when the outline of a person appeared before him. It gestured for him to come. They stood face to face in silence. Jasper examined the figure, desperately trying to identify it, but no face came into focus. The appearance of the figure brought on a battle that raged inside him, enlisting every emotion he ever felt. His emotions struggled for freedom, but Jasper held them close. He pulled them so close they fused inside him, forming a single, powerful feeling—love.

"Jasper," said Animus.

"Yes?"

"What do you see?"

"I think it's my mother."

Animus didn't answer.

"Where am I?" asked Jasper, never taking his eyes from the figure.

Animus held his silence.

Doubt whipped through Jasper's mind, and he began to question his beliefs. Standing alone with the figure, his beliefs fractured, leaving him struggling for understanding.

"God?"

The deep, familiar voice of Animus entered his mind. When Animus spoke, his voice transformed, becoming the gentle soothing voice of his mother.

"Jasper," she whispered.

"Yes, Mom," he replied, and just thinking the words filled him with unspeakable joy.

"It's only what you believe that matters."

The light that had enveloped Jasper faded slowly before finally disappearing completely. His mother materialized in front of him, and Jasper opened his eyes for the first time in his existence.

PREVIEW OF BOOK TWO

HUNTED

CHAPTER 1

JUMP

The last amber rays of sunlight slipped beneath the surface of the ocean, giving birth to a warm Hawaiian evening. Heat continued to radiate from the ink-black lava rocks like the embers of a fading fire. No breeze could be felt; the air was void of the familiar musky scent of the ocean, replaced with the sweet fragrance of frangipani. An unprecedented calm held the water in its grip, thwarting even the smallest of waves from reaching the shore. Darkness gathered as Christine stood on the edge of the cliff, peering into the tranquil water.

"What are you waiting for?" said the voice inside her head.

"What?" she replied and snapped her head around, expecting to see someone.

"Do it!" said the voice.

"I can't."

"You want to, don't you?"

"I do but..."

"Jump!" commanded the voice.

"I can't," she repeated, the tears racing down her cheeks.

"You must."

"Jasper… I'm afraid."

"Don't be."

Christine closed her eyes and stepped off the cliff, leaving her anxiety embedded in the rock. A smile filled her lips as a childlike laugh rushed from deep inside her, fueled by the euphoria of the fall. All sensation of time vanished. Christine was certain the Hand of God carried her to the water, for it felt like hours before she reached the surface. No cool wind poured over her skin, and there was no sound of air filling her ears. She cut through the surface of the water like an Olympic diver, sliding effortlessly into the ocean.

Christine opened her eyes when the warm salty water enveloped her. The swarm of bubbles streaming past her face dissipated like a curtain opening in a theatre, allowing the last remnants of the surface to fade from view. Complete darkness surrounded her. Absent was the urge to breathe, and she remained motionless, her senses held a prisoner of the vacuum she had entered.

"Jasper, where are you?" she asked, but only silence remained. "Where are you?" she repeated, anger evident in her thoughts. The silence was absolute.

Suddenly, the darkness was punctured by a pinhole of bluish-white light. A sharp pain accompanied the appearance of the light. Christine lowered her hands towards her waist in an effort to quell the ache originating from below her ribcage.

The diffuse light continued to expand towards her like an approaching subway train. The pain grew in unison with the light, radiating out from her stomach and growing more intense. The underwater silence was broken by a faint rhythmic pounding. It too began slowly like the beat of a drum but increased in intensity with the light. She was convinced it was her heart about to explode.

Christine focused on the light as it approached in an effort to distract herself from the growing pain. Her incredible physical condition was no match for the burning agony ripping through every nerve in her body. Her mind begged for an end of the torture, and her body curled into a fetal position. Then she noticed it, the once single point of light had become two; like the eyes of a cat reflected in the headlights of a car. Christine grabbed the top of her knees, sinking her fingernails deep into her flesh as the lights came closer into the darkness.

***

"Christine... Chris..." said the soft voice of her mother, Sandra Anderson.

Christine's eyes remained closed when Sandra put a hand on her head. Sandra slid the sheet off, uncovering her daughter's sweat-soaked body still clenching her knees.

"Honey, you need to get up," said Sandra while she pulled back Christine's sun-bleached hair off her face. Like surfacing from a dive, Christine's eyes and mouth opened simultaneously as she inhaled a deep breath.

"Mom?" said Christine with panic in her voice.

"Yes."

"I had the same dream, but it was worse."

"How so?"

"The light wasn't really a light—it was a pair of eyes. And this time the pain was terrible, like some kind of monster eating me from the inside."

"Don't worry, it's only a dream."

"But it's so real," she said fighting back her tears. Christine drew upon her faith for support and rarely cried. The twenty-plus years surfing the waves off Kona had carved Christine physically, but her faith in God remained the foundation of her strength.

"You need to eat something," said Sandra, not able to hide the concern spilling from her crystal blue eyes, the very same eyes as her daughter's. "You haven't had a thing since yesterday."

"I'm not hungry."

"Christine S. Anderson, you listen to me, you will eat something this morning even if I have to spoon-feed you myself," raged Sandra in an effort to get Christine to eat.

"Okay, I hate it when you call me that. I'll get something after I shower," she replied, knowing she was going to lose the battle based on the tone of her mother's voice.

"Fine, I'll get it ready. What do you want?"

"Just some fruit, a piece of toast and…"

Christine's request was interrupted by a knock on the front door.

"I'll get it, you go get cleaned up," said Sandra as she walked to the door. When she opened it, a plain-clothes police officer stood on the porch.

"Hello, Officer," Sandra said, spotting the officer's police badge hanging from her breast pocket.

"Good morning, ma'am."

"Can I help you?" asked Sandra in a surprisingly relaxed voice.

"I'm Officer Sorren. Do you have a daughter named Christine?"

"Yes. Is there a problem?"

"No. Is she home?"

"Yes, but she's in the shower, can I help?"

The officer looked at Sandra and decided to begin her questioning.

"Do you know a Jesse Struger?"

"Yes. Why?"

"Have you seen him recently?"

"No, he hasn't been around in weeks. Is everything okay?"

"His family is looking for him. They haven't been able to contact him for the past two weeks and…" continued the officer, but she stopped mid-sentence to answer her radio.

"Excuse me, Mrs. Anderson, I have to leave. Please have your daughter call us if she has any contact with Mr. Struger.

"Of course, immediately."

"Thank you," said the officer as she swiftly made her way to her car.

***

Christine entered the bathroom and walked directly to the shower, avoiding her reflection in the mirror, as she had been doing for the last two weeks. She turned on the hot water and waited patiently for the steam to fill the room, rendering the mirror useless. The past two weeks had left Christine emotionally and physically debilitated. Each morning the sight of herself in the mirror sent her racing to the toilet, nauseated to the point of throwing up. Her naked body unleashed a flood of memories beginning with the image of Jesse holding a bloodied piece of wood and ending with the morning her mother had found her naked and shivering on the sands of Kua Bay.

Time offered Christine no relief from the anguish and confusion of that horrible night. Her uncontrollable attraction to Jasper, a guy she had known for less than an hour, remained steeped in confusion. *Why did I covet him? How could I kiss him?* Their naked bodies were entangled and on the brink of consummating their carnal attraction when Jesse had delivered the fatal blow. *How could he do it?* she thought, and the image of Jasper played over in her mind.

Christine's thoughts focused on Jesse as she left the shower feeling lightheaded. *Where is he now?* Suddenly, another thought concerned her more, and her mind overflowed with anger toward her mother.

Why won't she talk about it?

ABOUT THE AUTHOR

 As a young boy growing up in the Okanagan Valley in beautiful British Columbia, Canada, Mark spent most of his youth roaming the surrounding hills looking for the next perfect fly-fishing opportunity. His love of nature and the outdoors influenced his education, and Mark went on to complete a Bachelor of Science degree from the University of Windsor and a graduate diploma in Environmental Toxicology from Simon Fraser University.

Now a senior scientist working for the Canadian government for more than twenty-five years, Mark conducts cutting-edge research on new and emerging environmental issues. He has traveled the globe extensively, speaking at scientific conferences and presenting his research. Mark has published many scientific papers but *The Convergence Series* represents his first work of fiction. When asked what made him want to write fiction, Mark replied, "Because my sons asked me to." Mark still resides in British Columbia with his two boys, where they enjoy trolling the waters of the Pacific Northwest in search of that elusive Tyee.

THE CONVERGENCE SERIES

Please visit www.MarkSekela.com for details about the other books in the Convergence Series.